'A gutsy tale well-grounded in local colour'
The Times

'Bleak, brutal and timely'
Financial Times

'A new and original pair of detectives . . .
it has the ring of truth'
Independent

'A melting-pot mix of mystery'
Sunday Express

'An intricate story around the lives of ordinary
people and the devastation that is caused when people are
not what they seem . . . A good read, very enjoyable'
Eurocrime

'A skilled and experienced writer'
Shotsmag

Also by Barbara Nadel

Hakim and Arnold Mysteries

A Private Business

The Inspector Ikmen Series

Belshazzar's Daughter
A Chemical Prison
Arabesk
Deep Waters
Harem
Petrified
Deadly Web
Dance with Death
A Passion for Killing
Pretty Dead Things
River of the Dead
Death by Design
Dead of Night
Deadline

The Hancock Series

Last Rights
After the Mourning
Ashes to Ashes
Sure and Certain Death

BARBARA NADEL

AN ACT OF KINDNESS

A Hakim and Arnold Mystery

Quercus

First published in Great Britain 2013 by Quercus Editions Ltd
This paperback edition published in 2014 by Quercus Editions Ltd

55 Baker Street
7th Floor, South Block
London W1U 8EW

A CIP catalogue record for this book is available
from the British Library

ISBN 978 0 85738 780 6
EBOOK ISBN 978 0 85738 779 0

10 9 8 7 6 5 4 3 2 1

Printed and bound in Great Britain by Clays Ltd, St Ives plc

Typeset by Ellipsis Digital Limited, Glasgow

To my husband, who is still here,
still putting up with it all and to my son
who is a constant source of inspiration

Part One

1

It looked like nothing. A tiny piece of paper that spiralled down towards the floor on a parachute of dust. She could have ignored it. If it hadn't landed face up she certainly would have.

It was a black and white photograph of a woman. Nasreen picked it up. Dark-haired and unsmiling, the woman looked somewhat like her aunt Shahana. But there was something more European about this face. The eyes were heavy, reminding her of the eyes of some of the Romanian boys she saw flogging fake Adidas tracksuits in Queens Market. Too thin and plain to be what Nasreen always thought of as typically Italian, there was a kind of beauty in the woman's face but it was not of an obvious or comfortable nature. This was someone who, though far from old, had done a lot of living. And even though the image had faded over time, Nasreen could see that the eyes were full of pain. She turned the photograph over in her hands and wondered what had happened to this woman.

Nasreen had been sanding down the front door when she'd spotted it, an ancient paint-encrusted lump stuck to the door-frame. To begin with she'd thought that it was merely a build-up of paint. The house hadn't been repaired or decorated for decades and she and Abdullah had found layers of paint and wallpaper that probably dated from the 1940s. But this lump was different.

As she'd chipped away at it with her scraper, Nasreen had seen that it was some sort of capsule fixed to the doorframe. About the same length as a wide, flat lipstick it was attached by screws, forced through metal loops at either end. She went into the house to find a screwdriver. When she returned, she gave the thing a tug and it came away easily from the rotten wood of the frame. The photograph had floated down to the floor from behind it. Someone had hidden it there. Why?

Nasreen and Abdullah had only just taken possession of the house and were both still excited to be home owners. But, due to the state of it, they hadn't moved in and were still living with Nasreen's parents a few streets away. Until they managed to make the place habitable, things would have to stay that way.

Abdullah called down from the bathroom, where he'd been knocking out a sink the colour of stewed tea. Now the banging coming from upstairs stopped. 'How you getting on?' he shouted, over the top of the CD player belting out Paul Simon's 'Graceland'. His accent always reminded her a little of that comedian Peter Kay. It made her smile.

'OK,' Nasreen yelled back.

'I've got the sink out. Now I'm going for the bath,' he said.

'I'm still scraping off paint.' Nasreen didn't tell him about the paint-encrusted lump or the photograph. She put them both into the pocket of her jeans, like secrets. She didn't know why.

Lee Arnold knew that his assistant Mumtaz Hakim wouldn't join him when he went out to get his lunch from the chippy. Saveloy and chips. He'd explained to her what a saveloy was and that the ones he bought contained no pork products. He'd told her that this kind of saveloy had been created for the Jewish immigrants, and was made of beef and cereal.

'You should try it,' he said now, 'with chips. You eat chips. Everybody eats chips.'

She smiled. 'I'm just not hungry. Maybe another time.'

'My treat,' he tried again. She'd lost weight in recent months and Lee was worried. He wanted to ask her if she was alright, but she was a private person and it was difficult. She hadn't taken any time off work and she was performing well. But the dark circles underneath her eyes bothered him.

He shrugged. 'OK.' He put his jacket on and made his way towards the office door. 'Call me on me mobile if you change your mind.'

'I will.'

He knew she wouldn't. He ran down the metal stairs leading from the front door of the Arnold Detective Agency and in to a rough back alley behind Green Street, Upton Park. A burst of Greek bouzouki music from George the Barbers heralded his arrival on one of London's liveliest streets. In spite of his concerns about his assistant, Lee Arnold smiled.

One way or another, Lee had been around Green Street all his life. As a kid he'd come with his mum and his brother to Queens Market for fruit, veg and the odd turn around the junk shops. As an adult he'd walked it to the sound of bangra music, past ornate jewellery emporiums run by Sikhs. He'd broken halal bread with owners of money-exchange agencies, restaurants and mobile phone shops. His favourite pub, the Boleyn, still stood at the far end of Green Street, on the Barking Road, and the chippies still sold saveloys, wallies and his favourite fish, rock eel. Managing to get an office on Green Street when he'd set up in business had been a bonus.

Lee lit a cigarette and began walking south towards the chippy.

He tipped his head at an old white bloke who scowled back. He'd been a fence, and probably still was. When he was a copper, Lee had arrested him twice.

The sky was as grey as a sewer rat's tail. London weather. It neither thrilled nor depressed Lee, it just was, and in its 'just was-ness' it represented comfort. His thoughts drifted back to Mumtaz. Since she'd joined the Arnold Agency, Lee had gradually been given access to a very lucrative market in troubled Asian ladies. Mumtaz helped them pursue errant husbands, looked into the backgrounds of prospective in-laws, and offered them a familiar and at the same time forceful woman with whom they could discuss their problems. Ever since she'd arrived just over a year before, Mumtaz Hakim hadn't missed a beat.

Lee stamped out his first fag on the ground and lit another. He knew that Mumtaz had financial problems. She was a young widow with a step-daughter and she lived in a house that was too expensive for her. Clearly things hadn't yet got so bad that she'd had to move because she was still in it, but she wasn't happy and whatever was causing her misery was making her pale and gaunt. Lee wanted to tackle her outright about it but something held him back, which made him feel impotent and also vaguely guilty. He knew that if Mumtaz had been a white woman he wouldn't have hesitated to ask her what was wrong.

There was no point going to Lee for more money because he didn't have any. Mumtaz and Lee had always shared the book keeping and she knew what he did and didn't have in the bank. The business was prospering but overheads were high and Lee had recently had to update his camera equipment as well as the office computer systems.

Mumtaz looked at her mobile phone and wondered, not for the first time, about calling her father. Her latest payment wasn't due – yet – but it was only a matter of days away and she was broke. There was just enough food in the house for dinner and Shazia could well have to go in to college with leftovers. She looked hard at her phone again. What would her father say if he knew? What could he do?

She knew that if she told him about her predicament, he would certainly help her with the mortgage. But it wouldn't be easy for him, he and her mother were old and they needed every penny. No, she couldn't take money from them. And anyway, even if she did, what would paying the mortgage do on its own?

Her two brothers were also out of the question. They were young men, quick to anger, and if they found out what was really happening to their sister they would be furious. And that, Mumtaz knew, could only end badly – for her brothers.

No. There was only a single realistic course of action and that was the one she had taken the previous month. She extracted a sheet of paper from the office printer and made a list. A lot of her jewellery had already gone and she didn't want to touch that again for a while. In her head she roamed around her house looking for things she could live without. She wondered whether items like toasters, microwaves and soft furnishings were actually worth selling. Mumtaz baulked at the idea of selling any of Ahmet's carpets. Her late husband had not been a man of taste – except when it came to carpets. Two Persian and three Afghan remained out of what had once been a considerable collection. Could she bring herself to sell those? If she failed to make the next payment there was more than just an increased rate of interest at stake.

The entryphone buzzed, interrupting her thoughts. Mumtaz

got up from her desk to answer it. She heard a man's voice then saw his face on the monitor. She recognised it immediately. He was called Naz Sheikh.

'Hello Mumtaz,' he said. There was a smile in that voice which made it even more oily than usual. He must have seen Lee go out.

Mumtaz stared at him on the CCTV monitor. She wasn't even frightened any more. Not for herself. She didn't answer.

'Just a friendly reminder about your obligation,' he said. 'The end of the week. You know what—'

'You'll get it,' she said as calmly as she could.

'Just making sure, you know, for the sake of your—'

'You'll get it,' Mumtaz reiterated. 'Go away.'

Naz's face broke into a big smile. He enjoyed what he did, and that made it much worse. To be so young, so handsome and yet so . . . Mumtaz didn't have the words for what he was. She watched him as he turned and walked back down the metal steps, back to whatever he did with the rest of his time. The silver panels on the sides of his trainers caught what little light there was left in the cloudy London sky.

The first thing that John Sawyer had noticed about Helmand had been the smell. He'd struggled to describe it for months until he finally came up with 'seven shades of shit'. Lieutenant Reeve had once asked him to list the seven shades. He'd said, 'Goat, sheep, man, woman, child, chicken, fucking bastard Taliban, sir.'

Lt Reeve had lost his head less than a week later. He and two others out on patrol, blown into thousands of pieces by the 'fucking bastard Taliban'. John had seen it. Walking fifty metres behind, he'd got away with a face full of his mates' blood. Everybody said how lucky he'd been. And he'd agreed with them.

A month, maybe a bit more, had passed then. Out on patrol again – some village in the arse-end of nowhere. He didn't know its name, he never had. Just like he'd never known the girl's name. John shook his head as he tried to forget about all that and concentrate on the present. Now, keeping low in the garden undergrowth so that he couldn't be seen, John watched the young, beautiful woman scrape away at fifty years' worth of paint on that rotten old doorpost. He had wanted to talk to her ever since he'd first seen her, but he had to be careful not to let her see him. If she did her husband might go mad and chase him away, and he didn't want that. John didn't like frightening people, even by accident.

Back in the horror of his past, the girl had frightened him because she'd been bleeding. It wasn't easy to say where from but it looked to John as if she had been shot or stabbed in the abdomen. He told the Afghan translator to ask her if there was anything they could do to help but he'd been reluctant to do so. John remembered that feeling of impatient agitation he'd had then. Sergeant Willets had told him to 'fucking pipe down'. But then he'd ordered the translator to ask the girl what was wrong.

'Don't do too much.' The man – the woman's husband's voice – ripped through the present and across the ruined, tangled garden. John lowered his head.

'I won't,' the beautiful woman said. Then he heard her scrape, scrape, scraping again. In Helmand he'd tap, tap, tapped his foot as they'd waited in fifty-degree heat for the girl to tell the translator why she was bleeding.

'She says it's nothing,' the translator had said. They'd talked in the local language, Dari. There was no contact on any level with English. They could have been saying anything. The girl, whose head was almost completely obscured by a scarf, began to walk on, blood dripping down her exposed ankles as she went.

And then the translator had said the fateful words, 'She must go back to her husband now.'

John closed his eyes, as if by shutting out the grey London light he might also somehow shut out what had happened next in Afghanistan as well. Tears seeped from the corner of his right eye. Then he heard the present reassert itself again. The beautiful woman called out, 'Abdullah, I'm going to get some cold drinks. What do you want? Coke or—'

'Fizzy water,' the man said. 'That'll do me.' He had a northern accent and if John hadn't been screaming inside he might have found it funny. He was, he had been, the type of bloke who found almost anything funny. But back in Helmand on that hot day he'd turned the girl around, taken the scarf off her head and looked into her eyes. Only after that had everything changed.

2

Abdullah didn't like her working at their new home on her own, but Strone Road was close to her mum and dad's house and Nasreen was anxious to get on. The place was such a mess, it would take them months to make it livable. Her mum wasn't happy about her act of defiance. 'If your husband comes home here and you're still out at the house I won't lie for you, you know,' she'd said as Nasreen left.

It was late afternoon now, the day had turned warm and Nasreen felt happy as she walked out into her garden. She wouldn't do any more paint scraping today. There was a hideous old sink outside the back door that she wanted to move. But before she did that, she would sit down on one of the deckchairs that Abdullah had brought for them and turn her face to the sun for a moment. Looking up, she caught sight of the back-door frame and the mark where she'd removed that odd lump with the photograph behind it, both still in the pocket of her jeans. She took them both out and looked at them.

The woman was difficult to place in terms of age. Clearly she wasn't old, but whether she was thirty, forty or even fifty was difficult to tell. Her expression was serious, on the edge of severe, but Nasreen felt a warmth towards her. Maybe the woman was someone who had lived in the house long ago? Abdullah had the deeds and she could maybe ask him to look into who had lived there before them. She'd just started to scrape some of the layers of paint away from the lump when the noise of something snapping behind her made her look round. There was a man, tall, scruffy, his hair and beard in long brown hanks. His eyes looked right through her.

The girl had been twelve at the most. Younger than his little sister.

'What's she doing with a husband?' he'd asked the translator.

The man had looked anxious and shifty – John had never trusted him. 'It is the custom here for girls to marry when they are young,' he'd said.

'She's a kid!'

Sergeant Willets had put a hand on John's arm. 'Leave it, Private.'

'Leave it?' He'd grabbed the girl and she'd screamed. John closed his eyes against the remembrance. But a voice in the present made him open them again

'Who are you? What do you want?' the beautiful woman said.

She had her hands on her abdomen and her voice quavered. He could see that she was scared.

'I er, I . . .'

'This is my house,' Nasreen Khan said. 'You shouldn't be here.'

John looked away.

'You should go home,' she said. He didn't answer. 'You do have a home . . .'

'I live in lots of places,' John said. 'Sometimes here.'

'Here?'

'I live in the shack,' he said.

She clearly didn't understand what he meant, so John pointed through the densest part of the tangle of trees and shrubs towards the back of the garden. She said, 'You mean the wood pile at the bottom of the garden?'

John said, 'I can show you if you . . .'

'No!' She took an abrupt step backwards. 'No. I think you should go.'

John couldn't remember when he'd first found the shack. The coppers had moved him on from his old billet down in Silvertown some time in the winter. Then there'd been the shack, Central Park sometimes, occasionally down by the river.

'Where will I go today?' he said to himself rather than to her.

'I don't know,' she said. 'Where do you come from?'

John said it entirely without thinking, 'Helmand province, Afghanistan.'

And Nasreen Khan's heart changed in an instant.

It was a slow day – a slow week as it went – and Lee let Mumtaz go home early. Whatever was upsetting her wouldn't be helped by sitting in the office with not much to do. She had a couple of appointments booked for later in the week – a missing husband and a background check on a potential bride from Leeds – so things could pick up. But Lee had bugger all. Clearly the upcoming Olympics were having an adverse effect upon infidelity in Newham. Lee let himself into his Forest Gate flat and put his keys down on the telephone table in the hall. From his living room he heard a low, cawing sound followed by a high-pitched rendition of that famous West Ham United anthem, 'I'm Forever Blowing Bubbles'. Christ, he'd taught that bloody bird well!

Lee took his coat off and walked into the living room. The mynah bird eyed him with his usual slight suspicion.

'Evening Chronus,' Lee said. He rubbed the bird's blue-black head with his fingers and Chronus stopped singing and shouted, 'Up the 'ammers!'

Lee laughed. 'You're a poor brainwashed fucker, aren't you?'

'Bobby Moore! Trevor Brooking!'

Lee went into the kitchen and took a bottle of diet Pepsi out of the fridge. He poured some into a glass and drank it straight down. He wanted a pint of bitter, or gin, or anything that would get him out of it for a bit, but that was out of the question. He walked back into the living room and put the TV on. It was all gloom as usual: Egypt still in turmoil, the endless civil war in Syria, another British squaddie killed in Afghanistan. Then there was the farce of the London mayoral elections. Bumbling Boris Johnson, the clever, posh boy, not-so-idiot, or Ken – there go my Socialist credentials – Livingstone. He'd have to vote for someone, but who?

His mobile rang. He picked it up and saw that it was Vi. He put it down again and let it ring out. She'd been a bit keen lately and he wanted to nip it in the bud. It was all very well sleeping together occasionally but Lee didn't want a girlfriend. Well, he didn't want Vi Collins to be his girlfriend. The phone stopped ringing. Vi didn't leave a message and Lee thought again about Mumtaz. Not for the first time he wondered whether he could pay her more. Thanks to the internet and modern home security systems, people were doing some forms of private investigation themselves. Not always well, but they were doing them. And that included some of Mumtaz's covered Asian ladies. He'd thought about a career change, but where, if not to private investigation, did an ex-soldier, ex-copper go? The wonderful world of security? Lee had turned his Roman nose up at that years ago. Nights spent wandering about outside dodgy factories chasing down illegal immigrants jumping out of lorries? No chance.

The telly showed a picture of the squaddie who'd just been killed in Helmand province and Lee felt his blood pressure rise. They'd called the conflict he'd fought in the 'First' Iraq War. Then there'd been the 'Second' Iraq war and now the endless Afghan campaign. It made him mad. When was it going to end, for Christ's sake?

Nasreen gave John a bottle of fizzy water she'd bought earlier in the day. He took it gratefully and drank it down.

'Thanks.' He smiled at her.

'It's no problem,' Nasreen said.

Nasreen knew a little about men like John, if that was really his name. He was one of those ex-soldiers that were sometimes spoken about on the TV. Unable to adjust to civilian life after the rigours of Afghanistan, they drifted, homeless and often ill, on the outside of society. Her cousin Abbas had fought in Helmand. He'd lost an eye and his faith and was hiding from his nightmares in drug abuse. Before she'd married Abdullah, she had done some temporary office work for a mental health charity which had tried to help sick soldiers. She'd been touched by some of their stories, which had chimed with what Abbas had experienced. She knew that most people, for all the talk of the soldiers as 'heroes', didn't give a damn.

'The thing you call the shack . . .' she began.

'At the bottom of your garden,' he said.

'It's just a woodpile.' She paused. She still wasn't entirely easy being on her own with him in her ruined garden, with evening coming on. If Abdullah ever found out he'd lose his mind. 'My husband and I bought this house in an auction six weeks ago,' she said. 'How long have you been coming here?'

He didn't know. Nasreen looked down the tight, rough tunnel John had forged to get from his 'shack' and into the part of the garden nearest the house and she said, 'Did you rearrange the woodpile to make a shack out of it?'

'A bit,' he said. 'It was something, a structure, once. But it collapsed, I reckon. It's old.'

Although she knew what he was talking about, Nasreen couldn't see much apart from branches and leaves. Again John asked her if she'd like to see his shack, and again she declined. At the end of the garden there was nothing of interest except the high wall that enclosed the old Plashet Jewish Cemetery. And if John suddenly 'lost it' or went for her, down there, no-one would know. As if reading her thoughts, he said, 'Why are you here? On your own?'

'Why do you ask? Why shouldn't I be?'

'You've always been with your husband when I've seen you before.'

'He's gone to work,' she said, then thought that maybe that was a stupid thing to say when she was alone with an unknown man. 'He's a lawyer,' she added. 'He works strange hours. He could be back any minute.'

But John had drifted off. 'Why are you here?' he repeated.

Nasreen changed tack. She pointed at the old sink by the back door. 'I wanted to see if I could move that,' she said.

John looked at the large, heavily stained Butler sink. There was even what looked like the remains of a tap on the side of it. 'On your own?'

It did look heavy and she wasn't sure how she was going to move it, or even why she wanted to move it. It was probably just a case of striking one more thing off the long list of tasks that needed to be done in the house and garden. It wasn't easy for her or Abdullah, living with her parents. Everyone was perfectly civilised and polite but she knew it was a strain – especially for her husband.

'I'll move it for you, if you like,' John said.

'Oh, no it's not your—'

'It's no problem.' He walked past her, his eyes fixed on the knackered old sink.

He took hold of it, a hand on either side. His fingernails were black, she noticed. He tugged and pulled and Nasreen began to feel guilty that he would strain himself. Suddenly he stopped and turned a red face towards her. 'It's plumbed in,' he said.

Nasreen went over to see for herself and, yes, the old sink was attached to a pipe. 'That's odd isn't it? To have a sink outside?'

John looked vague again. 'I don't know,' he said. 'Maybe. You'll have to get a plumber, I think.'

'Yes.' She looked up at him. He was well over six feet tall and behind all the hair and the unkempt beard, he had the look of someone kind.

'What do you do for food, John?' she asked.

Dinner was a basic dhal with rice. Luckily Shazia had been anxious to finish her homework so that she could watch TV later and so the food, or lack of it, hadn't bothered her much. Mumtaz was so glad that her stepdaughter was enjoying college. She was just anxious that nothing should stop her from doing so.

Now that the girl was up in her bedroom doing her work, Mumtaz could roam the house looking for things to sell. She'd given up on the idea of selling kitchen equipment; it just wasn't worth it. Even one of the many canteens of cutlery that Ahmet, her husband, had liked so much would barely fetch the price of a week's shopping. Mumtaz went from the kitchen and into the room Ahmet had called 'the games room'. It was where he'd sat with his friends, smoking, drinking and playing poker. Even with his friends, for fivers and tenners, he played it badly. With other people it was worse. She opened the large teak chest in the corner by the window and took out a bundle enrobed in sheets of tissue paper. She laid it on the larger of the two card tables and began to unwrap it, removing layer upon layer of thin, white tissue – a modern and, she felt, deserved mummification.

Her red wedding sari came into view. Made of banarasi silk and decorated with zari and buta work, it was a sari fit for a Bollywood superstar. Ahmet had spared no expense and Mumtaz and her family had been dazzled. How happy she'd been! Not even a scowling Shazia, resentful that – as she saw it – Mumtaz had usurped her dead mother, could spoil her big beautiful wedding. Rich, handsome and generous, Ahmet had been the perfect bride-groom and her female cousins – and even some of her aunts – had been openly jealous of her. And although she had been nervous about her 'first time' alone with her husband, Ahmet had been so gentle it had been wonderful. Her father and mother, she had felt back then, had chosen carefully and well. But within a year she'd wished Ahmet dead.

She looked down at the dress with nothing but contempt. She'd take it to one of those vintage shops at the northern end of Brick Lane so beloved by those young white people known as 'hipsters'. If she stuck to her guns, she'd get a good price for the sari. Also, it would probably be bought by someone who would do some-thing self-consciously ironic with it. Some boy would make it into a jacket to wear to the pub or a girl would team it with a pair of combat trousers and a bag made out of old tractor tyres. The thought of its defilement pleased her. She went into the teak box again and found her wedding shoes and the heavily jewelled bag she had used at her wedding.

Her mobile rang. Mumtaz took it out of her pocket and looked at it. She put it down on top of her wedding sari. It was always like this when a payment was coming up. Relentless.

3

First she took him some mutton biryani and chapatis, but Nasreen quickly learned that John had a sweet tooth. Her mum made good baklawa which she took him, and he had a particular weakness for halua. She bought some from one of the shops on Green Street.

Whether or not she and Abdullah were working on the house, she'd go there most days and put a small box of food out for John just in case he was around. If she was alone they'd talk, and he'd tell her how much he'd liked the Afghan people and how sad he'd been to see so many of their beautiful buildings in ruins. She told him that if her husband was around she would hide his food in the long grass just in front of the trees.

'You seem a bit afraid of your hubby,' he said to her one day. 'Why is that?'

'John, it isn't your business,' she said, but she smiled.

He'd said he understood. Nasreen wished that she did too. Her husband was a good man.

When she was with Abdullah, sneaking food out wasn't easy even if they were taking something to eat for themselves. He always wanted to look in the bag to see what she'd packed before they left her parents' house. She had to pretend to have eaten more sweets than she had which had made Abdullah tell her that she should watch her weight. 'Just because you're pregnant doesn't mean you can eat all day long,' he said one day when she appeared to have eaten all the baklawa they had brought with them.

Nasreen had become pregnant as soon as she married Abdullah. They were both pleased, although Nasreen felt that buying a house *and* having a baby at the same time was probably a bit much. Abdullah had a good job, but he insisted on doing the renovation work on the house himself. It wasn't easy on either of them, but the less money they spent on it the more they'd have for the new baby. Still, Nasreen couldn't help thinking that he could at least have employed someone to do the heavy work. While she scraped paint and stripped layers of ancient wallpaper, Abdullah pulled out fireplaces and removed sinks, kitchen units and ancient built-in cupboards. Sometimes, after spending all day at the house, he would be exhausted. Renovation coupled with his job was too much for him, although Nasreen had learned early on in their marriage that her husband didn't listen to any form of dissent. That she loved him and worried about him was, she sometimes felt, irrelevant to him. But then her father was of a similar type – if rather more gentle. He'd worked through two heart attacks so far and there had been nothing anyone in the family had been able to do about it.

Nasreen, for some reason she didn't fully understand, told John about it.

'It's because men are stupid,' he told her. 'We're always challenging ourselves and it's bonkers. That's why there are wars, because men have to front up to other men. We're programmed to do it.'

Yet Abdullah wasn't some empty-headed alpha male who was always ready for a fight. He was educated, a qualified lawyer, and he loved her passionately. But he was also very jealous and he didn't like it if she spoke to or even looked at other men. It was only recently that she'd been able to get him to laugh about the teenage crush she'd once had on Will Smith when he'd been in *The Fresh Prince of Bel Air*. He'd been jealous of the Hollywood star for weeks. She'd asked him, 'Don't people have crushes on film stars and musicians in Bolton?'

He hadn't answered. But then Abdullah didn't talk about Bolton much these days. When they'd first been introduced, his Uncle Fazal was with him and they'd talked about their old home town. Many people had moved to Bolton from Pakistan and Bangladesh in the Fifties and Sixties to work in the Lancashire cotton mills. Now the mills were all but defunct and people found other work, or went on the dole. Abdullah's uncle had moved to London in the Eighties and Abdullah had lived at the boarding house in Poplar that Fazal owned when he'd first come to the city in 2005. As far as Nasreen could tell, her husband had only been back to Bolton once since he'd left: when his father died in 2011. His people were not like hers, they weren't close.

Lee hadn't expected to see Martin Rogers, not in the Boleyn. A pub with pretensions was more his style, or a wine bar or lap dancing club. But there he was, sitting at a table by the door, while one of his minders loudly ordered a bottle of champagne. Marty Rogers only drank champagne, or rather that was the legend that he liked to put about. Lee looked down into his diet Pepsi and 'did invisible'. He'd been to school with Marty and his brother Sean but had no wish to speak to him. Lee had never arrested either of them, which was a shame.

'Don't tell me you ain't got Cristal!' the minder bellowed at the barmaid. Another Custom House scrote that Lee remembered from his youth, called Dave something or other. Twat had to know that a place like the Boleyn wouldn't have one of the most expensive champagnes in the world.

'We've got Moet,' the barmaid emphasised the 't'. 'Take it or leave it.'

Clearly Sandra, the barmaid, didn't live in any of Martin and Sean's shonky old properties otherwise she might have made a few calls to try and find some of Marty's preferred tipple. The Rogers', together with their 'business' partner Yunus Ali, were landlords that harked back to the days of Rachman. If you didn't pay your rent you got a visit from their 'boys' or, even worse, Marty's wife Debbie, a shoulder-padded, fag-wielding stick of malice known to be handy with a sharp instrument.

'Oh, I'll have the Moet,' Marty pronounced it without the 't'. 'I don't mind.'

Sandra took a bottle of champagne out of the fridge and said, 'Don't force yourself.'

'Oh, darlin', I can slum it for once.' Marty laughed.

He was clearly in an expansive mood for some reason, although Lee was still in the dark as to why he was in the Boleyn at all. An old geezers' pub that went bonkers with West Ham fans whenever a match was on couldn't possibly be his scene. Lee sipped his Pepsi, wishing it was a pint of bitter. Marty Rogers had always made his skin crawl.

Dave the minder paid for the champagne, popped the cork and took it over to his boss. Sandra had given him two glasses, but he only picked up one. Marty had never been a great one for sharing, not even with his brother. But then Sean had never been big on sharing either. They were both fucking psychos. Lee drained his glass and stood up to go outside for a fag. Marty Rogers's minder was sitting across the pub from his boss, drinking ginger ale and looking pissed off.

Lee had to pass Marty as he walked towards the door into Green Street. He couldn't stop himself from sneaking a peek at him. Marty, his dead green eyes refusing to smile in tandem with his mouth, raised his glass to Lee and said, 'Hello there, officer.'

Lee didn't hang around to see what Marty wanted, if anything. He got out of there, lit a fag and made his way to his office. For a moment back there the Plaistow air had smelt bloody foul.

Nasreen wasn't at the house, even though she must have been earlier. She'd left him a box with some chicken curry and rice and a Mars bar. She was a lovely lady. In some lights she looked a bit like the girl whose dead face he had cried into as the dust blew over Helmand. Shot by a Talib sniper, they said, but John had known better. Her husband had done it, or rather, had it done by someone else. Everything inside John's head screamed. Even now the memory of his own impotence in that situation made him claw the ground underneath him in frustration. When this didn't help, and for no reason he could properly articulate, he began to dig.

He dug in time to scraping noises that came from the house, it helped him to focus. Her husband worked in the house, only rarely in the garden. But that thought made John nervous. This billet had been so quiet and secure and in the short time that Nasreen had been bringing him food he'd hardly had to kip elsewhere at all. What would he do when it all came to an end? Because it would. Like Nasreen, her old man knew about the woodpile, he wouldn't put up with some homeless type living in it if he found him . . .

When the scraping stopped, Paul Simon tracks belted out of the house. John stopped digging. For a while there was just music and then, when it stopped, he heard what sounded like footsteps on the stairs inside the house. John turned his head.

Abdullah was very good looking. Tall with black hair, he had that light brown skin that people reckoned spoke of Kashmiri blood. When John had first seen him he had thought that Abdullah was probably mid-forties but Nasreen had told him that her husband was thirty-eight. John watched as Abdullah sat down on the step outside the back door. 'Fuck!' he said. He never swore when his wife was around, and he never smoked in front of her either. Now he took his cigarettes out of his pocket and lit up. Lawyers like him were generally stress-heads. In fact people with money seemed to do little else but stress out as far as John could see. His fingers dug into the clay as he stayed motionless on all fours beneath the flimsy roof of his shack. He didn't want Abdullah to see him. He didn't want any sort of confrontation.

'Fuck! Fuck! Fuck!' he heard Abdullah say. So far he had rarely come into the garden, but whenever he did it was to let off steam in some way. Last time John had seen him he'd kicked the shit out of that old Butler sink by the back door. He'd stubbed his toes and sworn like a sailor.

Back in Helmand, the girl's seventy-year-old husband hadn't looked even slightly phased when John had finally caught up with him outside the fly-blown house he'd been visiting. John had known that the old man could speak English because he'd heard him do it. It was night-time and John had lain in wait for him for hours. If he'd just pummelled the crap out of him and said nothing, she might have lived. But that was something he only knew with hindsight. At the time, he'd felt he *had* to say those things – those things about how he had hurt her, how he was a pervert, how he didn't deserve to live. But had he done it for her or for himself? And if he had his time over again would he do the selfsame thing?

John couldn't think about that and so he began silently clawing at the earth again. Abdullah smoked and looked around himself with an arrogant sneer. Then he threw his cigarette butt across the garden and went back inside the house. John was sure that he hadn't seen him, but he shook with fear nevertheless. His hands, almost on their own, began probing ever deeper into the ground as he looked at the cigarette butt that Abdullah had casually thrown away and wondered whether he should break his cover and take it. He hadn't smoked for weeks and he suddenly felt the need of it. Caught in a bind of desire and fear, John scrabbled at the earth still more violently, his ever increasing movements accompanied by grunts and sobs of frustration. If he didn't get a hold of himself, Abdullah would hear him and then that would be the end of it for him. But then his fingers touched something that made him look down and for just a moment, John's shaking stopped.

Then it started up again. More violently than it ever had done before. Paul Simon sang about Scarborough Fair.

The woman was nothing like Mumtaz had imagined she'd be. For a start she was white. She wore Western clothes and her problem was nothing to do with either her husband or her children.

'It's my little sister,' she said as she took the cup of tea that Mumtaz had made her. 'I think she's on the game.'

She was called Mrs Mirza and she looked about forty. With her long blonde hair and pale blue eyes she was one of the whitest people Mumtaz had ever met. She lived in Forest Gate with her husband, a Pakistani-born taxi driver. Ayesha, or Mary – Mumtaz could choose to call her by either name – had found out about Mumtaz on what she called the 'umma telegraph'.

'That's one of the great things about being a Muslim,' she said. 'You get help. We all help each other and that's priceless.'

Mumtaz, who was well aware of the power and utility of the worldwide Muslim brother and sisterhood known as the umma, smiled in spite of herself. That was usually the case but . . .

'Why do you think that your sister might be a prostitute, Mrs Mirza?' Mumtaz asked.

She leant across the desk. There was no-one else in the office. Lee was out at lunch, but Mrs Mirza clearly felt that she had to lower her voice. 'Well, you know how it is, these days,' she said. 'What with all the cuts and everything. Wend, that's me sister, Wendy Dixon, well she's on her own with three kids, know what I mean?'

Mumtaz, on her own with one child, understood more than Mrs Mirza could imagine. It had been almost two weeks now since she'd sold her wedding dress to a shop called *Retro Rocks!* on Brick Lane. A woman called Lilith had told her that saris were going to go 'viral' in the summer and had bought the dress on the spot. What Mumtaz had got for it after, surprisingly, no haggling at all, had paid off half her debt – for last month.

'Yes,' Mumtaz said.

'None of the kids' dads are interested,' Mrs Mirza continued. 'She can't get a job. She's tried, but she's got no certificates or nothing. She had her eldest at sixteen, she'd never been to work. But everything's gone up – food, fags, rent.'

'Yes, but why do you think that—'

'She's never in of a night,' Mrs Mirza said. 'Leaves Dolly, that's her eldest, fifteen, to look after the two little 'uns. I know people who've seen her in pubs, giving all the men the old come on, you know. One time, she was so skint she didn't even have the price of a packet of nappies for the baby. Then about three months ago that all stopped.'

'That was when you noticed your sister had started going out at night?'

'You've got it,' Mrs Mirza said. '*Inshallah*, I'm totally wrong and she's found some money in the attic or something, but I don't think so. There's no actual bloke on the horizon as far as I can tell. I'm worried.'

Mumtaz nodded. 'Yes.'

'I want to find out what she's doing so I can stop her before it's too late,' she said. 'That life, well, it's a one-way ticket, and if she's having to do that just to pay that slime of a landlord of hers . . .' She shook her head. 'Me and Wazim, that's my old man, we'd rather Wend and the kids moved in with us if that's what it takes.'

'So you'd like us to follow her?'

'Well not you, obviously,' she smiled.

'Why is that?'

Mrs Mirza blushed a little now. 'Well, you're a covered lady. Our Wend, she goes into pubs.'

'And you think that I can't?' Mumtaz asked.

Mrs Mirza's eyes widened.

'Just as you choose not to cover your head, I may uncover mine when I need to,' Mumtaz said. 'I may also go into a pub, for my job. Provided I don't drink alcohol, which I don't, that's fine. Mrs Mirza, you are obviously a woman of faith and so you will know that Islam is a very practical religion.' She smiled. 'If you would like me to take this case, I will be happy to work for you and do whatever I have to in order to find out the truth about your sister.

Let's start with you giving me her address and the name of this landlord, please?'

Mrs Mirza looked relieved. She gave her Wendy's address in Plaistow. 'The landlord's called Sean Rogers,' she said, 'and he's a right, if you'll excuse the expression Mrs Hakim, bastard.'

When John was little and he'd dug about in the back yard, his granddad had always told him off. 'Keep on digging like that and you'll end up in Australia. And leave my bloody daffs alone while you're at it!' But John had always carried on anyway. Granddad hadn't really minded that much and, anyway, as a kid John had always been besotted by the idea of buried treasure. Now he dug because it comforted him and because it meant that sometimes he could get into the hole that he dug and hide there. Except that he couldn't get into *this* hole. *This* hole was way too scary.

4

'Amma, are you sure?' Shazia said.

She'd been asking to stay overnight at her friend Maud's house for weeks but Mumtaz had refused to let her – until now. Unbeknown to her stepdaughter, it had taken Mumtaz a while to check out Maud's family. For some reason, that Mumtaz now knew was Maud's father's redundancy, they had moved from a house in Shepherd's Bush to a rented dump in Plaistow. They were nice people, who had initially struck Mumtaz as rather too good to be true. But the father, though out of work now, was an academic and the mother a struggling mid-list author. As far as Mumtaz could tell, they didn't have any skeletons in their cupboards.

Working in private investigation had made Mumtaz, who was cautious by nature, even more so. And when it came to her stepdaughter, Shazia, she was fanatical. She had good reason to be – and not just because the girl was only sixteen. Mumtaz's creditors, including the odious Naz, used the threat of harm to Shazia as a lever. In spite of Shazia not being her own blood, Mumtaz loved her. They shared a bond of pain forged at the hands of Ahmet Hakim who had beaten and raped them both. Even from beyond the grave he still made their lives hard. Theirs was a connection that was never going to be broken, not by anyone.

'Yes,' Mumtaz said. She'd spoken to Maud's mother, Christine, who had assured her that the girls would not be going out. They were going to watch DVDs and listen to music. Not having Shazia for the evening suited Mumtaz's plan to see what Wendy Dixon might be getting up to. Wendy lived two streets away from Maud's house in Patrick Road. According to Mrs Mirza, Wendy always went out on a Saturday night and was rarely home before dawn.

'Get your stuff together now and I'll take you to Maud's for eight o'clock,' Mumtaz told Shazia.

Shazia ran upstairs before Mumtaz could change her mind. Where her father had been laissez-faire about his daughter's social life, Mumtaz was strict. But she was kind too. Ahmet had been anything but that.

Mumtaz looked at the old Nissan Micra sitting on her drive and, just for a moment or two, pined for Ahmet's Mercedes. She knew it was shallow but she couldn't help it. The Nissan was probably the dodgiest company car in London but Mumtaz was glad of anything, especially when Lee was paying for the petrol and the upkeep. But it did look a mess.

'We're gonna watch *The Hurt Locker*,' Shazia said, as she ran down the stairs carrying a small rucksack. She spoke with that rising inflection which drove Mumtaz crazy. She had to keep on reminding herself that a lot of the kids did it as well as many people of her own age. After all, she told herself, at thirty-two, she was still quite young herself.

'Isn't *The Hurt Locker* about US soldiers in Afghanistan?' Mumtaz asked.

'Yeah. Maud and me are doing a module on colonialism,' Shazia said. 'Afghanistan's an example of cultural colonialism isn't it?'

Mumtaz frowned. 'That's a tough question, Shazia. It depends on your point of view.'

'Yeah, but as a Muslim . . .'

'As a Muslim I strongly disapprove of the Taliban. That isn't Islam, that's just violence and misogyny.'

'But isn't NATO imposing its western brand of democracy on Afghanistan?'

'Some Afghans want it,' Mumtaz said.

'But some want the Taliban.'

'And most, probably, want something in-between. It's a difficult issue.' But she was glad that Shazia was thinking about it. Time was, when she was back at her old private school, all she ever thought about were her clothes and what people thought about them.

It was raining again. Nasreen stood at her parents' dining room window and looked out at their soaked little garden. Her mind drifted to her own garden and John.

She'd never seen what he called his shack up close but she knew it couldn't be waterproof. What was he doing now, she wondered? Abdullah had been at the house for most of the afternoon. Then, just before seven, he'd come back, showered, and given her a present – an emerald ring that must have cost a fortune. He sometimes gave her things like that, out of the blue, and although she was invariably delighted, she didn't always know what to say to him. Instead, she'd kissed him and then pulled him towards their bed but he had rebuffed her advances, albeit gently, as he so often did. They'd only had sex three times since their wedding night and it made Nasreen sad. Now her husband had gone out to meet a client with his boss.

In one way Nasreen was glad that she didn't have to attend any of Abdullah's formal meetings – some lawyers' wives were always at social events with their husbands. Of course, when their new home was ready, she would have to entertain, but at the moment she couldn't – working on the house and being pregnant took it out of her. She'd only spent the morning there, just enough time to rub down a door and leave John some naan bread and a couple of samosas, but she hadn't seen him. It hadn't been raining then and so he'd probably been out and about. She hoped he'd managed to retrieve the food and eat it before the heavens opened.

Nasreen took the ring her husband had just given her and locked it away, with all the other baubles he had bought her, in her jewellery box.

Mumtaz watched from across the street as Wendy Dixon went into the pub next door to East Ham tube station. She was wearing an animal print catsuit in what looked like Lycra and a pair of very high-heeled shoes covered in red glitter. Mumtaz phoned Lee, who was about to follow Wendy. He opened the door and disappeared inside. He must have caught sight of her at once because he muttered into his mobile, 'Christ, she looks like a tranny.'

Mumtaz was going to follow him. She didn't like going into pubs on her own, but at least Lee was there, even though they weren't going to acknowledge each other. Mumtaz would order an orange juice, find somewhere to sit and watch the woman. Lee would watch Mumtaz's back. This wasn't usual practice, but when Lee had discovered that Wendy Dixon was a tenant of the Rogers brothers, his internal alarm had gone off. A young, single mum, possibly owing money to those bastards, possibly on the game, could mean that Wendy was working for Sean Rogers. He and Marty had run a lot of girls back in the day, when shoulder-padded Debbie had been their madam. They'd never actually got done for it, but it was well known they were still in the business.

Mumtaz pushed the door open. It was a smallish pub, characterised by stripped pine furnishings. She felt odd not having her head covered. It was a bitter-sweet feeling. On the one hand, as a devout Muslim she actually enjoyed wearing her scarf. At the same time, her uncovered head brought to mind her life before her marriage, which had been a happy time. Without her scarf Lee told her that she looked Italian or Spanish – others sometimes mistook her for eastern European. Either way it meant that she blended in easily with the pub's mixed clientele. No-one would recognise her. Muslim women in Newham didn't go into pubs, and to almost everyone else her headscarf made her invisible.

Wendy Dixon was standing at the bar. She called the barman over and ordered something called 'Sex on the Beach'. Mumtaz knew this was a cocktail. Briefly she caught Lee's eye – he was further along the bar from Wendy, towards the back of the pub. When Wendy left the bar, Mumtaz went up and ordered her juice. The joint wasn't jumping. There was only Wendy, a couple of teenage girls, a few old blokes and two serious-looking men – one white, one Asian – sitting at a table and talking quietly. Wendy went over to the white man, who was middle aged and a bit thick round the gut. The Asian was younger, leaner and good looking. As she approached them, the white man leered at her. Mumtaz paid for her drink and found a seat that allowed her to watch them. The pub was quiet enough that she could hear them too.

The white man spoke. 'Looking proper juicy tonight, Wendy,' he said. His voice was rough and there was something in its tone that registered with Mumtaz as contempt.

Wendy didn't reply. She drank whatever 'Sex on the Beach' was through a straw. When she'd first entered the pub there'd been a spring in her step, all gone now. The white man drank lager from a pint glass while the Asian sipped something green from a tall tumbler. Wendy's shoulders slumped forwards as if she was trying to close herself in on her considerable breasts. She almost looked ashamed of them.

Mumtaz's phone rang. It was Lee.

'I'm in the toilets,' he said. 'Thought I'd better tell you about who Wendy's sitting with. Not that I know who the Asian bloke is, but the white one is Sean Rogers, her landlord.'

'Right.' He'd told her some details about the Rogers brothers and their business partner Yunus Ali when she'd first run the case by him.

'I know Sean and his brother Marty a bit,' Lee said. 'You and me can carry on with the separate act, but I'm not leaving you on your own with this. Sean's a vicious psycho. If Wendy is working for him or just having sex with him, she's not in a healthy place.'

'No.'

The Asian man was smiling at Wendy now, but none of them were speaking.

Suddenly the relative quiet inside the pub was shattered. Police car sirens tore into the night like swords, rushing past the pub and up towards Forest Gate.

People, kids usually, were always getting into the old cemetery at the bottom of Majid Islam's garden. It drove him crazy. He was forever trying to catch whoever was doing or planning acts of desecration because it was wrong and because it offended him. He shone his torch in front of him and then behind. Still panting from the effort of scaling the wall, jumping down the other side, and then calling the police, he put his mobile phone back in his pocket and shouted, 'I know you're still in here, you bastards!'

But he immediately chastised himself. Whoever they were, now he'd alerted them. It was a Jewish cemetery and it attracted both far-right white supremacists and testosterone-fuelled Muslim jihadis. What scrawling a swastika on a gravestone dated 1904 did to alleviate the suffering of the Palestinians was beyond Majid, but some people seemed to think it was a good idea. Majid and his family had had to listen on more than one occasion to the sound of people whooping with delight as they desecrated the graves of the innocent. One time Majid had hauled himself on top of the wall to be greeted by the sight of white men and Asians knocking down gravestones and then fighting amongst themselves. As now, he had called the police.

But this time was different. This time he'd heard fear in the voices on the other side of the wall. Someone, maybe a woman, had screamed. Once inside the cemetery, he thought he saw a figure disappearing over the main gates onto High Street North, though he could still see movement among the gravestones. Now he could hear sirens in the distance which meant the police were on their way. He narrowed his eyes and looked into the rain-soaked darkness. If he could get his hands on just one of them, and manage to hang on, he could give him to the police who for once might do something. Majid was not a big man and he was scared, but he was also worn out from years of caring about something that few others seemed to give a damn about. What harm were the dead doing to anyone?

Using his torch to guide him, Majid began walking through the gravestones towards the main cemetery gates where the police would come in. The gravestones were tightly packed. Jews had once been numerous in the area and Plashet Jewish Cemetery had provided a last resting place for their dead for generations. Not any more. Occasionally someone came and opened it up for relatives or basic maintenance, but that was all. Majid thought about his own father buried thousands of miles away in Pakistan and fought to hold back his tears. To have a place to come to honour a dead loved one was a right, and anyone who interfered with that was little more than a beast.

He heard the front gates rattle and saw the dark outline of a figure outside the cemetery. The police. 'I'm coming!' he shouted as he began to run towards the gate. 'Some of them may still be here!'

He heard the chains attached to the padlocks that secured the front gates clanking as the police unlocked them. There were more police gathering now, more figures seen through the darkness and rain. Then suddenly Majid's foot caught on something and he tripped. It was fortunate that he didn't hit his head on a gravestone as he fell towards the ground. For a moment he was grateful just to be conscious and unhurt. But when he saw what he had tripped over, he wasn't so sure. Majid jumped to his feet.

'My Frank just texted to say the coppers are up at the old Jewish Cemetery,' the barman, who Sean Rogers called 'Queer Teddy', said.

'So?' Sean said, without concern.

Teddy went on cleaning the table and made no comment. Mumtaz, watching them all, slid her eyes over to connect with Lee's, when she saw Sean Rogers turn around and address him.

'I bet you had a few call-outs on the old Plashet boneyard back in the day, didn't you, Lee?'

Up until that point Sean hadn't acknowledged that Lee was

even on his radar. Lee knew that Sean liked to do his creepy, gangster act and he was good at it – just like his brother.

'Once or twice,' he said.

'What you doing in this shit hole?' Sean asked as Teddy looked theatrically offended. 'Who you watching?'

'Can't a bloke go into a pub and have a drink?' Lee said.

'Ah, but you don't drink, do you, Lee,' Sean said. 'Diet Pepsi, nectar of the recovering alkie, down the old Boleyn, that's you.'

'Maybe I needed a change. Saw your brother in the Boleyn a while ago. Now that's not his stomping ground, or yours.'

The Asian man sitting opposite Sean stood up. Sean's attention switched from Lee to him.

'What's up?'

The man shrugged. 'Bit poorly.' He didn't look it.

Sean's cold eyes immediately lit on Wendy Dixon's face.

'Mmm. Bit 1970s I suppose,' he said.

The Asian man walked out of the pub without looking back.

Mumtaz watched as Sean Rogers leaned across the table towards Wendy.

'I don't think that nouveau hippy look is working for you, darlin',' he said loudly.

Wendy stared down into her drink. It seemed that Sean Rogers had lined Wendy up for the Asian but he hadn't been too impressed. Sean had either been selling or giving Wendy to the other man, who had clearly refused his 'gift'.

Mumtaz saw Sean reach across the table and take one of Wendy's wrists in his hand. He squeezed, digging his nails into her flesh. It must have hurt her, but Wendy didn't make a sound.

5

Detective Inspector Violet Collins was knackered. She'd been in bed when she'd got the call to go out to the Plashet Jewish Cemetery on High Street North. It was the first time for months that it'd been just her, the telly, a ready meal and a packet of Marlboro, all in together for an early night. But that was just a distant fantasy now. She looked through the rain at her DS, Tony Bracci.

'A regular stiff you told me about, but what's this?' she said.

She pointed to a skeleton that lay beside the body of a man who looked to be in his late twenties or early thirties.

'I've no idea,' said Bracci. 'Maybe he was grave robbing?'

It was a possibility. The dead man, with his straggly hair, torn clothes and filthy, food-caked beard looked rather less like a white supremacist and more like a crusty eco-warrior. They didn't tend to dig up the dead in Vi's experience. She looked around the old cemetery, trying to remember where her dad's mum was buried.

'Hardly the Valley of the Kings, is it,' she said.

'No.'

'So where's the bloke who found the body?' she asked. The rain was relentless, and looking through it at Tony Bracci's round, habitually disappointed face made Vi squint.

'Over here.' Tony led her towards one of the high brick walls that enclosed the cemetery. A group of coppers stood there beside two men. 'He's called Majid Islam. He lives on Shelley Avenue. Always making complaints about people mucking around in the cemetery.'

'I know him, this place backs on to his garden.' As she drew closer, Vi saw a tired looking middle-aged Asian man with a blanket round his shoulders. Beside him, being held by a couple of constables, was what looked like a cartoon of a far-right thug except that his build was slight. A swastika tattoo covered one side of his neck. Vi ignored him and looked at the Asian who, in spite of the blanket, was shivering.

'Mr Islam.'

He moved towards her, his voice trembling. 'Yes?'

'You might not remember me, I'm DI Collins,' Vi said, 'from Forest Gate.'

'Oh, yes. Hello.'

'Hello. You discovered the body?'

'I fell over it,' he said. Then he corrected himself. 'Them. The man and the skeleton, I . . .' He swallowed. 'I'm always chasing people out of this place. There should be some sort of guard.'

'So you dialled 999?'

'From in here,' he said. 'I was in here when I called. I saw them, people, running about. I saw at least one get over the gate and get away.'

'You shouldn't really climb in here you know, Mr Islam,' Vi said. 'It's dangerous.'

'I know that!' He shook his head. 'And believe me, most of the time I wouldn't dream of getting in here. The wall is high . . .'

Vi looked at it. It had to be at least eight feet tall.

'But this time I heard someone scream,' Majid Islam said. 'I was in my house, in my dining room, and I heard screaming coming from here.' He shrugged. 'So I put a ladder up against the wall, and then I saw them.'

'How many were there?' Vi asked.

'Three that I saw. One I saw get away, the other must have got away and this one . . .' He turned to face the figure with the swastika. Majid Islam moved in closer to DI Collins. 'They're always of that type,' he said. 'That, or they're jihadi boys.'

Of course they were. Who else would break into a Jewish cemetery except white rights nutters and al Qaeda fanboys?

'Do you know the dead man at all, Mr Islam?' Vi asked.

'No.'

'Not a neighbour or . . .'

'I think he looks like a homeless person. He does to me,' he said.

'And do you know that person?' She indicated the figure with the tattoo.

'No!'

'By "know him", I mean have you ever seen him before?'

He considered the question for a moment. 'No, I don't think so.'

'Thanks, Mr Islam,' Vi said. 'When SOCO have finished we'll be able to take you home. Until then, I'm sorry, but we're going to have to keep you here.'

He said nothing, clearly not happy, but resigned. Vi and Tony Bracci moved forward until they were standing in front of the skinhead being restrained by the two constables. A pair of the sharpest, bluest eyes Vi had ever seen looked at her with loathing.

'So what's your story then?' she asked.

The skinhead tried to pull an arm free and then spat down on the ground.

'Charming.'

One of the constables said, 'She doesn't speak English, guv.'

'She?! Are you sure?'

'Yes, guv.' The constable who was speaking looked embarrassed. 'When we grabbed her to stop her escaping, we . . .' He nodded towards the figure's chest, covered in a loose, hoody top.

Vi tried not to laugh. 'So if she can't speak English, what can she speak?'

'Dunno.'

'Well, find out.' Vi looked at the swastika proudly displayed on the girl's neck. 'It's bad enough we have to put up with our own scumbags without importing the bleeders. And we need to know what she knows about our body.'

'Yes, guv.'

Vi turned to Tony Bracci. 'I want everyone in every house that backs onto this cemetery spoken to, Tone,' she said. 'I know that wall is high but it ain't soundproof.'

'No.'

'Do it.' She waved him on his way, then watched as the Scenes of Crime officers erected a tent over the body and the skeleton. Tangled together they lay on top of some poor-looking graves, marked only with simple plates and surrounded by stones.

Vi looked around the cemetery, darkness now illuminated by SOCO's powerful lamps. The wall was high, but it was still possible for people in the surrounding houses to see what was happening from their upstairs windows. And hear.

She looked at the tent that now covered the corpse and the skeleton and found herself feeling very cold. The body of the homeless bloke, or whoever he was, was one thing, but the skeleton was quite another. And it looked old. Nana Faye, her grandmother, was buried somewhere in Plashet. Vi's hand came up and stroked the Star of David and the Cross she wore together on a thick gold chain around her neck.

From the very first time Wendy had told Sean she couldn't pay the rent, she'd done everything that he or Marty ordered her to. To begin with it had mainly been blow jobs for their clients. The Rogers' and Yunus Ali had a string of girls they liked to offer to men they wanted to get in with or impress. The women were often the Rogers' tenants, usually behind with their rent. Nearly all the properties they managed were the sort that had young single mums living in them. Most of the girls were younger than Wendy. She'd watched Sean eyeing up her fifteen-year-old, Dolly. At that point Wendy had effectively offered herself up as what Marty called a 'pig'. Basically she'd do anything for the men Sean made her go with, and for Sean himself. That Asian man hadn't wanted her, so she'd have to pay the rent by going with Sean instead.

After Sean had sated his frustrations on her he wiped his dick on an old handkerchief which he threw on the ground.

'You could at least make a few noises like you're enjoying it,' he said, as he watched Wendy put her catsuit back on.

'You got what you wanted,' Wendy said. She couldn't be downright rude to Sean but she could state the obvious and get away with it. Just.

'My brother's wife'd knock you into shape,' Sean said as he zipped up his fly.

Debbie Rogers was known for her brutality and just the mention of her name made Wendy's heart pound.

Seeing her fear, Sean laughed. 'Oh, don't worry, I won't give you to Debs just yet,' he said. 'But me and Marty are having a party next Saturday night where I want you to make up for what you never done tonight.'

Sean and his brother were fond of what they called 'Blind' orgies. Sean's house in Ongar had a room that could be completely blacked out, into which he'd put a selection of his girls. Men, including Sean and Marty, would go in and take whatever girls they wanted. She and the others would have to satisfy whatever needs these men had all night long. Then they'd have to clean the place up afterwards. But if that was what it cost her to keep Dolly safe, then that was a price Wendy was prepared to pay.

Before she went back to the pub, Wendy looked up at the small, frosted glass window of the ladies toilets. They backed onto the yard, and although she'd told Sean that someone in the loo might hear them, he'd been too anxious to fuck her to care. The window was slightly open now. She was sure it had been closed before.

There was a lot of interest in what was happening in the old Jewish cemetery, but very little information. No-one that Tony Bracci had spoken to so far had, apparently, seen or heard anything, apart from Mr Islam's wife and his teenage daughter. Mrs Islam had told him that 'a lot of people round here are blind and deaf when it comes to that cemetery.' The most he got out of anyone else was an old Sikh who just said, 'BNP! BNP!'

Outside one house, a gang of Asian youths lurked in hoodies trying to look hard. Ignoring them, he knocked on the door of the house at the end of Colston Road. It was eventually answered by a young white woman with a baby on her hip. He held up his badge and said, 'Police.'

'Oh,' she said, 'what do you want?'

Tony picked up an accent in there but he didn't recognise it.

'Just wondering if you heard any noises coming from the old cemetery earlier this evening?' he said. 'Maybe you saw someone climbing over the wall?' The side of the house and the garden were bordered by a new section of wall that had been built to block up an old second entrance.

'Over the wall?' Her eyes widened. She was blonde and small and Tony rather fancied her. 'No, that's crazy,' she said. 'No, I heard nothing. Baby cries, you don't hear anything else.'

He moved on down Colston, briefly into Shrewsbury Road and then onto Strone Road, which had the largest number of houses backing on to the cemetery. Through the rain and the darkness Tony looked up at the houses that surrounded him. They were all of a type, Edwardian terraces, like so much of the borough. Hard though it was to believe now, Newham, or West Ham as it had been known, had been built as a rather genteel suburb, intended to house clerks and their families from the docks and the City. But it had soon turned into an ocean of poverty like Whitechapel, Bethnal Green and other manors 'out east'. And Olympics or no Olympics, it hadn't changed that much. House prices could be as high as they liked, but while people filled their front yards with old mattresses and flats meant for six people housed twelve, Newham would still be Newham. Tony knocked on a door that looked as if it had had acid thrown at it, and waited for someone to answer.

'He might as well have done her in front of the whole pub,' Lee said as he put a cup of tea down in front of Mumtaz.

Wendy Dixon had walked home after Sean Rogers had sex with her round the back of the pub. He'd told her to 'fuck off' while he got in his Daimler and drove away. Mumtaz had watched

Wendy drag herself down a wet High Street North. She'd wanted to give the poor woman a lift even though she knew that she couldn't. Shortly afterwards she'd met up with Lee back at the office.

Lee sat behind his desk. 'You got it all on camera?'

'Yes.' It had been vile. Sean Rogers had just slammed himself into her. Mumtaz remembered such encounters herself. The only way to deal with them was to pretend that you weren't there.

Lee said, 'Good.'

She'd had to stand on one of the toilets and hold the camera up to the gap between the back window and its frame. Luckily no one had come in. She wondered if all the trouble had been worth it. Now her client would know that she'd been right about her sister, but so what? Would that change anything for Wendy?

'I'm afraid that Mrs Mirza, Wendy's sister, will use our evidence to try and get her and her children to go and live with her and her husband,' Mumtaz said.

'That'd get her away from Sean Rogers,' Lee said.

'Yes, but why should *she* have to move?'

Lee looked at her and smiled. Mumtaz wasn't naive but sometimes her sense of justice made her sound like she was. 'Because she's Sean Rogers's tenant and if she isn't paying her rent then the law will be on his side. You know that.'

Mumtaz sipped her tea.

'And even if we did tell the coppers that Sean is screwing one of his tenants in lieu of rent, what do you think they'll do? Wendy'll support him anyway, she'll have to if she wants to stay in one piece.'

'I heard him talk about wanting her to be at a party he's holding next weekend. She'd have to "make up" for what she hadn't done this evening.'

'With the Asian guy?'

'I assume so. Lee are you sure that DI Collins wouldn't find this interesting?'

'She would if Wendy Dixon would shop Sean Rogers,' Lee said. 'But she won't.The Rogers boys and Yunus Ali own hundreds of properties in this borough and if you can find any one of their tenants who is prepared to grass them up, then you're better than Forest Gate's finest. Rogers and Ali are a crime empire and it takes time and extraordinary courage to take an empire down.'

Gangsters. Of course. Mumtaz's throat felt dry and she cleared it with a cough. 'I'll call Mrs Mirza in the morning.'

'Good.'

Mumtaz had asked to meet up at the office before they went home because she'd needed to talk about what she'd seen at the back of that pub. She didn't want to take those images home with her. But Lee's assessment of Wendy Dixon's future was so bleak she could hardly bear it. She changed the subject. 'What about the police being called out to the Plashet cemetery,' she said.

Lee shrugged. 'Again,' he said. 'Something else that just goes on and on and on.'

'Anti-Semitism?'

He shrugged again. 'Who knows? But whatever it was it must have been bad because when I drove past earlier, the coppers were still in there. A lot of coppers, judging by the number of cars parked outside.'

6

The woman he'd cuffed and then taken back to Forest Gate nick told Tony Bracci her name was Kazia Ostrowska and she was twenty-five years old. She obviously supported a Polish football team called Wisla Krakow, since she wore a Wisla Krakow tee-shirt, scarf and arm bands. She also had a grasp of the English language that she hadn't exhibited when they'd first caught up with her the previous night. She sounded, Tony thought, a bit like the pretty blonde woman he'd spoken to when he was doing house to house on Colston Road.

'I don't care for Jews, but I never killed no-one,' Kazia said.

'What were you doing in the Plashet Cemetery in the dark?'

Kazia turned her face towards the duty solicitor who was representing her and said nothing.

'I'll take that as a "no comment" then,' Tony said. He looked down at his notes. 'Considering the fact that Wisla Krakow are not playing any games in this country at the moment and you don't live here, why are you here, Miss Ostrowska?'

'My brother, he lives in Leytonstone. I tell you this I think.'

'Yes,' Tony said. He looked at his notes again. 'Lech Ostrowski, your brother, is a cook.'

'A chef,' she corrected. 'I come for holiday.'

'For almost three months?'

'Why not?' She shrugged. She was beyond thin, yet had a sort of sinewy muscularity that suggested time spent in a gym.

'Who was with you in the cemetery last night?' Tony asked.

'No-one.'

'Oh, come on Kazia. We have a witness who saw at least two other people. Who were you with?'

'A witness?' she said. And then she laughed. 'A Paki.'

Tony saw the duty solicitor flinch. 'I don't know a great deal about Polish football violence and far-right racist politics but I'm aware they're connected.' He'd seen a documentary with Ross Kemp, who used to be in *EastEnders* and had knocked about with a load of Polish football thugs for enough time to make a programme about it. They were serious people. 'You've said you don't like Jews. You were in a Jewish cemetery—'

'The man who was dead, he was white,' she said. The expression on her face was almost blank. She could have been talking about bus times. 'So the Paki killed him. Easy.'

Even if Tony hadn't known that Majid Islam had handed his clothes over to forensics without a murmur, he still wouldn't have believed he'd killed the man in the graveyard.

'I don't think that our witness killed anyone,' Tony said.

'You think I did.'

'I didn't say that.'

The man without a name had been stabbed in the back. Considerable force had been applied, according to the pathologist. Kazia looked as if she both did and didn't have it in her. The clothes she'd been wearing the night before were also being examined by forensics. But like Majid Islam's, they'd showed no signs of blood.

'I need to know who you were with last night, Kazia,' Tony said. 'Give me their names. If they're a bit tasty we'll protect you.'

'I was alone. How many times . . . !'

He looked into her eyes. They were as blue and as cold as an Alpine lake. Her lips curled as she regarded Tony with something approaching humour. 'I want cigarette now,' she said.

Mumtaz was on the phone to Ayesha Mirza. Still talking, she picked up her car keys. As soon as she'd finished the call, she'd have to go and pick up Shazia.

'If you like I'll come round to your house tomorrow morning, I can show you the footage,' she said. 'But it isn't for the faint-hearted. I'm sorry.'

At the other end of the line, Mrs Mirza sighed.

'Christ, I knew our Wend was into something horrible. Every-one knows what Sean Rogers and his brother are, but to do that to our Wend . . . I've got to get her and the kids out of there.'

'But you must be careful, Mrs Mirza,' Mumtaz said. 'Wendy owes Sean Rogers rent or she wouldn't be doing this.'

'Then I'll pay it off for her, I'll—'

'Rogers may want to charge you interest on what she owes,' Mumtaz cut in. She wanted to add *I know all about this* because that was exactly what had happened to her with Ahmet's debts, but she managed to stop herself. Her problems with the Sheikh family, the gangsters her husband had associated with, were not Mrs Mirza's. 'It could be at an extortionate rate. Say nothing until you've seen the footage and then speak to Mr Arnold, he was a policeman and he knows the Rogers brothers. He will advise you.'

She eventually agreed to this and Mumtaz managed to end the call. She walked out of the house and looked at the shabby little Micra on her driveway. When Ahmet had been alive they'd had not only the Mercedes, but a gardener too, *and* she'd had all her jewellery back then . . . But what had gone along with all that had not been so pleasant. She looked at the battered old car and smiled. She was about to open the driver's door when Mr Higgs from across the road, the one Ahmet had always called the 'Leftie', stopped trimming his hedge and called out to her, 'Did you hear they found a man dead in the old Jewish Cemetery?'

John's shack was barely a structure at all. Made out of a hood of tangled branches and creepers, it hung between two trees that butted up against the cemetery wall. The branches, which didn't belong to the trees, were clearly old and dead and, at some point, someone had thrown a sheet of polythene over them.

Underneath the canopy, on ground that was churned and damp from the recent rain, was a rolled up sleeping bag, a candle that was half burnt down and a tobacco tin. How did John survive?

Feeling like a burglar, Nasreen ducked down into the shack. The sleeping bag was covered with a camouflage pattern and she wondered whether it was John's old army one. She opened the tobacco tin and found only a couple of Rizla papers. She hadn't realised that John smoked. She closed the tin again and unrolled the sleeping bag. There was nothing in it except a spider. Nasreen looked at the uneven surface and she wondered how he ever slept there. She didn't know anything about the man who had been found dead in the cemetery. It might be John, but it might not. Yet she knew she should tell the police about the man who sometimes lived in her garden, a few metres from the graveyard, and was now nowhere to be seen.

But then there was Abdullah to consider. She'd kept quiet about the ex-soldier at the end of their garden for a good reason. What would he say if she suddenly went to the police with a story about keeping a homeless man in food?

Lee went into the Boleyn at lunchtime. Usually on a Sunday he went to his mum's place in Custom House, but she'd been invited to a friend's for lunch and Lee didn't want to spend any time alone with his brother. Roy Arnold, Lee's older and only sibling, was an alcoholic. In that respect the Arnold boys were the same, except that Lee had managed to stop drinking. Roy, on the other hand, reeked of cheap cider, was lairy most of the time, could be violent and ligged off their mother at every opportunity. Lee hated him with almost the same passion as their mother loved him. He only gave him the time of day at all because of her.

So he read the Sunday papers in the pub, ate a plate of chips and drank more diet Pepsi than he should. Occasionally he went out onto Green Street for a fag. The rest of the time he chatted to various people he knew both on and off the manor. A lot of them were old men, mates of his late father, plus the odd West Ham fan and someone Lee knew to be one of Vi Collins's snouts, a bloke in an electric wheelchair called 'Murderer' Noakes.

Wilf Cox, one of Lee's dad's old friends, bought Lee a Pepsi and himself a pint of bitter. As he walked over to the table where Lee sat flicking through the *Observer*, he looked over at Noakes.

'Dunno who's supposed to be looking after Murderer these days,' Wilf said, as he put Lee's drink down in front of him. 'But he smells of piss.'

Lee knew that Murderer had carers in twice a day, or he always had done.

'Shouldn't let him out smelling like that,' Wilf said. He sat down and looked idly at a bit of Lee's paper. 'Bleedin' country's going to pot. Run by rich boys for rich boys. But no-one cares about the poor anymore do they? Look at old Murderer. I mean I know he was in that bike gang—'

'The Hells Angels.'

'Yeah, but now he's a cripple and nobody wants to know!'

In principle Lee agreed with what Wilf was saying. He hated the cuts the government was making to public services, he hated the resultant unemployment and the complete absence of punishment for the big City financiers who had brought about the economic crisis in the first place, but Murderer Noakes was hardly the epitome of want. He'd come off his bike back in 1979 while riding to some Angels orgy out in Hertfordshire. He'd had every benefit and perk the State would give him. On top of that was the money Vi Collins bunged him from time to time for keeping his ear to the ground. If Murderer smelt of piss it was possibly because he wanted to.

Wilf read the cookery section of the *Observer* while continuing to witter on about politics. Lee's own thoughts were still with the events of the previous night. Mumtaz had been right about Sean Rogers. Something needed to be done about his business practices. Sean, Marty and their silent partner Yunus Ali had been abusing their tenants for years. There were loads of stories about how they put young girls out on the streets, how they gave them as presents, and rumours about orgies, drugs, protection, and their occasional spats with the Asian Sheikh brothers organisation. Years ago, Marty's wife Debbie had allegedly cut girls for failing to please their customers. Now it seemed Sean took the lead. But how to get either Wendy Dixon or any of the tenants of Rogers and Ali to grass on the bastards was a puzzler. There wasn't enough property on the manor as it was and so the poor were pushed into ever smaller and more squalid spaces for more and more money.

The door from Green Street burst open and everyone in the pub looked up. Framed in the doorway was a middle-aged woman holding a roll-up in her right hand. She was swaying. 'I need a light for me fag,' she said. 'Anyone got a light for me fag?'

Wilf said, 'Christ,' but Lee stood up and took his lighter out of his pocket.

'You can't smoke in here, Cheryl!' Maureen the barmaid yelled.

'Yeah, I know that, I . . .'

Lee braved the hum of cheap cider that always came off Cheryl's clothes and led her outside. She was, as usual, arse'oled. 'I went to Mass, but they chucked me out,' she said.

'Stick your fag in your gob,' Lee said, 'and I'll light it.'

Once Cheryl had had kids, a husband and a life. But then her husband had lost his job, then she'd fallen out with him, then they'd lost their home and Cheryl had gone on the booze. Now she was homeless and drunk while her husband and her kids lived in some damp flat in Barking. She put her roll-up in her mouth and sucked hard as Lee lit it.

'Ta, darling.'

'You're welcome,' he said.

He was just about to go back into the Boleyn when she said to him, 'You know they found a dead body up the old Jewish Cemetery last night?'

'Yes,' Lee said. 'Terrible.'

'Not really,' Cheryl said. She burped. 'He was grave robbing.'

Lee walked back towards her. 'Who was?'

'The dead geezer.'

'How do you know he was grave robbing?'

Cheryl smirked. 'Can I have a Kronenbourg?' she said.

She was always ligging booze off everybody, using all sorts of weird stories. Even through the booze Cheryl knew that Lee was an ex-copper and that stories about crime would get him going.

'You can have a Kronenbourg if you tell me,' Lee said. 'Story first, Cheryl.'

She swayed. Stained teeth made a brief appearance as she smiled.

'Because they found him with a skeleton.'

'Who did? The coppers?'

'Yeah. Can I have that beer now?'

'No, not yet. How do you know this, Cheryl? And why should I believe you?'

Cheryl put a finger to her nose and tapped it. 'Because I was up there, you stupid arse.'

'Where?'

'The fucking cemetery.' She waved a hand in the air. 'They was talking about it. I was walking past.'

'The coppers?'

'Yeah.'

'When?'

'I dunno. It was dark.'

'What did they say?'

'Fucking hell, don't you listen?' Cheryl said. 'They said the stiff had been grave robbing. He had a skeleton. Can you get me a beer?'

Vi was alone in the cemetery. She'd asked for a moment by herself and so SOCO had gone off to have a break. She didn't have a clue where her Nana Faye was buried. She remembered her dying but she hadn't gone to the funeral. She'd only been eight and Nana

Faye hadn't liked her anyway. Or rather she hadn't liked her mum. Her dad's people had been Orthodox Jews and so her gentile mum had never gone down well.

She looked around at the gravestones but it was hopeless. The inscriptions were in English as well as Hebrew but half of them had been worn away or vandalised. Nana Faye had called Vi's mum a 'gypsy' because she was Irish. She'd felt keenly and bitterly the dilution of her own Jewish blood. Vi's dad, her son, had hated her for it. But in spite of this, Vi was relieved that it didn't seem as if their unknown dead bloke had dug anyone up from the graveyard. The Polish skinhead girl they held in custody was denying any sort of involvement too and, so far, the forensic evidence from her clothes didn't point to any either. SOCO had already checked out the one pathetic camera on the site, but it hadn't shown anything of interest. But if the skeleton hadn't come from the graveyard, where *had* it come from? And why had the dead man been lying beside it when Majid Islam tripped over him?

Vi looked around the cemetery. She put one hand up to the Star of David around her neck but she knew that she was as much of an intruder there as the Polish girl had been.

7

Monday morning was dull, but at least it wasn't raining. Nasreen sat on the back step looking at the tangle of trees and bushes that concealed John's shack. To distract herself from thoughts of him, she took the photograph and the thing it had been hidden behind from her pocket and looked at them again. It was weird to nail a photograph behind something like that, on a doorpost. Maybe Abdullah would know what it was. He was the one who'd chosen this house, after all. He had to know more about it than she did. But did he? He'd bought the house at auction, which meant that he'd only viewed it very briefly and in a group of other potential buyers. As far as Nasreen could tell, it had been the price that had attracted him to it more than anything else. Although why that should have been of concern to a man who bought her emeralds she couldn't always square in her mind. But since they'd got married, and particularly after she became pregnant, Nasreen had found it hard to talk to Abdullah. If he wasn't busy, he was distracted, and if she talked about something he wasn't interested in, he would cut her off.

They'd met, indirectly, via her father's brother, Uncle Salim. He lived in Poplar where he owned a boarding house that was used by men who had come to London to work. All the landlords in the area knew each other and Uncle Salim was particular friends with a certain Fazal Bashar, who had his very personable nephew Abdullah staying with him. A thirty-seven-year-old lawyer from Bolton, Abdullah had impressed Uncle Salim from the start. After consulting Fazal Bashar and Nasreen's father Imran who, like her mother, was a liberal, western-leaning person, Uncle Salim had introduced Nasreen to the young lawyer. The attraction between them had been immediate. Within weeks they had announced their engagement.

During the months leading up to the wedding, Abdullah had taken Nasreen everywhere. They'd been to high-end restaurants run by celebrity chefs, to cinemas and theatres. Together they had chosen the most beautiful wedding cake and wedding rings, which Abdullah had paid for with his gold credit cards. But as the wedding day approached he had, she'd noticed, become nervous – and increasingly jealous. Later, he'd put extra pressure on himself by buying the house. He'd told Nasreen it was a bargain because it had been empty for so long and he just couldn't let it slip through his fingers. However, there was something else too. Unlike her, Abdullah had no real family. She'd only ever, briefly, met his uncle Fazal once. Abdullah was an only child, both his parents were dead and, although he was paying his share when it came to the wedding, he was ashamed that he was doing it on his own.

'But can't your uncle help out?' Nasreen had asked him when he'd told her. 'Don't you have cousins or whatever?'

But he'd said, 'No, there's nobody. I left Bolton because there was no point in being there anymore. Everybody was gone.'

'What about friends?' she'd said.

Abdullah had shaken his head. 'All the local lads were losers,' he'd said. 'When I went off to uni I lost touch.'

It was strange, this smallness of family. Even Nasreen's relatives, who basically lived very English lives and had few children, were still numerous. Abdullah was such a lonely soul, she felt her heart ache when she thought about it. 'Well, you can share my family then,' she'd said.

But he hadn't. Abdullah, though polite and courteous to her family, had little to do with them beyond niceties. Most of the time he was at her parents' house he either watched TV or listened to his father's old Paul Simon CDs in their room. It was clear from all the frantic activity that he put into it that he wanted to get their own house ready as soon as possible so that he and Nasreen could leave her parents' place and move in. She wanted that too, but she also wanted to talk to her husband. She looked at the photograph of the woman and wondered how old it was. It was black and white, but it could have been thirty or sixty years old. She had no idea. Maybe John would know? But then she remembered that she didn't know where John was.

'I couldn't have him like that at home,' the woman told Vi. 'Not like that. Not in that state. Even his girlfriend left him.'

'Why?'

'Because he was violent! Because he couldn't get what had happened out there out of his head! Because the mess in his brain spread out across every room in my house. Why should I live with that? For Afghanistan? I don't care.'

The woman was called Rita Sawyer and she'd just identified the man they'd found in Plashet Jewish Cemetery as her son, John Sawyer. Around fifty, Mrs Sawyer was thin and sun-dried in the way that only people who sunbathed or went abroad a lot were. Together with her husband and a teenage daughter, she lived in Manor Park.

'Tell me about John, Mrs Sawyer,' Vi asked.

'What do you want to know?'

Vi wanted to know whether John Sawyer had ever been a member of any sort of far-right or anti-Semitic group and whether he'd been nuts enough to dig up a skeleton. But she said, 'What was he like? As a son? You mean before Afghanistan or after?'

'Both.'

Rita Sawyer sighed. She wore clothes that were at least twenty years too young for her. A mini-skirt in electric pink and a zebra print top that showed her wrinkled cleavage. Vi, whose sartorial tastes were rather more conservative, was half appalled, half lost in admiration. 'John was a bit of an 'erbert when he was young,' she said. 'He never done well at school, couldn't concentrate. But he liked sports and he was good enough at home with his sister and me and Ken. He thought about things.'

'What things?'

She shook her head and grimaced, as if the memory she'd conjured was too painful for her. 'Hunger, all that Live Eight stuff, homeless people. Always on the side of the underdog. Got sick of hearing it sometimes.'

'Why did he go into the army?'

'Couldn't get a job,' she said. 'He learnt to drive when he was seventeen and Ken wanted him to do the Knowledge.' Vi knew that Ken Sawyer drove a black cab. 'But he never wanted to. He drifted into a bit of mini-cabbing but he never liked it much. One of his mates was going to Afghanistan and the next thing, he'd joined up.'

'What did you think about that?'

'I thought it was up to him,' she said.

'So what happened when he came home . . .' She wanted to say 'damaged' but in the end she said '. . . unwell?'

Rita Sawyer shifted uncomfortably in her chair. 'Well, he was a nightmare. Awake most of the night, wandering around the house and then flopping down on the Chesterfield at some God-forsaken hour of the morning, spilling his tobacco all over the coffee table. If you said anything to him about it he'd go berserk. Shouted right in his sister Shania's face, on about how all what he'd done out in Afghanistan was wrong, about injustice.' Vi saw her wince as if in physical pain. 'Then when Lisa left him – that was his girlfriend – he really lost the plot. He stopped washing, wouldn't eat, shouted and cried all the time. Ken took him down the doctor's, but they wouldn't do nothing except give him some pills what he never took.'

'What pills?'

'I dunno. Pills. I thought they put people like that somewhere, but not any more. They have to be looked after in the "community". I tried his old regiment but they didn't want to know. Something happened to him out there, something he wouldn't talk about.' She looked up at Vi and her eyes were challenging. 'What was we supposed to do? Have him destroy what we took thirty years to put together? My daughter was frightened of him.'

Poor John Sawyer. He wasn't the first soldier to go feral on the streets of London. According to Rita Sawyer, he'd left, been chucked out or whatever almost a year ago. Since then he'd been seen by his family on Green Street, High Street North, East Ham and wandering about talking to himself on Wanstead Flats and in Central Park. Vi reckoned she'd probably seen him. But John hadn't been a great drinker. He hadn't come to her attention for lobbing a cider bottle of piss at anybody, unlike some of the more lairy ex-soldiers.

'Do you know where John stayed or slept?'

'No.'

'You must've been curious about him, Mrs Sawyer.'

She took it as a criticism. 'You try living with what we had to live with, getting no help from no-one and then you criticise me, you mare,' she barked

It wasn't often that Vi looked away from an interviewee. Was this woman's apparent hardness real or a defence mechanism? She'd just turned back to look at Rita Sawyer again when she saw a single tear slide down her face.

When Mumtaz arrived at Ayesha Mirza's house in Forest Gate, everyone was out. Suspecting that the woman hadn't forgotten their appointment so much as ignored it, Mumtaz got in the Micra and drove to Patrick Road in Plaistow. And sure enough, there she was in Wendy Dixon's front garden.

'You and the kids have gotta come with me!' Mrs Mirza called up towards a top-floor window.

Wendy Dixon, leaning out, shouted back, 'Fuck off, Mary, you don't know what you're talking about!'

'You making money _that_ way,' Ayesha Mirza said. 'You can't do it Wend. You can't. Think of the kids.'

Mumtaz, appalled, if not surprised, that Ayesha Mirza had done the opposite to what she had advised, got out of the car and went over to her. 'Mrs Mirza . . .'

The woman turned and looked at her, her face red with anger and frustration. 'Oh, Mrs Hakim,' she said, 'what—'

'And don't think I give a shit what your fucking al Qaeda mates think either!' Wendy Dixon yelled as she looked at Mumtaz.

'Wendy, you . . .'

Mumtaz put a hand on Ayesha Mirza's arm.

'Come and get in the car and we'll talk,' she said. She wanted to say to her, *You still haven't seen the footage you've paid me for. Look at it and then tell me whether you can judge your sister or not?* But she didn't. A couple of Wendy Dixon's neighbours were peeping through their curtains at what was going on in the street, and one of them had come out of her front door to have a look.

Ayesha Mirza looked at Mumtaz, 'But . . .'

'Come on,' Mumtaz said. 'Let's go for a coffee somewhere.'

The woman let herself be led to the car while Wendy Dixon shouted, 'Go on! Fuck off!'

At the end of Patrick Road, where it met Tunmarsh Lane, Mumtaz saw a big BMW with blacked-out windows. It was the sort of car that gangsters often drove. People like the Sheikh family. Naz Sheikh, that good looking, lethal psychopath, was in charge of collecting 'her' debt for his equally ruthless father and brothers. If any of them were in that car now she hoped they would have an accident.

'Ayesha,' she said, 'I have to ask, did you tell your sister that you'd had her followed?'

Ayesha shook her head. 'No.'

'So what did you tell her?'

'Just that I knew what she was up to with her landlord. She didn't deny it. She just pushed me out the flat. I offered her and the kids to come and live with Wazim and me, I said all I wanted to do was help her.'

She was genuinely baffled. Clearly Ayesha had lived a much more sheltered life than her sister – and had listened to nothing Mumtaz had told her on Sunday.

'But it isn't as simple as that,' Mumtaz said. She was heading for Prince Regent Lane and then on down to Silvertown and the little cafe in the Thames Barrier Park. She liked it down there, it was quiet and anonymous. 'Your sister owes her landlord, Sean

Rogers. Even if you do take her and her children out of that house, he will come after her.'

'But if he's putting her on the streets . . .'

'She'd have to make a complaint to the police herself,' Mumtaz said. 'According to the law, at the moment she is in the wrong because she owes him money.'

'How much?'

'I don't know. But these people charge unbelievable rates of interest.'

'How can they do that?'

Mumtaz shrugged. 'It's legal,' she said. 'The only way forward for Wendy would be for her to go to the police and report the abuse. But I can tell from seeing how she was just now, she won't do that. My boss, Mr Arnold, has never known anyone press charges against the Rogers brothers or any of their associates. That's the thing with gangsters, Ayesha, nobody ever tells. That's where their power comes from: other people's silence.'

Just talking about it, about herself, made Mumtaz want to cry. Ahmet had gambled, literally, with the Sheikh family and he'd lost. Now she was selling everything she had to pay the interest on that debt and keep a roof over her own and Shazia's heads. And just like Wendy Dixon who kept her mouth shut about the Rogers brothers, she wasn't saying a word.

Lee could find nothing about any skeleton or bones in the local paper. He'd gone to the newsagents in Green Street and bought the *Newham Recorder* but there was no mention of bones being found in the Plashet Graveyard. There was just a sad little story about a man called John Sawyer, who'd been found stabbed in the back on Saturday night. He'd served in Afghanistan apparently. He was only twenty-seven, had been homeless and mentally ill and no-one had given a damn. A few of Lee's old mates from Iraq had ended up like that. He hadn't. He'd joined the police, lost his marriage and become addicted to booze and painkillers. Serving one's country was an honour that came at a price, Lee thought as he watched a cold rain lash down on Green Street.

There was no picture of John Sawyer in the newspaper, but Nasreen knew that it was him. His age seemed about right, he'd been a soldier in Afghanistan and he'd been homeless. It had to be John. Abdullah came in from the garden, soaked through.

'The guttering needs doing,' he said.

Water had suddenly poured through the open bathroom window.

'Oh.' She put the newspaper down.

'Anything in the *Recorder*?' he asked.

'Not much,' she said. She should have said *the homeless man who used to live in our garden is dead,* but she couldn't. If Abdullah found out she'd known about a man living in their garden he'd subject her to protracted interrogation. If he knew she'd fed John, his questioning would be furious and, she feared, without end. His jealousy of other men, in her experience, knew no limits.

Soon after they'd married, one of her cousins, Rafiq, had come to stay. Rafiq's father had spent a lot of time working away from home. His mother was dead, and Rafiq had often stayed at Nasreen's house when they were children. He was like a brother to her. As soon as he arrived they'd reverted to how they'd always been with each other – mucking around, joking, laughing loudly. Then Rafiq had tickled her, just for a laugh.

There was nothing in it, but Abdullah hadn't taken it that way.

He'd pulled them apart and then he'd hit Rafiq, hard. Neither Nasreen nor her parents had known what to do. None of them had seen Rafiq since.

As Abdullah walked past her into the living room, he briefly touched her shoulder. It was an affectionate touch and she wanted to turn to him, kiss him. But she daren't because by this time she was crying. John was dead and no-one knew why – but she feared her own terrible thoughts. Surely, even if Abdullah had found John in the garden, whatever had happened she as his wife would have been the first to know? Nasreen's next feeling was one of shame. Whatever else he was, Abdullah was her husband and she owed him trust and loyalty.

8

'Where'd you hear about a skeleton, Arnold?' Vi Collins asked Lee as they sat out in the cold in the garden of the Golden Fleece. Lee had had the morning off to take Chronus to the vet – he'd been off his food for a few days. He'd met Vi as he was going out to his car after depositing the mynah bird back in the flat. She'd offered him a drink and the Golden Fleece was the nearest boozer. He'd taken her up on her offer and then he'd asked her, naming no names, about the weird little bit of intel Cheryl the alkie had given him outside the Boleyn, about a skeleton found with the body of John Sawyer in the Plashet Jewish Cemetery.

'I just heard,' Lee said.

'Well, you must've heard from some sort of nutter,' Vi said.

'So there isn't any skeleton?'

'I chose my words very carefully, Arnold,' Vi said. 'I talked about "a" skeleton, not "the" skeleton.'

'So you're saying that the whole skeleton thing—'

'"A" skeleton,' Vi repeated. '"A" as in "a".'

Even though Cheryl the alkie was a notoriously unreliable source of information, Lee could read Vi Collins and so her inability to *actually* answer his question by talking about 'the' skeleton was telling. Somewhere a skeleton existed which Vi knew about; however, whether it was directly related to the Plashet

Cemetery was not something she wanted to discuss. Lee knew that he couldn't pursue it and she was on her guard now. He'd just salt that little bit of information away in his head in case he needed it sometime in the future.

'So what you up to this afternoon?' Vi asked. She was drinking diet Pepsi like he was, so she must be officially on duty.

'Going back to work.'

'Mmm. So how's your parrot? Is he sick or just moody?'

Chronus had been a gift from Vi, who knew full well he was a mynah bird. But she always called him a parrot and Lee had stopped correcting her years ago.

'Moody,' he said. The vet had been unable to find anything wrong with the bird and had concluded that he was just simply showing off in order to get more treats or different food. Lee spoiled him, but then Chronus had become what Vi had intended him to be – Lee's surrogate child. When she'd brought the bird into his life, Lee had been mourning the loss of his wife who had divorced him and his daughter who had left with her, and he was battling addiction to booze and pain killers. He'd still been in the police then and Vi had wanted to help. She'd also fancied the pants off him. They'd slept together a few times over the years and Lee knew that by taking him for a drink she could either be angling to go back to his place, less than a minute down the road, for some afternoon delight or she was having a bit of fun watching his discomfort. Either way he wasn't in the mood, and anyway Mumtaz was on her own in the office.

He looked at Vi and she smiled. 'How about we . . .' she began.

'I can't,' Lee said. 'I've gotta get back to Green Street.'

She shrugged. 'Fair enough.'

'And you've got to get back to your Plashet corpse – and that skeleton,' Lee said.

'I've told you it's not "the"—'

'Oh, methinks the lady doth protest too much,' Lee said, as he rose to his feet. He began to walk away but then he stopped. *Ah what the hell?* Then he turned, winked at her and said, 'You coming or what?'

'With you?'

'Who else you got on the go, Vi?'

She gave him a killer glare and stood up. 'I'm on duty, Arnold, sorry.' Then she put a fag in her mouth, lit it and began to walk towards her car. 'Shoulda said yes the first time, honey,' she said to him over her shoulder. 'No second chances here.'

Lee Arnold laughed. She was such a fucking tease.

Nasreen had heard of a lady, a Muslim, who helped women with problems. Her mum had mentioned her, and she'd heard her name spoken in a local shop: Mrs Hakim. She was a private detective and it was said she could sniff out a bad husband or an errant daughter-in-law the way other people sniffed out dry rot in old houses. She worked with an Englishman who was very good looking. Mrs Hakim was a widow but she was young, and some thought beautiful. Nasreen felt anxious about going to see such a person. She couldn't talk about Abdullah – she didn't have the courage. Not yet. What if the woman contacted him and told him what she'd done?

No, she'd have to find some other reason to go to the office on Green Street. She needed time to work out whether or not she could trust this Mrs Hakim. Maybe her reason for going to see her could be something to do with the house? She remembered the metal capsule that looked a bit like a lipstick she'd taken off the doorpost and the picture that she'd found underneath it.

Nasreen rooted through her handbag to make sure that the photograph and the object were still there. They were. She left her parents' house and made her way up the road to Green Street. She'd already decided not to breathe a word about John.

Naz Sheikh liked four things in life: women, flash clothes, cars and his job. The latter consisted of working for his father, Zahid, and his older brother Rizwan. They had a property development company as well as a sideline in lending money. The money had to be secured on something of course, like a house or a car – or a wife.

He dialled the number on his iPhone and put it up to his ear. As he listened to it ring, he looked up at the window of the office above George the Barbers, and he saw her pick her up mobile. Lee Arnold was still out and so he expected her to be forthright.

'I've paid you,' Mumtaz Hakim said tersely. 'What do you want?'

'Just reminding you about the date for next month's payment,' he said. 'It's the sixteenth.'

'I know that,' she snapped. 'Leave me alone.'

He could just see her features fall into a scowl.

'Making sure there's no mistakes,' Naz said. 'I'd hate to—'

'Spare me your insincerities,' she said, and cut the connection. He watched her throw her mobile down on her desk and then she disappeared from view. Shame. Although older than he was, she was a tasty-looking woman. That said, if given the choice between her and her stepdaughter Naz would be a bit stumped. The kid was cute.

*

Nasreen put the strange metal object on Mumtaz Hakim's desk and placed the small photograph alongside it.

'You found this on one of the back doorposts?' Mumtaz asked.

'Yes.' Nasreen was surprised at quite how young Mrs Hakim was. She'd imagined her to be pretty but a bit motherly too. But, like they said, she was beautiful. 'I'd like to find out who she is, if that's possible.'

'Mmm.' She looked up. 'Do you own your house, Mrs Khan?'

'My husband does, yes.'

'Because previous owners will be listed in the deeds and then there is the Land Registry.'

'Yes, I know.' She could have asked Abdullah to look it up, but she wouldn't. 'My husband is very busy,' she said. 'I don't want to bother him with this.'

'OK.' She gave Nasreen a look as if she didn't quite believe her.

'I'm three months pregnant,' Nasreen said. She knew this didn't explain anything, but she felt compelled to say it anyway. 'I'd like *you* to look into it.'

'Very well.' She smiled. She wore the most beautiful rose-coloured headscarf that was tied in such a stylish way it almost made Nasreen want to wear one herself.

'I've money.'

'Of course.' Mumtaz smiled again. 'Now can you tell me if you know anything at all about your house. Anecdotal stuff is fine.'

Abdullah had bought the house effectively on his own at auction. 'It was empty for a long time,' Nasreen said. 'Years.'

'Do you know who your husband bought it from?'

'A firm of solicitors held the deeds, I believe.'

'Do you know which one?'

Nasreen didn't and it made her feel stupid. 'No,' she said. They'd been married when Abdullah had bought the house and yet she'd let him get on with it like some sort of helpless village woman. Her mum wasn't like that. Although in public her mum always covered her head, like this Mrs Hakim, she was very much the mistress of her own destiny. Sometimes, Nasreen felt, her father was the junior partner in their relationship. Had she taken a step back into the past when she married Abdullah? Or was she simply reflecting a trend for increasingly traditional relationships that seemed to be growing in some sections of the Muslim community?

'May I keep the photograph?' Mumtaz Hakim asked. 'And the . . .' She picked up the metal capsule.

'I don't know what to call it, either,' Nasreen said. 'Yes, you may.' And then something occurred to her, something her mother had said when Abdullah had bought the house. 'One thing I've heard is that a man lived in our house alone for many years.'

Mrs Hakim began to write this down. 'Do you know his name?'

'No, but my mum said he was white.' She bit her bottom lip. Her mother had advised her against buying that particular house. 'She said that whenever she saw him, he looked very sad.'

It wasn't easy for Mumtaz to distract herself from thinking about her own problems. A visit or a phone call from any one of the Sheikh family, especially Naz, always shook her up. Her feelings about him had always been ambiguous because, although he threatened and hassled her for money, Naz had also been the author of her freedom. As he'd plunged that knife into Ahmet's chest back when she'd never even heard the name Sheikh, she had, in gratitude she told herself, wanted to give herself to him. In reality she had simply experienced a moment of pure, selfish lust. She began to sweat and, to take her mind off him, she looked at the photograph that Nasreen Khan had given her.

The woman in the picture didn't look modern. Her hair, which was dark, was pulled back from her face, maybe into a pony tail or a bun. She looked about mid-thirties even though her features were what Mumtaz could only describe as 'tired'. The woman had something about her that Mumtaz recognised. Here was someone who had lived – not always in a way that she had enjoyed.

The office phone rang and she picked it up. A male voice said, 'Lee there?'

Mumtaz was a little taken aback by the terseness. 'No,' she said. 'Mr Arnold is out. Do you want to leave a message?'

The man gave a sigh of frustration. Mumtaz looked at her watch. It was one p.m. Lee had been taking Chronus to the vet, but he'd been gone a long time. She hoped that the mynah bird was OK. She knew how much he meant to Lee.

'Tell him that Brian Green called,' the man said. 'I've tried his mobile, but it's off.'

If he had Lee's mobile number, then Brian Green was either a client or he knew Lee well.

The office door swung open and Lee walked in carrying a couple of cappuccinos. 'Sorry!' he said as he entered, 'I—'

'Oh, he's just walked into the office, Mr Green. If you'd like to wait a moment, I'll transfer you,' Mumtaz said.

'Ta, darling.'

She put Green on hold. 'How's Chronus?' she asked as she watched Lee sit down at his desk.

'A grumpy little sod,' he said. 'But not ill.'

'That's good. I've a Mr—'

'Brian bloody Green,' Lee said. 'Yes, I know. Switched me mobile off in the vet's, forgot to put the bleeder back on again. Put him through, Mumtaz.'

She released the call.

Lee said, 'Hello Brian, how's tricks?'

Mumtaz went back to looking at the photograph and the odd, paint-encrusted lump that Nasreen Khan had found it under. She'd never seen anything like it before. She picked it up and weighed it in her hand. It was heavy. Lee, she noticed, was watching her.

9

The Polish girl was a tough nut. She stuck to her story, insisting that she'd been in the Plashet graveyard alone and denying that she'd seen anyone in there except Majid Islam. Both Tony Bracci and Vi Collins doubted her story. There were a lot of footprints in the cemetery that didn't belong to Mr Islam, Kazia or the victim. But so far there were no other witnesses. Except one. Lee Arnold had told Vi that someone had told him they'd overheard coppers talking about a skeleton. He wouldn't give her a name, but she'd spoken to a couple of the uniforms who'd been on duty outside the cemetery gates that night and she'd come up with someone. While Tony Bracci went off to talk to Kazia's brother Lech for a second time, Vi walked down to the Duke of Edinburgh pub on Green Street. She wanted to talk to Cheryl Bines, and the Duke or the Boleyn were the only stable points in her life. Where Cheryl actually lived was a mystery.

Vi didn't go straight in to the pub. Instead she stood on the opposite side of the road, looking in the window of a shop that sold fabulous Asian costume jewellery, rhinestone-encrusted handbags and scarves of every colour, texture and size. Run by a couple of Sikh widows, it was a magnet for fashion-conscious, traditional Asian girls. Vi looked across at the pub. No sign of Cheryl yet, but if she ran true to form, she'd be out pretty soon.

Sure enough, ten minutes later Cheryl came stumbling out of the Duke, swearing her head off. Vi crossed the road.

'Hi, Cheryl,' she said.

Cheryl looked up at her with red, hostile eyes. 'Fuck off, lesbian!' she said. Then realising that she might just have alienated someone she could lig off, she added, 'Sorry, sorry. I'm just . . . I'm . . .'

'Do you want me to buy you a beer?' Vi said.

'They've fucking chucked me out!'

'Yeah, but I can go in and buy you a pint, can't I? We could both have a drink outside then, couldn't we?'

'That'd be very nice of you, very nice,' Cheryl said.

Vi went inside the pub and bought herself a diet Pepsi and a pint of Kronenbourg for Cheryl. Whether she'd get any sense out of her, Vi didn't know but one more pint wouldn't make any difference.

When she came out, Cheryl was trying to make herself a roll-up but only succeeded in spilling tobacco over the pavement. Vi took the makings from her, built a decent fag and gave it to her. 'Cheryl,' she said, 'couple of our lads saw you up round the old Plashet Cemetery the other night, when we found the body of John Sawyer.'

Cheryl looked at Vi through the accumulated years of booze and drugs, not appearing to remember her.

'You a copper?'

'Yes, Cheryl, Vi Collins,' Vi said. 'You know, DI Collins?'

'Oh. What do you want then? I haven't done nothing.'

'No-one says you have.' Vi sipped her Pepsi. It was horrible. How could Lee drink the stuff all day long? 'Cheryl, you were at the cemetery—'

'I never killed that bloke, I—'

'No-one says you did,' Vi said. Cheryl, although sometimes quite lairy, was incapable of actually inflicting wounds on anyone except herself. 'But did you see anyone come out of the cemetery?'

'Well, the coppers and—'

'No, before the coppers.' One of the officers had told Vi that when he'd arrived, Cheryl had been outside the front gates of the cemetery, drinking from a can of Special Brew. 'You were outside the cemetery before the coppers arrived. Did you see anyone come out of the cemetery before they got there?'

'There might have been someone.'

'Someone? Who?'

'I dunno,' Cheryl said. 'If I had another beer—'

'No more beer unless you tell me what you remember, Cheryl.'

Majid Islam had seen what looked like a man vaulting over the cemetery gates and into High Street North, but he hadn't been close enough to give the police a description and there was no-one else who could corroborate his story. Except maybe Cheryl.

'Take your time,' Vi said. 'Was it a man or a woman? Black, white . . .'

'Oh, he was white,' Cheryl said.

'He?' Vi repeated what Cheryl had said to her just to be sure.

'Yeah, like a sort of a bovver boy,' Cheryl frowned. 'Big boots . . . or was that his feet? Or was he a girl?'

Vi felt deflated. Typical bloody alkie nonsense. Didn't know which way was up.

But then Cheryl did something that Vi had experienced various addicts do before. She suddenly came out with a small detail. 'Had a ring in his nose like a bull,' she said. 'Caught the light from me can as he jumped over the gates.'

*

Nasreen Khan called Mumtaz before she had a chance to call her. 'The previous owner of your house, before the firm of Wright and Baily LLP, was a man called Eric Smith,' Mumtaz told her. 'He was known to be a bit of a recluse. There's not a huge amount more that I can tell you at the moment, although I can tell you that Eric's father, Reginald Smith, owned the property before him.'

'Were there any women in the house?' Nasreen asked.

'There was Eric's mother, Lily,' Mumtaz said. There was something else too, but she didn't have time to go into that now. It didn't involve a woman and so it was not strictly germane to the investigation. 'Nasreen, I have an appointment in a moment. Can I call you back later?'

'Yes, of course.'

The door-bell rang. Mumtaz said goodbye and stood up to open the door.

Ayesha Mirza looked terrible. She had purple shadows underneath her eyes that made her look as if she'd been punched. She sat down heavily in front of Mumtaz's desk and said, 'Wendy rung me up and told me she don't want to see me no more. She won't even see me mum!'

Perhaps Wendy wanted to protect them, Mumtaz thought. If she could, she would probably like to cut off from her children too. But Sean Rogers may have some sort of hold over them – the way that Naz Sheikh had his eye on Shazia. Mumtaz attempted to explain this to Ayesha but she just said, 'Can't nothing be done about Sean Rogers?'

All Mumtaz could do was repeat what Lee had said to her, 'I'm afraid you either take on organised criminals like Sean Rogers and his partners or you don't. And they play rough, Mrs Mirza.

If you make a complaint against them, they could come for you, your husband and your children.'

'But I can't just leave Wend! Not now I *know* she . . .' Her voice trailed off. She began to cry.

Mumtaz sympathised but was at a loss as to what she could do. Unless Wendy Dixon went to the police herself, or disappeared, she was stuck with Sean Rogers. And Mumtaz guessed that Wendy wouldn't take either of those options. But like Ayesha Mirza, Mumtaz was loath to do nothing.

Eventually she said, 'Mrs Mirza, I don't want to raise your hopes, because I don't know if there is anything we can do without Wendy's co-operation, but let me speak to Mr Arnold. He used to be a policeman and so he knows the Rogers family.'

Ayesha Mirza looked up through her tears and she smiled. Mumtaz smiled back, hoping that she hadn't encouraged the woman to have unrealistic expectations.

The pathologist's report said that the skeleton was female. Vi looked up from her reading.

'She's been dead over fifty years,' she said.

Tony Bracci had already seen the report while Vi had been out at the Duke of Edinburgh with Cheryl Bines. He'd tried to find Kazia's brother, but Lech Ostrowski had been out God knows where.

'The skeleton didn't come from the Plashet Cemetery,' Vi continued.

'No, guv,' he said. 'Gravestones have been vandalised, as per – swastikas, paint daubs, all sorts of abuse, but not the actual graves.'

'Huh!' Vi said. 'Well, right-wing nutters would, wouldn't they? Vicious but superstitious.'

'I know. Hitler was into all that occult business. Tried to get his hands on the Ark of the Covenant. Thought the Jews had some sort of secret.'

'That was *Raiders of the Lost Ark*,' Vi said. 'A film, Tone. But in essence you're right. A lot of the fascists are into magic and rituals and all that. They're all hung up on symbols and uniforms. Comes of having no lives and being bullied. Or not.' She looked back at the pathologist's report again. 'Adult woman,' she read. 'Over thirty . . .'

'Path clocked a lot of wear and tear on her,' Tony said.

'Mmm.' Vi, reading on, said, 'Reckons she worked hard.'

'We all work hard.'

'Physically,' Vi said. 'You know, like people used to in the old days. Not fannying around writing reports or worrying yourself into an ulcer. I mean doing washing by hand, hauling in coal from the back yard, walking miles to the shops and then bringing the stuff home on foot.'

'As you said, it's an old skeleton.'

Vi looked down at the report again. 'Yeah.'

'What do you think John Sawyer was doing with it?'

Her eyes still on the report, Vi said, 'What makes you think he was doing anything with it? Just because he was found with it, don't mean he had it with him when he died.'

'Maybe the perp found him digging her up and then killed him?'

'Yes, but he or she would've had to have found him elsewhere because the skeleton don't come from the Plashet Cemetery,' Vi said. 'And SOCO established that John Sawyer was killed in the

Plashet.' She looked up. 'Nothing missing from any of the other cemeteries on the manor?'

'Nah.'

'Try Tower Hamlets and Waltham Forest too,' Vi said.

Tony Bracci frowned. 'What? You think Sawyer could have brought her from Bow or somewhere?' He shook his head.

'Why not? Beyond lurking around Green Street and Wanstead Flats and a few parks we don't really know where John Sawyer went,' Vi said.

'Yeah. S'pose.'

Vi stood up. 'Any idea about how John got into the cemetery?'

'Not yet,' Tony said. 'What with the Poles or whoever they was, running about all over the place . . .'

'Pole,' Vi corrected. 'Just one, so far, Tone. Kazia.'

'Oh, yeah, but you know what they're like, they're—'

'All the same?' She laughed. Tony Bracci could be a terrible bigot sometimes. 'Unless Kazia coughs we can't assume that,' she said. 'The skill of course is to *get* Kazia to cough – without breaking her fingers.'

'Which is what her own coppers'd do back home.'

Vi shook her head. 'Don't start with the racist bollocks. It makes us as bad as them. Put out some feelers for a white rights type with a ring through his nose, will you?'

'A ring through his nose?'

'Yeah. Cheryl Bines saw a bloke with a ring through his nose jumping out of Plashet Cemetery on Saturday night.'

Tony raised his eyebrows. 'Sure she wasn't just having a moment, guv?'

*

Lee couldn't stop looking at the pond. Apparently it was stocked with koi carp, but it was the stone fairies skipping around the edge amongst the miniature conifers that had captured his attention.

'She's a lovely girl, my Amy,' Brian Green said. 'Looks after me, this gaff, herself. Know what I mean?'

Brian handed Lee a glass of diet Pepsi and sat down. His own tipple was some sort of red wine in a glass the size of a fruit bowl. They were in Brian's conservatory overlooking his garden, which didn't so much end as fade into the Essex countryside.

'How long have you been married, Brian?' Lee asked. He wanted a fag but he knew that smoking was not one of Green's vices. Booze, the odd line of coke, and smashing people's faces until their cheekbones cracked was more his style.

'Just over seven years.' Brian Green leaned forward until his massive head was just inches from Lee's. 'Seven-year itch. Know what I mean?'

'Yeah, but Brian, do you know whether Amy is actually being unfaithful to you or . . .'

'That's why I want to buy you,' he said. 'So you can tell me.'

Lee had known Brian Green for decades. Fifty something and built like an integral garage, he had been an old style gangster in the Kray/Richardson mould until he went straight in the early 1990s and moved into health clubs. However, 'straight' when it came to Brian Green was a relative term, and Lee knew that his gyms covered a multitude of sins. They funded this lavish house in Ongar as well as the activities of his twenty-something wife, Amy. The fairies round the pond had to have been her idea.

'What'll you do if Amy *is* playing away?' Lee asked.

'Depends who she's playing with.'

Lee watched Brian's small, grey eyes glitter over the top of his glass and he had to make an effort not to shudder. It was well known in police circles that Brian Green played rough. Born into poverty in Bethnal Green, like Ronnie and Reggie Kray, Brian had been the product of an Irish traveller and Jewish marriage. It had resulted in a sort of uber-Brit, a creature half man half bulldog, all malice. Oddly, he'd liked Lee even when he'd been a copper, though he'd never managed to buy him. Unlike now.

'Brian, I'll do it, provided you don't hurt her if it all goes tits up,' Lee said.

'Hurt my Amy? Why would I—'

'Brian, you knocked seven shades of shit out of Tina and we both know it.'

The grey eyes narrowed. Tina Bloch, Brian's first wife, had never brought charges when she apparently smashed herself repeatedly in the face against a doorframe, but it was well known that she'd had some sort of liaison with a waiter in Spain.

Although he was shaking inside, Lee said, 'I'll find out about Amy for you if you agree not to beat the crap out of her if she is messing around.'

Brian Green knew better than to plead innocence with Lee Arnold. He and Vi Collins had been the only coppers who had ever come close to nicking him and he knew that to try and pull the wool over either of their eyes was pointless.

'She won't get nothing,' Brian growled. Out in the garden, a vast string of multi-coloured fairy lights draped around a summer house, came on.

'Any divorce settlement you might make is up to you, Brian,' Lee said. 'But you have to understand that as well as being a PI I'm also still a copper.'

'You was a good copper, it's why I want ya,' Brian said. 'I know you'll be straight with me.'

'Alright, but there's a price,' Lee said.

'I'll pay you anything—'

'Beyond the cash,' Lee interrupted. 'I do what you ask, Brian, and you don't lay a finger on that girl, understand? You promise me that on your mother's life.'

10

Nasreen wondered what the man Mumtaz Hakim had told her about had been, if anything, to the woman in the photograph she'd discovered in her house. Was that face the face of Lily Smith, wife of Reginald and mother of Eric Smith, the one time reclusive owner of her new house?

Mumtaz had found out that Lily Smith had originally come from Poland. Together with her son, who had been called Marek Berkowicz, she'd arrived sometime after the Second World War. She'd married Reg Smith in 1948 and their son, Eric, had been born one year later. Nasreen had always been under the impression that Eric Smith had been an old man, but when he'd died in 2003 he'd only been fifty-four. She looked down at Abdullah who was asleep beside her and then back into the darkness that washed over her bedroom. Her mother had been right about the house that had once been the Smiths', it was rotten. It needed *so* much work, but it was something more than that too. Mumtaz had told her a boy, not much more than a child, had gone missing from that house. That boy had been, or was, Marek Berkowicz. In 1955, in the depths of a smog-coated December night, he'd disappeared from the house – *her* house – and had never been seen again. He'd been fifteen.

Nasreen felt her stomach tighten and, alarmed, she forced herself to try and relax for the sake of the baby. Back in 1955 the police had suspected Reginald Smith. Neighbours had told them that he didn't treat his stepson right and they'd dug up the garden looking for Marek's body. But they'd found nothing. No body, no blood, no Marek. He'd just winked out of existence, just like John had seemingly winked into existence when he first appeared in her garden. Until someone killed him. Again, Nasreen felt her stomach tighten and this time she got out of bed and went downstairs to the kitchen where she could be on her own with her thoughts and make herself a cup of tea.

Had she done the right thing when she'd given Mumtaz Hakim Abdullah's date and place of birth when she'd phoned? She'd failed to remember his late father's name, although she did know that he had run an electrical shop. Now that she trusted Mrs Hakim, Nasreen had her checking up on her own husband and she felt guilty. If only John hadn't been found murdered, maybe she could have just gone along knowing very little about Abdullah for the rest of her life. But his jealousy worried her. He had no family to temper it, no mother to scold him or father to listen to his fears and either agree with them or allay them. Had Abdullah found John in the garden when he was alone at the house and then killed him?

No. But . . .

Nasreen drank her tea and thought about how stupid that sounded. Why would Abdullah murder a man? Would or could he seriously believe that such a man could be a threat to him? She'd given John some food and drink, that was all. And yet she felt guilty – for doing it behind Abdullah's back and for asking Mumtaz Hakim to find out whether her handsome and generous husband was who he said he was. Why was she wasting her money like this?

*

It was the house that they wanted, that was clear. The Sheikhs could have no other agenda. Ahmet had put his life, and by extension her life and Shazia's too, in their hands. Mumtaz looked at the miserable little pile of jewellery in front of her on the table. That wasn't even going to pay the gas bill let alone her debt to the gangsters. Three of Ahmet's carpets had gone, and she knew that the other two weren't worth nearly as much. There were some other better pieces of jewellery, but was she obliged to sell her entire past now? She'd have to sell the house and she'd have to sell it to them. That was how it worked. That was where it was always going to end up anyway.

She, or rather Ahmet, had originally owed the Sheikhs £100,000 which he had failed to pay back. This had now ballooned to just over £400,000 and counting. And if she couldn't pay the £1,000 monthly interest fee, anything could happen. They'd take Shazia for a start. Mumtaz went cold. She'd offer herself to them ten times over rather than let them do anything to that girl. She had already suffered enough. But would they take her, a woman of almost thirty-three, in lieu of a sixteen-year-old? Of course they wouldn't. Mumtaz looked at the local paper and saw a house just like hers for sale for £530,000. She had to be able to get half a million for it. But not from *them*. They'd take it from her in lieu of Ahmet's debt and leave her and Shazia homeless. She'd have to pay legal fees and get her furniture moved to somewhere and she'd have no choice but to go home to her parents' place in Spitalfields. Shazia would hate it.

Nasreen Khan, had asked Mumtaz to find out whether her husband Abdullah was who he said he was. He had no family, no obvious roots, and she felt she couldn't entirely trust him. But even if one did know a man, could one ever entirely trust him? Her own husband had been a rich and respected man in the

Bangladeshi community, and she'd known his family before she'd married him. But he'd hidden what he really was: a gambler, a liar, a rapist and a child abuser. Just thinking about him made her feel sick. Nasreen Khan was in the dark and suffering who knew what at the hands of her husband. Mumtaz had known better than to ask. She might have frightened her away and then Nasreen would have done nothing.

She put the all but useless jewellery into her handbag and resolved to get what she could for it from a pawn shop. If the money would at least pay off the gas bill, then that was no bad thing. Even if they did get the house for basically nothing, the Sheikhs would make her pay any outstanding bills. For the moment, however, there was nothing to do but go to bed. She did look briefly at her phone and wonder whether she should call Lee. For months she'd thought about telling him she was in trouble, but she had yet to find the courage to do it. This time, like all the other times, ended in her leaving the phone where it was.

The girls all seemed to be drinking a cocktail called Porn Star. Malibu, pineapple, crushed strawberries, coconut syrup and ice. Just the thought of it made Lee want to gag. Nursing his diet Pepsi he stood at the end of the bar watching Amy Green and her mates get drunk. He felt like the dustiest suit in the wardrobe. Even being optimistic he had fifteen years on the oldest person in the place, the music was giving him a headache and the decor was only serving to enhance his discomfort.

'Take one of me and Dani!'

Amy Green was just a kid, and like a kid she was keen for one of her mates to take a photograph of her with another girl who was wearing a short bridal veil.

'Get in close then,' the girl wielding the iPhone said. Amy and Dani pushed their heads together and screeched. There was a white flash.

'Oh, my God, you've blinded me!' Amy spoke with that rising inflection everyone under thirty used. It had wheedled its way into the country, via Australian soaps apparently, and had now taken root in west Essex. Lee hated it with the kind of energy only a parent with a child who uses that form can do.

Amy and Dani looked at the picture their friend had taken on her phone. Amy's face fell. 'Oh, my God, I look so fat.'

'No, you don't, you look lush.'

'Do I?'

Dani put her hands on her hips and said, 'Course you do, babe. Would I lie to you? Would I?'

Amy laughed. 'Oh my God, I am like so ready for another drink.'

Another girl said, 'I'll get 'em. Do yous all want Porns?'

'Yeah.'

'Yeah.'

'And me.'

'Yeah, babe.'

The girl teetered over to what Lee had been reliably informed by a young man in an Italian suit was a 'genuine Swarowski crystal' bar and asked for 'Five Porns and all the trimmings.'

As he wrestled with his need for a cigarette, Lee wondered whether these people around him were actually genuine. At the insistence of his daughter he'd watched a TV 'reality' show called *The Only Way is Essex*. Now apparently, he was seeing it played out for real. People did fake tan themselves until they were orange, the girls did have fake tits and Amy Green and her mates said 'Oh my God' and 'like' *all* the time. Amy Green and her mates also flirted. The club, which was called The LA Lounge, was like one big mating ritual. Flirting and 'getting off' with people was the whole reason that it existed. Even Amy's mate Dani, whose hen night this was, was fluttering her fake eyelashes at every man and boy who passed her.

Lee successfully swallowed a yawn. If Brian Green hadn't given him a wad of cash to start watching Amy he would be at home listening to Chronus yelling about West Ham. But Brian, for all his faults, was a generous man and the financial temptation he'd put in front of Lee had been too great. The long and short of it was that, as usual, the Agency needed money. He wanted to give Mumtaz something extra too. Her mortgage, which apparently her late husband had taken out with some dodgy bank, was huge. She was selling things. He didn't know what, but most days lately she was coming to work with a bag full of stuff, going to lunch and then returning empty handed. He never asked her about it. The formality that had existed between them when she'd first come to work for him was no longer there. Back in the early days, she'd called him 'Mr Arnold' and had never even alluded to her private life. As she'd learned to trust him, Mumtaz had opened up – somewhat. But there were still things he didn't know about her and there was definitely more to her financial status than just a dead husband and a large mortgage.

'Looking good costs money.' Amy Green put her glass down on the table in front of her and flashed her eyes at a boy sitting opposite on one of the LA Lounge's 'signature' purple sofas.

'I know but you've well spent,' he said. All of Amy's friends laughed.

'Major,' Amy said.

The boy bought the whole lot of them Porn Stars then moved on, seemingly oblivious to what he'd just spent on a group of girls he didn't know. Lee wondered what he did and whether he could do it too.

By the time Amy and her friends left the LA Lounge they were all drunk and lairy and Dani and another girl called Micki had snogged a few lads. They'd all flirted, but nothing more than that. The baby-pink stretch limousine hired to take them all home was, Lee heard one of the girls say, 'brimming with champagne' and they fully intended to carry on drinking all the way home. Lee had a fairly extensive trip around Chigwell and Ongar, following the limo as it dropped the girls off at their respective houses. It was just his luck that Amy was the last on the list. On top of this, she spent fifteen minutes outside the house she shared with Brian in the limo. But when she got out she was waving a bottle of champagne about and so it wasn't difficult to work out what she might have been up to.

Amy staggered to her front door and scrabbled about in her vast handbag for her keys. Lee saw her mouth the odd curse. The limo still stood in the drive, but Lee couldn't see the driver except as a shadow behind the smoked glass windscreen. Amy, meanwhile, hoisted her massive bag up close to her face and put one of her hands beside the front door in order to steady herself. But as she did this she appeared to injure her hand, and said, 'Fuck that!'

The door to the limo opened and a tall, dark, powerfully built young man got out and looked concerned. Amy, smiling now, whispered something to him and then blew him a kiss.

11

Wendy looked at the picture of the young soldier in the *Recorder* and wished that she'd known him. His face looked soft and kind and it was hard to believe that he'd ended his days being murdered in some old cemetery up Plashet Grove. Wendy sorted her washing into whites, coloureds and sex clothes. The kids weren't allowed to see the latter, which she had to dry on the radiator in her bedroom – when she could afford to turn it on.

The weekend was looming and Wendy Dixon felt her heart beat more quickly just thinking about it. She'd told the kids she was going away with a mate. Dolly was quite happy to look after everyone provided there was food in the house, which there would be. The kids would eat even if Wendy didn't. Sean Rogers's sex parties were not heavy on food – not even of the nibbles variety. Wendy shuddered. In one way it was better that Sean's parties were held in total darkness but it was also even more frightening. When the sex was over and all the men were outside by the pool drinking she'd find herself wondering which ones she'd serviced. A sea of brutish, predatory men talking about the things they'd done.

Apart from the kids, Wendy was sorry about her sister, Mary, or Ayesha as she called herself these days. She meant well and

Wendy loved her and her husband, Wazim, who was a good man, but they didn't live in her world. The Asians she knew, weren't like Wazim. Men like Yunus Ali, the Rogers' business partner, and that family of gangsters, the Sheikhs. Some of them went to Sean's orgies and they all took bungs and bribes and broke people's fingers. Get behind with the rent and, just like their white counterparts, they'd be on your doorstep with either a baseball bat or an offer you most certainly couldn't refuse. Wendy, suddenly exhausted, sat down and she cried.

'Oi! Stop!'

Tony Bracci had seen the bloke his snout had told him about standing outside the Boleyn. Tony didn't know him, but he clearly knew Tony because the sight of him had made him run. Had the snout, a junkie known as 'Deserts Disease' (on account of the fact the palms of his hands tended to wander onto women's thighs), tipped off the bloke Tony was running after? To play both the police and the criminals was not an unknown tactic for a snout, especially one who was on the gear. The bloke, known as Bully, took off up the Barking Road towards East Ham like Usain Bolt. Tony Bracci, who was really more of a Gordon Brown style of runner, puffed and wheezed after him.

Tony was a long way behind. Bully, who did indeed have a ring through his nose, was, according to Deserts Disease, not so much a racist as a necrophile. Fantastic as it sounded, Deserts Disease said Bully had 'had' several fresh corpses up the East London Cemetery. But Deserts Disease was permanently off his neck, so who knew what he knew about anything. Up in front, Bully, who was twenty-five at the most, was pulling ever further ahead. Tony thought about stopping and calling for assistance, but he knew that if he did he'd never get going again. Bully slipped his skinny, white body between two black-clad Muslim ladies and then, briefly, looked behind him at Tony. And that, luckily for Tony Bracci, was Bully's undoing.

When Mumtaz entered the office she found Lee at her desk, fiddling with something.

'What are you doing?'

He looked up at her. In his hand was the metal capsule that Nasreen Khan had found on one of the doorposts in her new house. He was scratching away at the layers of paint. 'If I'm not too much mistaken, I know what this is,' he said.

Mumtaz put her handbag down on her desk and looked at Lee as he worked away at the lump with his fingernails.

'I saw something like this up at Brian Green's house last night,' Lee said. He picked a spoon up off the desk and used the end to whittle away at the paint. Mumtaz frowned. As ancient paint flakes fluttered down towards the floor, she saw a shape come into view. She gasped.

'A Star of David,' Lee said as he held the metal lump up. 'Which means that this is a mezuzah.'

'What's that?'

'Well,' Lee said, 'according to Brian, who, let's face it, is not even strictly Jewish, it's a container for some sort of Hebrew scroll that observant Jews have to have on their doorposts. Brian's father was Jewish and he lived with him for a few years before he died so Brian had them put on his doorposts.'

'So Nasreen Khan's house was once owned by Jews?'

'Yes. It could have been back in the 1900s when there were a lot of Jews around here,' Lee said. 'Although that photograph your client found underneath it looks more modern than that to me.'

Mumtaz sat down. 'I went back to the Land Registry records and discovered that the last individual the house had belonged to was a man called Eric Smith,' she said.

'Not very Jewish.' Lee put the mezuzah back on her desk. He'd called Brian Green first thing and told him about his wife hurting her hand on the thing on his doorpost and the blown kiss she'd made at her chauffeur. Brian had growled out the detail about the mezuzah. Lee had told Brian not to make assumptions about Amy and the chauffeur. She was the sort of girl who blew kisses at the bloody dog. But apparently Amy was going to be out with her mates again on Saturday and Brian wanted Lee to be there at a price that he couldn't even think about refusing.

'No, but his mother was Polish apparently,' Mumtaz said. 'Her name before she married Eric Smith's father was Lily Berkowicz.'

'That sounds Jewish to me.' Lee went into their tiny office kitchen, picked up the dustpan and brush and swept the paint shavings from the mezuzah off the floor.

'There was another son too,' Mumtaz continued, 'besides Eric, a boy called Marek.'

'From a previous marriage?'

'Must have been,' she said. 'The information I found about Marek Berkowicz on line was very scant.'

'Why would it be anything else? I mean he must be quite old now . . .'

'Wherever he is, yes,' Mumtaz said. 'Lee, Marek Berkowicz went missing from his home in 1955 when he was fifteen and hasn't been seen since.'

Lee, now back at his desk, said, 'I've never heard anything about that.'

'It was before you were born.'

'Yes, I know, but you hear stories as you're growing up, don't you?'

'But you come from the south of the borough.'

'Yeah.' Custom House, down by the old Victoria Dock. When Lee had been a kid it had been a whole distinct and separate community from places like Upton Park. Then the Docks had been alive and trips to places like Upton Park for Lee and his brother had been rare. 'My mum might remember,' he said. 'Or maybe me dad's old drinking mates.'

'I found one newspaper report,' Mumtaz said. 'From the *Recorder*. Marek went missing one night in December 1955. No-one saw him go, no-one knew where he might have gone. The police even dug up the Smith family's garden.'

'Mmm. Perhaps I'll speak to Vi. Her dad was Jewish.'

Mumtaz picked up the small photograph that had been hidden behind the mezuzah and said, 'I wonder if this is Lily Smith.' Then she looked up again. 'Lee, do you know what's written on the scroll inside this . . . mezuzah?'

'Not a clue. But it'll be in Hebrew and so neither of us'd be able to read it.'

'Oh, I wasn't thinking about opening it. I don't think that would be right. We're not Jewish,' Mumtaz said, and she put the mezuzah to one side.

'DS Bracci tells me he reckons you've a tale to tell, Mr Murray,' Vi Collins said, as she sat down in front of one Mark Murray aka Bully. A pale, skinny lad, Bully had apparently got his nickname because of the black metal ring that he'd stuck through his nose. It made him, he'd told Tony Bracci, look a bit like a bull. Tony Bracci felt it made him look like a twat.

Bully didn't say anything.

'What were you doing in the old Plashet Cemetery on Saturday night?' Vi asked. 'Fiddling about with the dead?'

He looked up at her from underneath heavy eyelids. 'I don't do that.'

'Don't you?' The notion that Bully was a necrophiliac had only come from that deadbeat Deserts Disease and so it was hardly gospel. But Vi had to see how Bully would respond.

'No.' He *looked* disgusted.

'So what were you doing?' Vi asked.

'Hanging out.'

'In a cemetery?' And then something occurred to Vi, something she'd once talked about to a drag queen she'd met on a night out up west. 'The old Plashet's not like Brompton Cemetery is it, Mark? Brompton Cemetery is well known as a place where men go to meet other men for sex . . .'

'I'm no fuckin' Iron!' Bully's face had gone from spotty white to spotty red in an instant. It either meant that he was deeply offended by the suggestion that he might be gay or he was so far in the closet he was out the other side.

'So why were you there?' Vi asked. 'Tell us and you can go. Don't tell us and . . .' She held up the very small wrap of cocaine Tony Bracci had found in one of Bully's pockets.

Bully looked at it with what could have been hunger in his eyes. 'You'll do me for that anyway.'

Vi, smiling, dropped the wrap onto the floor. 'You'll have to find that out,' she said.

Tony Bracci looked across at his superior nervously.

'Tell me the truth,' Vi said.

The boy had refused a Brief. He'd done that for a reason.

Bully moved his head to the left, then to the right, and he sucked his teeth. He said, 'I go to get laid.'

'Oh, so you—'

'Not by no man!' He sniffed. 'I like girls, you know what I mean?'

'In a graveyard.'

'Yeah, man!'

Bully was one of the whitest people Vi had ever met and yet, in common with a lot of young people, he spoke in a semi-Caribbean, semi-London/Essex dialect that, to her, sounded weird.

'Goth girls go to boneyards, yeah? They like to get laid on the gravestones and they are reem, man. '

'Easy, tiger.' Vi raised a hand. 'So let me get this straight, you go to graveyards to pick up Goth girls?'

'They'll do it with anyone as long as you do it on a tomb,' he said. Then he went red again when he realised what he'd just said. 'Not that I couldn't get laid by other girls but, you know, I like the Goth girls.'

'So is Plashet Jewish Cemetery a known place for this sort of activity?'

Bully looked back again. 'No.'

'So why were you romping about in there last Saturday night?'

For a moment he didn't say anything.

'Well?'

'I saw this bitch,' he said. 'Sort of gothy but also she had a swastika tattoo and other symbols and stuff on her garms, you know? She was vaulting over the railings into the cemetery and she looked at me like . . .'

'Like she wouldn't be averse to letting you slip her a length.'

'Eh?'

Inwardly Vi laughed. How quickly slang changed. 'Fuck her,' she interpreted.

'Oh, er, yeah.'

'So did you? Fuck her?'

Kazia Ostrowska had been the only female, as far as they knew, who had been in the Plashet Jewish Cemetery that night. Kazia it had been who was tattooed with a swastika.

'Did you fuck her?' Vi reiterated.

Bully put his head down again. 'No,' he mumbled.

'What?' Tony Bracci only pretended he hadn't heard. The little scrote had made him run, he was ripe for a bit of humiliation.

'No, I never,' Bully said. He looked up.

'Why not? If she give you the eye and all that?'

Bully sighed. 'Because she wasn't alone,' he said.

'Who was with her?'

He shrugged. 'Dunno.'

'How many of them were there?'

He shrugged again.

'Did you see what any of them looked like? Hear how they spoke?'

'Foreign.'

'What sort of foreign?'

'I dunno.'

Kazia was Polish and so it was possible she had been in the graveyard with other Polish people. The only other person who could definitely be placed in the graveyard was Majid Islam. Would Majid, a British-born Asian, have cried out or spoken in any other language apart from English in that context?

'Did any of the voices you heard sound Asian?' Vi asked.

'What like Pak—'

'Asian,' she cut across.

He thought for a moment and then he said, 'No. No it was like . . . foreign, you know.'

Like it or not, and even among those of a decidedly right-wing nature, Asian voices had become native to Newham, even when they were speaking Urdu or Hindi. Like the Jews before them, their language had become accepted. Now it was other European tones that were 'foreign'.

'No,' Vi said, even though she did know. 'And anyway what's this "it". How many voices did you hear, Bully?'

'Oh, just hers.'

'The girl you took a fancy to?'

'Yeah.'

'So you saw more than one person but only actually heard one foreign voice?'

'Yeah. But there was a bloke, a Pak . . . an Asian in there too,' Bully said.

Majid Islam, who had found the body.

'So what made you run away?' Vi said.

'Oh, that was the stiff on the ground,' Bully said.

'Which was?'

'Holding a fucking skellington. Fuck man!' he put a hand up to his head. He was sweating now. 'All on its own holding a fucking skellington!'

But if that was the case, then how had he seen Majid Islam? While Kazia and who knew who else cavorted around the grave-yard, according to Mr Islam, he had not moved from the dead man's side.

'So where was the Asian bloke you claimed you saw?' Vi asked.

'Oh, he was off on his toes,' Bully said.

'To where?'

He shrugged. 'I dunno,' he said. 'The railings? I was shitting myself at the skellington, what did I care? So you gonna do something with that wrap or not?'

12

It was difficult for Mumtaz to concentrate. The mezuzah kept on catching her eye. She was supposed to be looking into the background of Nasreen Khan's husband, Abdullah, but it wasn't easy. In spite of what she'd said to Lee, who had disappeared down to the Boleyn to try and meet up with some of his dad's old mates in order to help her, she wanted to take the back off it and look at the scroll inside. But that was so wrong. She could hear her father's rebuke in her head, *That's not for you, leave it alone!*

Growing up just off Brick Lane in Spitalfields, Mumtaz had been brought up with a strange view of Jewish people. On the one hand, the area her family lived in had once been Jewish, the mosque her father and her brothers attended had been first a church and then a synagogue. Her parents had Jewish friends, Mumtaz herself had once loved a Jewish boy when she was at university and yet hatred of Jews was common. White racist lunatics preached it, those who sympathised with the Palestinians and opposed Israel often resorted to it and some of her fellow Muslims felt that if you *really* followed Islam, then you had to do it. She disagreed. She could see why the Palestinian cause was a just one, but she could also appreciate why Israel existed and why it was so important to world Jewry. In addition, she'd worked out long ago that there were Jews and there were Israelis and the two were not necessarily the same. But did her sympathy for the Jews permit her to open that mezuzah?

Mumtaz turned back to her computer screen. So far her researches had taken her to Abdullah Khan's parents who had been called Mursel and Meena Khan. They'd lived just outside where Abdullah had told Nasreen he came from, the town of Bolton, in a place called Ramsbottom. She'd Googled some pictures of it and it was not what she had expected. Ramsbottom looked middle class and quite trendy. It even had a 'heritage' steam railway.

Mursel Khan had had an electrical shop in the middle of the town and had been something of a local character on account of his heavy involvement with the heritage railway. He had died, according to an article in a local newspaper, in 2011 at the age of seventy-one. His wife, Meena, had died in 1974, which was the same year in which her only child, Abdullah, had been born. She'd only been twenty-three. Mursel had not remarried. Thus Abdullah and Mursel had lived as, she imagined, a fairly isolated unit in what seemed to be a white, Christian town. Bolton itself, which was where Meena, if not Mursel, had been born, had a high proportion of Asian people and in the racially tense 1970s surely the Khans would have felt happier and safer living there. Mumtaz's father had told her about the 'Paki-bashing' that had gone on all over the country at that time even though she had no memories of it herself. Back then there had been a lot of activity against immigrants by far-right groups like the National Front. The British National Party, their successors, were still around but they usually operated in a far less confrontational way than they had in the 1970s. Long before the 1970s, back at the beginning of the twentieth century, the Jews had been treated badly too. Mumtaz's eyes, yet again, were drawn to the mezuzah. She looked away.

Abdullah Khan had, so he'd told his wife Nasreen, entered Manchester University's School of Law in 1992. Via the Law Society's website, Mumtaz learned that he would have done a three-year degree course, after which he would have had to complete a one-year postgraduate Legal Practice Course in order to qualify for a training contract with a firm of solicitors. Only after completing that contract would he have become a fully-fledged solicitor. That would have taken him up to approximately 1997/8. He had come to London in 2005 which meant that he had to have been working as a solicitor for about seven years prior to that. So why had he, when he first came to the city, stayed in a cheap boarding house in Poplar?

She'd been sick. It was the first time it had happened since Nasreen had learned that she was pregnant and it had come as a shock. It was after all barely still morning. But as she stripped thirty-year-old-plus wallpaper off the kitchen wall, she suddenly felt nauseous. Her mobile rang as Nasreen flung herself out of the back door and into the garden where she threw up her breakfast. As soon as she'd finished retching she felt instantly better. But she made herself sit down on the back step for a moment anyway.

Nasreen took deep breaths of the torrid London air. Looking up at the sky she could see that it was going to rain again soon. She couldn't help thinking that if John had still been alive she would have been embarrassed by what had just happened, but comforted too. John would have been concerned, he had been kind. He'd killed people and yet he'd also been very kind. How could that be?

Nasreen heard her mobile phone bleep, letting her know that

she had either an ansaphone message or a text. It was probably from the person who had called while she was throwing up. She didn't much care. It could wait. Oddly, she was elated all of a sudden and she wanted to enjoy it. Being sick, even more than the test results she'd got from the doctor, meant that she really was pregnant.

'Once I'd found that body, I didn't leave it for an instant, I can assure you,' Majid Islam said. 'Such strange people cavorting around in the graveyard. Who knew what they might do to it?'

Vi Collins's officers had told her that Majid Islam had been standing over the body when they'd arrived and she had no reason to disbelieve either them or him. The only jarring theme to the melody was being provided by a cokehead and general oddity known as Bully. But Vi had to check his story out.

'Apart from the girl we arrested did you see anyone else in the Plashet Graveyard that night?' Vi asked.

She'd gone round to Islam's house, keeping it informal. As Plashet Cemetery's unofficial guardian, he was alright with the police and she wanted to keep him on side.

Majid Islam twirled his tasbeeh beads around his fingers and said, 'I saw a boy jump over the gate.'

'But there were three figures in the graveyard when you got there weren't there, Mr Islam?' Vi said. 'That's what you told us. The girl, the boy who jumped the gate and . . .' She shrugged.

'I don't know,' he said. 'I saw a figure and then . . .' He snapped his fingers.

'Did you get any sort of idea about whether it was male or female, white or . . .'

'Oh, no, it was just an impression,' Majid Islam said. 'A silhouette.' Then he paused for a moment, his face creased into a frown. 'But I suppose I would have to say, at a pinch, that he was a man.'

'Why do you say that?' Vi asked.

He shook his head. 'I don't really know. An instinct perhaps you'd say?' He looked over at his fifty-inch television screen which was playing children's afternoon programmes to no-one and said, 'Perhaps it was the way that he moved?'

'Which was?'

'Like a man.'

'Which is how?' Vi asked. She'd often been told she walked about like a bloke when she had flat shoes on.

He held his hands out. 'I don't know,' he said. 'I know it when I see it. But I can't be sure.'

Vi left Majid Islam's house and went back to the station. Both Kazia and Bully had been released on bail pending possible charges, but there had been nothing – forensic or otherwise – to connect them to either of the bodies in the graveyard. There was Majid Islam who was an unlikely culprit on account of his history with the graveyard and some shadowy figure that could have been male. Where had he gone? And had he, this shadowy figure, actually been the 'Paki' that Bully had seen running away from the bodies when he approached them?

He hadn't jumped over the gate into High Street North and it was unlikely that he could have hidden in the graveyard during the time she and all the other coppers had spent in there. Logically the only way he could have got out of there without being seen was over that fucking wall. Visions of Spiderman invaded Vi's mind. She replaced them with more sensible pictures of ladders.

When Tony Bracci came in from his protracted smoking session out in the car park she said, 'I think we need to have another look at the wall around the old Plashet Cemetery.'

'We've had a look at the wall, guv,' Tony said. 'We looked at it when we found John Sawyer. There was nothing to see.'

'Not at ground level, no,' Vi smiled. 'We need to get on top of it, Tone.'

'Oh.'

'It's alright,' she said. 'I'm not asking you to do something I wouldn't do myself.' And then she added. 'In theory.'

Her phone rang, and while she answered it Tony Bracci pulled a face. He didn't like climbing any more than he liked running. But she waved him away. As he left he heard her say, 'Well, Arnold, I haven't heard anyone mention the Smiths of Strone Road for at least twenty years. You got a client down there, have you?'

'Why aren't you at work?' Nasreen was surprised to see her husband come through the front door. She was pleased to see Abdullah but also a little nervous. He didn't like her working at the house on her own in case she had an accident or felt faint. She wouldn't tell him about the sickness.

'I have to do some odds and sods over the weekend,' her husband said. 'So I took myself off early. It's Friday.'

Nasreen stopped scraping weird moss-green wallpaper off the dining room wall. 'Don't you have clients to attend to?'

He shrugged. Then he said, 'What you doing here? I went to your mum and dad's and they—'

'I just wanted to get on.'

'So what did you do?'

He didn't trust her, she could hear it in his voice. Did he know about John maybe? Did he think that she was having some sort of affair with John? But John was dead.

'Just some scraping,' she said.

He looked at the walls of the dining room. 'Fun?'

'No, but it has to be done.'

'Mmm.'

Nasreen particularly fancied Abdullah when he was all suited up for work – as he was now. Although completely inexperienced sexually before her wedding night, Nasreen had nevertheless educated herself extensively in the art of sex via books, friends and films. Abdullah had known what to do as she had expected and so her first time had been exciting and painless. She'd wanted him so much. After he'd taken her virginity she'd ached to carry on. But he hadn't wanted to. Now, looking at him, she wanted him even though she knew that part of such a voracious desire was due to her hormones. She walked over to him and kissed him on the mouth and she felt his dick harden against her leg.

When he finally disengaged from her he said, 'That was nice.'

She took one of his hands and put it on her breast. 'There could be more . . .'

He smiled. 'Maybe when we go back to your parents . . .'

They hadn't had sex for over a month. 'There are things we could do here,' she said.

'Yes, but it's not very hygienic and—'

Nasreen got down on her knees and opened his fly.

'Nasreen!'

'Oh, Abi, I really want to do it!' she said as she reached for his cock.

But he pulled away. 'That's disgusting!' he said. 'That's not what married people do!'

'Yes, it is!' Nasreen said. Kneeling on the floor in front of him she felt pathetic now, but she still made her point. 'Oral sex is normal.'

His pale face became red. 'It's disgusting and dishonourable. You're my wife, the mother of my child, not some whore!'

Nasreen began to cry. 'But Abi, I want our sex to be wonderful,' she said.

'By doing . . .that?' He did up his fly.

'Yes, if you . . .'

'But I don't,' he said. He moved away from her completely. He looked at her with disgust. Didn't he realise that even if what they occasionally did in bed satisfied him completely, she wanted more? Didn't she have a right to more?

And then suddenly he was sitting on the floor beside her, kissing her hands. 'I care for you and our baby more than anything else in this world,' he said.

'Then why . . .'

His eyes were so intense and so passionate they stopped Nasreen in her tracks.

He put his hands on her shoulders. 'Because we don't need all that,' he said. 'Our love is pure, we're good Muslims you and me, Nasreen. Sex is good but it's for babies, you know? It's to make the baby we're making now. Anything else is dirty and disrespectful – to you. Don't you see that?'

How could he be so passionate and yet at the same time so sexually unadventurous? And why was he bringing up religion? Sure they were both Muslims but neither of them were shalwar khameez wearing types. It was one of those moments, which were increasing, when Nasreen didn't understand her husband.

'You know I love you. You know I'll give you everything—'

A noise from outside interrupted him and Abdullah, frowning, said, 'Sounds like someone in the back garden.'

'Who?'

He stood up.

'I'll go and see,' he said. 'You stay here.'

Still on her knees, Nasreen slowly rose and it was then that her phone rang. This time she picked it up.

'Nasreen,' she heard Mumtaz Hakim's confident voice on the end of the line.

'Yes?'

'Are you alright?'

She must have heard the tremor in Nasreen's voice. 'Yes fine,' Nasreen lied.

'Nasreen, a question,' Mumtaz said. 'When your husband first came to London why did he stay in the ZamZam boarding house in Poplar? It seems odd to me that a solicitor of some years practice should do something like that.'

Nasreen said, 'His uncle owns the boarding house.'

'Oh, I see.'

And yet Nasreen felt that she didn't – not really. And neither – really – did Nasreen, not now she came to think about it. Why *had* Abdullah stayed in that dirty place? It wasn't as if he even liked his uncle. Nasreen saw Abdullah coming back in from the garden. 'I have to go,' she said and ended the call.

As he walked into the dining room, Abdullah Khan looked very formal indeed. His suit, straight and smooth again, his hair neat.

Nasreen said, 'What's going on? In the garden?'

For a moment he appeared to be lost in thought and then he said, 'Oh, it's the police.'

'What are they doing? Where?'

'They're on the back wall,' he said. 'I think it's got something to do with that body they found in the graveyard. You know, the soldier.'

'Yes.' Nasreen put her arms around her shoulders and hugged herself.

13

'The Berkowicz boy just disappeared,' Wilf Cox said.

The barmaid, Maureen, picked his empty pint up off the table and said, 'Same again?'

The old man looked expectantly across at Lee Arnold who said, 'Yeah, thanks Maureen. And I'll have me usual.' He handed her his Pepsi glass.

Now that the game had started the Boleyn was very light on football fans of any description and so Lee and Wilf could talk. Lee had been trying to catch up with the old man since the previous day, and later this evening he had to go to a no doubt designer perfume-scented place called 'Spicey's' in Billericay for another obbo on Amy Green. He'd decided to fortify himself in the blokiness of the Boleyn first. It was an added bonus that Wilf had turned up – he rarely did on a match day – so Lee had taken the opportunity to ask him about the house on Strone Road where that client of Mumtaz's had found a mezuzah.

'Police looked everywhere,' the old man continued. 'Dug up gardens and everything. People whispered about the stepfather, what was his name? Reg. About Reg.'

'Why?'

'You mean aside from the fact that he was his stepdad? He was a bit of a lout, Reg Smith, as I remember him.'

'Drinks.' Maureen put Wilf's pint down in front of him and gave Lee his Pepsi.

'Ta, darling.'

Wilf continued, 'He had his own son by Lily by the time the other boy went missing.'

'Eric.' Mumtaz and Vi had told him the bones of the story.

'Yes, Eric.' He shook his head. 'He was weird. Living in that house all them years all on his own after his parents died. People said he was guarding that first boy's body in there – until they forgot about it.'

'Guarding it for who?'

'The memory of his dad? His mum? I dunno,' Wilf said. 'But then Eric died years ago – he weren't that old even though he looked it. Far as I know, nothing was ever found in that house.'

'So Marek Berkowicz could have run away just as the family said.'

The old man shrugged. 'Possibly.' Then he said, 'Here, fancy a fag?'

They both went out onto Green Street which, in contrast to how it had been earlier on when it was riddled with football fans, looked a bit like some recession-hit high street in the Midlands. Only the occasional roar of the crowd from the Boleyn Ground broke the one noise that was always around: traffic.

Lee lit up first. 'What about Lily Smith?' he asked. 'Remember much about her?'

Wilf frowned. He lowered his voice. 'She'd been in the camps.'

'What? Like Auschwitz?'

'Belsen,' the old man said. 'We, the British, liberated it in 1945. Reg Smith was one of the soldiers first in. Piles of bodies so high they cut out the sunlight, people said. No wonder Reg took to the bottle.'

'But he brought Lily back from Germany with him?'

'And the boy.'

'Marek.'

'Yes.'

'Do you remember what Lily looked like, Wilf?'

He puffed on his fag and then he smiled. 'Like a little fairy, she was.' he said. 'A nice pretty lady with long, blonde hair. I thought she was German – you know, proper German – not a Jew. My mum told me not to speak to her because of it – until she realised, like.'

Wilf was sure that Lily Smith had been blonde, but the little picture that Mumtaz's client had found behind the mezuzah had been of a dark-haired woman. Who was she? For the moment at least, it seemed unlikely that she was Lily Smith.

'Actually, my mum got to know Lily Smith a bit before the boy left,' Wilf said. 'She, Mum that is, she always said that Lily Smith was quality.'

Lee frowned. 'You mean . . .'

'She come from a well-off, educated family.' Wilf shook his head. 'Dunno what her first husband was like, but Reg Smith must have been a come-down.'

'He saved her,' Lee said.

'Oh, well that was the story, yes,' Wilf said. 'Her and the boy was close to death on the floor of some hut and Reg took them out of there. That's what my cousin Arthur always said anyway, and he knew them well.'

'What, Arthur Dobson?' Lee asked.

'Yeah.' Wilf shook his head. 'We could ask him if he weren't in hospital.'

Lee, who knew Wilf's much older cousin a little bit, said, 'What's he in there for?'

Wilf leaned towards him and whispered, 'Cancer.'

'Oh. Sorry.'

Across Green Street the lads in the local barber's shop came out onto the pavement for a smoke and one of them, Kumar, waved at Lee.

'Alright, mate,' Lee called out.

'Yes, yes.'

Lee turned back to Wilf. 'You said that your mum knew Lily Smith until Marek went missing. What happened after that?'

'Oh, Lily Smith never went out again,' Wilf said. 'Only once, which was when she was took out feet first in a box. Buried in the old Plashet I think.'

'When was that?'

He shrugged. 'Must've been sometime in the 1960s. Eric went to the funeral of course, and I have heard it said that that was the last time *he* ever left that house.' Vi had told Lee that Eric Smith had been a recluse. 'Then he died,' Wilf said, 'and then the place just went to rack and ruin. Arthur'd know more about it than I would, but . . .' He shook his head. 'Not a good house that one, I wouldn't live in it. Here, Lee, is it true it's been bought by some young couple?'

The woman behind the toughened glass window looked down at the ring with nothing but contempt. Mumtaz said, 'It's a one-carat solitaire diamond.'

The woman shrugged as if to say, So you're another skint woman with another one-carat diamond, so what?

'We have to verify it,' she said. She put the ring that Ahmet had bought Mumtaz for their first wedding anniversary in a battered cardboard jewellery box and passed it to an old man who sat behind her. 'Can you move out the way so I can serve the next customer?'

Mumtaz stood aside to let a big-haired woman, who looked like she was probably a traveller, push a load of gold chains underneath the toughened glass and say, 'Eighteen carat.' Her economy of speech and her tone made Mumtaz feel that she hated what she was doing. That was understandable.

Mumtaz had come to Manor Park to sell her final piece of valuable jewellery because the pawn shops on Green Street had become too familiar and public and she needed to go somewhere anonymous. This place, however, made her shudder. Part of a chain that had expanded massively since the onset of the credit crunch of 2007, it dealt in anything anyone might want to sell. It was the sort of establishment that attracted men in their early thirties pushing babies in buggies, looking to sell guitars that had once been imbued with their dreams.

The woman behind the toughened glass took the traveller's chains wordlessly and then she beckoned Mumtaz back to the counter.

'Our expert says we can advance you eight hundred on it,' she said.

Mumtaz remembered what Ahmet had paid for the ring, because he had been the sort of man who told a woman such things. *Look, I paid three thousand pounds for this, for you!* he'd said as he'd hurled it at her after she'd said she'd rather have a few less beatings than a ring for their first wedding anniversary. Now it was the last valuable piece of jewellery that she had, it was the most beautiful and she hated it. It was a no brainer.

'OK,' she said.

The woman behind the counter began to fill out paperwork and quoted a figure that Mumtaz would have to pay if she wanted to keep the ring 'in'. She knew that unless some miracle happened she'd never redeem it, and nor did she want to, not for herself. The only reason to pawn it at all was so that maybe one day she could redeem it to give to Shazia. The girl had no jewellery from her own mother; Ahmet had sold that long ago.

Once she'd completed her business, Mumtaz put the eight hundred pounds in her purse and left the shop as quickly as possible. Once outside, even though it was raining and grey, she breathed more easily.

Some of the girls she'd seen there before. A lot of them were eastern European – generally of the blonde, long-legged variety – who sat in one corner of the room talking and laughing among themselves. Over Wendy's side of the room were two black girls whom she knew, and four others, white and British, that she didn't.

Sean Rogers's house wasn't beautiful but it was fabulous. The girls had been put into what Sean called the 'Granny Flat' which was an apartment on the first floor of the pool house. It had a vast living room, two bedrooms and two bathrooms. This was the 'holding pen' where the girls who would provide Sean and Marty's business associates with 'entertainment' that night would prepare themselves with fake tans, perfume and make-up. The Rogers had their reputations to think about while Wendy just concentrated on how much this would knock off her debt.

She was wearing a thong, a bra and a pair of six-inch wedges which took her to almost six feet tall. There were mirrors all over the living room and she sat in front of one to do her make-up and put on her false eyelashes. A black girl, Harmony, smiled at her, but it was a leggy East European who came and sat down at the mirror beside her.

In comparison to this fake-tanned girl, Wendy was pallid. Her face looked grey and for a few moments her own deathly pallor gave her pause.

'This waterproof is very good.'

Wendy looked to her left. The girl, blonde and unsmiling, was offering her a tube of foundation cream.

'Is a little dark for you but it do not run,' the girl continued. 'Take it.'

Wendy took it. 'Thank you.'

'Do you work here before?'

'Yes,' Wendy said.

'Is very nice house.'

'Yes.'

A house with a room that would later be darkened and packed to the ceiling with bodies fucking and being fucked like pieces of meat.

The East European shadowed her eyes in green and then picked up a set of false eyelashes with a pair of tweezers. 'I would like to live in a house like this one day,' she said.

Wendy didn't answer. All she wanted was her own flat with the kids in Plaistow.

'But I must have a lot of sex before I can do that,' the girl continued.

Was she a professional prostitute? The few East European girls Wendy had met before at Sean's parties had been, like this girl, very calm about it all. But then maybe that was just how they were. Coming from poor places like Romania and Albania maybe you did whatever you had to to survive . . . But then wasn't Wendy's own situation rather like theirs?

'Anyway, perhaps we meet rich men who want to keep us or maybe marry,' the girl said. She saw Wendy shudder and she asked, 'You don't like?'

'I don't want to marry a bloke like that,' she said.

'But if he is rich . . .'

'Even if he is rich,' Wendy said. The other girl had put her false eyelashes on now, Wendy was just getting going with hers.

'Why not?'

'Because to marry a bloke I'd have to love him, and I can't love anyone who abuses me.'

The girl stopped what she was doing and turned to Wendy. This time she smiled. 'When I see you come here I see there is fear in you.'

'I've been before and it's . . .'

'It is a way for women like us to survive. You would not be here if you had trouble with that.'

In the past, Wendy had always fought shy of these foreign girls. She'd found them unintelligible and even a bit cold. This one was no different, but she had a nice smile. 'What's your name?' Wendy asked.

'Is Tatiana. You?'

'I'm Wendy.'

'Wendy.'

'Yeah.' Tatiana smiled again and the feeling that Wendy had that she could talk to this girl increased. 'I've got kids,' she said. 'Children.'

'Ah.' Tatiana's face became grave. 'The same for my friend Masha.' She pointed to one of the other East Europeans, a slightly smaller girl with red hair. 'You do for them.'

'Yes.'

Tatiana put a friendly as opposed to a sexual hand on Wendy's knee. She said, 'Children make life different, harder. But Wendy, maybe you still find rich man even with children? Even if you don't really want. Is good, eh?'

Abdullah's answer to her question had made perfect sense.

'Yes, I'd been practising up north for a few years but I didn't know how London'd work out for me,' he'd told Nasreen, 'so why spend a load of money on property? Uncle Fazal's place was fine, and it meant that eventually I could buy the house in Strone Road for us when it came on the market.'

She'd wanted to ask him about the rest of the money that he'd made because, even as quite a young solicitor, even up north, he must have made a fair amount. But she hadn't. And now he was gone. Out working, something to do with drawing up a contract for some businessman in south London, he'd said.

Nasreen, alone in her bedroom at her parents' house, thought about that word that Mumtaz Hakim had said to her. *Mezuzah.*

It was Hebrew – so it was Jewish – for that cylinder she'd found on the post beside the back door of their new house. Apparently it contained some sort of scroll that was meaningful to Jews and was part of the traditions they had around living in houses. The small picture behind the mezuzah could be of the woman who had lived in the house years ago, the mother of the odd, reclusive man who, she understood, was Jewish. But Mrs Hakim had not been sure, and was still in the process of finding out more about that family. She was also looking into Abdullah's background. Not even Nasreen's own mother knew about that, and just thinking about it made her feel guilty.

But when it had just been Abdullah and her, his past had not been an issue. He'd been handsome, employed in a good job and he'd loved her: loved her enough to make her pregnant, and so there was now another life to consider. She had to know who her baby's father really was. All the little things that had either not added up or made sense to her about Abdullah had to be addressed.

All the stuff about respecting her and keeping her away from 'unnatural' sexual practices set off many alarm bells for Nasreen. She knew that there were some deeply religious men who really believed that and treated their wives like empresses, but a lot of men used the 'you're too pure' argument to go and do 'dirty' things with Western women or with prostitutes. She had sincerely wanted to be more sexually adventurous with Abdullah, but what had really hurt when he'd rebuffed her advances had been the thought that he was getting what she was offering elsewhere. He was away a lot.

As yet, Mrs Hakim had found out little about Abdullah that Nasreen didn't already know. If she found nothing, then all well and good. But then was it? Even if Mrs Hakim found nothing bad in Abdullah's past, that didn't mean that he wasn't doing what he shouldn't in the present. If that happened, should she have him followed to these business meetings he attended?

She'd had a conversation, once, with John Sawyer about his time in Afghanistan that had stuck in her mind. John had, albeit indirectly, started her thinking about Abdullah and the doubts that she had, in all honesty, always had.

While stationed near a small village in Helmand province, John had seen a girl of twelve running, crying and bleeding into the dust. She'd looked as if she'd been attacked, which she had, by her husband. Given in marriage to a seventy-year-old man, the girl had had her virginity taken roughly. Later, John had come across the husband at a house in a neighbouring village where a troupe of *bachabaze* boy dancers was appearing. Dressed as girls, the young boys, or *bachas*, had then been taken for sex by the men who had paid them to dance. John had caught one of them with the girl's seventy-year-old husband. No doubt doing what the old man would never have asked his 'wife' to do, the boy had been petted and kissed by the old man afterwards. He'd then tossed him a low-value note and the boy had run away. John beat the 'husband' up when he went outside the courtyard of the house to relieve himself. He'd made the mistake of telling him just why he considered him to be a filthy, psychopathic rapist, not fit to be a husband to anyone, much less a child, while he punched and kicked him.

Only days later, John learned that the old man's wife had died. Apparently she'd been shot by the Taliban, but John knew better than that. The old man had killed the girl in order both to retain his honour in the face of a foreigner who clearly cared on some level for her, and to punish John. When John told Nasreen about it, he had cried. He'd said that men in Afghanistan used women simply as baby makers. John hadn't known about her sex life, but what he'd said had made Nasreen think.

Was she just a 'baby maker' for Abdullah? If so, how would her life be when she moved out of the security of her parents' home and into that strange, unhappy house in Strone Road?

14

There were three girls in the swimming pool, all naked, playing catch with a football. Around the pool a load of scantily clad middle-aged and old men leered at them. It was, Wendy felt, a bit like watching a scene from a cheap 1980s porn film. When, she wondered, will a naked German with a moustache arrive to fix the outflow?

The blind room hadn't started yet and so far she hadn't had to do anything except allow herself to be fondled by any man who wanted her. No-one had taken enough coke or drunk enough booze for all their inhibitions to disappear. But it wouldn't be long. The sky was blackening and the laughter and the talk were getting louder.

Wendy walked past the pool and then wobbled on her wedges onto the finely manicured lawn that led down, so Sean said, to a stream at the bottom of the garden. If she could spend a few minutes just looking at something pleasant before it all started she might feel better. But for some, it seemed, the sex had already begun.

Watched by Marty's wife, the vicious and terrifying Debbie, Tatiana was kneeling down in front of a man twice her age, who then roughly assaulted her mouth. Debbie, urging the girl to 'do better', spanked the man's bottom to increase his pleasure. Once Debbie had threatened to kill Wendy when she'd refused to let some man who looked like a pit bull terrier bugger her.

Now just the sight of Debbie made Wendy shrink back into the small amount of cover afforded by some trees. She couldn't help Tatiana. Nobody could. If Debbie noticed you, then you suffered because that, as well as watching her husband have sex with other women, was what Debbie liked.

Shaking, Wendy looked at the row of fir trees behind the stream that marked the limits of Sean's property, and fantasised about making a run for it. But she couldn't. If she went, what would Sean do to the kids? What specifically would he do to Dolly?

'Would you like a drink?'

Wendy didn't turn around at first because she thought that whoever was talking couldn't be addressing her. Girls at Sean and Marty's parties were just for sex, they weren't for wooing with promises of drinks. But if he wasn't talking to her, then who was he talking to?

Wendy turned around and saw a man who was more her age than most of the blokes she'd seen so far. And although she couldn't see him properly through the unlit dusk she gained an impression that he was handsome.

Before she'd thought it through, Wendy found herself saying, 'Who are you?'

Asking men at Sean's parties who they were was strictly forbidden. They could be judges, captains of industry, in entertainment – anything. Sean and Marty always promised their rich and famous guests complete anonymity, it was how they entertained and did business with them.

Wendy opened her mouth to say that she was sorry but the man pre-empted her. 'I'm Paul,' he said. 'Would you like a glass of this champagne cocktail? It's proper nice.'

*

Lech Ostrowski had told his sister Kazia not to go anywhere near the Plashet Cemetery. He'd said he shouldn't go to East Ham at all. But then Bully had called her up and she fancied him and so she'd gone.

When she got there, just as Bully had said, there were no police. He'd sent her a text to let her know he'd meet her inside and so Kazia walked down to Colston Road and knocked on the door of the house where her friend Dorotka lived. Bully had a meeting with someone somewhere else first and he'd told her he'd probably have some gear. It was irresistible.

Once over the wall beside Dorotka's garden, Kazia scoured the graveyard for Bully. She'd met him the previous year at a BNP rally in Luton. Dorotka had encouraged her to come over to Britain for the rally, and so she'd gone with her and a group of skinhead boys from East Ham, including Bully. If the police hadn't been protecting the Luton Pakis they would have taken them down. Kazia didn't understand why the British allowed so many of them to come to their country and also protected them. Sometimes she found the British very soft and stupid. Even Bully, for all his fascist opinions, could be cowardly. When the police had arrested him he'd just given in to them like a pussy.

Kazia took a small torch out of her pocket and shone it on the ground. Everywhere she looked there were those blocky Hebrew letters on gravestones. She looked for Bully. She didn't know how he'd got in last time and assumed he had his own method just as she did. He'd vaulted the gates to get out. There were no cameras at the gates, only one at the back of the cemetery. Bully said someone had tipped off the police about him.

When Kazia became aware of that slight but familiar smell in the air, it made her smile. Bully's meeting had come good and he had some weed. First they could get fucked in the head and then they could shag each other stupid. She thought about calling his name but then she felt that it would be more fun if she just crept up on him and maybe pulled the ring in his nose or something. Following the cannabis smell as it strengthened, she found herself veering towards the south side of the cemetery. And then she saw him. Kazia had to put a hand up to her mouth to stop herself from yelling.

Dressed, as they always were, in shalwar khameez and waving some beads around his wrist with one hand was that Paki who had got her arrested. Oblivious to his surroundings, he was smoking a massive joint. Bully was nowhere to be seen but Kazia's evening had just cheered up considerably.

Lee felt his heart sink. There was no way of wrapping up the fact that Amy Green was having an affair, even in his own mind now. Quite how he'd put it to her husband, he didn't know. Although he'd never been convicted of murder, Brian Green had killed people in the past – Lee knew it, everyone knew it.

In a far distant corner of 'Spicey's' car park, Amy and the driver he'd seen her with outside her house were kissing up against a tree. Amy's skirt was so short that Lee could see one of the man's hands was down her knickers and she was, in turn, making noises like she was having an orgasm. Discreet was not a word that either of them clearly had any sort of acquaintance with. Lee felt conflicted and then he felt angry. How could either of them be so fucking stupid? If Amy Green felt she had to have more carnal fun than Brian's wrinkled todger could provide then why couldn't she have been a sensible girl and found a way to meet her bloke somewhere nice and off the beaten track?

People's stupidity never failed to depress Lee Arnold. Just when he thought he'd plumbed the depths of human ridiculousness, along came something even more pathetic. And what was he supposed to do now, he wondered, as he watched the driver unzip his fly and lift the squealing girl onto his knob? He had a duty to his client to tell him the truth, but knowing how Brian could be, and what he was capable of, gave Lee a headache. Should he tell Amy and her beau to just pack it in or he *will* tell Brian? Would it help to tell the girl just what Brian might do to her if he ever found out?

Lee didn't see the BMW 320 convertible until it was halfway across the car park doing about fifty. He did see that it was headed for the couple shagging up against the tree, but by the time he'd opened his mouth to warn them, it had slammed into them. It reversed quickly, just once, so it could smash into them again, but by this time they were almost certainly dead.

Part Two

15

'Why?' Vi Collins handed Majid Islam his personal effects and began walking with him towards the Station's back exit.

Majid Islam shrugged. 'Can a man not have a small vice?' he asked.

Here was a man who presented himself as the virtuous guardian of the Plashet Jewish Cemetery. He didn't drink, eat pork, smoke fags or go out. He portrayed himself as a person who didn't 'do' vice.

'The only regret I have is that everyone will point the finger at me now,' he continued. 'If Muslims are found to have vices everyone does that.'

'You set yourself up as a paragon of virtue, Mr Islam,' Vi said.

'And yet if I were an atheist or a Christian . . .'

'Look, I know what you mean, Mr Islam,' Vi said. 'People will jump on this story about you because you're a Muslim. I'm not a fool, I know what goes on. But you've only got yourself to blame.'

'Because I smoke a little cannabis from time to time?'

'And because you were doing it in that cemetery.'

He looked outraged. 'You'd rather I did it in my home? Around my kids?'

'No, of course not!'

'I thought I wasn't doing any harm,' he said. 'I work for myself, it's stressful and living near to the cemetery—'

'But you were found.'

She swiped her station pass over the sensor that unlocked the inner back exit door.

'I don't know . . .'

'You were seen,' Vi said.

'By whom? I was alone.'

'I don't know,' Vi said. 'As I told you, it was an anonymous tip-off.'

Vi swiped her pass over yet another key pad to unlock the outer back door, which buzzed as they both walked through it. Out in the rain-soaked car park he said, 'So what happens now?'

'You've been charged and so you're free to go,' Vi said.

Majid Islam walked away, head down, his hands in the folds of his shalwar khameez. He'd said he hadn't been smoking cannabis the night he'd found John Sawyer's body and the skeleton, but was he telling the truth? As a habitual cannabis smoker, could he actually be trusted? Bully had talked about an Asian who had apparently 'left' the body of John Sawyer after doing God alone knew what to it. Could that Asian be Majid Islam after all?

But then Islam had been the one who had called the police in the first place, so to effectively shop himself didn't make any sense. Also, there had been no significant forensic evidence on him. However, John Sawyer had died, according to the pathologist, many hours before Majid Islam had found him. Could Mr Islam have murdered Sawyer much earlier, changed his clothes, and then returned later in order to very publicly 'find' his body?

Vi hadn't been able to discover any sort of connection between

Majid Islam and John Sawyer the first time around. Apart from the fact that Islam didn't approve of the war in Afghanistan there was none.

Lee was shivering slightly. Mumtaz put the cup of tea she'd made him down on his desk and said, 'Drink it while it's hot.'

He didn't reply but he followed her advice. He'd been questioned about what he'd seen in 'Spicey's' car park by the Essex police for hours. They'd wanted to know why he'd been in the car park, what he'd seen and whether he'd got the registration number of the car that had killed Amy Green and her lover, Dale Champ. He had.

Lee had been completely honest with the coppers who had taken him up to Chelmsford HQ for questioning. He'd told them about Brian, what he'd seen Amy and Dale doing up against the tree and as much as he could about the car that had killed them. What he hadn't managed to clock was the driver of the car. He had feared it might be Brian, but whatever else he was Brian Green was no fool. To employ him to watch Amy and then kill her on only the second obbo wouldn't make any sense.

He'd told Mumtaz some details about what had happened when he'd phoned her to let her know about the previous evening. It was she who had suggested that they meet up at their office even though it was Sunday. Now he told her the rest. She said, 'So where is Mr Green now?'

'He had to identify his wife's body,' Lee said. 'Then the coppers had him in for questioning.'

Mumtaz shook her head. 'Even if she was being unfaithful . . .'

'I'd've been amazed if she hadn't been playing away.' Lee shook his head. 'Brian can be charming, don't get me wrong, but he makes Andrew Lloyd Webber look attractive and he is almost old enough to have been Amy's granddad.'

They sat in silence for a few moments. Love and lust were emotions so frequently born of moments of madness. When Mumtaz had first seen Naz Sheikh, when he'd walked towards her husband with murder in his face, she'd been horrified by her own lust for him. Then she didn't know him and she'd kept any details about her husband's murderer secret from the police in order to protect him. He'd killed her tormenter *and* she was attracted to him. But now that she knew Naz, hatred had overwhelmed all her other feelings.

'So do the police have any idea about who might have killed Mrs Green and her lover?' Mumtaz asked.

'No, but it's early days,' Lee said. 'They have to follow up on the number plate I got for them and see if it's kosher, *then* they have to find out who knew about their affair and who could've been pissed off about it. Brian's obvious, but I don't know who else. Maybe lover boy Dale had a missus? Or a boyfriend . . . That whole glossy Essex world is so fucked, er, messed up.'

'In what way?'

'In the way that nobody's who they seem. They've all got fake boobs, fake teeth, fake hair. I think a lot of the friendships they seem to have, which tend to be all lovey-dovey and over the top, are fake. Some girl takes her top off for some dirty old man to take her photograph and suddenly she's a glamour model. Know what I mean?' He shook his head. 'Any one of them might have secretly hated Amy and her boyfriend.' Lee leaned back in his chair and rubbed his reddened eyes with his fingers. 'Anyway that's me unemployed again on Monday. Thank God you've got some on.'

Mumtaz looked over at her computer screen which she had

abandoned while she'd gone to make them both tea. 'Yes, the information you passed on to me about Nasreen Khan's house in Strone Road was interesting.'

'About the Jewish family?'

'The Smiths stroke Berkowiczs, yes. But if your contact was right and Lily Smith was a blonde, then the photograph behind the mezuzah can't have been of her.'

'Maybe there was another woman in the house.'

'Your contact didn't say that there was?'

'No, and nor did Vi, but I didn't ask.' Lee drank the last of his tea. 'I will.'

'Thank you. But I don't think that Nasreen is so exercised about the picture as she was,' Mumtaz said. 'Now she seems to think that her husband is not all she thinks he is.'

'In what way?'

'He has no family, which is very unusual in our culture. And so Nasreen, and her parents, have had to take whatever Abdullah Khan has told them about himself at face value.' She looked at her screen again. 'For instance, he is a solicitor and yet when he first came down to London from Lancashire he stayed at a cheap boarding house that was run by his uncle.'

'I can understand that,' Lee said.

'Yes, it makes some sense until you factor in that he had apparently been practising law for some years. So he can't have been poor.'

'Maybe he stayed in the boarding house to help his uncle out.'

She shrugged. 'He would have been helping his uncle out more if he had obtained tenants for him. And anyway, Abdullah was in the boarding house for some years. Lawyers are highly prized in our culture and it would be shameful if a lawyer lived as a poor person. So there is that,' Mumtaz said. 'Then there is the fact that when he did finally buy a property, in spite of surely having saved some money during his time in the boarding house, Abdullah bought the cheapest house, at auction, in Newham. Do you see?'

'Yeah. So you think he's got a gambling habit? A woman somewhere?'

'I don't know,' Mumtaz said. 'Nasreen has not as yet instructed me to follow her husband. But this I do know . . .' She looked back at her screen again.

'What?'

'No person named Abdullah Khan, resident and practising in Newham, is listed with the Law Society,' Mumtaz said.

Wendy Dixon didn't know what to do. She couldn't fathom how she'd survived one of Sean Rogers's parties unscathed. In fact she'd spent the time with just one man, Paul.

Beyond the fact that he was dark and sexy, Wendy didn't know anything about him. He *was* attractive, and although he hadn't hurt her or treated her like shit as the rest of Sean's friends and associates generally did, he had wanted some dirty sex. But for once, because he was polite and he was fit, Wendy had been into it herself. He'd *asked* her to do things. Not even the fathers of her children had done that.

Wendy got out of the posh car that Paul had summoned up to take her home and she made a point of thanking its young Asian driver. It had been early and so most of the other party-goers had been in bed or flaked out in that hideous blind orgy room when she'd left. And although Paul hadn't said anything about wanting to get her away from Ongar before all the rank old men decided they wanted just one more shag before they left, she knew he'd got her out quickly on purpose.

He'd liked her, he'd said so, and she knew she'd given him pleasure. Wendy could be mechanical at sex, but she could also be good at it. They'd fucked almost all night, there'd been top quality smoke and they'd done it in one of Sean's best guest rooms. He'd even let her sleep.

Just once she'd thought that maybe Paul was some sort of imposter who'd broken into Sean's house and taken advantage. But some time in the early hours of the morning, Marty had opened the door to the room and looked at them. Then she'd seen him nod at Paul. She hadn't known what that had meant and just the memory of it made her anxious. Then she looked up at her bedroom window and saw Dolly, holding baby Stuart in her arms, and Wendy smiled. She felt such warmth for her kids at that moment!

Was this, she wondered, what being in love was like?

Her phone rang. It was Sean. Wendy ignored it.

Nasreen was learning new things. She'd been sick again that morning and, unlike the first time it had happened, she hadn't really felt better since. So she'd stayed in bed and once she'd started to feel a little brighter, she'd entertained herself on her laptop computer. Her parents were having a quiet Sunday with their newspapers and Abdullah still hadn't returned from his latest business trip.

After checking her e-mails and a quick glance at Facebook, Nasreen decided she would look up some information on mezuzahs.

The first thing that struck her about the Jewish information sites was that the word God was never actually shown. Expressed as G-d, it struck her as weird until she compared it to the commandment against physical representation of human beings and animals that existed in Islam. Those who were orthodox and followed the Koran to the letter as well as abiding by rules added via Hadith, wouldn't even photograph their own children. This G-d thing was the orthodox Jews' version of that. The name of God should never be written or spoken.

A mezuzah, she read, contained a parchment with verses from the Jewish Holy book, the Torah, written on it. These verses made up what was called the *Shema Yisrael* which was a special prayer which began, 'Hear O Israel, the Lord our G-d, the Lord is One.' Again, parallels with Islam were clear to Nasreen. The *adhan*, or Call to Prayer, always began: *Allahu Akbar! Ash-hadu an-la ilaha illa llah* – God is Great! I bear witness there is no God but God. What was the difference there? Some Muslims she knew had this thing about how different the Jews were to everybody else. Nasreen had never knowingly met any Jews but even this small piece of information about them was enough to convince her that they were not a million miles away from Islam.

The mezuzah parchment had to be prepared by a scribe and written in indelible ink with a quill pen. Having mezuzot on doors fulfilled a *mitzvah* or commandment to Jews from God. It had to be placed at shoulder height and if the household was an Ashkenazi one then it had to slant towards the property, if a Sephardic home then it pointed straight up towards heaven. The 'lump' that Nasreen had found on the back doorpost at Strone Road had been painted over so many times it was difficult now to remember whether or not it had slanted. And did it matter anyway? Ashkenazi and Sephardic were just different branches of Judaism, like Sunni and Shi'a Muslims. What she did know, however, was that she had only found one mezuzah in the house. According to the websites she was looking at, really orthodox

Jews would have a mezuzah on every doorpost there was, even cupboard doors. But then if Mrs Hakim was right about the family who had lived there before, it had only been the wife, Lily, and her son Marek who had actually been Jewish. Maybe the Christian husband, Mr Smith, hadn't wanted to have mezuzot all over the house . . .

In Israel it seemed, mezuzot had to be affixed to doorposts as soon as a family moved into a new home. But out in the diaspora there was always a hiatus of thirty days, in order to allow time in case the family had to move again: legacy of a persecution Nasreen knew she could never understand. Her uncles sometimes talked about the 'Paki bashing' of the 1970s but it didn't compare to gas chambers. Her husband was one of those Muslims who said that it did, but Nasreen couldn't agree with him and so 'Jews' were not a topic of conversation between them.

And then Nasreen read something that made her smile. The purpose of mezuzot was basically to remind people of the continuing presence of God in their lives. But it had another purpose too. Every mezuzah fixed to a doorpost added to the divine protection given by God to people everywhere. It was, as one writer put it, 'an act of kindness' to humanity. Nasreen felt that was incredibly beautiful.

16

Mumtaz looked at her office telephone. She should call Nasreen Khan. It was Monday morning, a work day, and so she had no excuses left not to call.

The door buzzer went.

Lee walked over to the entryphone box on the wall and looked at the monitor. 'Come in, Brian,' he said as he released the office door lock.

Brian Green, the bereaved husband, walked slowly into the office. He was a big man, whose shoulders slumped and whose skin was grey and pitted with acne scars. More significant than his physical defects, however, was his demeanour, which was that of someone who had had the spark of life forced out of them. Brian Green was empty.

He took Lee's proffered hand and said, 'Hello, mate.'

'Brian, I'm . . .'

Brian Green looked over his shoulder at Mumtaz. 'Hello, darlin',' he said.

'I am really sad to hear about your loss, Mr Green,' she said.

'Thank you, love, that's appreciated.' He turned back to Lee and said, 'Can we talk? About the weekend?'

'Yes, of course, Brian.'

Although Lee and Mumtaz generally had the door between

their two offices open all the time, there were occasions when that wasn't desirable. This was one of them. As Brian Green closed the door to Lee's office behind him, Mumtaz heard him say, 'The number plate of the car what killed Amy was a fucking fake.'

She heard Lee draw in breath and then she heard no more. Before she could think for any longer about what she had to say, Mumtaz called Nasreen Khan. When the young woman picked up, she sounded terrible.

'Nasreen? What's the matter? Are you sick?'

'I've just been sick,' Nasreen panted. 'Morning sickness.'

Of course . . . she was pregnant. Mumtaz would have to tread carefully.

'I found out some more details about your house in Strone Road,' she said.

'Oh?'

'Yes. Lily Smith, you know the Jewish lady who was the mother of the boy Marek who disappeared . . .'

'Yes?'

'She lived in the house with her son, Eric, until sometime in the 1960s when she died. Her husband Reg predeceased her. But Nasreen, the main thing I've found out about Lily Smith is that she was a blonde.'

'So she's not the woman in the photograph?'

'It's unlikely,' Mumtaz said.

'Oh.' She sounded a bit disappointed, but only a bit.

Mumtaz took her courage in her hands. 'However, your husband, Abdullah Khan . . .'

'Yes?' This time her voice had more tension in it. Then she said, 'He's at the house today, sanding floorboards.'

'Nasreen, there's no easy way to say this but I think it's possible that Abdullah has been lying to you about what he does.'

'What? At the house?' She was clearly rather woozy from being sick.

'No,' Mumtaz said, 'about his job. I've searched for his name on the Law Society's register of practising solicitors and I cannot find anyone called Abdullah Khan who matches the profile you have given me. Which firm does he work for?'

But all Nasreen said was, 'There has to be a mistake!'

Mumtaz had expected this response. 'I will check again,' she said, 'but I don't think so, Nasreen. Can you tell me which firm of solicitors your husband works for?'

'They're based out in Essex,' Nasreen said.

Mumtaz had assumed that Abdullah Khan worked for a local firm but that wouldn't change how she searched for him much. 'And the name?'

'Rogers and Ali,' Nasreen said. 'The senior partner is a man called Sean Rogers.'

Wendy slammed into the television, sending it crashing to the floor. She heard Dolly scream.

'When I call you, you answer me, right?' she heard Sean say as he punched her in the side of the head. 'Just because one of my business acquaintances decided to have you all to hisself at my party, don't think that you don't still owe me.'

Wendy struggled to clear the blood out of her mouth. She looked at Dolly whose eyes were as big as space. She'd never met Sean Rogers before, Wendy had made sure that she hadn't. But that morning, straight after breakfast, he'd just kicked the door down and let himself in.

'Paul,' she mumbled.

Sean ignored her. 'I want you, up the pub tonight at seven,' he said. He looked at Dolly and smiled. 'Couple of my friends want to fuck your mother,' he said.

Wendy watched, horrified, as Dolly's little face just collapsed. She'd never told her what she did, of course she hadn't!

'You pay what you owe me by playing pig for men I need to keep on side,' Sean Rogers said. 'You don't get brownie points for persuading some geezer to go down on you all night long.'

There was nothing to say.

'Getting a bit fucked off with people trying to rip me and my brother off. Fucking arse'oles on the make, tarts like you!' He kicked her in the ribs. Dolly screamed again, 'Don't hurt my mum!'

But he did it again. Dolly launched herself at him – arms chopping, teeth grinding. To Wendy's horror, he caught her in mid-air and then pulled her towards him and smiled. Dolly's face went white.

Lee had expected Brian to pay him for his services in cash. He was old fashioned like that.

'I just hope the coppers'll get whoever killed Amy,' Lee said, as he led Brian to the office door.

'And the boy.'

'Yes, and him.' Lee had told the police about what he'd seen Amy and Dale Champ doing in Spicey's car park just before they died, but he hadn't discussed it with Brian. Now he wondered what, if anything, he had been told.

'He was gonna take her home,' Brian said. 'Bring her back to me.'

Lee, for once, was stumped.

'She'd left her mates in the club and she was coming home,' he said.

Amy and Dale hadn't been anywhere near his limo when they died. Surely Brian had to have been told that? Surely the police had to have told him that the couple had been in each other's arms when they died? When the bodies were autopsied it would be obvious that they'd been having sex. For a moment, Lee thought about telling him himself, but then he changed his mind. It wasn't his responsibility and he didn't work for Brian any more.

Brian Green left and, after Lee had spent a few minutes outside the office having a restorative fag, he said to Mumtaz, 'I couldn't tell him.'

'That his wife was having an affair?'

Lee sat down in the chair opposite Mumtaz's desk. 'He suspected her which was why he employed me. But to confirm that? For sure?'

'If she was having sex at the time of her death, the police will know,' Mumtaz said.

'Yeah. And maybe they've already told him?' He shrugged. 'Maybe Brian's in denial.'

'Would it be in character for him to do that?'

'Partly,' Lee said. 'Or rather, that's my reading of Brian inasmuch as I *can* read him. Old-time gangsters like him are good at hiding things. What he knows and what he don't know are not easy things to discover. There's kudos involved too, see. Brian can know that Amy was playing away from home and that's alright, but he wouldn't want anyone else to know.'

'He was happy for you to know.'

'Because I was working for him and so he was by definition buying my silence,' Lee said. 'We keep our gobs shut on a professional basis.'

'So Brian Green may or may not be deluding himself?'

'Absolutely.'

Mumtaz was struck by how like Nasreen Khan the old gangster was in that respect. When, at the end of their earlier conversation, Mumtaz had asked whether or not Nasreen wanted her to continue her investigation into the background of her husband, she had said that she didn't. She didn't believe what Mumtaz had told her about Abdullah. She didn't want her to look any further into the Smith/Berkowicz story either. Mumtaz could keep the mezuzah and the tiny picture. And then Nasreen Khan had said a very emphatic 'goodbye'.

So now they were both without work. But then the front door buzzer buzzed, and it kept on buzzing as if the person outside's life depended upon it, until Lee got up and answered it.

Nasreen had been sick again before she left her parents' house to go to Strone Road. Her mother, concerned, had said, 'You really should lie down, dear. You are very pale.'

But Nasreen had ignored her. For some reason, that Hakim woman had lied to her about Abdullah. Of course he was a solicitor! He talked about his legal studies and about cases he'd worked on in the past all the time. But then something was making her almost break into a run to see her husband, and it was not desire. Why would Mumtaz Hakim lie? It was a question that kept on playing over and over in Nasreen's mind as she hurried along the rain-dappled streets of East Ham. Why would she lie? What would be the point?

Walking along Colston Road, she saw a policeman and a woman in plain clothes knock on one of the doors and she wondered whether it had anything to do with John Sawyer's death. They hadn't found his killer and she still hadn't confided her fears about the possibility of Abdullah having been involved. And nor would she, not until she'd cleared up this business about her husband's employment. There had to be a rational explanation for the discrepancy between what Abdullah had told her and what she'd learned from Mumtaz Hakim. But then, if she had been so sure of him, why had Nasreen even asked Mrs Hakim to look into his background? She looked down at her pregnant belly and she knew why.

As she picked her way down the convolvulus-strewn front path and let herself into the house Nasreen regretted telling Mumtaz Hakim that she could keep the mezuzah. It belonged with the house. Perhaps when she went in to pay her bill she'd ask for it back. Maybe she'd even ask Mrs Hakim to continue her researches into the previous owners of the house. That remained unfinished business.

Nasreen had thought she'd hear the sound of the sanding machine as she came in, but the house was silent. She walked from the hall and into the dining room. What she saw in there was unexpected and disturbing. Where once there had been an original Edwardian fireplace that they had both agreed they wanted to keep, now there was a great, raw gash in the wall. Not only had the fireplace gone but most of the chimney breast seemed to have followed it. Nasreen looked at one side of a soot-stained shaft, her mouth open.

'It had to go.'

She turned and saw him standing behind her, panting, a pickaxe in one hand. He smelt of smoke and now she saw that something out in the back garden was burning.

'I thought you were sanding . . .' He'd even removed some of the floorboards.

'Everything was damp.'

'But we agreed . . .'

'I know you wanted to keep the original stuff, love, but I had a look at it. It were rotten. That's why I'm burning it now,' he said. He put the pickaxe down on the floorboards and smiled. 'We can get a lovely gas fire in there,' he said. 'Contemporary.'

'But . . . the original features.'

'I told you, they were rotten.' His face changed in that way it did when she talked about any other man, or sex. Nasreen's breath became a little bit more ragged. 'We can get some sort of Edwardian replacement in there if you want,' he continued. 'But the more I think about it, the more I think we should go modern. I think it'd be nice to make one big room down here.'

Again, they'd agreed early on that they would retain the original form of the house, with a separate dining room and living room. She was about to say something to this effect when he pre-empted her. 'What you doing here anyhow? You were sick this morning, you should be resting.'

'I feel better now,' Nasreen said.

'Good.' Sweaty and wearing a tee-shirt that was ripped in just the right places to show off his abs, Abdullah looked good enough to eat. He also looked scary.

Nasreen said, 'I came to help. I thought you were sanding.'

'So did I,' he said. 'But then I took a look at that fireplace . . .' He shrugged. 'This is graft, Nas . . .'

'Yes, but I'd like to help.'

Maybe if she stayed around him for long enough she'd get the courage up to ask him just exactly what he did for his company, Rogers and Ali.

'I wouldn't mind a cold drink and maybe a butty,' he said.

'A sandwich.'

'If you want to be posh, yes.' And then he smiled.

For a moment, Nasreen relaxed. This was the old Abdullah, who had wooed her with passion and humour. It was into that one relaxed moment that she inserted the question, 'Then, when I get back, maybe you can tell me about what you've been doing?'

His face instantly darkened. 'Doing where?' he said.

Nasreen swallowed, her throat suddenly dry with tension. 'At work,' she said. 'You were away for most of the weekend.'

'Yes, on business,' he said. His face still dark, he turned away from her, picked up the axe from the floor and hit a piece of brick that jutted out from the ruined fireplace. 'Making money to keep you happy and for this fucking house.'

'I didn't know where else to go!'

Mumtaz put a cup of tea down in front of Ayesha Mirza and said, 'Just take a few breaths and drink some tea, then tell us about it.'

'Thank you.' She wiped her eyes with a tissue. Lee, now back in his own office, looked through the open door at Mumtaz, who indicated that maybe he should close it and give her and the woman some privacy. But Ayesha Mirza had other ideas.

'Oh, Mr Arnold can hear what I've got to say too,' she said, after she'd taken a few sips of tea from her mug. Lee picked up his chair and joined the ladies.

'Alright, Mrs Mirza,' Mumtaz said, 'tell us . . .'

'Dolly phoned me, that's our Wendy's eldest,' she said.

'This is about your sister, Wendy Dixon.'

'He beat her up!' she said.

'Who?'

'Me sister, Wendy!'

'No, who beat your sister Wendy up, love?' Lee said.

'Oh.' She took another sip of tea. 'Her landlord,' she said.

'Sean Rogers.'

'Yeah!'

'Why did he beat her up?' Mumtaz asked.

'I don't know,' Ayesha Mirza said. 'Dolly rang me and said that the landlord had just beat her mum up and the telly was broke. I went over. Dolly said she never knew why it happened, even though she did. But I thought it was about what that pig makes Wend do, and then when I spoke to Wendy eventually she said that she'd gone to some sex party of his where she never had enough sex with enough men – or something.'

'So he beat her up for that?'

'Yeah. I told her, Wend, that she had to go to the police now that she was in such a state and the telly was broke, but she said no. Then when she sent Dolly off to go and get some fags for her from the old woman next door, she told me that Sean Rogers had directly threatened her daughter. She said she had to do what he wanted 'cause she was frightened for Dolly.'

'Do you know what he wants Wendy to do to "make up" for the party?' Mumtaz asked.

'Well, she wouldn't tell me, but Dolly did,' Ayesha said.

'And what was that?'

'She's to meet him in the pub on High Street North him and his people always go to,' she said. 'Sean and his brother use it like a sort of an office' so Wendy says. He wants her to have sex with a couple of blokes.' She looked first at Mumtaz and then at Lee. 'I don't know what time or nothing. She won't go to the police. She told me not to go to the police.'

Lee leaning back in his chair his arms across his chest said,

'And I can't fault her for that. Sean Rogers and his brother are very dangerous people and your sister owes him money.'

'She does.'

'She could go the whole police protection route if she was prepared to grass Sean up and give the law everything she knows about him and his sex parties and his violence – and maybe the names of other girls he's abused, and possibly even trafficked into the country. Sean, to my recollection, always liked foreign women. But that's a big risk.'

'Mr Arnold, I'm not being funny, but going with who knows who or what tonight is a risk too,' Ayesha said. 'Wend's on the Pill, she says, but there's worse things to catch than another baby and I can't see any of these men having condoms in their wallets.'

'No.'

'So what we gonna do?' Ayesha said. 'I can't just sit about and wait for my sister to be abused – again.' Mumtaz looked expectantly at Lee who realised that, as the ex-police officer on the team, he was expected to provide some sort of solution.

Tony Bracci had thought that the girl had been the baby's mother when he'd knocked on that door in Colston Road the night John Sawyer's body had been discovered. But Dorotka Walensa wasn't baby Henry's mother, she was his nanny.

'Someone made an emergency call from the landline in this house on Saturday night at 8.46 p.m.,' Vi said. 'Mr and Mrs Bancroft, your employers, were out at a concert and so, assuming it wasn't baby Henry, that just leaves you, Dorotka.'

The girl was blonde and pretty but her face was pulled into a scowl.

'That call,' Vi continued, 'led directly to the arrest of a man we found smoking cannabis in the Plashet Jewish Cemetery. And while we're pleased that we managed to collar someone smoking illegal drugs, we are concerned that whoever phoned us was either in or watching a graveyard where we found the body of a man who was murdered only last week. We're not accusing anyone of anything . . .'

Her phone started to ring and Vi looked at its screen to find out who was calling her. She decided she had to take it.

''Scuse me,' she said to Dorotka and to PC Finn who had accompanied her to Colston Road. She left the tastefully middle-class living room, belonging to a chartered accountant and his architect wife, and wandered up the staircase to what she hoped was the bathroom. She could do with patching up her lipstick. She answered the call.

'Lee,' she said.

'Vi,' he responded.

'What can I do for you, gorgeous?'

'It's about Sean Rogers,' he said.

She stood on the first-floor landing and saw the bathroom straight ahead of her. She went in.

'Invoking the Devil today are we? What about him?' Vi asked.

'I've got a situation, with a client and Sean Rogers,' Lee said.

'So? What you want me to do about it? Your client want to shop Sean, Marty and the fragrant Debbie?'

'No, of course . . .'

'Then I'm at a loss as to how I might help you, handsome.'

'Then pin 'em back and listen,' he said.

And then, while Vi repaired her lipstick in front of the Bancrofts' bathroom mirror, Lee Arnold explained – no names – that the sister of a client of his might be in danger from Sean and his friends.

When he'd finished she said, 'Look, I'm busy at the moment, but I'll ring you back later on this.'

He sounded miffed but he said, 'Yeah, alright, thanks Vi, I appreciate it.'

She was going to end the call with a bit of mild flirtation and had even started to smile in anticipation of it. But then, in one of the bedrooms, she saw something that both made her frown and struck a chord in her mind. When she went downstairs she said to Dorotka Walensa, 'So you're a Wisla Krakow fan are you, Dorotka?'

'Yes.'

'You know, I know another girl who's a big Wisla fan,' Vi said. 'Do you know someone called Kazia Ostrowska, Dorotka?'

17

In the 1950s, London had been another city. It had been dark and smoky and boarding houses had had notices in their windows saying 'No blacks or Irish.' Sadly, racism hadn't disappeared in the intervening years but life had become easier for people from foreign lands. Mumtaz's father, Baharat, hadn't arrived in London until the 1960s, her mother Sumita, not until 1970, but they both remembered how the old '50s city had lingered on.

'There were still holes where bombs had dropped in the Second World War,' Baharat told his daughter. 'Children used to play in those holes. Can you imagine? And then every so often someone would find an unexploded bomb.'

Mumtaz had been due to visit her parents, with Shazia, and although part of her had wanted to stay with Lee while the police observed Wendy Dixon, she was also glad to be away from the situation. Much as she felt for Wendy, the inevitability of what would happen depressed her. Vi Collins would observe Wendy going with whatever men Sean Rogers ordered her to go with and then they'd contact her to offer her a deal, which she would refuse. Rogers and Ali, property developers, purveyors of loans, pimps and women, were powerful and vicious. They were also, at the most basic level, men, and sadly that was all too pertinent because women feared men. Nasreen Khan feared her husband, who also worked for Rogers and Ali. Mumtaz smiled at the circularity of her own thinking. What, she wondered, did Abdullah Khan do for the Rogers brothers? Was he their own, personal lawyer? If he was, then he wasn't doing a terribly good job. A cheap house in East Ham was hardly the reward given to a man of power.

'Mumtaz, are you listening, or am I talking to myself?'

She looked up. 'Oh, Abba, I'm sorry. I was miles away.'

'You ask me to talk to you about the old days and then you drift off!'

'I'm sorry.'

From her place, scrunched up in a chair over by a window, Shazia looked over at Mumtaz and raised her eyebrows. Being in that old house in Spitalfields was always a trial for the youngster. But one evening every week she had to put up with it.

Mumtaz, who had indeed asked her father about the 'old days', said, 'Abba, I know that a few Jewish people do still live here, but were there many when you first arrived?'

'Oh, yes,' Baharat said. 'I myself knew a Mr Klein, a family Rosenberg and my first employer here, Mr Braverman, was a Jew.'

'Did you ever meet anyone who had been in a concentration camp?'

The smell of mutton biryani hung tantalisingly in the damp air. Sumita Huq, Mumtaz's mother, would delay serving food until everyone was almost mad with culinary desire.

Baharat said, 'Concentration camp? No. I believe that some Jews came to this country after the war, some of whom had been in the camps. But most of the East End Jews had been in London for generations. Now they all live in Ilford or Finchley or some such.'

'Do you think that Jews who had been in the camps would have stood out?'

Baharat thought. 'Probably,' he said. 'But why all of this interest in Jews and concentration camps? Did you not study about all that at school?'

'Yes.'

'So?'

'So, I am just interested, Abba.'

'Ah. Private detective.' He tapped the side of his nose with his finger. Mumtaz inclined her head in agreement.

Nasreen Khan was no longer paying her to look into the lives of Reg Smith and his Jewish wife Lily, but Mumtaz was still intrigued by those lives. How had Lily Berkowicz and her son Marek managed to adjust to life in the UK after Belsen? How had they survived the camp? And what were their relationships like with Reg Smith? Did either of them actually love him or had it all just been about gratitude?

Ignoring his daughter's thoughtful silence, Baharat continued, 'You ask would foreign Jews have stood out in the old days? Not to look at maybe and only if they didn't speak any English. When the uneducated come from Bangladesh it is the same thing. If they can speak the language they can do things and pass amongst people without comment. If they can't, then the silly buggers must rely on their family members who can make themselves understood.'

Although only formally educated until the age of twelve, Baharat Huq nevertheless considered himself a man of learning, mainly because he had always spoken English and because he read multiple newspapers. One of his favourite sayings was *How can one get a balanced view of the world unless one reads The Guardian and The Daily Mail?*

'And then it is that they start with all the jihad talk,' Baharat said. 'They come here, knowing nothing of this country and they want to start jihad immediately. Uneducated and with no under-standing of Islam!'

Mumtaz shook her head. Her father had it fixed in his mind that only recent, non-English-speaking immigrants from the sub-continent wanted to destroy Western society and impose a Cali-phate. She knew a few boys who had been born and bred in the UK who were enthusiastic about that. Religious zealotry was not limited to those with no education. But Mumtaz hadn't just come to see her parents to socialise with them or talk about mid-twen-tieth-century Jewish immigration.

'Abba, is it OK if I go to my old room for a few moments, please?' she asked.

He shrugged. 'This is still your home.'

'I think I've still got my copy of *The Complete Works of Shakespeare* here.'

'Oh, one cannot do without Shakespeare! Go! Go!'

She knew that he'd never read a word of Shakespeare in his life. 'Thank you, Abba.'

She stood up, noticing that Shazia was frowning at her. There was a *Complete Works* at the house in Forest Gate and they both knew it, but Mumtaz couldn't think about that now. Once the meal had started she wouldn't be able to leave the table except to go home. She had to get into her old bedroom, pick up her old complete works and look for some Mughal coins her Uncle Asif had given her when she was little. They had to be worth something.

He was still angry with her when they went to bed. Nasreen

reached out to touch him when she thought that he was half asleep, but even then her husband pulled away from her.

They hadn't exactly had a row back at Strone Road, but he had shouted at her for questioning him. He'd said some horrible things about her parents, accusing them of poisoning her mind against him even though she'd not actually got anywhere near to asking him about what he did for a living. All she'd done was ask him about what he'd been doing.

Of course she had been digging, but he hadn't known that. He hadn't known what Mumtaz Hakim had said about him. Although Nasreen still didn't believe what the private detective had told her, she nevertheless felt that Abdullah's reactions to her questions had been overly confrontational. But then he'd always been volatile, even – as she thought about it now – when they'd first met he'd been so very keen to pander to her every whim that he'd come across as a bit of a desperate case. Her friends, Julie and Rachida, had found him 'over the top'. Not that she'd seen either of them since her wedding.

Just before they'd gone to bed, Abdullah had broken his silence to her with, 'We'll move into the new house the day after tomorrow.'

She'd been horrified, but she'd said nothing: just turned away from his fierce, disapproving eyes and got into bed. The new house was still a wreck! What was more, Abdullah was now knocking down the wall between the living room and the dining room. Against everything they had agreed, he was turning their home into a modern house. Nasreen fought not to cry. There was plenty to be done at the new house and there were few places to rest; and now that morning sickness had become a regular feature, she needed a quiet place in which to recuperate. But there was nothing to be done. Abdullah wanted them to move in and so move in they would. Now that she was married, her father wouldn't interfere. Nasreen was Abdullah's wife and therefore his responsibility and his property now.

'You know as well as I do that she'll say she went willingly,' Vi said.

It was just gone one in the morning and she was in Lee Arnold's Forest Gate flat, drinking tea and talking about Wendy Dixon.

'And I can't prove nothing,' Vi continued. 'She had a black eye and was walking a bit unsteady before she went into that flat on Forest Road with them two blokes.'

'How long was she in there?' Lee asked.

'Three hours. But she come out much the same as she looked when she went in.'

'Did you know either of the blokes?' Lee asked.

'I knew one,' Vi said. 'Do you remember George White? Conman.'

'Bad one,' Lee said. 'Did a lot of time.'

'Tried to get some book deal on the back of having once met Reggie Kray when he was in Maidstone. One of the blokes was his son, Norman.'

'Don't know him,' Lee said. 'What's he do?'

'Norman and the other bloke do maintenance on rented properties for local landlords.'

'Including the Rogers.'

'Yep.' Vi lit a fag. 'And Sean particularly likes to keep those who work for them sweet. Give incentives. Know what I mean?'

'Keep quiet about the illegal gas boilers and galloping mould in the flats and we'll pay you well and give you the odd free shag.'

'That, or they asked Sean for Wendy specifically,' Vi said. 'I mean if she owes him money, which we know she does, she's his now to do what he wants with. I checked out the address of the flat and it too belongs to Sean.'

'Could be him and his brother keep it as a "love nest", Lee said, scowling. 'Fuck, it's like something out of fucking Dickens!'

Vi laughed, a deep, scarred, mirthless rumble. 'Welcome to free-market Britain,' she said. 'Bye-bye council houses, hello land-lords who'll charge you what they like, put 2,000 percent interest on your debt if you default and put you on the streets.'

'So what can we do about it?'

'Nothing.'

'I thought you were going to contact Wendy Dixon? Offer her some sort of deal?'

'I said that to make Mumtaz feel better,' Vi said. 'Wendy Dixon won't take a deal! She might tell Sean Rogers I offered her one and I can't risk that. How's it going with that investigation Mumtaz was doing into the old Smith house by the way?'

'Ah, well it's funny you should say that—'

Her phone rang. She took the call, listened, and then said, 'That's good. I'll be there.'

'So, what . . .'

Vi stood up. 'Unless Wendy Dixon comes to us and fingers the Rogers' there's nothing I can do. Not unless she's assaulted or raped and she reports it.'

'Mmm . . . But you know that Mumtaz's client's husband works for the Rogers'.'

'What, the Smith house, Strone Road?'

'Yes.'

Vi narrowed her eyes. 'Interesting.' She stood up.

'You off?' Lee asked.

'Tony Bracci has found something I was looking for,' Vi said with a smile. She walked towards Lee's front door.

He said, 'So that's Wendy Dixon over and done with then is it, Vi?'

She turned, smiled and said, 'Oh, I didn't say that, Arnold. I would never say that.' And then she left.

If the Rogers brothers and their business parter, Yunus Ali, had ever been off Vi's radar they were certainly back on again now.

Kazia Ostrowska refused to speak any language but Polish. So at three in the morning, Vi had had to organise a Polish/English translator. But once communication had been established, Kazia gave them the silent treatment.

'Your friend Dorotka told us you used the landline in the Bancrofts' house to tell us about Mr Islam and his cannabis habit,' Vi said. She hadn't. Dorotka Walensa, in spite of her little girl looks, had proved to be a much tougher nut to crack than Kazia had been. She'd been silent treatment from the start. But then, as Tony Bracci had told Vi, he'd expected nothing less from a dyed-in-the-wool Wisla fan. 'They're beyond nuts,' he'd said. 'It's like they're all in the SS or something.'

Vi leaned on the table between her and Kazia and said, 'And the only way you could've seen him was if you went inside the Plashet Jewish Cemetery, which you're not supposed to, are you Kazia.'

The girl said something to the translator who said to Vi, 'No comment.'

'Oh, the no comment game. How original.' Vi leaned back in her chair. She was knackered. After taking Dorotka in earlier that afternoon she'd done an unofficial obbo for Lee Arnold, and now she was back with Kazia Ostrowska and what seemed to be an attempt to smear Majid Islam's character.

'Doesn't bother me, I've got all night,' Vi said. 'We've a recording of the voice that made the emergency call on Saturday night and if it matches yours . . .' She looked up at the girl, who remained impassive. 'It's up to you. But let me give you a little snapshot of what's going on in my mind at the moment, shall I?'

The translator, aware that Kazia could both speak and understand English, did not translate Vi's words.

'I've got a theory about why you were in the cemetery . . . But whatever you were there for,' Vi said, 'you came across Majid Islam smoking weed. You saw him, he didn't see you, but you recognised him as the bloke who'd called us out the night we found the body of John Sawyer and the skeleton. The bloke who got you arrested.'

Kazia said nothing.

'And you know what I think you saw that as? An opportunity,' Vi said. 'Smear Mr Islam's character, muddy the waters around his testimony and get you and also Bully Murray completely off the hook for John Sawyer's murder.'

This time Kazia looked confused.

'Oh, didn't I explain?' Vi said. 'It's my belief that you and Mark Murray knew each other before the night when we found the body of John Sawyer. He told me some crap about following you in there because you gave him the come-on outside the cemetery. But you wouldn't follow someone into a graveyard for sex just on a look, would you? What was it, Kazia? Met him up in East London for a bit of alfresco nookie before, had you?' She watched the girl colour. 'Kazia Ostrowska,' she said, 'you are going to have to talk to me if you don't want me to charge you and your boyfriend with murder.'

18

Mumtaz thought that Shazia had forgotten her key. It wouldn't be the first time. With the doorbell frantically playing 'Greensleeves' over and over again, she opened the door.

'Hello, Mrs Hakim.'

He had his fingers around her throat before she could even breathe. Naz Sheikh kicked the front door shut behind him and pushed her back towards the living room. The conflict that existed between her fear and her anger rendered Mumtaz temporarily dumb. Then she felt his other hand on her breasts.

'Stop that!'

He carried on. 'But we both know that you love it, Mrs Hakim,' he said. 'Why else didn't you give the police my description when I stuck your old man like a pig on Wanstead Flats? Not just because you hated him, was it?'

'I hate you!' She did. But when Naz Sheikh had killed Ahmet Hakim on Wanstead Flats just over a year ago, she'd hated her husband more.

He pushed her up against the doorpost.

'You're just your father's thug!'

He ground his hips into hers. 'Your father is a gangster and so is your brother!' she said. Although the Sheikhs hadn't put her on the streets in order to service what were really Ahmet

Hakim's debts, threats against her and Shazia were constant.

'I can't wait to get my hands on that daughter of yours!' Naz said into her face.

'Never!'

'I'll have you too, Mrs Hakim,' he breathed at her. His words were rasping and harsh now as if he were really having sex with her. Mumtaz felt her stomach turn. She wanted to push him away, but if she did that she didn't know what he'd do.

'Not that I like older flesh,' he continued. 'I like young things. Even if they're damaged – like your daughter.'

'Leave Shazia alone,' she said. He knew all about what Ahmet had done to his daughter and yet he had no compassion. She was just a whore in his eyes, a whore who had called her own father to her bed.

'Do you have our money, Mrs Hakim?'

'It isn't due yet,' Mumtaz said. 'I won't give it to you until the due date.'

'Yes, but do you have it?' He tightened his grip on her throat while he rubbed himself up against her.

Almost vomiting with disgust she said, 'Yes, I have!' And then she pushed him away from her. Instantly she knew she'd done the wrong thing.

'Oh, Mrs Hakim,' Naz said. 'You're going to regret you rejected the attentions of a real man.'

'You can't arrest either Mark Murray or Kazia Ostrowska. Where's your evidence?'

'They were in the graveyard . . .'

'In vaguely fascist mufti at the wrong time,' the superintendent said. 'You've no witnesses, no forensic evidence, DI Collins.'

'There's Majid Islam.'

'A cannabis user.' Superintendent Venus looked at Vi for the first time since their conversation had begun. 'Can you afford to trust his word?'

'Because he smokes a bit of weed, I should distrust him?' She wanted to follow that up with *Him and half the country?* But she didn't.

'Mr Islam has often called us out to incidents at the Plashet Cemetery because his house backs onto it,' she said. 'He's a nice man, sir.'

'A nice man with a Class B drug habit,' the superintendent said.

'Yeah, but sir . . .'

He carried on walking along the corridor in front of her, his straight, stiff back like a brick wall in her path. 'Let the Polish girl go, DI Collins,' he said. 'Firm evidence has to be in place before we bring anyone down. Big or small, I don't care. Clear?'

'Yes, sir,' Vi said, but not before she'd flicked the Vs at his back. Childish but necessary. He didn't like her because she was middle aged, she drank and she smoked. She didn't like him because he did press-ups in his office, sniffed around after young female officers and was a total twat who'd only got his job because of who he knew. Not that he was wrong, in principle, about firm evidence.

Vi went down to the cells to tell Kazia Ostrowska the 'good news'. Kazia hadn't killed John Sawyer and she knew it. It was unlikely that either Mark Murray or Majid Islam had either. But she had a notion that one of them maybe knew, or had at least recognised, who had killed the soldier. Mark Murray was keeping a low profile but she knew where he was.

If Wendy closed her eyes she could still see what those two men had done to her. She kept her eyes open.

With the exception of Dolly's dad, who'd been a soldier who had buggered off abroad, the only man who had ever been gentle and sexy with her had been Paul. As those two dogs had been savaging her, she'd tried to keep her mind on him.

But then they were just hideous old maintenance men. Paul had been a business associate of the Rogers brothers. A professional of some sort, Wendy imagined – a doctor, maybe, a lawyer or an accountant. But then Paul hadn't been different from them because of what he did, he was different because of who he was. He was nice, and Wendy really wanted to get to know him.

'Nasreen, you know that if you feel ill I can be at your new house in a moment.'

Nasreen looked at her mother and then she hugged her. She knew she didn't approve of this move that Abdullah had imposed upon her so suddenly. She let her mother go and put some blouses from her wardrobe into a cardboard box. 'Thank you, Amma, I'm sure I'll be fine,' she said.

But her face told a different story and her mother shook her head with impatience. 'Why does he want you to go now, Nasreen? Why all of a sudden now? The house isn't ready.'

'He wants us to be together, as a couple, Amma.'

'But people live with their families in our culture. It's what we do. I know Abdullah has no family to speak of but he is still a Muslim, he is no different from us.' She sat down on Nasreen's bed. She was only twenty years older than her daughter and she still looked very young. 'Why this rush?'

'Amma, I don't know why Abdullah wants us to move tomorrow,'

Nasreen said, and her eyes filled with tears. Her mother stood up and hugged her. 'Oh, my girl,' she said, 'is everything alright? Are you telling your Abba and me everything? We only want your happiness, Nasreen, only that.'

'And I only want your happiness too, Amma,' Nasreen said. Abdullah had given her the choice of either doing as he told her or suffering the ignominy of divorce. Not that she could tell her mother or her father that. It was bad enough that she knew her husband would abandon his unborn child rather than not get his own way.

'You know your father has always been a very good man,' her mother's voice broke across her thoughts. 'I had a difficult time giving birth to you, Nasreen. You know this. But what you don't know is that it was Abba who decided that we should not have any more children.'

Nasreen had always thought that she'd been an only child because her mother had been incapable of having further babies.

'Abba couldn't bear to put me through such an ordeal again. I would have done it,' her mother continued, 'but he was quite fixed on the idea that I should suffer no more pain.'

'We are very lucky to have my Abba.'

Her mother stroked Nasreen's hair. 'Your father is a good Muslim.'

'I know.'

'He honours women,' she said. 'But there are men who do not. They use religion as an excuse to drag up all sorts of terrible customs from the past . . .'

'Abdullah isn't like that.' He hadn't been. Abdullah had lived a modern life and they'd had a lot of fun together when they'd first met. How and when had he changed? He'd been jealous right from the start, but he'd never blamed her for that. He wasn't blaming her for anything now. But he was still pulling her away from her parents. *It's the house,* Nasreen thought, *he has changed since the house!*

But Nasreen had a lot to do and little time to spend questioning what her husband might be thinking or why. She remembered that there was a suitcase underneath her bed that was empty. She bent down and dragged it out under the pained gaze of her mother.

Something had happened to Mumtaz. Lee could tell just by looking at her. It wasn't that she was any different physically from how she always was – even her voice and her expressions were as they had always been. Only her eyes gave whatever it was away. There was nothing behind them. It was like looking into the gaze of a psychopath – and Lee had clocked a few of those in his time. For some reason, she'd closed down.

But now she was doing paperwork. Preparing a bill for the woman who'd asked her to look into her husband's past and then backed off. A final bill, just like the one she'd already typed for Ayesha, the sister of Wendy Dixon.

What was the point of going any further for Ayesha? There was none. She now knew for certain that her sister was a Tom, and she also knew that unless Wendy shopped her own landlord it was going to stay that way. For all the fanfare that blasted out about 'Stratford City', '2012' and 'regeneration', Newham remained a place still marked by the vices that came with poverty: gang violence, prostitution, drugs and protection rackets. Come the end of September when both the Olympics and the Paralympics were over, would the little that the outside world had seen of the borough be forgotten? Lee couldn't help but think that it would. Except for Westfield, the great big, fuck-off shopping centre.

'Lee, I need to make more money.'

It came out suddenly. Lee looked at Mumtaz, her head was still down over her paperwork. They'd been here before. Back in 2011 she'd got into a state about her mortgage, which was with some dodgy organisation her late husband had chosen. Mumtaz referred to them as 'criminals'. He got up, walked over to her desk and sat down in front of her.

'How much do you need?' he asked.

She looked up at him with those empty eyes which now looked slightly offended. They'd rarely talked money before. She'd never wanted to. But in spite of what she'd told Naz Sheikh, she was short on next month's payment by seven hundred pounds and she had nothing of value left to sell – and that included her uncle's Mughal coins.

'Is it your husband's dodgy mortgage?' Lee asked. 'I know you're not happy about telling me who it's with or you would have done so already, but if words need to be had . . .'

'No.' She smiled. 'No, I need to earn more, Lee, for my expenses.'

'Well, how much more? Give me a figure.'

'We have no clients,' she said.

'We'll get them. Something always comes along.'

'I need that to be a certainty,' she said.

'"Are you being leant on by someone?' Lee asked. 'These "criminals"—'

'No! I told you—'

'I know what you *told* me, but—'

'Lee, I can't manage on what I'm paid,' she said. 'I will have to look for another job.'

It was like being smacked.

'Another job? What?'

'Anything that pays,' she said.

He wasn't an idiot, he knew that he didn't pay either himself or Mumtaz much more than minimum wage, but she'd managed at first. What had changed? 'What they want you to pay this month, Mumtaz?' he asked.

She turned her head to one side.

'I've watched you take things out at lunchtime and then come back empty handed. I know the signs and so do you. Tell me what they want?'

Still she didn't look at him. 'Lee, I like this job very much,' she said. 'I'm telling you I might have to go if I get more money elsewhere because I respect you. But I have to earn more money. For what, is my business. But that is the end of it.'

The weird eyes had gone now and she was crying.

'Mumtaz . . .'

But she held up a hand to ward off his sympathy. 'No, no Lee, I will have to look elsewhere. I am so sorry, I . . .'

'For God's sake will you just tell me what you need! Or tell me who they are and I'll . . .'

He'd leaned over her desk and taken her chin between his thumb and finger before he'd even thought about it. But then he saw the fear in her eyes and he immediately let go. He got up and walked away from her desk. 'What do they want this month?'

'It doesn't matter, it . . .'

'Mumtaz, you tell me you're looking for another job.' He turned to face her. 'Then you won't give me a chance to compete. Christ, I thought that you and me was business partners, I thought you and me was friends . . .'

'Seven hundred pounds,' she said.

He looked at her, his eyes fixed in obvious shock.

Then she said, 'So there, you can do nothing about it.'

He didn't say a thing.

'And even if you could, what about next month, the month after that? And after that? Lee, my debts are a bottomless pit.' Still he said nothing and so she pushed it further. 'And the seven hundred pounds I need this month isn't even all of it. As you've noticed, I've been selling things. Now there's nothing left.' There was a silence, into which she added, 'Except the house.'

Lee sat back down in front of her again. 'And if you sold the house . . .'

'If I sold the house and got a good price for it, I may be alright,' she said. 'But that's very unlikely, Lee, in this financial climate.'

'So you're stuck.'

'Yes, I'm stuck,' she said.

'So if you're stuck anyway, what's the point of going off and looking for a new job that'll only pay you a couple of hundred quid more a month than I do, at the most?'

She didn't want him involved. 'I can't ex—'

'I'll get seven hundred quid out of the business account now,' he said.

Mumtaz felt her eyes widen.

'I won't take no for an answer,' he said. He stood up. 'You don't have to pay me back.'

'But . . .'

'Not yet,' he said. 'We'll take it month by month. I'll give you the money this month and then if you've a shortfall next month then you can—'

'I can't do that!' Mumtaz stood, smoothing a hand agitatedly across her headscarf. She paced.

Lee went back to his desk and put his jacket on. Watching him, she said, 'Where are you going?'

'Like I said, to the bank.'

'No!' She put an arm up to stop him from leaving. It rested on his shoulder in what looked almost like an embrace. 'I can't let you, Lee! I just can't!'

He gently moved her arm out of his path and said, 'Unless you let me sort out the bastards who're threatening you, this is the way it's going to have to be. This is the way I'll make it.'

19

Now there was a sight for sore eyes: Majid Islam deep in conversation with Zahid Sheikh – and both of them smiling. That wasn't right. Since when had Majid Islam been thick with any of the local gangsters? *But then,* Vi thought, *since when had Majid Islam smoked cannabis?*

John Sawyer's body was due to be released to his family later on that day and there were no words of comfort that Vi Collins could give them. John was dead and they still hadn't arrested anyone for his murder. She tried to comfort herself with the well-known fact that the friendless and dispossessed always presented a challenge if they were suddenly found dead. There was no-one to ask about their habits, their likes and dislikes, where they went and where they didn't.

That John had been killed in the Plashet graveyard was no help at all. There'd been no signs of anyone climbing over the walls except for Majid Islam, Mark Murray – Bully – and Kazia Ostrowska. John had been stabbed so there had to be blood, but there wasn't any, except at the site of his death. Why hadn't he fought his attacker? It had to have something to do with the blow he'd received to the head before he was stabbed. Either he'd come to the cemetery unconscious somehow or he'd just materialised, dead, in the cemetery – with a skeleton in his arms. And where *that* had come from was anybody's guess. It certainly hadn't come from the Plashet and Vi was still waiting for DNA tests.

Everyone who'd been at the scene had been weird in some way – even Majid Islam, the erstwhile protector of the cemetery. None of them were what could be described as 'regular' people, but had any of them killed John Sawyer? No. Given that neither Kazia, Majid Islam or Mark Murray had any blood or fibres of any sort from John Sawyer's body on them, it was unlikely.

And so that left just one possibility, the unknown man that none of the people involved claimed to have seen properly. The third man. She pulled up Bully Murray's mum's address on her computer system.

She was looking in the window of Topshop. All around her Westfield Shopping Centre buzzed with the sound of people. A couple of young girls looked at her and giggled, probably wondering why someone like Wendy was staring at a load of teenage clothes. She liked denim shorts over thick tights and she had the body to carry them off, but she was skint. She'd walked from Plaistow to Stratford so she could wander around Westfield because she was bored. She didn't even have enough money for a cup of tea, especially not at the prices they were charging in there.

She turned away, about to look for the toilets and possibly get a drink of water, when she saw him. He was coming towards her. Paul. Wendy, in spite of herself, blushed. What was she going to say to him? What did you say to a man you'd had sex with AND liked?

For a moment it seemed as if he'd not recognised her. He walked past her without so much as a flicker of recognition in his eyes. But then, just as she turned to watch him go, he turned to look at her and then he smiled. He walked over to her. 'What are you doing here?'

'Oh, I'm, er . . . I . . . I'm window shopping. You know . . .'

He smiled. 'Not buying?'

Wendy shook her head. She knew she had to look dead scruffy in comparison to the bejewelled, scrubbed and hair-dressed vision he'd had sex with at Sean's place. She'd only put make-up on to cover up where Sean had knocked her about.

'I've been thinking about you, you know,' he said.

Wendy felt herself blush again. 'Oh, that's nice.'

He leaned down so that his lips were level with her ear. 'We had some fun, didn't we?'

She didn't answer. He smiled. Then he said, 'Would you like to go for a coffee?'

Again she was embarrassed. 'Oh, I don't have, er . . . I'm not . . .'

'I'll pay,' he said. He took her arm in his and began to walk towards one of the exits.

Wendy was confused, but she didn't say anything. If he was going to buy her a cup of coffee then that was a good thing, wasn't it? She'd dreamed about meeting him again.

About a hundred metres before the exit, Paul suddenly veered off to the left and began to pull her towards the toilets. 'Just pretend you're sick,' he told her.

'Pretend I'm . . .'

'Not very well.'

There wasn't a queue for the toilets in the Ladies but some women were at the sinks, washing their hands and fixing their make-up.

'Heave as if you're throwing up!' Paul hissed.

Wendy looked at him as if he was mad.

'Heave!'

She heaved. It hurt and because she didn't really feel sick at all she found it funny. At a run now he pulled her past the women at the sinks saying, 'Sick! Sick!' to all the startled ladies that they ran behind, until he pushed her into a cubicle at the far end.

As soon as he'd locked the door behind them he put his hands down her top and fondled her breasts. Wendy responded immediately by unzipping his fly.

Nasreen Khan put the cash on the desk in front of Mumtaz. 'It should all be there,' she said.

Mumtaz smiled. She motioned towards the chair in front of her desk. 'Please sit down, Mrs Khan,' she said. 'Just while I count the money out and then print you a receipt.'

'I don't need a receipt.'

In case her husband found it? Mumtaz briefly caught the eye of Lee Arnold, who was apparently engrossed in his paperwork in the other office, but Nasreen missed the look that passed between them and sat down.

'I don't have much time,' she said. 'We're moving into the new house, Abdullah and me.'

'It won't take long.' Four hundred pounds in twenty-pound notes. Mumtaz made her way through the pile methodically, if not at speed. 'You know that your husband works for some very unpleasant people,' she said.

What Nasreen Khan chose to do with the information she was being given was up to her, but Mumtaz was determined she should have it. Mumtaz herself had her eyes open with the Sheikhs. It didn't help her pay her debts, but it did mean that she was prepared for anything.

'The Rogers brothers and Yunus Ali are bad people,' Mumtaz said. 'And if they're using your husband's legal knowledge to—'

'That's no longer your concern,' Nasreen said. She looked pale and suddenly more pregnant than she had before. Mumtaz finished counting.

'I know you don't want a receipt because you are afraid that your husband will find it.'

'I . . .'

'Hear me out,' Mumtaz said. She switched to speaking Bengali. Whether Nasreen was aware of Lee's presence or not, she wanted her to feel safe.

'Nasreen, you came to me because you had concerns about your husband. I have not managed to allay your fears, but I can still help you if you need me.' She pushed one of her cards across the table at Nasreen. 'Please . . .'

'No!' She pushed the card away.

Mumtaz gave Nasreen a small parcel and said, 'But you must have this.'

'What is it?'

'It is the mezuzah from your doorpost.'

Nasreen visibly cringed. She wanted to take it but then again she didn't want to either. 'I can't take that,' she said. 'My husband . . .'

'It belongs to your house, Nasreen,' Mumtaz said. She pushed the parcel towards her. 'Take it.'

For a moment she hesitated, but then she picked up the parcel.

Mumtaz switched back to English again. 'Thank you for your business, Mrs Khan.'

Nasreen rose, but as she did so, Mumtaz took one of her hands and, in Bengali, she said, 'I am your friend. You know where I am.'

Nasreen Khan left. Mumtaz looked across at Lee.

'I didn't understand half of that,' he said.

'I was trying to make her feel at ease,' Mumtaz said.

'If her husband is the Rogers' tame solicitor then she has to be careful.'

'My research showed that no-one called Abdullah Khan, aged thirty-eight and from Bolton, Lancashire, is a practising solicitor in this area,' Mumtaz said.

'Maybe he was struck off the Roll.'

'Struck off the Roll?'

'Prevented from practising,' Lee said. 'If it's a barrister they are disbarred, a solicitor is struck off the Roll. It wouldn't surprise me. A lot of crime firms like Rogers and Ali use struck-off solicitors. They generally know a few struck-off doctors too. They're useful if one of their soldiers needs patching up. But they only use such people as and when.'

'But according to Nasreen, Abdullah Khan goes to work every day.'

'Then maybe he does other things for them too. I don't know any Abdullah Khan in connection to the Rogers brothers. But then they tend to keep those around them close and shady. People work for them, then they don't, then they do again. Sean in particular likes to keep things mobile.'

'Nasreen thought that Rogers and Ali were a firm of solicitors until I told her that they were property developers and landlords of the worst kind,' Mumtaz said. 'Her parents are quite well off, respectable people who would never have come across such characters.'

'Mmm, well Rogers and Ali don't do much business in the Asian community. That's the Sheikhs.' He looked up.

Mumtaz looked down. 'If not living a lie as such, Abdullah

Khan is not telling his wife the whole truth.'

'But if she doesn't want us to continue investigating him, what can we do?'

'Nothing.'

'If people don't want you to do things or they won't tell you stuff . . .' He shrugged.

Mumtaz knew that he was talking about her. He'd given her seven hundred pounds of the company's money to give to people she hadn't named. Mumtaz still didn't want him to know. She didn't want him involved, even though she imagined that now he'd given her the money he would be watching her as closely as he could.

Bully Murray was pleased with himself. The Filth seemed to have backed off and although Kazia was fighting shy of him, he had some weed and a bit of whizz so what did he care? Anyway she'd been stupid to finger that Paki just for smoking a bit of blow. He was glad he hadn't met her in the graveyard on Saturday night. He'd been on business that was proving to be lucrative. It had given Bully an entree into the big league. Soon, if he played his cards right, he'd have more than just drugs. Marty – he let him call him Marty – had hinted at maybe even a job. It was lucky he'd recognised that face in the graveyard, luckier still that Marty felt that information was worth something. Bully had almost allowed that old sack DI Collins to get a name out of him; lucky he'd pulled back just in time.

Bully lived in south East Ham, on Mitcham Road. But this evening he was going out. He planned to spend the evening at the Tollgate Tavern up by Asda in Beckton. To get there he had to walk past East Ham Jewish Cemetery down Sandford Road. The cemetery gates were closed that time of night but there was a little access road up to them, where the man who owed Sean Rogers a very great deal of money stood and waited, trembling a little from time to time, until Bully Murray came into view.

The benefit of surprise was all with the man. For seemingly no reason, he caught Bully round the shoulders and pulled him into the access road. For a few seconds Bully fought, grunting occasionally until finally he yelled out, 'Who the fuck are you?'

The man, his shalwar khameez flapping wetly around his thin legs in the damp springtime air, hissed, 'You get greedy, man! This what happen! This a message from Sean and from Marty!'

'What?' Bully could see that the man had to steel himself to hit him. The man smashed his fist down into Bully's face. It glanced against the ring in Bully's nose. The man's hand, as well as Bully's nose, bled.

Bully fought back. He was stringy and not very strong, but he managed to land a blow on the man's cheek. The bone inside cracked. The man howled but he carried on hitting. He said, 'They'll hurt my family, I must do this, I . . .' So Marty hadn't responded well to Bully's little adventure into blackmail. Suddenly afraid, even though the other man was so much smaller than he was, Bully wondered if he'd been sent to just rough him up or more. Bully, in his stride now, landed a second blow on the side of the man's head. The man staggered.

'Not so fucking brave now, are you, Paki!' he said. 'A fucking message from Sean and Marty? What kind of fucking messenger are you? Eh?'

Bully hit him again. Then one more blow to the head and he was on the ground. Useless tosser. If this was the best that Sean and Marty Rogers could do then maybe Bully didn't want to be associated with them anyway. Bully, on his feet now, kicked the man in the groin, and while he scrunched up in a foetal position he kicked him in the back. Bully did see the man put a hand into the pocket of his waistcoat and grab hold of something but he didn't pay it any attention. Bully pulled at one of the man's shoulders to make him lie flat on his back.

'You know I don't want to hurt you but I have to,' the man said.

'You couldn't hurt pussy, mate,' Bully said.

'I have . . .'

'Little wrestling move this,' Bully said, as he stood over the man. Then he just threw himself on top of him. The man, still holding onto the knife, felt it go through the wall of Bully's chest. Then the man, in spite of the fact that he knew it had been inevitable, screamed.

'You need rest,' Abdullah said.

But the room he led Nasreen into was far from restful. There was a bed in the middle of it, but the walls were full of holes and some of the floorboards had been removed. She looked at him with what she knew was a horrified expression on her face. But he ignored it.

'You mustn't get tired or our baby'll suffer.'

The bedroom was cold. And the bathroom, where she'd just been, had provided no more comfort even though he'd put a new suite in. It was still full of dust, mess and holes. When she could speak, she said, 'I can't sleep here.'

'Why not?' He wasn't angry, which was what she had feared, he was calm. But then when she didn't answer him he reiterated his question. This time his voice had an edge. 'Why not?'

Nasreen swallowed hard. She'd had to really push down that

awful fried chicken he'd brought for their dinner. Sitting in that unheated kitchen, the plumbing from the sink exposed, had been like camping out in a war zone.

'Abdullah,' she said, 'this place isn't ready. It's cold and there are holes and dust everywhere. We should go back to my parents.'

She saw his face harden. It did that when they had sex too. It made him look as if he was on some sort of mission that he had been forced to accept against his will. Before, when they'd made love on her wedding night, he had treated her with absolute tenderness. But most of that had very quickly and suddenly gone.

'I don't think so.' He shook his head. He pulled the bits of fabric that served as curtains across the windows and said, 'Your mum and dad were driving a wedge between us.'

'No, they weren't.'

'Then why all the questions about my job? You know what I do because I told you.'

'You work for Rogers and Ali.'

'Solicitors,' he said.

'Are they?'

'Of course they are!' He walked towards her. 'Who told you that they weren't?'

Nasreen felt her face go hot, but she said nothing.

'Your fucking parents.' Abdullah raised his top lip in a sneer. 'Talking lies to you, Nasreen. I know why.'

She looked up at him.

'Because I twatted that fucking cousin of yours, isn't it? Rafiq?'

'No!'

'Yes, it is,' he said. Then he took one of her wrists in his hand. 'You're my wife now and so you listen to me. Not your mum, or your dad or some fucking sex-starved cousin.'

'He isn't . . .'

He pushed her in front of him, onto the bed. 'This is your home, I'm your husband and you do as I say.'

Nasreen hated herself. She'd got a degree, she'd worked in responsible jobs and earned her own money and now she was letting herself be treated like this. 'I . . .' She stopped. He had his hand raised above her and she cringed. She'd thought she'd chosen well. 'I . . .'

This time she didn't get away with it. She'd spoken once too often without his permission, and he struck her full in the face with the back of his hand. Nasreen tried not to give him the satisfaction of making her cry, but her eyes wept without her intervention. Against all the signs when they'd first met, Nasreen had not chosen her husband well.

Part Three

20

Four months after Amy Green was killed, Lee Arnold couldn't decide whether he admired Brian Green or not. Even when he'd been an 'active' gangster, there'd always been something likeable about him. Maybe it was all part of the genial giant act? Lee knew it was a load of bollocks and that Brian, barely roused to anger, could – and would – break a man's arm with his bare hands. But he had an affection for him anyway and this party, the first since his late wife's wake back in May, was Brian showing the world that he was still in the game.

As well as his brother Mike and his family, Brian had invited staff from his five health and boxing clubs, some of his most promising young athletes and a few old faces that Lee recognised from both his own and Brian's pasts: men getting on in years with cauliflower ears or the odd false eye, and one old chap with a broken nose who Lee knew had done a few favours for the Krays. It was an odd mixture – some kids rapping in one room, a couple of old girls talking about turning tricks up Kings Cross in the Sixties in another.

This being summer, of course it was raining. Lee looked out of Brian's patio doors at his sodden garden, and at Amy's little fish pond now bereft of fairies. But Brian didn't like people smoking in his house and so he'd have to go out there for a fag. There was only just so much interest that a glassful of cranberry juice could hold for anyone. He left it for half an hour, but when the rain failed to abate he went out. He was quickly joined by a woman power-dressed à la 1980s in bright red and matt black. Lee recognised her immediately, but was surprised to see her at Brian's gaff. 'Debs,' he said.

She lit her cigarette, a gold-collared St Moritz, with a gold lighter and looked at him out of heavily kohl-rimmed eyes. 'Hello, officer,' Debbie Rogers said. 'If I'd known Brian was gonna invite the Old Bill . . .'

'Private detective these days, Debs,' Lee said. 'But I imagine you know that. You're a smart lady.' She didn't smile. Looking at her, Lee couldn't tell how old she was, but then he'd never been able to do that. She'd married Martin Rogers sometime back in the 1980s. Word at the time had been that she'd had a good ten years on him, but nobody actually knew or, probably Lee thought, dared to ask.

'You here with Marty?' Lee asked, once the silence between them became unbearable. 'I've not seen him.'

'Maybe he's avoiding you.'

He smiled. 'I didn't know you and Marty were thick with Brian.'

'We're not.'

'But you're here.'

Debbie puffed on her posh fag. 'It's respect, innit,' she said.

'For Brian's wife?' She looked at him with slow, lizard-like eyes. 'Know her did you, Debs?'

'No.' She paused. 'But I know you saw her die.'

Lee looked down at the ground. He hadn't known Amy Green at all and what he had observed about her had only proved what an airhead she had been. But she'd also been young, pretty and full of life. Whatever she'd been doing that night, she hadn't deserved to die.

'Don't wanna talk about it?' Debbie's concern could have been for real or she could have been sneering at him. Either way Lee wasn't bothered.

'No,' he said. Then he changed the subject. 'Sean here?'

'Somewhere.'

Sean Rogers had a house just up the road. It was in that house, so Wendy Dixon had told her sister Ayesha, that he had sex parties. Lee wondered whether Brian had ever been to one. Unlikely. Brian had always been a one-woman-at-a-time sort of a man. Lee thought about having another fag while he was outside in the rain and then decided against it. Thoughts about Wendy Dixon had led his mind back to Mumtaz. Two of the women she'd tried to help back in the spring, Wendy Dixon and Nasreen Khan, had seemingly disappeared off the face of the earth. Lee knew it still bugged Mumtaz, although on this particular Saturday afternoon he knew she had more pressing concerns.

'You should've put it up for sale way before the Olympics,' Shazia said. 'Then you'd've got loads of money for it. Now there are missiles on people's roofs and everything, and everybody's getting really stressed.'

Mumtaz and Shazia watched as a man in a woolly hat put a 'For Sale' sign up outside their house. It had taken weeks of soul searching by Mumtaz to find a way to tell Shazia that she'd have to sell the house and all the girl had said was, 'Cool.'

Of course Shazia didn't know *why* Mumtaz was selling the house, beyond the fact that 'we can't afford it anymore'. Only Lee, who had lent her money for two months and couldn't afford any more, knew that Mumtaz couldn't carry on being financially drained, even though he didn't know by whom. What she knew he'd surmised, however, was that selling the house on the open market was a risk. Those she 'owed' had wanted to buy it at a knock-down price – that had always been the Sheikh family's plan.

Mumtaz looked up and down the street to see whether anyone was watching the man put the sign up, but no-one was about. It was raining too hard.

'Can we move to Stratford?' she heard Shazia say. The girl had walked away from the window now and was sprawling across one of the living room sofas.

'Why do you want to move to Stratford?' Mumtaz asked. The leafy quietness of Forest Gate came at a premium. Why would anyone want to give that up for the concrete jungle that was Stratford?

'Is it so you can just nip out to Westfield whenever you want?' she asked.

'No!' Shazia tossed her thick hair over her shoulders slightly petulantly. 'No, it's because there are some way cool flats in Stratford now. They have like, gyms and porters and everything.'

Mumtaz smiled. 'Do we need gyms and porters and everything?'

'Well, where were you thinking of buying a house then?' Shazia asked.

Mumtaz wasn't thinking of buying anything, not until she knew what money she would have available. She'd put the house up for sale at £500,000, which was a price that reflected its somewhat neglected state. The Sheikhs would have taken it off her hands for £400,000 but that still left her in debt. At £500,000 she'd come out of the deal with about £50,000 and no debts. With that she'd be able to find a nice place for herself and Shazia to rent.

'Well, I thought another place around here, but smaller,' Mumtaz said. 'There are some really nice little houses on Radley Road and around that area.'

Shazia pulled a face.

'What?' Mumtaz asked.

'They're full of old people,' she said.

'So?'

'So I don't want to live around a lot of old people.' She hauled herself up off the sofa. 'Still think you'd've got more money if you'd sold a few months ago. *Everybody* wanted to live in east London then. Now the Olympics are just giving everyone terrors.'

Shazia wandered out to the kitchen, no doubt to raid the fridge. The girl had been right about prices though. Now just under two weeks away from the Olympic opening ceremony, no-one was shopping for houses. Most people were spending most of their time sheltering from the non-stop summer rain. What if the Olympics turned out to be just one big washout?

Although not interested in sport in any way, Mumtaz hoped that it wasn't, for the sake of the athletes. But if the skies wouldn't clear then what was anyone to do? She looked out into the rain again and willed someone, anyone, to come along quickly and buy her house.

Nasreen looked up at the cracked ceiling above her head and tried to imagine that it wasn't there. Beyond it was the roof and then the sky. She could hear that it was raining outside even though she couldn't see it. But that didn't bother her.

Her belly was huge now. The baby was due in two weeks' time and she still knew so little. Her mother came to visit so seldom that she always forgot to ask her about babies. She didn't ask her mother much about anything, or even talk to her often, not with Abdullah in the room. And Abdullah was always in the room, the one reasonably respectable room downstairs, when her mother and father came to the house. Her father even seemed to think that Abdullah's protectiveness of her, as well as his devotion to apparently endless DIY, was laudable in some way. Her mother, she knew, felt differently. Her mother's eyes looked sad every time she saw her and how she had to live.

Alone in that house, in that terrible bedroom, day in and day out, with only Abdullah for company, was turning her into some sort of mindless blob. All she did was eat, sleep, go to the toilet. She no longer read or even watched the television. There was no television in the bedroom. She was just a thing with one purpose: to give birth. And when Abdullah was out, she was a thing that was fixed to her bed by handcuff ties.

She'd known it was wrong because the kids were at home. It was also unwise to let people know where she lived. But Wendy had had to do it.

They'd met, she and Paul, in Central Park. Since that first time at Westfield she'd met him on a weekly basis. Always somewhere anonymous. Sean didn't know and he wasn't to know. Paul, although he wouldn't tell her exactly what he did, had some sort of business which meant that he had contact with Sean, so he had to know that she still went to Sean's parties and had sex with men for him all the time. But he never said anything and he hadn't gone to any more parties.

Wendy could hear Dolly singing to the other kids through the walls and through her own gasps and squeaks. She wanted to feel guilty, but with Paul inside her she couldn't. This wasn't anything like the tricks she turned for Sean, this made her feel alive.

Later, when she lay in his arms, feeling his sleeping breath rising and falling beneath her, that was when the guilt had come upon her. If Sean found out she was fucking a bloke she knew outside of her usual 'work', he'd go off his nut. Where was Sean's cut in what she was doing? He'd punish her. How could she put them all at such risk?

Paul opened his eyes and he looked at her. She reached for him but he pushed her gently away. 'Let me watch you do yourself,' he said.

She'd put on 'shows' for him before. Just having him watch was enough to make her hot. As she touched herself, Wendy saw him lick his lips and so she lowered herself onto him. He'd used a condom before but this time she wanted him to come inside her. For a moment he looked alarmed but then his desire overtook him.

When they'd both recovered their breath, Paul said, 'That was a bit risky.'

'It'll be alright,' she said. Next door the kids were jumping on the furniture.

Paul looked at her with desire again. 'I want you all the time,' he said. 'But that was . . .'

'I won't get pregnant or nothing,' Wendy said.

'You on the pill?'

'Course.' She was, but she wasn't always on the ball with it. That day and the day before she'd missed it. She bent down and kissed his chest. Then suddenly she said, 'Don't you have a woman to give you love?'

And for the first time since she'd met him, she saw his face change. It morphed into something she could easily recognise as the type of face that lived around Sean and Marty.

In her job Vi Collins had always known that you lost far more cases than you won. Bully Murray's killer had tried to hang himself again, and again he had failed. He was called Abduljabbar Mitra and ever since he'd been arrested – in spite of admitting his guilt immediately – he'd been trying to kill himself. A woman who bought her greengrocery from his shop on Green Street had seen him running away from the scene of the crime with blood down his shirt. He hadn't been difficult to track down. In fact it was almost as if, Vi felt, Mitra had wanted to get arrested. Why, she couldn't imagine. Mitra was a family man with much to live for. His business wasn't doing too well – whose was – but he appeared to be managing. Why had he messed all that up?

Abduljabbar Mitra had told the police he'd got into a fight with Bully Murray. The thug had hurled some racist abuse at him and he'd snapped. He'd attacked Bully who had taken out a knife which Mitra had got hold of and used against him. That was the story. But was it the truth? Apart from the fact that the forensic team reckoned that the knife was Mitra's – it had only his finger-prints on it – Vi had a bad feeling about his story. Why would he put his entire life, including the future of his wife and kids, in jeopardy like that? Why was he trying to kill himself?

But it was all academic anyway. Mitra had owned up to killing Bully, albeit in self-defence, and so he was a convicted killer, all bar the shouting. But still it irked Vi. Not because she pitied the late Bully Murray – she'd hardly known the bastard – but because he'd been indirectly associated with another case of murder that was still outstanding. John Sawyer's.

Four and a half months had gone by since the Afghanistan vet's death and London had voted Boris Johnson in as Mayor again. Leeds, like the 'other Paki man' Bully Murray had apparently seen in the graveyard that night, had fizzled out. Majid Islam had been cautioned about his cannabis use and Kazia Ostrowska had gone back to Poland. They'd even finally issued details about the skeleton to the press, but still no information about either of them had emerged.

And things were not set to get better any time soon. Word had come through from the assistant commissioner that the company that had been employed to provide security at the Olympics was not going to be able to deliver. So it would come down to the poor old coppers after all, backed up by the army. Less than two weeks away.

Vi was about to go home for the evening and try to forget all about it in front of the telly, when her phone rang. One of the constables on the front desk told her that there was a young lady who wanted to see her. Apparently she had a problem that wouldn't wait.

21

It took Lee a while to recognise the old boy in the wheelchair. It was only when Wilf Cox came into the Boleyn just before midday that Lee realised the geezer was Wilf's cousin, Arthur. The last thing that Wilf had told him about Arthur was that he was in hospital with cancer. Lee had thought he was dead.

Lee, nodding at Arthur, said to Wilf, 'I thought he was . . .'

'In remission,' Wilf said, and put a silencing finger up to his lips.

It was a slow, wet Sunday in the Boleyn and Lee had spent much of the morning reading the papers. Then Arthur had come in, his wheelchair pushed by a woman of about fifty. Then Wilf had joined them. Now he asked Lee to come over and 'make a party of it' and so he did. The woman, it turned out, was Arthur's daughter, Ella.

It was Wilf who brought up the subject of Lily Smith. 'Here, you knew Eric Smith's mum, Lily, didn't you, Art? Strone Road, and all that business with that missing kid back in the Fifties?'

Although Lee hadn't forgotten the mezuzah that had come from the house where the Smiths had once lived on Strone Road, or the little picture of the woman that Nasreen Khan had found behind it, it hadn't been at the forefront of his mind for some time.

'Shocking!' Arthur Dobson shook his head. His voice was very breathy and hoarse. Lee guessed that his cancer was possibly in his lungs.

'Lee here, you know old Rosie Arnold's boy, he's interested in all that, aren't you son?'

Lee wasn't that bothered about the Smiths, the mezuzah or the story of the missing boy Marek any more, but he said that he was.

'The kid died,' Arthur Dobson wheezed.

'What, Marek?'

'Must've,' he said. Then he leaned forward in his wheelchair and whispered. 'The coppers found blood in the kitchen.'

Lee had heard that the police had dug up the Smiths' garden back in 1955 but nobody had ever said anything about finding any blood.

'Lil Smith reckoned it was hers, and Reg did knock her about . . .'

'Maybe it was hers,' Lee said. 'The coppers never found a body did they.'

'No, but back then . . .' Arthur shrugged. 'There was a smog as thick as snot the night that boy went missing. Reg could've chucked the kid in his wheelbarrow and dumped him just about anywhere. On the tube tracks, in one of the cemeteries, anywhere.'

'But no body was ever found.'

'Don't mean Reg didn't kill him,' Arthur said. 'Lily and the other boy, young Eric, they was out that night at the pictures up East Ham. It was just Reg and the older boy. Oh and the sister . . .'

'The sister?'

'Lil's,' Arthur said. Then he frowned. 'But then she must've gone before, now I come to think about it. I can't remember the police ever questioning her afterwards.' He looked up at the ceiling. 'What was her name, now?' Then he shook his head impatiently. 'Gone.'

'So where did the sister come from?' Lee asked.

'Oh, somewhere in Europe,' Arthur said. 'I dunno where. All I do remember is that she'd been in a camp too, so people said. Not Belsen. Maybe Auschwitz.'

'They were Polish.'

'Oh, yes.'

Lee shook his head at the marvel of the story. 'So two sisters, two concentration camps and both of them survived.'

'Mmm.'

'Did they have any other sisters or brothers?' Lee asked.

'Lil and wotshername? No, I don't think so,' Arthur said. 'There was Lil, the boy . . .'

'Marek Berkowicz.'

'Him and the sister,' he said. 'She come, must've been about late '54. Then she left just afore the boy . . .'

'Marek.'

'Before he disappeared, yes. Hadn't seen Lil since the war and so it must've been a nice reunion for them both. Never saw her again, I didn't.'

'Did Lily?' Lee asked.

'Dunno.'

'Do you think that Marek could have gone back to Poland or wherever the sister went?'

'No, the sister went afore him. And anyway,' Arthur said, 'she wouldn't've gone back to Poland would she? Iron Curtain country by then, weren't it? And them being posh and all that . . .'

'Posh?' Wilf had said that his mum had told him Lily's family had been wealthy before the war.

'They'd been business people of some sort,' Arthur said. 'No, the sister must've gone to France or somewhere like that.'

'Couldn't she have gone somewhere else in England?' Lee asked.

'No, she was foreign,' Arthur said. 'She went somewhere foreign, I remember Lily saying.'

'What, to you?'

'No, that's what she told the police,' the old man said. 'Her sister had gone just before her son went missing, somewhere foreign.'

Mumtaz turned her phone off. Her landline had been cut off and so once the mobile was disabled, there was no way that they could call her.

As soon as the Sheikhs had found out she'd put the house on the market they had bombarded her with threats. Because she wasn't selling to them, she'd never find a buyer because they'd scare them all off – and even if she did, they'd make sure they were 'dealt with'. She'd still owe them, whatever happened.

The previous night, when the calls had been back to back, she had been scared, but then, amazingly, she'd slept and woken up with an entirely new perspective. She'd sell her own house in spite of the Sheikhs. And then, at just after midday, the estate agent had called to ask her if a Mr and Mrs Linn could come around that afternoon. She'd said that of course they could.

Mumtaz stood in front of the couple in the hall and smiled. Mr and Mrs Linn didn't look older than twenty-five and yet the first thing they'd said to her when they came into the house was how good they felt it was 'for the money'. And it *was* a bargain, given the size of the place, but to a pair of twenty-five-year-olds? Surely they couldn't afford such a barn of a place?

'Here on the ground floor we've got a living room, a dining room, a breakfast room, a games room and a kitchen, which also has a small utility room that used to be the old downstairs bathroom,' she said.

'Four bedrooms?' Mrs Linn asked.

'Yes, two with en suite and then a family bathroom,' Mumtaz said. 'There are also two of what used to be servants' rooms in the roof, and we've still got the old coach house at the bottom of the garden. That has a small studio flat on the first floor.'

Mr Linn, a thin young man with glasses, consulted his estate agent's details sheet. 'Garden's only ninety feet by a hundred and twenty.'

'Right.'

He looked at his wife. 'Rather pokey,' he said.

The young woman blushed at his ham-fisted attempt at belittling the house and said to Mumtaz, 'Can we look around?'

'Of course.'

She led them into the kitchen. If Mr Linn had any thoughts about trying to reduce the price of the property, he could think again.

'The appliances – gas cooker, fridge, washing machine and dishwasher – are included in the price,' Mumtaz said.

Mrs Linn smiled, her husband said, 'It'll need updating.'

'And then again, I can take the appliances if you wish,' Mumtaz said through gritted teeth. Mr Linn, she felt, watched too many property programmes on TV. People on those things always seemed to walk into spectacular kitchens and declare that they 'needed updating'.

The front doorbell rang. Shazia was up in her bedroom doing her homework and listening to 'Plan B' on her iPod, so Mumtaz excused herself to the Linns and went to answer it. She was ready if it was Naz Sheikh or any of the other members of his clan. But still her hands shook as she unlatched the front door.

'Lee!' Every muscle in her body relaxed as she looked into his face.

'I've been trying to call you, but you've been unavailable,' he said. 'I was worried . . .'

'Oh, I have people viewing the house,' Mumtaz said. 'But come in.'

'Oh, well I . . .'

'Come in! Come in!'

He stepped over the threshold. 'Mumtaz, do you remember that Nasreen Khan woman and the mezuzah she found on her back door? You know, the Jewish thing with the little picture behind it?' There was an excitement in him that was unusual for Lee.

'Yes? Lee I have to go and see to my—'

'I might know who the picture is of,' he said.

'Oh, but Lee, I don't have it any more. I gave it back to Mrs Khan.'

'I know,' he said, 'but . . . Look, I'll wait till you've done with these people and then we'll talk.'

'OK.' She was taken aback, and it was a Sunday, which was her day off, but Mumtaz was intrigued. It had been months since she'd so much as thought about Nasreen Khan, but she and her mezuzah, not to mention her husband, had been unfinished business. 'Go and sit in the living room and I'll be with you as soon as I can,' she said.

Lee went into the living room and Mumtaz made her way back to the kitchen. Just before she walked in she heard Mr Linn say to his wife, 'It's the smell of curry Abigail, it gets into everything.'

*

'The Boxer', 'Sound of Silence', 'Cecilia' – Nasreen knew them all by heart. She'd been listening to them for months. Abdullah's father had been a big Paul Simon fan. He'd grown up with his music which, so Abdullah said, had consoled his father after his mother's death. Or rather that was what he used to say. On this occasion, his story was different.

'When she left him, he only had me and his music.' Sitting at the rickety structure that passed for a kitchen table, Abdullah watched Nasreen cook.

She fried off spices and then added onion and garlic. Her wrists hurt where she'd been tied to the bed for most of Saturday and her heart pounded with fear. 'Your mother died.'

He didn't contradict her, but he looked at her from underneath his thick eyebrows with resentment. 'She wasn't there.'

She couldn't bring herself to agree with what he was saying but she couldn't face challenging him on it either so she remained silent. The shift from the idea that his mother had died when he was a baby to the notion that she had somehow abandoned him and his father, had grown over the past six weeks or so. With it had come more playing of Paul Simon, more smashing up of the kitchen and an instability that frightened Nasreen. Months ago, Mumtaz Hakim had confirmed that Abdullah's mother had died just after she'd given birth to him. Not that Nasreen could ever tell Abdullah about Mumtaz.

She added lamb to the onion, garlic and spices. Whenever he was out, she was imprisoned because he said he feared that she'd run away, just like his mother. He couldn't bear the thought of having a motherless child, he said. As her husband, if he wanted her to stay indoors then she had to stay indoors and yet she'd married Abdullah as an equal – or so she thought.

But then wasn't there also something in his eyes that told her he wasn't right in his mind? All the bashing about of the house, even back when they'd first bought it, had been excessive. Now it was even worse. Now he was smashing up walls he'd already smashed up months before and made good. Why was he doing that?

Nasreen stirred her curry. She couldn't say anything to her parents. Her dad had a heart condition and she didn't know how he would take it. And she was frightened about how Abdullah would react. Would he smash them all to pieces like the walls? Her mind clicked one stage further and she wondered, *Did he kill John?*

She still thought about John Sawyer. Abdullah had cut down most of the trees in the garden now, leaving part of the old shack that John had lived in open to view. He never talked about it and Nasreen never brought the subject up. It just stood out there naked and frightening in its emptiness.

Abdullah stood up, walked over to the CD player and put 'The Boxer' on again. Nasreen fought to retain her composure. He was driving her mad. He was pushing her closer to hating him every single day. Was that what he wanted? Was that why he left her on her own for hours on end almost every day? Nasreen remembered what Mumtaz Hakim had said about the company that Abdullah worked for and she wished she'd taken her words more seriously. Were Rogers and Ali in fact a bunch of criminals and, if they were, did Abdullah work to protect them whatever they did? Was he even a lawyer? According to Mumtaz there was some doubt, but what could she do about any of that now?

Nasreen added chilli paste and coriander leaves. 'I do hope that you like this,' she said, without raising her eyes to her husband's face.

'I hope I do too,' he said. There was an implicit threat in there but Nasreen took her courage in her hands and ignored it.

'I just want to please you,' she said.

He got out of his chair so quickly that it fell over backwards behind him. He shot a hand up to her throat, grabbed it and squeezed. He leaned forward and looked into her eyes, searching. 'I do hope this isn't some sort of way you think you can get me to have sex with you,' he said.

'No . . . of course . . . not,' Nasreen spluttered. It was difficult to breathe. 'Why would . . .'

'Because it's what women do,' he said. 'They tempt. They lead men astray.'

'I'm not . . .'

'Even pregnant they do it. It's disgusting.' Abdullah let her go. He walked back to the table and sat down. 'You have no idea,' he said, without looking at her, 'how it was to be a child in a house with no mother.' And then he added something that he'd never said before. 'My father was a very bad person. She shouldn't have left me with him.'

'Lily Smith had a sister,' Lee said.

Mumtaz put a mug of tea down on the coffee table in front of him. The Linns had finally gone and she was now free to talk.

She sat down.

'She came the previous winter, old Arthur Dobson thought, and then left just before Marek Berkowicz disappeared. He seemed to think that the sister had come from France.'

Mumtaz leaned back in her chair. 'Did he know the sister's name?'

'No. Didn't really know much about her at all except that she'd been in a camp too. Not Belsen, he didn't know where. But he was pretty sure that this woman was dark haired. I was thinking the woman in the photograph . . .'

'But why put her image behind a mezuzah?'

'To keep it safe? Keep it hidden? Protect it? I don't know,' Lee said. 'But the Khan woman was interested, wasn't she.'

'Oh, yes,' Mumtaz said. 'Although I don't know how much. I think her real concern was her husband. She used the photograph she found as a way to engage my attention. Then she brought up the husband. I think it was difficult for her. Nasreen is a bright girl and her husband had clearly omitted to tell her that his bosses were a firm of gangsters.'

'Rogers and Ali.'

She shrugged. 'She must be due to have her baby soon.'

'Then maybe you should pay her a visit – when her old man's out of course,' Lee said.

But Mumtaz shook her head. 'I don't think so, Lee,' she said. 'Nasreen was clearly frightened of her husband and if I interfere it could make things worse.'

'But if he's out . . .'

'Men like that have eyes everywhere,' she said. 'I couldn't put her at risk.'

'Yeah, but if it was just a social call, it'd be OK, surely?'

She shook her head again. 'No, Lee, trust me on this, it's best left alone,' she said.

'Like the identities of the people you owe all this money to?' He couldn't help himself.

'Lee . . .'

'I only want to help,' he said.

'Yes, but you can't.'

'Why? Because they're your own people? Because—'

'Whether they are "my own people" or not, is neither here nor there,' she said, her face reddened now with both embarrassment and anger. Why did Lee and so many other white people think that they had some sort of right to pry into everyone's private business? Was nothing off limits to them? 'It is my concern,' she said. 'Ahmet was my husband and so it is up to me to deal with those business associates that he owed money to and—'

'If he owed money to a crime firm—'

'He owed money to people I call criminals but then I am—'

'You're as bad as Nasreen Khan, protecting bloody scumbags!' And then he shook his head and put a hand up to his temples. He'd said too much and he knew it. 'I'm sorry. It's not my business.'

'No, it isn't,' she said, but she didn't raise her voice. He meant well, but the world of Ahmet's financial obligations to the Sheikhs was somewhere he could not go – not least because her guilt meant that she couldn't possibly take him. She had wanted Ahmet to die.

'Oh, hi Lee.'

And now Shazia had come downstairs. She broke the tension immediately.

'Hi Shazia,' he said. 'How's it going?'

She flopped her long thin body down onto the sofa beside him and said, 'A levels.' She shrugged. Then she looked at Mumtaz, 'So Amma,' she said, 'did those people like the house?'

22

The 'Super', as was his custom, didn't even look at them. Vi Collins and Tony Bracci stood in front of his desk observing his back. It was Monday morning and he wasn't enthusiastic. But then Tom Venus had never taken any risks in his professional life. He kept that side of his character for his personal relationships with younger women.

'Sean Rogers is having one of his sex parties at his gaff in Ongar this Saturday night,' Vi said.

'Which he is perfectly entitled to do provided those attending are consenting adults, and no money is changing hands.'

'And our intel is that he's shipping in a fresh bunch of East European girls.'

'Which again—'

'Just because some of 'em can come here legally now doesn't mean that they don't still get trafficked for sex,' Vi said. Venus had to know that was what was happening, he was just too cautious to do anything about it. 'Sir, the girls our informant told us were coming are Russian,' she said. 'Not EU citizens. They can't work here.'

'And most of them won't be able to speak any English,' Tony Bracci said.

'No, so Sean and co are going to exploit them,' Vi said. 'Sir, if we catch Sean and Marty red-handed with these girls, we can have a go at taking them down. People trafficking—'

'And if the girls, who don't speak English, won't inform on them?'

'Our informant will,' Vi said. 'She does speak English.' She'd called herself Tatiana, although whether that had been her real name Vi didn't know. But the girl had told her about torture, about sexual abuse by a woman Vi recognised as Debbie Rogers, and had stated emphatically that what had been done to her had not been consensual. She'd become what was known as one of the 'pigs', women who would do anything and everything.

'You *think* your informant will, DI Collins,' Venus said.

'I think she will too,' Tony Bracci said. He'd been in on the second interview Vi had had with the girl, and although he was overstating his case by saying he felt she'd be as good as her word, he was desperate to bring Rogers and Ali down. He'd seen a few of the girls that they'd 'worked' with before – in hospital – and he'd never heard any of them speak, until he heard Tatiana. But he'd read a lot of gut-churning accounts of their wounds.

'Our informant says he keeps the girls' passports in his safe at his house,' Vi said. 'She's seen him put them in there.'

'Yes, but—'

'Sir, we can bring Rogers and Ali down.'

'When you bring down an empire, DI Collins, you have to be very sure you are in the right. Because empires have teams of rapacious and very smart lawyers who can twist the notion of things like consent, collusion and entrapment into barely recognisable creatures that have the ability, metaphorically, to kill us. Do you understand?'

'Yes, sir.' Vi looked briefly over at Tony, who flashed her a very small smile. 'But we know they run brothels on this manor.

According to our informant, some girls are picked from the brothels for the parties.'

'I don't like Sean and Martin Rogers and Yunus Ali operating on our patch any more than you do, but an observation of the one you propose is not without its complications. And then we have the Olympics to think about. That must take priority over everything.'

'I'm aware of that, sir.'

'And because the property in question is in Essex then we will have to gain the support and co-operation of Essex police.'

'I know that.'

Venus rubbed a hand against his chin and sat down behind his desk. Small-time crooks and hustlers were really his thing. Men of power like Sean and Marty Rogers made him feel nervous, and he had what amounted to a morbid fear of lawyers that went back so far into his past nobody could now say what its origin had been. Why anyone, least of all Venus himself, had ever thought he was suitable for a high-pressure nick like Forest Gate was well beyond Vi's ken. Tony Bracci liked to use a blanket term for why Venus was where he was, which was 'politics'. All Vi and Tony knew was that having him as their superior was a fucking great pain in the neck if you wanted to get something done a bit pronto.

'I will consult with Essex,' the Super said.

'That's a great leap forward, sir, thank you,' Vi said.

He looked at her and scowled but he didn't say anything. He knew of old that reacting to Vi Collins's little straight-faced sarcasms wasn't worth the trouble. Vi and Tony celebrated by going out into the car park for a smoke.

'You can see how the public can sometimes think we're in bed with the villains, can't you,' Tony said.

'He's right to be cautious and he's right about the kind of lawyers Rogers and Ali would have at their disposal,' Vi said. 'But there are faster things than him in the morgue, yes.'

'Do you think he'll go for it, guv?'

Vi shrugged. 'I dunno,' she said. 'I hope so. If not, everything I told Tatiana I'd do for her is going to fall on its arse and I don't, as you know, Tony, like being made to look a liar.'

Sean had called Wendy first thing on Monday morning and so ruined her day.

'I want a little piggy for my party on Saturday night,' he'd said. 'You up for it, are you?'

She'd said yes, because she'd had no choice, and he knew it. She'd tried hard not to take it out on the kids but she'd failed. Sometimes she wondered why Paul wasn't at Sean's parties any more, but she never had the balls to ask him. In her head, he wasn't going to Sean's any more because he had fallen in love with her, but she knew inside that it wasn't true. A man like that had to have a wife or a girlfriend. She was just the 'bit on the side'.

Wendy looked down at her stomach and wondered whether she could be up the stick. She hadn't taken her pill that day or the day before. She'd lied to Paul, she'd deliberately encouraged him to come inside her. She wanted his baby. If you had a baby you had a bit of the man who had made it forever. Even though she couldn't admit it, even to herself, Wendy knew that Paul would go sometime. In the end, everybody did.

It wasn't often that Mumtaz had to visit a home where the woman didn't leave the house at all, but it happened occasionally and it always depressed her. This lady, an Irishwoman by birth, was the wife of a Syrian she suspected of being unfaithful to her. Her husband worked away from home in a Cash and Carry place in Walthamstow for most of the time, and so it had been quite safe for Mumtaz to visit her at their flat in Manor Park.

The woman, who would only give her name as Zinat, was a true and pious Muslim and, although she wanted to divorce her husband if he was playing away, she told Mumtaz that she would still never go out. Even alone with Mumtaz, she covered her face and wore gloves on her hands and socks on her feet so that absolutely none of her flesh could be seen. Mumtaz told Zinat that she would arrange for one of their male freelance operatives to follow her husband for a few days and try to determine where he went when he wasn't at work.

Coming out of Zinat's flat to a rain-battered, grey London lunchtime, Mumtaz was going to drive back to office when she changed her mind. And although she had told Lee that she would not be visiting Nasreen Khan's house on Strone Road, that was where she ended up.

She parked across the road from the house and tried to see if she could detect any movement inside. But with curtains up at all the windows both upstairs and downstairs, it was impossible to tell. She didn't want to call if Nasreen's husband was in. Her presence might jeopardise Nasreen's safety. So what was she to do?

The house to the right of the Khans' property – which was separated from it by an alleyway – looked empty. Some of the windows were broken and there were several old mattresses dumped in the front garden. Mumtaz decided to do some property viewing. She got out of her car and crossed the road. Not a sound came from either house and so she walked up the alleyway between the rain-soaked properties.

Both houses had back gardens that, to Mumtaz, were substantial. No doubt Mr Linn would have described them as 'pokey' but they weren't. What they were, however, was in a state. Both gardens were overgrown, although Nasreen's did show signs of work in progress. Some trees had been cut down and some patches of earth cleared. At the back of the plot, next to the wall that surrounded the cemetery, there were the remains of what resembled a terrible old shed. There was also a Butler sink just by the back door. They were quite 'in' with the young, stylish and 'ethical' and Mumtaz wondered why the Khans hadn't either installed it in their home or sold it. She looked up at the back of the house. They hadn't done much to it considering they'd bought it at the beginning of the year and lived in it for the last three months or so. It looked really unkempt, almost derelict.

It was also completely silent, with not so much as a shadow showing in any of the windows. Perhaps Nasreen and her husband were both out?

Mumtaz walked back down the alleyway and crossed the road to go back to her car. Looking up at the bay window on the first floor she saw a gap between the curtains but she couldn't see anything beyond it. Aware that she was being watched now by a group of small brown children in the front garden of the house two doors from Nasreen's, Mumtaz got in the Micra and drove away. When she was only halfway down Strone Road her phone rang and she pulled over and answered it.

'One of her neighbours called it in,' Vi said.

Lee, on the other end of the line, put his head in his hands. 'Poor Mumtaz.'

'At least her and Shazia were out.'

'Yeah, but it's small comfort really, isn't it?'

Vi had been in the control room when news had come in that the windows of the house belonging to Mrs Mumtaz Hakim were being shot out by a masked man with an airgun. An armed response unit had been despatched, but by the time they got there the shooter had gone. Every window at the front of the house had been shattered.

'Do you know who might do such a thing?' Vi asked.

'No.' He didn't, but he strongly suspected it had more than just a little to do with whoever Mumtaz owed money to.

'Mmm.' She paused for a moment, then she said, 'Here, Arnold, the Rogers brothers, Sean and Marty?'

'What about them,' Lee said. 'You think they hit Mumtaz's house?'

'No! Don't be daft!'

'Debbie Rogers I saw at the weekend,' he said.

'Did you? Where?'

'Brian Green had a party on Saturday at his place in Ongar. A sort of "I'm still here" after the death of his wife.'

'Oh yeah, which you witnessed, didn't you?'

'Yeah.'

'Green's retired now, ain't he?'

'So he says.'

'So what's he doing inviting the Rogers?'

'Sean Rogers is his neighbour,' Lee said.

'Mmm. Lucky Brian.'

'You could say the same for Sean Rogers,' Lee said. 'Brian's no angel.'

'No, but he's served his time,' Vi said. Brian Green had been to prison on three occasions. 'Sean and his family have only ever been inconvenienced for a short while.'

Lee smiled. Vi had a bit of a soft spot for 'old fashioned gangsters' – those who did bank jobs, slept with British 'tarts' and thought the Internet was a kind of sex aid. Sean and Marty Rogers, with their carefully crafted companies and their desperate women sourced from all over Europe, were far more savvy.

'I should get over to Forest Gate,' Lee said.

'There's nothing you can do, Arnold,' Vi said.

Lee put his jacket on while holding the phone up to his ear with one shoulder. 'I can be there,' he said, and put the phone down.

Chipboard was placed over the shattered living room window and nailed down. Mumtaz watched it darken the room and she felt despair. How was she ever going to sell the house?

Her phone rang and she saw the number she'd called before come up on the screen. She answered. 'Oh, hello, Christine. Thanks for getting back to me.'

She couldn't bring Shazia back into this. Once she'd seen the damage and spoken to the police, she'd called Shazia's friend Maud's mother to find out whether she could stay there for the night. The girls were pretty inseparable now and were currently in the West End for the day. After a few pleasantries, Mumtaz said, 'Christine, I'm so sorry but we've had a bit of trouble at the house. The police are here now. Some hooligan has shot our front windows out with an air rifle and I don't want Shazia to come home until I can get the glass cleared up and can feel a little bit more secure. Would it be OK if she stayed over at your house tonight?'

Christine said that Shazia could stay with them for as long as she liked.

Relieved, Mumtaz said, 'I'll bring her things over later if that's alright. I'm so grateful, I really cannot say.'

It was as she was ending this call that Mumtaz saw Lee walk past the constable at the front door and come inside.

'Mumtaz.'

She put her phone down on the sofa beside her and stood up. 'Lee, you didn't need to . . .'

He put his arms out to her and then, when he drew close, he just rested them lightly on her elbows. 'This is terrible,' he said.

'Done by some boy for kicks the police reckon,' she said. She tried to smile but her face wouldn't move.

Lee took her arm and led her back to the sofa. They sat down. Behind them a Scenes of Crime officer was examining the back wall of the living room.

Lee looked her straight in the eyes and lowered his voice. 'You need to tell me the truth even if you won't tell them,' he said, nodding his head towards the officers. 'Who did this?'

'It was a boy, they say, a—'

'Don't even try to bullshit me.' He didn't move his fierce gaze from her face. 'If you'd been here, or Shazia . . .'

'Don't!' Tears came, but she wiped them away with the edge of her headscarf. 'We are all in the hands of Allah and mercifully He saw fit—'

'Yeah, but you have to help him out you know, Mumtaz,' Lee said. 'This time the man upstairs was looking out for you, but what about next time? God helps them that help themselves, you know.'

'And yet we are all in the hands of Allah and whatever it is our fate to—'

'How can it be your fate to be bled dry, or even murdered, by a bunch of scumbags? Eh?' He moved closer to her, so that he could whisper. 'You're a good person.'

'No, I'm not!'

The fierceness of her rebuttal startled him and, in turn, it alarmed her. She put a hand up to her mouth, suddenly afraid that if she didn't what she'd done to Ahmet would just tumble out and disgust him.

'Look,' he said, 'I can't pretend to understand any of this religious business. All I can do is say it like I see it, and I see you as a good woman who works hard and does her best for her kid. That's it. Whatever your husband did shouldn't still be affecting your life now.'

Mumtaz didn't say anything. The police had taken a description from her neighbours of the man who had shot her windows out. It had almost certainly been Naz. She imagined him enjoying doing it.

'But I can't force you to do anything that you don't want to,' Lee continued. 'I know that you won't tell your family about this and I won't try to persuade you otherwise. I know, remember, how people are around organised crime.'

She looked round, checking that none of the police officers were listening.

'Now, like it or not, I'm staying here,' he said. 'I don't care where you put us, on the sofa, up the bloody chimney for all I care, but there's no way that you're going to be on your own in this house tonight.'

She had all sorts of arguments against this idea assembled in her head, not least of which was her reputation, but she gave voice to none of them. After a moment's thought she just questioned, 'Us?'

'I can't leave Chronus on his own overnight,' Lee said. 'He'll scream the flat down.'

23

Bloated, her feet swollen with fluid, Nasreen felt like a cow that needed to be milked. In addition to that her arms were dead, but that was not connected to her pregnancy. No, that was *him*. Again Abdullah had left her handcuffed to the bed all day, and this time she had wet herself.

She thought that he would be furious when he saw what she'd done, but he didn't say a word. He changed the sheets and told her to have a shower. Then she had to cook. While she did that, he began hammering at the walls of the small utility room behind the kitchen. Nasreen fried off her spices and then she added onions, garlic and tomatoes. When there was a pause in the hammering she said, 'What are you looking for?'

It had occurred to her more than once that all the hammering and breaking down of the fabric of the house had to be about more than just remodelling the place, but she'd never given voice to her suspicions before. The hammering did not recommence. With shaking hands, Nasreen added chicken to the pan. She stirred, watching the meat begin to brown and caramelise. And then there was a pain at her throat as her head was wrenched sharply backwards.

'I'm not looking for anything,' Abdullah said. 'What makes you think I'm looking for summat?'

Although her first urge was to back down immediately, Nasreen said, 'Because you keep making holes in the walls.'

'I'm cutting out rot,' he said.

She swallowed hard, it was difficult to talk with your head almost at right angles to your neck.

'You don't question me.' He pulled her head back still further, one agonising centimetre more, and then he let her go. The chicken in the pan sizzled furiously and Nasreen smelt a faint burning. She turned the gas down.

Now back over by the table, he switched his CD player on and 'Scarborough Fair' drifted into the room again. He said, 'The only reason I can see for this lack of respect is that you've been talking to your fucking mother.'

As well as being untrue, under these present circumstances this was impossible. Nasreen's shell of self-preservation cracked. She'd not been raised to be anybody's meek and terrified wife. 'And how would that happen eh?' she said. 'Tied to the bed with no phone to—'

'You cannot be trusted.'

'*I* cannot be trusted?' She stirred her pot, the sharp smells of cardamom, curry leaves and cumin making her eyes begin to water. 'What is *wrong* with you? Why are you treating me like some sort of—'

He hit her so hard that she fell sideways onto the floor. It was just luck that she didn't take the pan of boiling food down with her.

He screamed into her face, 'You daft cunt! What you trying to do to me, eh? With your endless yack, your fucking family, your fucking friend in the fucking garden!'

He wasn't *like* a lunatic, he was one. His face was red from shouting, his eyes bulged and now she knew that he'd known about John.

'So you killed him, did you?' she said. 'My friend in the garden? That was you, was it?'

He didn't say anything.

Emboldened by his silence, in spite of the pain in her back and her side, Nasreen said, 'Because somebody killed him. Was it you? Was it?'

He stood up and for a moment she thought that he might be about to kick her. But instead he said, 'When the baby's born you can fuck off.'

'Oh, don't worry about that, I will,' Nasreen said.

And then he smiled. 'Oh, but not with the baby,' he said. 'I'll take that.'

'No, you bloody won't!' Nasreen put a protective hand over her stomach. 'You think I'd leave my baby with a psycho like you?'

His smile turned into a laugh. Nasreen began to feel cold. Maybe if she'd kept on appeasing him he would have eventually let her have more freedom and she could have escaped. But now that time was long gone. As he moved towards her, Nasreen tried to pull her legs as far up towards her body as she could.

He pulled down the cooking pot onto her feet and burning hot spices and chicken scalded her legs. Nasreen was suddenly in so much pain she couldn't even scream.

Vi watched the house in Manor Park whenever she could. She saw it as protecting her investment. The girl Tatiana had come to her to shop Sean, Marty and Debbie Rogers. Vi had trusted her about as far as she could shove her and so she'd followed her home. Now she kept an 'eye'. The house where Tatiana lived with two other girls wasn't obviously a brothel, but then operators like Sean and Marty were too clever to run loads of girls out of one house. Apparently respectable, the girls were just like any number of eastern European women in the borough. But Vi knew the signs: men arriving and leaving at odd times, permanently closed blinds, girls leaving to go places in the middle of the night . . . And then there was Dave.

Dave Spall was a great big ox of a thing who'd been employed as one of Marty's minders for years. Like Marty he came from Custom House, where he'd built a reputation as a dirty fighter. Dave'd do just about anything to win. He smashed heads because he liked it, and Marty Rogers gave him free rein to do just that. In return, Dave seemingly allowed Marty to treat him like shit. Wherever they went together, Dave had to sit or stand outside the door or across the room, and although the Rogers brothers gave a lot of their employees perks Dave always appeared to be exempt. Vi had a theory about this, which went back to a time when Dave and the Rogers boys were kids. Dave, though no angel, wasn't a psycho like the others. He wasn't as clever as they were either. They'd frightened him into submission at an early age and now they were all too old to change.

Dave didn't often do anything much without Marty, but he did visit this house in Manor Park. So far that first evening, she'd seen him twice – with flowers. Who they were for and why, Vi didn't know. But if they were for Tatiana, she had to wonder whether Dave knew that the girl grassed up his bosses. As Vi watched, Dave came into view with flowers, and a big smile on his fat face.

Or had Marty finally let Dave have the odd free shag? It didn't seem likely. Dave was the male equivalent of one of Sean's 'pigs' – someone who would do anything, however degrading, to please.

Vi frowned. She thought she'd sold the idea of raiding Sean Rogers's place in Ongar to Superintendent Venus, but even if she hadn't, she knew she wanted to do it.

Vi watched Dave Spall go into the house and heard a female voice squeak with what sounded like joy. As a general rule, Vi tried not to get too excited about bringing villains down, but in this case she couldn't resist a small shiver of pleasure. The Rogers brothers, together with their business partner Yunus Ali, had preyed upon the poor of the borough for long enough. Get rid of the Rogers, then she could start on the Sheikhs; and maybe by the time she retired there'd actually be a power vacuum in Newham for once. But then Vi frowned at the thought. Vacuums were dangerous things.

She saw a light come on behind the blinds in one of the rooms upstairs and she wondered whether Dave Spall was getting a shag. And then she wondered whether Marty knew about it.

'Mumtaz?'

She'd been trying to let herself into the kitchen as quietly as she could, but she'd clearly failed.

'Go back to sleep,' she whispered. 'Everything is fine.'

He pulled himself upright against the back of the sofa. 'Yeah, but . . .'

'Sssh! You'll wake Chronus.' She opened the kitchen door just as the bird opened one eye and then the other.

'I'm forever blowing bubbles,' he screeched, 'Pretty bubbles in the air . . .'

'Oh, Christ.' Lee switched on the reading lamp that Mumtaz had placed on the coffee table. By the light of it, with his hair on end, he looked comically bizarre.

'Shut up, Chronus!' Lee said.

Mumtaz laughed. 'Oh goodness, Lee, what is he to do? You taught him that song.'

She walked into the living room and rubbed the bird's head. Usually when confronted by strangers, Chronus went quietly into his shell, but not with her. 'Trevor Brooking!' he cawed.

'He just wants to please you,' she said.

'Yeah.' Lee shook his head.

'Bobby Moore! Geoff Hurst!'

'Yes, enough now!' Lee said, holding a warning finger up to the bird. 'Enough!' He moved back away from Chronus just a bit, his eyes still on the bird's. 'God Almighty, I don't know why I have you sometimes, you're nothing but trouble.'

Mumtaz, still stroking the bird, said, 'Oh, you'd be lost without him. He's your little boy, aren't you, Chronus?'

Lee flopped back down on the sofa and pulled the duvet that Mumtaz had given him up to his chest.

'Well, seeing as we're all awake, how about some ginger tea?' Mumtaz asked.

'What, like the stuff from the health food shop?'

'No, no, no. Proper ginger tea, like we make in Bangladesh,' Mumtaz said, 'with proper ginger.'

'Blimey, isn't that a bit hot?'

She smiled. 'No, it's actually very soothing. But if you'd prefer something else I do have ordinary tea or hot chocolate.'

She knew that Lee really liked coffee but she hadn't had any of that in for months. All but the most disgusting incarnations cost too much.

'Oh, I'll try some of your ginger wotsit if you're having some yourself,' Lee said.

'That was why I came down,' Mumtaz said. 'Do you want sugar in your tea?'

'Yeah, thanks.'

While Lee calmed the bird down, Mumtaz went into the kitchen, sliced a ginger root, added loose tea and poured hot water over it. It needed to steep for at least five minutes and so she left it to itself and went back into her living room. For a good minute, unobserved by him, she watched Lee stroke and comfort Chronus back to sleep. There was a very gentle side to him that belied his big copper's feet and sometimes aggressive demeanour. That he was in her house at all – she was only an employee – was proof that he was a good person who cared about others.

He turned away from the bird now and looked at her. 'I think he's off,' he whispered.

Mumtaz smiled. She walked over to the chair that was opposite the sofa and sat down. 'You have a way with him,' she said. 'I'll have to call you the Bird Whisperer.'

Lee shook his head. 'He's just a big soft twit,' he said.

There was a pause and then Mumtaz said, 'Nothing's happened.'

'I didn't expect it to,' Lee said. 'Organised criminals aren't stupid. It's why they're successful and why people like you protect them. Not stupid equals dangerous, I know that.'

'Lee, there is no way I'm going to—'

'I know you won't tell me who they are,' Lee said. 'But you have to know, Mumtaz, that I'll find out.'

She felt herself go cold inside. He was a private detective and an ex-policeman, he'd find out in the end. And then what? Mumtaz did what she always did when she didn't want to face up to something, she changed the subject. 'Is Chronus eating properly now?' she said.

But Lee's eyes continued to hold her eyes, making it impossible for her to look away. 'You have to face up to it sometime,' he said. 'I can't be here every night. What happens when I go? When you're alone with Shazia? When they do more than shoot your windows out while you're at work?'

Mumtaz stood up. 'Must go and get the tea,' she said. 'It'll be ready now.'

He lifted her up and held her in the cold water in the bath until her calves and feet were covered. Nasreen screamed. He muttered at her to be quiet, too shocked by what had happened to say any more. Abdullah didn't know himself why he'd pulled the cooking pot down onto her legs. It had been stupid, and now here he was saddled not only with a pregnant woman but with a woman who was injured too. How was he going to deal with that?

He couldn't let anyone into the house. When she went into labour he'd just have to take her to the hospital and then stay with her until it was over. But then what would they make of her scalded legs? The skin was already starting to come off, revealing the raw flesh beneath. What would he tell them about that? He'd have to make sure she said it was an accident.

'It was an accident,' he told her, as he heard her gasp in agony.

'No!' she panted. 'It wasn't!'

He looked into her eyes and this time he didn't see any hurt, only fury. Abdullah felt every nerve and muscle in his body contract away from her. It was like the first time he'd met her, when she'd just been a rather beautiful idea. He hadn't loved her. That had come later and, later still, it had gone. Now she was secondary to the baby she carried, which was secondary to the house. He was running out of time.

Abdullah took Nasreen out of the bath and placed her on a towel he'd laid on the bare bathroom floor. She looked up at him with disgust and then she moved onto one side and groaned. He wanted to leave her there but he knew that if he did that her legs would end up sticking to the towel. He had to put some sort of cream on them. He looked in the bathroom cabinet, which was on the floor, but the only suitable thing he found was a small tube of Savlon. It was supposed to be for minor cuts and burns, but it would have to do. Nasreen whimpered and grunted as he picked her up to carry her to the bedroom and then, when he smeared the cream on, she cried with pain.

'Why are you doing these things to me?' she said. 'Don't you love me?'

He evaded both questions. 'You're my wife.'

What was love anyway? Women when mothers were sacred, but one couldn't love such creatures, not as a man. To love women involved having sex with them. He remembered the first time with Nasreen, and how her eyes had unfocused when he'd entered her. She'd been so beautiful and if he closed his eyes he could almost taste her breasts on his tongue. But then she'd become pregnant.

Thinking about how she had been, he felt horny. Once he'd finished putting cream on her legs, he pulled her arms up and tied them to the headboard.

'Oh, God,' she gasped. 'You can't . . .'

'I have to go out to get more cream,' he said.

'I need a doctor!' Nasreen said. 'Can't you see!' She wept. 'What are you trying to do, kill me?'

If he didn't get himself sorted out he'd burst. Hot now, he turned to leave the room.

But Nasreen called after him, 'Are you trying to kill me, like you killed John Sawyer?'

For a moment, his back turned to her, Abdullah stopped. But then he ran down the stairs and out of the house.

24

The day Sean Rogers had come to the flat and broken the telly he'd also let a genie out of a bottle, because now Dolly knew what her mum did. It was Saturday afternoon and Wendy was putting her make-up on in front of her dressing table mirror. She'd have to leave soon, for Ongar.

Dolly, sitting on Wendy's bed, said, 'Aren't you scared?'

'This time, no,' Wendy said. She turned around and smiled at Dolly. 'No, Paul'll be there this time, Doll.'

Paul, her mum's new boyfriend, had something to do with the landlord. Dolly didn't like him. She'd seen her mum bouncing up and down on him through a crack in her bedroom door. Every time he came round they spent every minute screwing.

Wendy turned back to the cracked dressing table mirror and put on her fake eyelashes. She'd only just seen Paul but, even though it was going to be at one of Sean's parties, she was desperate to see him again. Not only was he good looking and hot, he seemed to love her body even though, at times, he could be cruel.

'Does he make you come?' Dolly asked.

Wendy turned back to look at her daughter again. She was used to Dolly and her twelve-year-old brother Frank swearing, but this was new. 'Doll!'

The girl shrugged. 'I don't like him,' she said.

'What, Paul? What's he done? He don't work for Sean Rogers, he's you know, like a businessman who works with him.'

'But if he works with him then he must be a gangster,' Dolly said. 'Anyway, I don't like him.'

Angry, Wendy turned back to her mirror and said, 'Nobody asked you to.'

'Well, that's good then, ain't it?' Dolly got up and left.

Alone, Wendy carried on with her make-up routine. When she'd finished, she just sat and looked at herself for a while. She'd never see thirty again, and even then she didn't look that good for her age. What she did have going for her was all to do with how good she was at sex. Wendy looked down at her stomach, encased now in skinny jeans, and wondered how she'd managed to get them on. Either she was really bloated or she was pregnant.

The glaziers had just gone when Lee arrived at Mumtaz's tree-draped house. He'd timed himself to get there just as they left, but he had someone else with him too. When Mumtaz opened the door, she saw Lee first and then, looking down, she saw an old man in a wheelchair.

'This is Arthur,' Lee said, as he pushed Arthur Dobson across the threshold and into the hall. 'And he's got a story you might be interested in.'

'Hello, love,' the old man said.

If she were honest, Mumtaz was somewhat taken aback by the sight of an elderly stranger in a wheelchair coming into her home, but she welcomed Arthur warmly and did her duty as a hostess by making tea for him and prising what remained of their biscuits away from Shazia. It was Ramadan now and so food and drink were prohibited to Mumtaz during the hours of daylight.

'I went to see the wife's sister the other day,' Arthur said, 'after I spoke to Lee here. So all that stuff we talked about old Reg Smith and his wife Lil was fresh in me mind.'

Much as Lee knew that Mumtaz had to confront what was happening to her, he also knew that she needed some distraction, and Nasreen Khan's mysterious old house continued to provide that. Arthur Dobson had contacted him, although coming to Mumtaz's house had been entirely Lee's idea. As the old man spoke, Lee kept one eye on the street outside, which was dingy and grey.

'So anyway the wife's sister, she's in a nursing home up Manor Park – I don't get to go unless me cousin Wilf takes me – but she ain't funny in the head or nothing. But like my Helen was, she's Jewish, like.

'Your wife's sister.'

'Evelyn, yeah. She remembers Lily Smith well, she went to her funeral. But more to the point, she remembers her sister too,' the old man said. 'And she give me a name.' He took a small piece of paper out of his pocket, which he held a long way away from his face to read. 'Sara Kaminski,' he said. 'And that name, Kaminski, that was Lil's name afore she got married.'

'Well, that's er . . .' Mumtaz didn't really know what to say. It was good to be able to put a name to the face on the picture behind the mezuzah, if indeed that was Sara Kaminski. However . . .

'Ah, there's more,' the old man said. 'The Kaminskis wasn't just anybody. They was rich. According to Evelyn, the father of the girls was a big jeweller in Warsaw, but then they lost everything to the Germans in the war – or so you might think. But Evelyn said that Lil once told her that unlike her and her son, her sister never went to no concentration camp.'

Mumtaz looked at Lee. 'I thought you said that the sister did go to a camp.'

'It now seems that was an assumption,' he said.

'The sister bought her way out,' Arthur said. 'She paid the Nazis to let her go. That's what Lily told Evelyn. There was a lot of bad blood between them two because of it.'

'She used the jewellery from her father's shop?'

'Must've done,' Arthur said. 'Lil weren't at home by then. She was off married to a bloke called Berkowicz who died in Belsen.'

'Do you know if Sara tried to help her?' Mumtaz asked.

'Gawd knows.'

Mumtaz felt a little bit nauseous. Surely Sara Kaminski had to have tried to help her sister Lily and Marek? Hadn't she? But Lily and Marek had been almost dead by the time Reg Smith found them in Belsen. And yet if Sara Kaminski had abandoned them, why had she apparently been welcomed by Lily to her house in Strone Road?

'Sara come here in late 1954, stayed till sometime in 1955,' Arthur said. 'And according to Evelyn, Lily was glad to see her.'

'But I understand that just after she left, Marek disappeared,' Mumtaz said.

The old man shrugged. 'You thinking that maybe Sara took him with her?'

'If Sara had money . . .'

'What d'you mean? That Lily sold Marek?' Lee asked.

'No, not precisely,' Mumtaz said. 'But Lily had married Reg, with whom she had a new child, Eric. At the time, back in 1955, some of the police believed that Reg Smith didn't like Marek very much. Maybe Lily thought that he'd have a better life with her sister.'

'Yeah, but if she gave the kid away then why were the police called out on a Missing Person gig?' Lee asked. 'Surely if Marek went abroad with his aunt then there was no need for the law to get involved.'

'Mmm, I can see that.' Mumtaz put her chin in her hands. Then she said, 'There's something not right with that story.'

'Which is why I brought Arthur to see you,' Lee said. 'I think there's something missing.'

'What?'

'I don't know.' Still looking out of the window he narrowed his eyes. 'But it's . . .' Lee stood up quickly and began to run.

'Lee?' Mumtaz jumping up too followed after him. 'Lee? What?'

But he was out of the living room, into the hall and out of the front door, way ahead of her.

'Some bastard with a fucking mask on!' she heard him yell, as he ran into the street.

Sean Rogers was immensely pleased with himself. He usually looked very satisfied with his lot, but this was way beyond that. Even Marty's wife Debbie noticed.

'What's with you?' she asked him as she casually looked at a pair of Ukrainian teenage girls having sex on a makeshift stage in the middle of Sean's lounge. The party had been going for a couple of hours now and things were hotting up.

Sean didn't answer her. Years ago he'd had a short fling with Debbie, before Marty had married her. The woman was beyond cold and she hadn't changed in the intervening years.

'There's some judge in the blind room so I put a foreign girl with fake tits in with him,' Debbie said. 'I'm assuming we need him.'

'You can never have too many high court judges,' Sean said. Then he asked her, 'Where's my girl from Plaistow?'

'With your best boy, as usual these days,' Debbie said. She sneered. She didn't practise the kind of favouritism that Sean and Marty sometimes indulged in.

'Just because he can terrify people . . .' she began.

'Useful skill,' Sean said, and then he laughed. 'You have it too, Debs. Anyway I respect him, he takes care of my business, I take care of his, and he's grateful. I like that. Let him have his fun. He's taken with the little slag for some reason. But don't worry, Debs, I won't let it go on.'

'What? Because she owes you money?'

'And because he's mine too. I like him but he still owes me.' Sean smiled. 'Don't worry, Debs,' he said, 'I've not gone soft or nothing.'

When Lee came back he was out of breath and empty handed. The masked man who'd been peering into Mumtaz's living room window had all too easily out-run him. He had been, Lee rationalised, not much more than a kid.

Arthur Dobson said, 'No luck, son?'

'No,' Lee gasped, and sat down on the sofa while Mumtaz went and got him a glass of water.

When she came back, Arthur said to her, 'Too many kids with nothing to do but cause bother these days.'

Mumtaz had expected the old man to carry on with a plea for

them all to do National Service, but he didn't. Lee drank his water between panting.

And then out of the blue, Arthur said, 'Maybe she was dying.'

Lee frowned, while Mumtaz asked, 'Who?'

'Sara Kaminski,' Arthur said, taking their thoughts back to the original topic of conversation. 'Lee, you said that the photograph of the dark-haired woman was hidden behind that mezuzah thing in the Strone Road house.'

'Yeah.'

'Well, maybe it was some sort of memento,' the old man said. 'It'd explain why Lily spoke to that Sara and was alright with her even after all what she done by not sharing her money. If someone's dying all that sort of thing don't mean nothing – believe me.'

Lee knew that Arthur was dying and so he clearly understood what he was talking about.

'But even if Sara was dying, that still doesn't explain Marek,' Mumtaz said.

'Maybe he went to wherever it was she come from to help to take care of her,' Arthur said.

'So why didn't he come back when she'd died? Why call out the police? No, that doesn't make any sense,' Mumtaz said. 'Sara came here, she stayed with her sister, she left and then Marek disappeared. Sara and Marek are unconnected.'

'They never found a body,' the old man said.

'No.'

'Not just here but nowhere in the country,' he continued. 'No-one who ever fitted that boy's description.'

'Then maybe it hasn't been found yet or perhaps it *is* abroad somewhere,' Mumtaz said.

'Unless old Marek's out there somewhere,' Arthur said.

'What?'

'Out there,' he reiterated. 'Because he run away. He'd be old now but . . . Eric Smith was never normal you know,' he said. 'Shut up in that house for years on end sitting on secrets.'

Other people had alluded to the possibility that Eric might have known more about Marek's disappearance than he ever let on. Had someone in that house killed Marek and then disposed of his corpse somewhere? Mumtaz thought about the skeleton that had been found in the old Plashet Cemetery at the same time as the body of that war veteran. But that had belonged to a female. And anyway the police had searched the gardens of all the houses in Strone Road at the time.

Sometimes girls screamed during one of Sean's parties. But not like this. This was terror. The music from the sound system downstairs had stopped. Wendy watched Paul's face pale. He got out of bed and ran across the room to the door, which he opened just a crack.

'What's . . .'

'Sssh!' He held a finger up to her. Wendy, still in bed, assumed a discontented silence. Whatever was going on downstairs had nothing to do with them. All she wanted was more of him.

But Paul resolutely stood by the door and she saw his face stretch into a grimace as he attempted to hear what was happening downstairs. Then suddenly his face dropped.

'It's the bloody filth,' he said. He closed the door as quietly as he was able and tiptoed across the floor, picking up the clothes he had discarded earlier.

'What you gonna do?' Wendy said.

'I'm getting out of here,' he said. He put his trousers on, then his shirt and his jacket which she could see had a gun in one of its pockets. Then he began looking for something, in wardrobes and on the dressing table.

'What you looking for?' Wendy whispered.

But he'd found a scarf which he tied over his mouth and nose.

'What's gonna happen to me?'

He looked at her as she sat up in the bed, the duvet pulled up to her chest. He looked out of one of the windows and then, slowly, opened it. 'If Sean and Marty are going down, you'll be free,' he said.

He flung one leg over the windowsill and lowered himself down onto the garage roof below.

'Open the safe, Sean,' Vi Collins said.

Sean Rogers smiled and then said, 'Now if only I can remember the combination . . .'

'Don't fuck me about – sir,' Vi said.

They were in Sean Rogers' office, a hardwood-lined copy of what he imagined the headquarters of an international business empire would look like. Burgundy Chesterfield sofas seemed to be everywhere. It even smelt, Vi noticed, of brandy. Together with a couple of uniformed officers, she was with Sean and his brother Marty, who both looked very relaxed about the warrant she carried to search the house and its environs. In the rooms beyond the office, Tony Bracci and another team of uniforms were attempting to calm a load of screaming girls and prevent guests – known villains, high court judges, doctors, solicitors – from leaving.

Sean Rogers waggled his fingers in emulation of an old-time safe cracker limbering up to do a bank job and then he turned the dial three times to the left, twice to the right and then once to the left again. He pulled the door open and stood to one side.

'I dunno what you're looking for, but knock yourself out,' he said.

Vi peered inside the safe and then removed its contents, which consisted of two cardboard folders and a jewellery box. With Sean and Marty in front of her she opened the box, which predictably contained cheap-looking expensive jewellery and then she looked inside the folders. They contained the deeds to the house, Sean's passport and birth certificate and about two thousand pounds in cash.

'Me float,' Sean said by way of explanation.

Vi was furious. But she had to contain herself. No other passports. She hadn't seen Tatiana when they'd burst into that gruesome orgy room. It was possible she was in some other part of the house they had yet to search. At that moment Vi felt that if she found her, she'd bloody kill her. If she found her. A distinct stench of 'set-up' was beginning to invade Vi's nostrils, just as Venus had said it would – the fucking bastard. He'd given her her head, against what he described as his 'better judgement', and now here she was, in a house full of naked judges but no passports and, so far, not even one small wrap of coke.

Vi looked at the uniforms and said, 'Search the place. All of it. ID every girl you find. Passports, work permits, you know the drill.'

The uniforms left.

Debbie Rogers came in, smoking a green cocktail cigarette. Vi hadn't seen her for a number of years, but she hadn't changed a bit. She still had a face you could crack marble on. She looked tense. Vi nodded in her direction, 'Debbie.'

'DI Collins.' Debbie sat down on one of the Chesterfields. 'What you looking for?' she asked. 'This is a private party here, you know.'

'A private party where half the guests are eastern European Toms. Right.'

'Toms?' Debbie shook her dyed head and said, 'Oh no, DI Collins, they ain't Toms. No money changes hands here. All these people are our friends.'

'So your mates are having a freebie.'

Debbie moved forward. Vi was assaulted by the overwhelming stench of Debbie's perfume. 'This is a private party for friends,' she said. 'Consenting adults.'

The orgy room and the vast living room were awash with sex toys, vials of poppers and various costumes designed to enhance people's sexual fantasies. Vi, wound up by Debbie Rogers' smug, bright red smile, left the office and joined Tony Bracci in the living room.

'There's a pool house wotsit in the garden so I've sent a group of officers out there,' he said. 'Passports?'

Vi shook her head.

'Fuck. You think we've been—'

'We'll need to have a word with Tatiana, if we can find her,' Vi said. And then she noticed the unprepossessing figure of Dave Spall, fully clothed, sitting in a chair.

Vi walked over to him. 'Mr Spall,' she said. 'Can I have a word?'

'What about?' He looked grey and drained.

'About your visits to a house in Manor Park,' Vi said.

'What house in Manor Park?'

She told him the address.

'So what?' he said.

'Why do you go there?' Vi asked. 'It's full of girls, from Eastern Europe.'

'What if it is?'

'Well, we think that they might be on the game,' Vi said. Around them officers took names, addresses and contact numbers. They looked at passports, turned out drawers, boxes and DVD cabinets.

Dave shrugged. 'They ain't Toms, they've all got proper jobs,' he said.

'How do you know? Got a girlfriend there, have you?'

He looked up at her with pale blue, pig-small eyes. 'Yeah.'

'What's her name, Dave?' Vi asked.

'Magda,' he said.

'She here tonight with you, is she?' Vi asked.

'As a matter of fact she is,' he said. He pointed to a red-head wearing a basque.

'You mind your girlfriend servicing a load of wrinkly old judges, do you?' Vi asked.

'It's just a bit of fun.' He smiled, but it was forced. There was a pain somewhere in Dave, but was it because of Magda?

'You know the names of the other girls who live with Magda?' Vi said.

'Olga,' he said. Vi waited for more but none came.

'Just Olga?'

'Yeah.' But he looked away and so Vi knew that he knew. He had to.

'I thought there were three girls in that house,' she said.

'No, only two.'

'I'd've hardly described the house as being full if there were only two girls in it, now would I?' Vi said.

'I dunno.' He shrugged again.

Vi smiled at him but then she was distracted by a shout from outside. It came from one of her officers.

25

It had all come down, finally, to Wendy Dixon. The plods from Essex who were supposed to have been securing the house and the garden had managed to let someone get past them. But then he, or she, had shot at them. They'd managed to retrieve a bullet from the side of Sean Rogers's house. But the rest of the operation had been a disaster. All the girls had their own passports with them, they all apparently worked, and the house had been so drug free that DI Vi Collins wondered if she'd inadvertently wandered into a convent. 'Just a group of consenting adults indulging their sexual fantasies', as Sean Rogers had told her. Nobody knew any shooter, and Sean's house had been as clean of firearms as it was of drugs. He'd known they were coming.

Vi had asked Magda about the girls she shared her house with but she hadn't mentioned Tatiana's name. Now a team was searching the Manor Park house for her. At one point in the early hours of the morning Vi actually wondered whether she'd dreamed the girl up. But now here was Wendy, who was crying. She alone had been found in possession of what remained of a joint which, she said, she'd brought to the party with her.

Vi looked across the table at Wendy and said, 'You weren't downstairs with the rest of the party guests, were you?'

They'd found her, naked, in a bedroom over the top of Sean's double garage.

'Who were you with?' Vi asked.

She shrugged.

'Anyone?'

Wendy said nothing.

Vi leaned back in the hard wooden chair and wished she could have a fag. 'I know what you are, Wendy,' Vi said. 'I've watched you being passed around. What is it Sean calls girls like you?'

Wendy looked up sharply through her tears.

'I know you owe him money,' Vi continued. 'But you'll never work your debt off, you know, not until you're too old and too knackered to be useful.' She leaned forward. She'd seen the Sean Rogers type many times over the years. 'But even then it won't end. When your body's like a sack and your face looks like mine on a bad day, he'll have you dealing blow or stashing hooky fags and booze. Your debt will never be paid. Who were you with in that room over the garage, Wendy?'

'No-one.'

'So you were just stark naked on your own?'

Wendy looked down again.

'Wendy, the Essex coppers who provided backup tonight saw a figure jump down off the garage roof and make a break for the woods behind Sean's house. It was that person who fired on those officers with a gun. That's a very serious offence, and if you are protecting that person you could be in a lot of trouble.'

Wendy said nothing and so Vi changed tack. 'If you won't think of yourself then think about your kids,' she said. 'If anything happened to you, what would happen to them? Eh? If you went inside or died, they'd go into care.'

'I've got a sister,' she mumbled.

'Oh, and you think your sister'd automatically get your kids?' Vi leaned across the table. 'Don't be stupid, Wendy. You know what the score is. They'd go into care. Deal with Sean and his organisation now and you can be free.'

There was a pause before Wendy Dixon laughed. 'You know that's bollocks,' she said.

'We'll protect you.'

'And how you gonna do that?' Wendy said. 'Lock us all in a bulletproof car? Sean and Marty kill people. I know it and so do you, even though you've never managed to catch them. You never will! They know everybody, they've got everybody . . .'

'They haven't got me,' Vi said. 'Wendy . . .'

'No! No,' she said. 'I . . . Look, just do me for the blow and let me go. I've nothing more to say.'

Vi shook her head. 'I think you're making a really big mistake, Wendy.'

'I don't.'

'If you'll just give us the name of the shooter.'

'What shooter?' Wendy said. 'There was no shooter. There was just men and me in that bed and—'

'Oh, fucking hell!' Vi put her forehead in her hands. 'No shooter, no Tatiana, no—'

'Tatiana. There was a girl called Tatiana, I met her once or twice,' Wendy said.

Vi sat up straight again. 'Blonde, Russian, tall girl.'

'Yes, lovely,' Wendy said. 'But I never saw her at Sean's last night.' And then she frowned.

Vi saw it and said, 'Bad memory, Wendy? Of Tatiana?'

'Oh? Oh, no.' And then she smiled. But Vi knew that it was false.

*

For the second night running Nasreen had been tied to the bed. In too much pain to sleep she'd peered into the darkness around her and wondered what was going to happen once the baby was born. Would he kill her? How could he get away with doing that? And yet he clearly hated her and so how could it end other than badly?

She heard him come in through the front door at some time she couldn't begin to guess at. He hadn't asked her to cook an *iftar* meal to break the Ramadan fast and so she was wildly hungry and thirsty. It was dark. In the silence she heard him talk to someone, or into his phone.

'It's sorted,' he said. Then, 'I'm cool, I'm cool.' Then there was a long gap before she heard him say, 'Look, I promised and I never go back on my word . . . What police station? Where?' Finally she heard him say, 'You own the house at the end of the day. Just give me another week.'

Nasreen felt her heart begin to race. What house had her husband been talking about? Their house? But that wasn't possible because they owned their house – didn't they?

Morning came, bringing with it a double dose of horror. Not only had Abduljabbar Mitra, the man who had murdered Bully Murray, finally managed to hang himself in his cell but Vi had also been obliged to give an account of her actions in Ongar to Superintendent Venus. He had not been impressed.

'So you're telling me,' he said as Vi stood in front of his desk, 'that ourselves and Essex committed valuable resources to an operation that only resulted in one caution for possession of a half-smoked joint?'

'Essex police officers were shot at . . .'

'They recovered the bullet, sir.'

'From a handgun, a pistol.'

'Yes. My informant is missing, sir,' Vi said. 'Tatiana.'

He looked up at her quickly and then looked down at the paperwork on his desk again. 'She played you,' he said.

'I don't think so, sir,' Vi replied. 'We searched the house where she lived in Manor Park and there was no sign of her at all. Everyone I asked about a third girl in that house denied flat that one had ever lived there.'

'Maybe they were right.'

'No, sir, I followed Tatiana, she lived there,' Vi said. 'And Wendy Dixon, the Class B, confirmed that she'd known Tatiana too. She existed.'

'Maybe she did, but you were played anyway, DI Collins,' he said.

'The Rogers knew we were coming, yes,' Vi said, 'that was evident from the moment I saw inside Sean's safe. But either Tatiana tipped them off or they got the information out of her somehow. I think that Marty Rogers' henchman Dave Spall was having a fling with her. I can't prove it, it's just a hunch . . .'

'Yes, well I think we've had quite enough of your hunches, don't you, DI—'

'Tatiana was no hunch, sir!' Vi said. She was angry now. Even if Venus didn't accept anything else, he had to accept that Tatiana was real and she was missing. She could very well be dead. 'The Rogers had a man with a gun in their house last night—'

'Which they deny and we cannot prove. I think you'll find that he or she cannot definitively be connected to the Rogers brothers.'

Vi ignored him. Of course the shooter had been connected. 'They've either killed Tatiana or shuffled her back to Eastern Europe,' she said.

'Yes, well . . .' He moved one piece of paper off his desk and replaced it with another. 'All that is by the by. I've had word from the assistant commissioner's officer today and we're definitely on for the Olympics. Because that security firm cocked up so royally all leave is cancelled and that is now our priority.'

Vi had known it had been coming. 'Yes, sir.'

'So tomorrow morning, bright and early.'

'Yes, sir.'

Vi left and went out on Green Street with the intention of buying an early morning samosa. And she could have done, had not the realisation that Ramadan had started last Friday made her have a fag at the back of the car park instead. Nobody needed to see some skinny white woman eating when they were trying to be pious. Her thoughts turned to the late Abduljabbar Mitra and she found herself wondering what had possessed him to take his own life during Ramadan, when Muslims were not only supposed to abstain from eating and drinking but also from sin in all its forms. He was a religious man, so to do such a thing had to be an act of desperation. Wasn't he afraid of God's punishment in the afterlife, or whatever it was called? There had to have been something in this life that was even more frightening .

26

The burns on Nasreen's legs had started to fester. She told Abdullah that she needed a doctor and antibiotics, but he didn't appear to hear her. It was Monday morning and he said he had to go out to conduct some business before he could come back and do more work on the house.

He stood over her with the handcuff ties and tried to push her arms up to the headboard, but she resisted him. 'I can't walk with these legs! For God's sake let me have my hands free! I can't do anything!'

He looked into her eyes, trying to work out whether she was telling the truth. Then he looked down at her legs and he knew that she was. He lowered his hands to his sides

'I need antibiotics,' she said. 'If I don't get them then the baby will die.'

He thought for a moment and then he said, 'But if I get them you'll only be able to take them at night.'

'Why?'

'Because it's Ramadan,' he said.

Nasreen gathered every iota of strength that she had and yelled, 'But I'm pregnant, I'm allowed to eat and drink! If you don't get them then your baby will die.'

He went on his way, leaving her rolling around on the bed, her body bent in agony. The baby could be dead already – it hadn't moved for at least a day now.

Mumtaz watched Lee eat something that she would normally find absolutely abhorrent. It was a white bun filled with fake cream and cheap raspberry jam. But she only had herself to blame and she knew it. Lee had offered not to eat or drink in front of her, but she'd said that she really didn't mind. She'd told Shazia exactly the same thing. Except that now she regretted it – bitterly. Getting up at four in the morning with the intention of stuffing your face until the sun rose didn't really work for Mumtaz. In the mornings she was often vaguely nauseous, while by the time she got home for *iftar* in the evenings, she was often past caring about food at all.

But she couldn't very well change her mind now and ask Lee to stop eating. He'd been so good to her that to rob him of the simple pleasure of a bun from Percy Ingle's was beyond the pale. Mumtaz looked down at the stack of bills on her desk that needed paying, and shuffled uncomfortably in her chair. She couldn't concentrate.

'Why don't you go down and get some more stamps from the post office,' Lee said without taking his eyes away from the photograph on his computer screen. 'I know we're low and there's a few bills to post out today.'

'OK.' Mumtaz got up and went to the safe to get petty cash. 'How many do you want me to get?'

'Couple of dozen,' Lee said. He pressed his keyboard to bring up another picture which he frowned at.

Mumtaz took a twenty-pound note out of petty cash and put it in her purse. She had just one appointment with a potential client later on that afternoon, so she knew she didn't have to hurry back. Lee clearly understood what she was going through and was fine with it.

'See you later, Lee,' Mumtaz said.

'See ya.'

She closed the door behind her and Lee Arnold let out a long sigh of relief. Being around Mumtaz when she was fasting wasn't easy, even though she never said a word about it to him. Lee took the bag he'd got from Percy Ingle's out of his drawer and put it on his desk. There were two other buns and an éclair to get through before she came back.

Paul had phoned to say he was fine, which was such a relief that Wendy almost cried. He'd gone on to say that he wanted to see her as soon as possible. She'd nearly gone mad with it. Make-up, perfume, making sure her legs were silky smooth.

Wendy paid Dolly to take the kids to the park for a few hours. She told her she needed to go shopping. Then, once they were out of the way, she went off to meet Paul. It wasn't far, although it still seemed like a funny place to meet. But he'd been insistent. Maybe he had some sort of kink for derelict places, but she didn't care. Wendy walked across the Barking Road and down Credon Road until she came to the walls of the old hospital between Credon and Western Roads. As instructed, she turned into Western and made for what had once been the main entrance.

Her gran had died at what used to be called Samson Street Hospital. Once a smallpox clinic, back in the 1980s it had become a place where people with dementia were 'stored', as Wendy's mum had put it. Then in 2006 it closed. Now its damp-riddled walls were threaded with convolvulus and ivy, and barbed wire sat in heavy rolls around gaps in the old metal gates that had once given entry to the hospital. One gap was unencumbered by barbed wire. Instead, there stood Paul, smiling at her.

Wendy smiled back. 'I can't decide whether this is a new kink of yours or what,' she said.

He put his fingers up to his lips. 'Sssh.'

'Oh, we not supposed to be here? I . . .'

'Sssh.'

He held a piece of bent metal aside so that she could get inside and then he pulled her into some bushes. She put her arms up on his shoulders and said, 'The coppers said you shot your way out. I heard a crack but . . .'

'I had to let off one round,' he said. 'The police took you to Forest Gate.'

'Yeah, but I never told them nothing,' Wendy said. 'I said that joint was mine. I got a caution.'

She kissed him but, oddly for him, he didn't respond. Then she noticed that he was sweating. He didn't usually sweat, not much at least.

'Are you alright, babe?' she asked.

He didn't answer but held her close, and although she was surprised she thought that having a hug was rather sweet. Even though she hadn't come for that.

She'd woofed her hair up so high and with so much spray that Wendy didn't feel the cold metal as it rested against her head. She heard him say, 'I'm sorry,' which did make her wonder, for just a second, what he was on about. But then he pulled the trigger.

It wasn't far to Strone Road and if Nasreen was in then she might be interested in what Mumtaz had found out about her house. It had been some time since she'd last tried to visit Nasreen and she could have gone into labour already, but Mumtaz wanted the walk. It would only have taken her five minutes to go to the post office and Lee needed rather more time than that to get through all the cakes he'd bought for himself from Percy Ingle's. He'd thought she'd not seen all of them, but she had. How he kept so slim she didn't understand. She walked down Green Street and turned into Strone Road. Nasreen lived right at the other end which, through the vague heat haze that was building, looked like miles away.

Mumtaz kept walking. The streets were quiet in spite of the fact that the children were on holiday. But then everybody had become accustomed to being indoors because of all the rain. Now it seemed to have stopped, just in time for the Olympics. For once, the Afghan women who wore burqas didn't seem to be soaked from the knees down.

As before, the house was quiet and when Mumtaz knocked on the front door a hollow sound came back at her from inside. It made her want to look through the letterbox and see if it was empty, but she resisted the temptation – for a few seconds. She knocked again and this time she did lift the letterbox flap. What she saw was worse than empty. The hall at least looked as if it had been bombed. Old wallpaper, lumps of plaster, wood and ancient paint splinters were everywhere. What had happened? She knew that Nasreen and her husband had been decorating the house back in the spring, but this looked as if someone had gone in and beaten the place up with an axe. Had they perhaps moved out and vandals got in?

Mumtaz put her mouth up to the letterbox and called out, 'Nasreen? Are you there, Nasreen? It's Mumtaz Hakim. I have some information about your house that you might find interesting.'

But nobody answered. Her voice reverberated through the shattered hall.

At first Nasreen thought she had to be hallucinating. Abdullah
had gone out and then there had been nothing until the voice.
Initially she thought that it had to be him. Then she heard it was
a woman's voice and she wondered whether he was just putting
it on to trick her. But then she'd heard that name. Mumtaz Hakim.

Nasreen's eyes began to water with tears. How and why had
Mumtaz Hakim remembered her when the rest of the world
seemed to have forgotten? She'd been a nice woman but Nasreen
remembered that they hadn't parted on the best of terms because
Mumtaz had tried to tell her that Abdullah was no saint. She'd
been right.

She heard her call again. 'Nasreen . . . ?'

If Abdullah found her at the house he'd go mad, but Abdullah
was out. Nasreen looked at her feet and wondered how she could
get over to the window to call back. For a moment, just the look
of her feet made her lose all hope. How could she stand on things
that were so red and sore and infected? The floor of the bedroom
was covered with plaster and wallpaper. Who knew what further
damage she'd do to her feet if she tried to walk? But did she have
a choice? If Mumtaz Hakim was outside her house, calling to her,
then she had to be the best hope that Nasreen had of getting
medical attention. Abdullah was supposedly getting antibiotics
for her, but how could she know whether he really was?

The muscles in her sides and across her back hauled her vast
body into a sitting position and for a second she just panted on
the bed. The first time she stood it was so painful that she

screamed. Her feet felt like balloons, walking on them a precarious act of balancing on agony. The route from the bed to the window was strewn with litter and muck and there was nothing for her to hang on to. Nasreen had just made up her mind to pull herself to the window when she heard Mumtaz's voice again.

'Nasreen,' she said, 'is that you?'

'Yes! Yes it is me! Please help me!' Nasreen shouted. 'Please!'

The sound she heard next was of breaking glass as a stone shattered the small window in the front door.

What had once been a beautiful young woman was now a creature crawling on the floor amongst gobbets of plaster and tumbleweed-sized bolls of dust. Mumtaz bent down and put her hands around Nasreen's shoulders. 'What has happened to you?' she said.

Nasreen wiped a string of snot away from her nose. 'He happened to me,' she said. 'You were right.'

'Abdullah?'

'I don't know who he is anymore.' She began to cry.

Mumtaz took her phone out of her handbag. 'We have to get you to hospital,' she said. She wondered why Nasreen's feet were so swollen and infected, but she also knew that she didn't have time to ask. Whatever had gone on, she had to get the young woman medical attention as soon as she could. She dialled 999 and asked for an ambulance. Once she'd given all the details she could to the operator, she turned back to Nasreen and tried to make her as comfortable as she could. She didn't want to risk moving her, so she just draped a blanket around her shoulders and propped her head up against a pile of filthy pillows.

'The ambulance'll be here soon,' she said. 'Then we'll get you and the baby to hospital.'

'The baby's dead,' Nasreen said. 'It hasn't moved for days.'

Mumtaz stroked her forehead and watched as the young woman sighed with something akin to relief underneath what she imagined had to be an unusually affectionate touch. 'You don't know that, Nasreen,' she said. 'Sometimes babies don't move very much during the last few days in the womb.'

As soon as she'd said it Mumtaz felt stupid. What did she know? She'd never had a baby.

'Mumtaz, I think that Abdullah has killed someone,' Nasreen said.

One thing that Mumtaz did know was true was that pregnant women often suffered from high blood pressure. She smoothed Nasreen's filthy hair back, away from her face, and said, 'Don't worry about that now. Just keep calm, Nasreen. We'll talk about all of this later.'

'He killed John Sawyer, I'm sure of it,' she said. 'He's jealous of everybody. John used to come to our garden sometimes. I used to leave food out for him. Abdullah must have seen me talking to him. If he even found you here . . .' Her chest began to pump in panic. 'Oh God, he's coming back,' she said. 'I asked him to get antibiotics for me and then he was coming back.'

'When?'

'I don't know,' she said.

Mumtaz looked at her watch. 'When did Abdullah go out?'

'I don't know. Some time ago.' Her head lolled back onto the pillows again.

Mumtaz rubbed one of her hands, which was hot and clammy. Nasreen would be lucky to get away with her own life given the extent of the infection in her feet. 'Ambulance'll be here soon.'

'Good.' She panted and Mumtaz took a handkerchief out of her pocket and wiped some of the dirt away from Nasreen's mouth and eyes.

'There.'

'Thank you,' Nasreen said. 'You know, he tipped a hot pan of curry over my legs.'

Mumtaz shook her head. 'Why?' Although as soon as she'd said it, she wondered why she'd asked – Abdullah was a man. Ahmet had once knocked her unconscious just for changing the channel on the TV without his permission.

'Because I displeased him,' Nasreen said. 'Because I hoped and prayed that he was better than that. But he wasn't.'

'Don't think about that now,' Mumtaz said, stroking Nasreen's forehead once again. 'Don't think about him now.' She leaned forward and kissed her on the head and then she smiled.

'Who are you? Get away from my wife!'

Neither of them had heard Abdullah come into the house and tiptoe up the stairs. Now he stood in the bedroom doorway, his face red with fury.

'Mr Khan, your wife needs a doctor,' Mumtaz said. So this tall, handsome, furious man was the lawyer husband. It was the first time that Mumtaz had seen him. She could imagine how he could easily have turned Nasreen's head. She knew the type. She stood up and walked over to him. 'I've called an ambulance.'

'Why? She's my wife.' He leaned towards her. 'Did you break my front door window?'

'I did,' Mumtaz said. 'Your wife was screaming out in pain. Someone needed to get to her.'

'You have to go now,' he said.

Mumtaz remained calm. 'No.'

There was a moment when he didn't seem to understand her.

Then he grabbed her arm in a grip that was as hard as death and pulled her towards him. Practised in the art of not giving men the satisfaction of hearing her pain, Mumtaz didn't murmur.

'Get out of here,' he hissed. 'Now.'

His fingers dug into her flesh, clawing through her jacket and her blouse. 'No,' she said.

And then they all heard the siren.

'Oh, they're here,' Nasreen said.

'Yes, they are.' Mumtaz turned to smile at her. Then she turned back to the infuriated man. 'Paramedics'll be coming in any moment now, Mr Khan,' she said. 'If you'd rather leave . . .'

And then he did something that Mumtaz had not anticipated. He put his hand into the pocket of his jacket and took out a gun.

The bullet exploded into the bedroom ceiling. Mumtaz covered her head with her hands and hit the floor. Then he shot out the smallest of the bedroom windows. Another explosion. Outside on the street she heard a man scream. Abdullah Khan said, 'It's too late for any of us to leave now.'

27

'I can't work out what it's for,' Vi said.

'Well, it's a festival of sport, isn't it,' Constable Roberts said.

'Yeah, but who wants it?' Vi dragged hard on her fag, in the full knowledge that Superintendent Venus could see both her and Roberts from his eyrie at the top of the police station. If he had been looking, which he wasn't.

Roberts, a young black copper originally from Notting Hill, said, 'David Beckham, Lord Coe, Boris Johnson . . .'

'Oh, so we should all go mad for sport because a bloke who calls his kid after a number, a Tory windbag and a man who looks like he's got a blizzard on his head says we should?'

Roberts shrugged. 'It is what it is,' he said. 'I'd like to be able to buy a flat back near me mum and dad but it ain't happening. Life's not fair, guv.'

She looked at him and shook her head. 'You must fucking hate Hugh Grant.'

He laughed. 'Oh, we had the Portobello Road effect years before that film came out. Anyway, I think the Olympics'll be good. We've got some great sportsmen and women in this country and by that I don't mean any dumb footballers.'

Vi laughed.

'Oh, it's crap though, isn't it, guv?' Roberts said. 'Some bloody boy paid £200,000 a week . . .'

'You're just jealous . . .'

'Well, yeah, maybe but . . .'

'Guv, you gotta come! Quick!' It wasn't often that anyone saw Tony Bracci run and it was never an edifying sight, involving as it did a lot of sweat and redness about the face. But this time he looked white bordering on grey. 'Tone?' She ground her fag butt out with her heel.

'Something's going on in East Ham,' Tony Bracci gasped. 'The Super's called out SCO19 . . .'

'So it's an armed . . .'

'We think so, yes,' Tony Bracci said. 'We've got to get to it. The Super wants us all in now.'

He turned and began running back towards the station. Vi and Constable Roberts followed.

Lee looked at his watch and wondered what was keeping Mumtaz. She'd been nearly an hour and he knew that the queue in the post office couldn't possibly be that long. He put the final bun into his mouth and went over to the window to look down into Green Street. It was a slow Monday during Ramadan and so there wasn't much movement. There was certainly no Mumtaz. But then he'd sort of implied that she take her time. She didn't have any appointments until the afternoon and business was slow. People were on holiday – cheating husbands were temporarily tolerated, wayward daughters curbed by the strictures of being in close quarters with their parents for two weeks and even moon-lighting workers were taking a break. Everyone who could had buggered off to get away from the Olympic influx.

Lee went outside and sat on the metal stairs to smoke. The weather seemed to be heating up, which was good news for the Games. Much as he didn't feel anything much about them himself, he hoped that they went well. He didn't want any incidents to mar the occasion. Over the years, London had had more than its share of terrorist outrages and bomb scares. When Lee had been a kid it had been the IRA, then later it had been offshoots from the IRA, then, in 2005, the day after the Olympic bid had been won, al Qaeda had taken their turn. Poor old city. When his parents had been children it had been bombed to bits, although maybe all of that 'poor old London' thing was on the wane now. Vast new apartment blocks had risen up everywhere, including in Newham, and flashy landmarks like the Shard on the south bank were giving London a whole new world city vibe. But that was only part of the story and Lee Arnold knew it. Down in Custom House, his mum still rented the same council house she'd had since before his older brother Roy had been born. She still bought her groceries off cheap markets and her household goods from pound shops. A lot of people were being left behind by the reality of shiny new London.

But then suddenly the calm, warm air was slashed through by what sounded like at least five sirens. Lee walked back into his office and looked out onto Green Street again. One police car whizzed past him, three others were coming out of the car park behind Forest Gate Police Station. Lee frowned. Maybe he'd been too quick to think that terrorist outrages in London were a thing of the past.

'Who are you?'

Mumtaz knew she couldn't own up to being who and what she

was. Lee had always taught her *If things get dangerous, you're any-thing but a PI.* If Abdullah Khan found out she was a private detec-tive, who knew how he would react? Especially if he realised that she had at one time been investigating him.

'My name is Habiba Anwar,' she said.

Abdullah Khan narrowed his eyes. 'I know you from some-where,' he said.

'I'm a friend of Nasreen,' Mumtaz said.

'She doesn't have any friends,' he said.

'She did have . . .'

'Before me?' He pointed the gun at her and smiled. 'I ruined her life.'

'Oh Abdullah, you didn't,' Nasreen said. The urgency in her voice told Mumtaz that on some level, although she clearly hated him too, she meant it. It was a trait that she recognised. Abdullah Khan motioned to Mumtaz to move. 'Sit on the bed.'

Still down on the floor with Nasreen, she didn't move. The ambulance siren had been quickly followed by other, slightly dif-ferent sirens that she suspected were the police. Abdullah Khan had shot a window out which the paramedics had to have both heard and seen. It had been difficult not to. But whatever the truth was, they hadn't even attempted to gain access to the house. Yet. Why had Khan done that? Had he just simply done it out of anger?

'Sit on the bed.'

'Your wife . . .'

'Just do as I tell you!' The shrieking of orders was as familiar to Mumtaz as his manipulation and violence. As Mumtaz rose and moved slowly towards the bed she fought to keep her loathing from her face.

He went to the window, looked out and then went back to the

bedroom door. Briefly his hand hovered over a CD player on a nightstand but then he seemed to change his mind about it. Not once did he even so much as glance at his wife.

'Nasreen told me that you went out to get antibiotics for her,' Mumtaz said, as she sat down on the Khans' bed. 'I think that she needs them now.'

'She can have them for *iftar*,' he said. He pointed to her handbag. 'Got a phone in there?'

'Yes,' Mumtaz said.

'Give it to me.'

She put her hand in her bag and took out her iPhone. He snatched it from her, threw it to the floor and then ground his heel into its screen.

'Your wife needs antibiotics now,' she said.

'She can wait for *iftar*.'

Mumtaz felt a cold prickling of her skin. 'Pregnant women and sick people don't fast during Ramadan,' she said. 'She is both.'

'She keeps Ramadan,' he said.

The similarities between Abdullah Khan and her dead husband Ahmet were racking up. He too had insisted they all keep the fast while at night he drank alcohol and sexually abused both her and Shazia. He'd known nothing of Islam and this man was the same. Such people were all about public show, while privately doing as they pleased because they were 'men'. Mumtaz said, 'That is ridiculous.' Then she looked at him. 'You are ridiculous. And why did you shoot a window out, eh Mr Khan? Is it because you're stupid?'

He darted forward like a snake and jammed the muzzle of the pistol into one of her temples. 'You dare to speak to me . . .'

'Oh, don't shoot her, please don't shoot her!' Nasreen screamed.

*

A bloke called Will had called them out. He was a paramedic from Newham General.

'I heard the shot,' he said. 'Then I saw a bloke at the top window with a gun.'

Vi Collins, Tony Bracci, and the paramedic team that had originally been called out to Nasreen Khan were in the house of a Mrs Janwari who lived opposite the couple. Mrs Janwari, an elderly widow, gave out cups of tea and bustled about making sure that everyone was comfortable.

'The patient's called Nasreen Khan, she's twenty-seven, eight and a half months pregnant and suffering from suspected septicaemia,' Will said.

Vi took notes. The house opposite was familiar. Lee Arnold had asked her about its history. It was where nuts old Eric Smith the recluse had once lived, and where an alleged employee of Sean Rogers, Abdullah Khan, now resided with his wife.

'Did Nasreen Khan call you out herself?' Vi asked.

'No.' Will looked down at his notes. 'That was a Mrs Hakim,' he said.

Vi felt her heart jump in her chest. Mumtaz. But then Hakim was a common enough name, she shouldn't rush to conclusions. 'Any first name for Mrs Hakim?' she asked Will.

He looked at his paperwork again. 'Nah.'

Although Lee's firm had had some involvement with Nasreen Khan some months back, Vi's understanding was that all that was over. She wondered why Mumtaz would be in that house now. If she was in that house.

'Thanks Mr Ross,' she said to Will. She'd have to call Lee Arnold anyway, just to be sure.

Vi picked up her phone, stood up and was just about to go outside to make a call when Mrs Janwari said, 'Oh, I know the name of the Hakim lady. I saw her knocking on the door of the Khans' house. She broke a window in their door, it was most strange. Her name is Mumtaz, she is quite a famous lady around here. A private detective, you know, a Muslim.'

Vi stared at her. 'You sure it's Mumtaz, Mrs Janwari,' she said. 'Yes.'

Tony Bracci raised his eyebrows.

Vi went out into the old woman's garden and wondered how she was going to tell Lee. Then she made the call.

He picked up almost immediately. 'Arnold Agency.'

'Lee . . .'

'Vi.'

She took a breath. 'Lee, I'm across the road from old Eric Smith's house in Strone Road. Couple called Khan live there now.'

'Yeah, that was the house that . . .'

'We think Mumtaz is in there with the wife . . .'

'Nasreen Khan.'

'Yeah, and the husband an' all,' Vi said. She took a breath. 'And Lee, he's armed.'

There was a long pause. She knew he wasn't one to panic. He was absorbing the information. Clearly Mumtaz wasn't with him or he would have just laughed. He said, 'Explains the sirens I heard. I'm coming.'

'Far end of Strone's blocked off,' Vi said. 'We've got two SCO19 ARVs in place, the Plashet Cemetery's full of coppers and we've got Venus at the scene.'

'Mumtaz is my employee,' he said calmly. 'And I'm ex-job. I'm coming.'

She heard a click as he ended the call. She went back in to Mrs Janwari's house and pulled Tony Bracci to one side. 'Lee Arnold's on his way down here,' she said.

'So it is his Mumtaz.'

'Yeah.'

'Venus wants this end of Strone completely evacuated,' Tony Bracci said.

'Where's he now?'

'Upstairs in the bog.'

'Get out and meet Arnold at the junction with Shrewsbury Road,' Vi said. He'd be coming from Green Street and so he'd have to cross Shrewsbury to get into Strone.

As if reassuring himself that he'd be okay out on the street, even with a gunman on the loose, Tony Bracci tightened his Kevlar vest around his middle. It also served to remind Vi that if Lee Arnold was coming onto the scene he should have one too. As Bracci made to walk out of the room she said, 'And get a vest off SCO19 for Lee Arnold. He might like to think he's immortal but I know better.'

'Guv.'

Tony Bracci walked out just as Superintendent Venus came down the stairs. He'd overheard their conversation and his face did not express approval.

'This is your old friend ex-DI Arnold?' he asked Vi.

'His business partner is in the house with the suspected gunman, sir.'

'And so you think that an ex-police officer who only knows one of the potential victims is an appropriate person to invite to this scene?'

'Yes, sir.'

'Well, I don't,' he said.

Vi saw the paramedics through the open living room door and she lowered her voice. 'Lee Arnold and Mumtaz Hakim did some work on finding out the history of the Khans' house a few months ago,' she said. 'They know the wife, Nasreen Khan. They know of the husband, Abdullah, who could be an employee of Sean and Marty Rogers.'

'Rogers and Ali?'

'Yes, sir.'

She thought she saw him shudder. Bad memories of the previous Saturday.

'I think we may be able to find out a bit more about the Khans from Lee,' she said. 'He could be very useful.'

He wore his 'doubtful' face.

'He's on his way, sir,' Vi said. 'I suggest we wait and see what he's got to say when he gets here.'

He took a moment and then he said, 'Alright.' Then he looked in at the paramedics. 'Are they staying?'

'They want to, yes, sir,' Vi said.

He sighed. 'Well, let's get this lady and her neighbours away from here at least.'

28

Abdullah moved the pistol away from Mumtaz's head and then shoved her so that she toppled over onto the bed. As she sat up, Mumtaz adjusted her headscarf and said, 'If you don't let Nasreen have antibiotics your baby will die. Do you want that, Mr Khan?'

He didn't say anything for a good minute. Things were happening down in the street – cars pulling up, the sound of running feet, the occasional crackle of a radio.

Mumtaz watched his face. Things had happened in ways that he hadn't anticipated and could not have wanted. And even though she knew that Abdullah Khan worked for the Rogers brothers in some capacity, Mumtaz didn't know what he did or why he would have a firearm. And why *had* he used it – on a window? She looked down at Nasreen, who was weeping now, and she wondered about what she'd said in relation to the war veteran who'd been found dead in the cemetery all those months ago. Had Abdullah Khan really killed John Sawyer because he was jealous of him? Sawyer had been a tramp, how could anyone be jealous of someone like that? But then her own husband had been jealous of everybody. She still remembered the day he had told the milkman never to come to their house again.

'Get her some water,' Abdullah Khan said. 'There's a glass in the bathroom.'

Mumtaz stood up. Abdullah pointed his gun at his wife's head. 'Try to leave and I'll kill her,' he said.

'And kill your own child?' She started walking past him, towards the bathroom.

'There's more than that at stake here,' he said.

Mumtaz stopped. 'What?' And then she looked around the bedroom and pointed at the walls. 'What's at stake, Mr Khan? Is it something to do with this house?'

He stared at her for a moment and then he said, 'Get the water and then my wife can take her antibiotics.'

Mumtaz went into the bathroom whose walls were pitted with holes big and small, some of which showed water pipes beneath. She took a dirty glass from the side of the sink and washed it. Then she filled it with water and walked back into the bedroom. As she entered she heard Nasreen say, 'What can be more important than our baby, Abdullah? Tell me.'

But he didn't. He put a tablet into Mumtaz's hand and said coldly, 'Give it to her.'

Families – whirls of mothers and babies, kids with toy guns, teenagers playing on games consoles, grannies, rough sorts in combat trousers and a typhoon of saris – escorted by police officers made their way round the Police Do Not Cross tape and the police cars that sealed Strone Road off from Shrewsbury Road and formed an orderly crocodile going somewhere. Lee saw Tony Bracci beyond the tape and called out to him. Tony beckoned him forwards.

Lee passed two white women in tight fitting T-shirts talking in a language he couldn't understand. He pushed past them, a couple of kids and a bloke with a tattoo of a dragon on his neck until he eventually got to Tony. For a moment neither of them talked, but looked at the eastern stretch of Strone Road. There were two armed response vehicles in the middle of the street. Crouched behind them on the northern side of the road were pairs of heavily Kevlared, helmeted and armed SCO19 officers.

Tony put an arm on Lee's shoulder. 'Here,' he said handing him a Kevlar vest. Automatically Lee opened it up and pulled it over his chest. They walked towards the cars and, as they got close, one of the SCO19 officers stood up and aimed his weapon at the windows of the Khans' house while Lee and Tony went inside Mrs Janwari's house opposite.

The old woman had gone now and her front sitting room was occupied by DI Vi Collins, Superintendent Venus and a man who looked like *Robocop*. Luckily, Lee had seen such officers before.

'This is SFO Dalton,' Vi told Lee. Then she looked at *Robocop* and said, 'Jim, this is ex-DI, now PI, Lee Arnold.'

The two men shook hands. Dalton said, 'You work with one of the hostages.'

'Yeah.' Lee turned to Vi and said, 'I tried to call Mumtaz on her mobile but it just rang out.'

Superintendent Venus, who had only worked with Lee for the last six months of his career in the police, said, 'Please sit down, Mr Arnold.'

Lee sat down in a soft armchair that was covered in wine-red velour.

'Mr Arnold, we think that your assistant and a woman called Nasreen Khan are in the house opposite with an armed man, who we believe is Mrs Khan's husband, Abdullah,' Venus said. 'The lady who lives in this house, Mrs Janwari, saw a woman she named as Mumtaz Hakim go into that house at approximately 10.45.' He looked down at his notebook. 'Then at approximately 11.05 a man

Mrs Janwari identified as Nasreen Khan's husband Abdullah arrived and let himself into the house. Mrs Janwari didn't see the ambulance, which Mrs Hakim had called for Mrs Khan, arrive ten minutes later, but the paramedics' TOA was 11.15. Can you tell me why Mrs Hakim went to visit Mrs Khan please, Mr Arnold?'

'I don't know,' Lee said. 'As far as I knew, Mumtaz went to the post office.'

'When was that?'

'About twenty past ten.'

'The post office on Green Street?'

'Yeah.'

'So weren't you concerned when she hadn't returned to your office – which I understand is also on Green Street – over an hour later?'

'Not really,' Lee said. 'I asked her to get stamps in the full knowledge that she'd probably look in some shops along the way for a while. She's a Muslim and it's Ramadan, she has to take her mind off food and drink somehow. She says she doesn't mind if I eat in front of her and I was eating a cream cake when she arrived this morning. But I was still hungry after I'd finished it. I'll be honest, I asked her to get stamps so she could go out and I could eat more cakes. We both knew what was going on.' Then he frowned. 'What's all this about firearms? Are the women hostages or what? What's the score?'

'Someone, we think Abdullah Khan, fired two shots, one of which broke a front bedroom window, out into Strone Road at about 11.18. Paramedic William Connor called it in and we responded with support from SCO19. No demands have been made by Khan so far, who has yet to make contact, and so the status of the two women is still unknown. Now DI Collins tells me that you know something about the Khans, Mr Arnold.'

'Nasreen Khan first came to us back in the spring,' he said. 'She wanted Mumtaz to find out who had lived in that house over there before her husband bought it. She'd found a mezuzah, a sort of a capsule with a prayer in it that Jews put on their doorposts. But this one had a photograph of a woman behind it. We found out that a Jewish woman who had been in Belsen concentration camp had once lived there with her English husband, but all that was by the by because later on Nasreen Khan asked Mumtaz to investigate her husband's background. Mumtaz felt that the husband was really what Nasreen had wanted investigated right from the start.'

'The mezuzah and the photograph were just an excuse?'

'Maybe. Although I think that Nasreen was genuinely interested in who'd lived in her house too.'

'What about the husband? What did you find out about him?' SFO Dalton asked. For him, a firearms officer, it was all about the man with the gun.

'Mumtaz did some digging and then I filled in a few gaps,' Lee said. 'Khan comes from an Asian family in Lancashire, where he said he did a law degree at Manchester University. That much we think is correct, but then it all gets a bit hazy. According to Nasreen Khan, her husband was a practising solicitor working for a reputable local company. Turned out he never qualified and he was working for Rogers and Ali.'

Venus looked over at Vi Collins who met his gaze with steady eyes. The abortive raid on Sean Rogers's house in Ongar still sat between them like an open sore. Neither of them so much as dared touch it. But both of them knew all too well that a shot had been fired by an unknown attendee at that party. Could that man have been Abdullah Khan?

'What Khan does or did for Sean and Marty Rogers, we never

got to,' Lee said. 'Mrs Khan refused to believe what we'd dug up and that seemed to be the end of that.'

'But you say you don't know why Mrs Hakim went to visit Nasreen Khan this morning?' Venus asked.

Lee shrugged. 'No. We'd recently had a bit more intel on the Jewish family who used to live in the house from an old bloke I know from the Boleyn pub. But my understanding from Mumtaz was that she wasn't going to pass that on to Nasreen Khan. She believed Abdullah Khan was the jealous type, know what I mean?'

'Do you think, Mr Arnold, that Abdullah Khan might be jealous enough to do his wife or others harm?' Venus asked.

'I don't know,' Lee said, 'I've never met him, and I don't think Mumtaz ever did until now. Like I said, Superintendent, I don't know what he does for Sean and Marty Rogers. For all I know he could clean out their swimming pool or chauffeur Debbie Rogers about when she's out on the piss. But then again he could be one of their enforcers, employed to terrorise their tenants. He could be dangerous, so I think it's important that we don't tell him who Mumtaz is. She won't have told him, that I do know. I train all my staff to protect their identities. As far as I'm aware, he never knew his wife was having him investigated and we want to keep it that way.'

'I understand.'

A crackle, followed by a voice from the radio that Dalton had been holding on his knee, stopped Lee in his tracks and they all watched while the Special Firearms Officer held it up to his ear. Once the speaking had finished, Dalton said, 'OK, on way.' Then he stood up. 'Somebody's come to the top bedroom window with a woman,' he said.

*

He held her jaws shut with one hand while, with the other, he jammed the muzzle of the gun against her head. 'Say one word and I'll blow your brains out,' Abdullah Khan said to Mumtaz.

On the bedroom floor behind, Nasreen rocked from side to side in agony. There was now some movement in her abdomen, so she said, and she felt as if she could be going into labour.

Abdullah opened the largest of the bedroom windows and Mumtaz saw two police cars plus at least eight officers in Kevlar vests down in the street below. Most of them held guns and all of them were trained on the window she was being pulled through.

'No-one'll get hurt provided you do as I say,' Abdullah shouted into the street.

The front door of the house opposite opened and a man in uniform emerged. Mumtaz felt the fear shoot through Abdullah Khan's body and he shrieked, 'Who's that?'

The man, a tall, middle-aged person in police uniform, called up, using a megaphone. 'My name's Superintendent Paul Venus,' he said. 'What's your name?'

'That's not important,' Abdullah said.

'I have to call you something.'

Mumtaz felt his pulse as it pounded through his hand and against her neck. He breathed hard twice and then he said, 'Call me Mursel.'

Mumtaz remembered that had been his father's name.

'Mursel it is then,' Venus said. 'Mursel, you have two ladies with you. I can see one of them now. Are both the ladies fit and in good health?'

'Yes.' He didn't miss a beat. Liar, Mumtaz thought, Nasreen is almost hallucinating she's in so much pain.

'Because the paramedic team who were called out earlier say

that one of the ladies might be pregnant and she might have septicaemia. Would it be possible for one of the medics to just look at—'

Abdullah ignored him. 'I wanna get to Heathrow,' he said. 'I want to fly to Dhaka.'

'Let's do some talking first, Mursel, shall we?' Venus said.

'I don't wanna talk. I want you to organise a flight for me to Bangladesh.'

'Yes, but we have to talk about that, make arrangements between us.'

Abdullah didn't reply.

'Do you have a phone there, Mursel?' Venus said. 'If I could call you on your phone I wouldn't have to shout and we could talk whenever you wanted to.'

There was a pause. Abdullah made little noises in his throat that sounded to Mumtaz like confusion. Then he said, 'Alright, but I'll need a minute to sort myself out.'

'That's fine,' Venus said. 'Take your time. You can ring me if you like. Shall I give you my number now?'

Mumtaz felt him take his hand away from her mouth and push her back inside the room. Then, one-handed, he searched his jacket pockets for a pen and something to write on. He pointed the gun at her head and said, 'Come here and take down this number.'

She walked forwards and picked up the pen.

'What's the number?' Abdullah shouted down into the street.

Mumtaz wrote it down. Then Abdullah shouted, 'I'll call you,' and closed the window.

On the floor, Nasreen whimpered, 'I think the baby's coming.'

*

Lee looked at his watch. It was nearly two-thirty, and still no further word from Abdullah Khan. Venus, who was a trained hostage negotiator, paced the floor of Mrs Janwari's living room. News about the Strone Road incident would be leaking out into the borough and beyond by this time. It was then that Lee remembered Shazia. It was the school holidays and she was either out with her friends or at home. Unless they were lucky and wrapped up the siege before nightfall, she'd have to be told and taken to Mumtaz's parents' house in Tower Hamlets.

'You know her well and so maybe you and Tone should go and pick her up,' Vi said when he told her.

'I'll ring her.'

While Lee rang Shazia, Vi spoke to Venus. 'Sir, if Khan is employed by Rogers and Ali, shouldn't we tap them up? If I know Sean and Marty they won't want this kind of trouble. I saw Sean's face when he heard that shot outside his house on Saturday night.'

Venus frowned. 'And what would we say to the Rogers brothers, do you think, DI Collins?'

'We can tell them that one of their employees has gone postal,' she said. 'They've a right to know.'

'Mmm.' He was doubtful. 'I don't want them contacting him. That won't help.'

'No, but sir, Sean and Marty should know Abdullah Khan better than anyone else we can get access to, and they won't want any bother. You know how they are. They'll give us chapter and verse if they think it'll benefit them in any way.'

Lee got off the phone. 'Shazia's at home,' he said.

'OK.' Vi turned back to Venus. 'DS Bracci could go with Mr Arnold to take Mrs Hakim's daughter to her grandparents' place while I tap up Sean and Marty,' she said. Venus sighed, and then nodded his head. 'Alright,' he said. 'But DI Collins, do not suggest for a moment that the gun Khan has might have come from the Rogers brothers.'

29

He'd heard about the ruin of an old hospital at Upton Park via a blog on the Internet. The blogger, known as Mother's Ruin, was some hipster photographer who sold prints of her Polaroids via a poncey shop on Spitalfields Market. But Gerry didn't care. He just went wherever the ruins took him, and his photographs – which were very carefully set up – were only for the enjoyment of himself and his friends. Posh people like Mother's Ruin were just trying to make money; Gerry, on the other hand, was all about preserving a London that was rapidly disappearing.

When he'd got off the tube at Upton Park he'd noticed there was a kind of excited frisson in the air, as if something amazing or awful was happening somewhere close by. But as soon as he'd left Green Street and, in line with Mother's Ruin's instructions, turned left down Walton Road and into Credon Road he'd forgotten all about that.

The old hospital, which had been called both Samson Street and Plaistow Hospital in its time, was on an island in the middle of four roads: Western Road, Credon Road, Bushey Road and Southern Road. But that wasn't really what he was interested in.

Gerry walked around the perimeter of the hospital until he came to the entrance on Western Road. Knotted with weeds and trailing ivy, the old gates were protected by rolls of barbed wire, but Gerry noticed that one of the rolls had been moved to one side. Maybe God or whoever was smiling down on him after all.

Moving a metal strut that had once been part of the main gate to one side, Gerry folded himself through the gap and then stood upright on a thick tangle of weeds. Pleased with himself, he took his camera out and began looking through the viewfinder for potentially interesting angles. There were fascinating bits and pieces everywhere – gateposts, tiles from the hospital roof, old dustbins, a generator shed – and also what looked like a red ribbon, which led off into a knot of thicker vegetation further towards the hospital. Gerry decided to follow it.

Then he saw her. At first she looked like some sort of 1960s mannequin in her mini-skirt, with her hair all bouffed up into a beehive like Amy Winehouse. Lying on the ground as she was, if Gerry hadn't seen that she didn't have a face, he would have thought that maybe she was just having a sleep. Instead, the shock of the look of her made him wet his pants.

'Was Abdullah Khan at your party in Ongar on Saturday night?' Vi asked Sean and Marty Rogers. They were in what they considered their 'local', the pub across the road from East Ham tube station. When Vi had called them they'd suggested they meet there rather than in their office on High Street South, which was, so they said, being 'done up.' They clearly feared the production of a warrant, but this time it wasn't about them.

'No, DI Collins, I don't recall that he was,' Sean said.

Vi looked at Marty.

'Can't remember Paul being there, love.'

'Paul?'

Marty smiled. It looked to Vi a bit like the particularly

unpleasant grimace a snake makes just before it strikes. 'Sometimes he calls hisself Paul, depending where we are.' Marty said. 'We have some Jewish business associates and they don't like the Muslim thing much these days, know what I mean?'

Vi ignored him. 'Where was he?'

Sean shrugged. 'I dunno,' he said. 'At home with his missus?'

'What does Abdullah Khan, or Paul, do for you? What's his job?'

Again it was Sean who answered. 'Oh, well as you probably know, DI Collins, Abdullah did train as a lawyer even though he never completed his course.'

They were rightly assuming that she knew certain pieces of information about Khan. They hadn't even tried to deny that he worked for them. But then Sean and Marty were clever people.

'So he advises you on legal matters?'

'He does a bit of that – and a bit of this too,' Sean smiled. 'He's very useful at sorting out issues we sometimes have regarding tenancies.'

Vi leaned across the table that stood between her and them and said, 'He one of your enforcers, is he?'

'Do we need a brief, DI Collins?' Marty asked.

She shook her head. 'I ain't got time,' she said. Out of the corner of her eye, she clocked Marty's minder, Dave Spall. He looked even more miserable than usual.

'Abdullah does a bit of rent collecting, which I'll admit can get lively at times, but never on his part,' Sean said. Then he leaned towards Vi and smiled. 'We get some right scum in our places these days, DI Collins, but I never countenance violence.'

She ignored his last comment. 'What else does Khan do for you?'

'He looks over tenancy agreements, leases, things like that.'

'Don't you have a proper lawyer to do that for you?' Vi asked.

'What, the day-to-day stuff? We'd be bankrupt if we had to use a brief all the time. Do you know what they charge?' Marty said. 'No, Abdullah's a good lad, a jack of all trades with a legal edge. We're sorry to hear he's not himself. But it's nothing to do with us. Can't think why he might have lost it. We've only ever tried to help the lad.'

'We bought that house for him,' Sean said.

'But he has to pay you back.'

'Oh, we have a business arrangement, yes,' Sean said. 'But that's how much we like him. We gave him the money to buy that house for him and his wife.'

And then a look passed between the two of them that Vi just couldn't read. She wondered if either or both of them planned to add anything to what had just been said and she thought that maybe at least one of them did. It was something about lending Abdullah money for that house, but Vi was fucked if she knew what. Then nothing more beyond niceties were said and shortly afterwards she left.

On her way out of the pub, however, she did just stop to have a brief word with Dave Spall.

'How's Magda?' she asked. That was the name that he'd given her as that of his latest girlfriend.

Dave looked up and said, 'Who?'

One-handed, Abdullah Khan sorted through a small sports bag full of phones. Mumtaz squatted on the floor beside Nasreen who, it now seemed, had not yet gone into labour – but it wouldn't be long before she did. Still Abdullah held the gun out in front of him, pointing at her head.

'You know I'm not going to leave Nasreen like this,' she said to him. 'So you might as well put that down.'

He ignored her, and continued training his gun on her. Then he found what he was looking for in the bag. It was an old Nokia 3310 mobile phone. He switched it on. A million miles away from the probably very flashy number he normally used, Mumtaz reasoned he was using this phone to call the police in order to keep up the fiction of 'Mursel'. It had been hours since he'd spoken to that police officer out of the window and Mumtaz wondered how the police were interpreting his silence.

He walked over to the windowsill and punched the number that Mumtaz had taken down for him into the old phone. Then he rang it and he said, 'It's me, this is my number.' And then he hung up.

Mumtaz saw him look at the walls and run the pistol down the exposed plaster. He looked at her. 'Do you know how to use a hammer?' he said.

'Of course.'

'I need you to do some labouring for me.'

'Knocking yet more holes in your walls, Mr Khan,' she said. 'What are you looking for in this house?'

And then, just for a moment, he laughed. 'If I told you, darlin', you'd never believe me.'

'Try me.' Nasreen had dropped into a fitful sleep and so Mumtaz stood up.

Abdullah Khan shook his head. 'Nah.'

'Up to you,' she said. 'But if you want me to work for you, I have to know what I'm looking for. If I don't, then how will I know if I've found it?'

He looked into her eyes. She could see that he knew she was right, but he was having a problem letting her into whatever secret he held so close. Did he, she wondered, like her, suspect that the police might be listening in to their conversations?

'I'll watch you,' he said eventually. 'I'll know when you find it.'

Lee and Tony returned to headquarters at Mrs Janwari's house. Shazia, now safely in the care of Mumtaz's parents, had wanted to come back with them but that, she'd been told, was impossible. They'd left her in tears, which Lee had found hard. Of course the kid was worried sick about her mother, but being in the line of fire herself wasn't going to help.

'She had a bank card on her in the name of Wendy Dixon,' Superintendent Venus told Vi Collins.

Lee, who had just walked through the door, said, 'Wendy Dixon? I know her. What's she done?'

'She's dead, Lee,' Vi said baldly. Her face was grey and looked heavily lined in the gloomy light of Mrs Janwari's living room.

'SOCO have been despatched,' Venus said. 'All we know at the moment is that the victim is female, possesses a bank card in the name of Wendy Dixon and she's been shot.'

They all looked at each other: Lee, Vi, Venus and Tony. Only Lee voiced what at least he and Vi were thinking, which was, 'Wendy Dixon worked as a Tom for the Rogers brothers.'

Vi narrowed her eyes. 'Could've known Abdullah Khan?'

'He's got a gun.'

'I'd be surprised if Sean and Marty didn't have guns somewhere too,' Vi said.

'Knowing Sean and Marty they're probably well hidden though, guv,' Tony said.

'Ballistic analysis will confirm the calibre of the weapon used to kill the woman and then compare it to the bullet we removed from the wall of Sean Rogers's house,' Venus said. 'In the meantime, Khan has finally made contact. We must now consider the women he is holding hostage and get food and drink to them. One of the women is pregnant. And even if Khan won't let her be treated medically we must ensure that she receives nourishment.'

Lee went over to one of the windows and looked up at the sky. 'Not dark yet, Superintendent,' he said. 'No point.'

'Oh, yeah it's Ramadan,' Vi said. 'But aren't pregnant women allowed to eat?'

'Yeah, you're right,' Lee said.

'I'll phone Khan now.' Venus turned aside to make the call while Vi, Lee and Tony went into the hall.

'So we just keep on turning up the Rogers brothers,' Lee said.

'Dave Spall, Marty's minder, was at the Rogers' favourite pub when I got there,' Vi said. 'I asked him about one of the girls at that house where my snout lived. The girl, Magda, was supposed to be his girlfriend but he didn't know who she was. He was going with my snout, Tatiana, I know it. But Gawd knows where she is now.'

'Gone ahead of Wendy Dixon, guv.'

'Maybe, but we have to prove it, don't we, Tone and with no body . . .'

'Maybe Dave Spall's a way in,' Lee said.

'How do you mean?'

'Well, Sean and Marty have always treated him like shit and if they *have* disposed of a girl that he was keen on . . .'

'Lee, love, Sean and Marty Rogers kill people who betray them,' Vi said. 'Dave's been with them two since school, as you know. What's gonna make him dob them in now, eh?'

Lee said nothing.

'Dave's got a kid over in Hackney,' Vi said. 'Sean and Marty'll know where. As they have with everyone, they've got Dave by the bollocks and he knows it. No, we have to get a connection, direct or otherwise, between Sean and Marty and something tangible. Wendy Dixon knew Tatiana, she told me herself, but with her gone . . .'

Venus, off the phone now, came into the hall. 'Khan is insisting they don't receive food and drink until the sun has set,' he said.

Lee shook his head. Nasreen Khan aside, Mumtaz struggled with the Ramadan fast anyway and after the day she'd had she'd be parched and weak and he was worried about her.

Venus looked at Vi. 'Get food organised with a local halal restaurant,' he said.

'Sir.'

'I'm going to go and speak to the neighbours who live on the left hand side of the Khans' property,' he continued. At present all the residents of the eastern section of Strone Road were holed up in the hall of Monega Primary School. He looked at Lee and said, 'I need to have ears in there now.'

The first time that Mumtaz hit the bedroom wall with the hammer Khan had given her, Nasreen woke up.

'What's going on?'

Abdullah Khan didn't even look at her. Instead he said to Mumtaz, who had stopped, 'Carry on. What are you waiting for?'

Mumtaz didn't move. 'Nasreen,' she said, 'she can't sleep through this.'

Abdullah raised his gun level with her head again. 'Do as you're told,' he said.

Mumtaz shook her head, but she did as he asked her. Weak

though she was, she found that once she got into a rhythm with the hammer she could make good progress. Old, brittle plaster flew off the wall with comparative ease revealing sometimes brick, sometimes wood or cladding or cavities behind. Every so often he would tell her to stop and then he would sort through the detritus on the floor and minutely investigate the section of wall that had just been attacked. Whenever he did this, when Mumtaz stopped to catch her breath, she could hear the sound of Nasreen crying. Whether it was out of distress or pain she didn't know, but just by the look of her it was clear that she wasn't in labour which was the main thing.

'Alright, go on.' Having looked and found nothing, Abdullah told Mumtaz to smash the wall again. She pulled her arm backwards and wished that she had the strength and the speed to run towards him and bash his skull in. But her eyes were barely focusing and her mouth and throat, starved of water, were so dry. She struck the wall.

Quite how many times Mumtaz belted that wall, she didn't know. But every time he looked and found nothing Khan became more agitated. At first he'd just looked nervous and run his fingers through his hair. But then, as time went on he became more vocal, muttering 'Fuck it!' underneath his breath and then, later still, shouting the same thing at the ceiling.

Mumtaz looked through the bedroom window and wondered if the darkness she was seeing outside was in fact real or just an hallucination brought on by stress, hunger and fear.

'Get on with it!' He shook her elbow and then rammed the muzzle of the gun against the side of her head.

Mumtaz moved her tongue to try and make some saliva and then she said, 'What are you looking for, Mr Khan? What is so important . . .'

He flicked her head with the gun and then said, 'We haven't got time for this! Work!'

But she couldn't. Her arms ached, her stomach growled and she felt dizzy. Still she made an attempt to do what he wanted, but as she drew her arm back to strike the wall again she fell over backwards onto the floor. 'What are you looking for?' she said weakly. 'What?'

He pulled her to her feet by the collar of her jacket and stood her up against the side of the bed. Then he put his face close to hers and he said, 'I'm looking for my only way out of here.'

'And what's that, Mr Khan?' There were strange fairy-like wisps on the periphery of her vision now. Abdullah Khan opened his mouth to speak.

A ring on the doorbell downstairs momentarily caught his attention. What she heard him say next, however, was to be imprinted on her mind for a long, long time to come.

'I'm looking for diamonds,' he said. 'Great big diamonds that once belonged to Jews in this house.'

30

Sumita Huq did what she usually did in times of trouble, she cooked. What she cooked was immaterial and so the food that she produced that night was completely random.

What was becoming known as the Siege of Strone Road had made not only the local but also the national news. Shazia, who had entirely lost her appetite, looked at the pictures of police cars in the middle of an East Ham street with big, horrified eyes.

'What can Amma have been doing there?' she asked no-one in particular.

Baharat, Mumtaz's father, toyed with a date and then put it back down on the tray in the middle of the coffee table again. 'Well, as Mr Arnold says, she was going to give the lady in that house some information,' he said. Then he added, 'I rather like Mr Arnold.'

But Shazia just stared at the screen, watching as a police officer took a tray of food to the front door of the house. She moved close up to the screen to try and see who came to the door to take the food, but the pictures were too blurry. A reporter kept on saying the words 'armed siege' which made Shazia feel sick.

As much to distract herself from what was going on in East Ham as anything else, Shazia said to Baharat, 'Do you think that Amma will be alright?'

She feared that he would come up with a load of stuff she

didn't believe about Allah – as her Amma would have done – but he just said, 'I don't know.'

Shazia looked at him. Baharat Huq was a religious man who prayed five times a day, abstained from alcohol and loved Allah, but in this case it was very clear that he didn't know what to do or say. When he did finally speak, however, he said, 'We must have faith,' as he stroked Shazia's hair.

Annoyed that religion seemed to be on the agenda again, Shazia knocked his hand away and said, 'Faith? Faith in what? Allah? My Amma is being held prisoner by a madman, what should I have faith in? Tell me.'

But Baharat just smiled and shrugged, and then he said, 'Have faith in whatever it is that works for you. Have faith in your Amma, my daughter.'

And then she saw just a tiny bit of moisture leak out of one of his eyes. She put her hand up to his face. 'Oh, I'm so . . .'

He took her hand in his and smiled. 'Don't be sorry,' he said to her. 'You are young and you are worried too. But have faith in my daughter, Shazia, we both know that she has never let you down.'

'There are four of them.'

Mumtaz noticed Abdullah Khan's ecstatic expression, while she held the mug containing plain lassi up to Nasreen's mouth. It was the first time she had seen his face express anything other than hatred, fear or contempt.

'Four pink diamonds,' Abdullah said. 'Or, actually, they are pink purple, which is the most uncommon and valuable colour that a diamond can be. Three are one carat, one is two. Can you imagine what they're worth?'

Grateful that Nasreen continued to have the sense not to reveal her real identity, Mumtaz put the lassi down and then fed her a little dhal.

'How do you know that these pink diamonds belonged to Jews?' Mumtaz asked. 'How do you know they even exist?'

But he ignored her questions and just said, 'When I find them, everything will be alright. They have to be worth a quarter of a million, easily. That's all I need.'

'Need for what?'

But this time he just stared at her. In her mind Mumtaz went over the known history of that house. Lily Smith, who had been Berkowicz née Kaminski, had come to the UK with her son Marek and nothing else. She'd almost died in Belsen, but Reg Smith rescued her and her child. That pink diamonds should have come to the house in Strone Road via Lily had to be impossible, but Lily had a sister, Sara Kaminski, who had somehow avoided transportation to the death camps. Had Sara Kaminski used her jeweller father's stock to buy her way to freedom? That was the story, but what wasn't the story, as far as Mumtaz knew, was that Sara Kaminski had somehow still had some very precious jewels when she'd come to England back in the 1950s. That had to be very unlikely – surely the Nazis would have taken them? And what was even more mysterious was what this had to do with Abdullah Khan, an Asian thirty-something from Bolton.

Mumtaz tore off a piece of chapatti and popped it into her mouth. 'How do you know about these diamonds?' she asked.

He looked at her, took a sip of water from one of the bottles the police had given them and said, 'That's not your business.'

'I think it is if I'm looking for them,' she said.

He aimed his gun at her face. Mumtaz shrugged, then looked down at Nasreen and said, 'Time for another antibiotic.'

Nasreen took the tablet with water and without complaint, then lay back on her pillows. Mumtaz asked her how she felt.

'Tired,' she said.

'In pain?'

'A bit.' She tried to sit up a little and Mumtaz helped her. 'But the baby isn't moving now,' she said. 'I'm so worried.'

Mumtaz didn't know what to say. Nothing she could say could possibly reassure Nasreen. So she looked at Abdullah Khan instead. In spite of his wife's distress he was completely impassive.

Only Vi and the Super listened in. Lee, Tony and a constable sat on chairs they'd brought up from the kitchen. The house next door to the Khans, which belonged to a single white man, was a rather *frou-frou* affair inside, with lots of frills and scallop decorations. Lee wasn't alone in thinking that the owner, whose bedroom they were now in, was probably gay, but nobody said anything – not because they were worried about what the others would think, but because Vi and Venus were listening, via the miracle of electronics, to what was going on in the bedroom next door. Just after the food had gone in, the banging which had made hearing anything impossible had stopped. Then they'd got voices.

After a while, Vi took her headphones off and handed them to Tony. She walked over to Lee. She whispered, 'Khan's talking about diamonds belonging to Jews hidden somewhere in the house. Know anything about that?'

'No,' he said. 'Except that Lily Smith, Reg's Jewish wife, was the daughter of a jeweller. And there was talk that her sister managed to escape the concentration camps by giving her old man's stock to the Nazis.'

'Is that true?'

'I dunno,' he said. 'But that was the sister, not Lily. She went back to Europe as far as I know.'

'We *are* in Europe, Arnold,' Vi said.

He rolled his eyes. They'd never agreed on this subject. She was a European and he just wasn't. 'On the mainland then,' he said. 'If the sister came here, then why leave diamonds hidden in that house? If she still had some, she might've given them to her sister, who hid them, I suppose. Old Reg Smith was fond of the sauce and if he'd got his hands on them . . .'

'You got any idea why Khan might know about it?' Vi asked.

'Not a scooby,' Lee said. 'Khan didn't come to London until Lily's son, Eric Smith, had been dead for years. What do you think?'

'I don't know either,' Vi said. 'But I do remember Eric and I know that the gossip around here was that he was hiding something in that house.'

'The body of Marek Berkowicz?'

'His half-brother, maybe,' she said. Then she shook her head. 'But the coppers scoured that house and its garden back in 1955. They found bugger all.'

They both went silent. The police had indeed taken the house on Strone Road apart in 1955. Marek Berkowicz had apparently evaporated. Then a thought struck Lee and he said, 'Here, do you know whether they had any of the old cemetery up when they dug the garden?'

'Not that I know of,' Vi said. 'I think they must've searched it, but I can't see why they'd do any more'n look for freshly turned earth or something. Anyway, there wasn't anything.'

'And the skeleton you found in there . . .'

'Was a woman,' Vi said. She shook her head. 'Sounds to me like Khan's losing it.'

And then the banging from the Khans' bedroom started again.

Once Mumtaz had made a big enough hole in the wall to satisfy Abdullah Khan she stood back and let him investigate it. Looking down at Nasreen on the floor, she couldn't bear her strained expression.

'Can't Nasreen lie down in another bedroom?' she asked. 'She can't sleep with all the—'

'No,' he said. Then he glanced back at the hole in the wall and added, 'Fuck! No, she needs to be where I can see her.'

Mumtaz saw that he was sweating and she said, 'Why are you so afraid of not finding these diamonds, Mr Khan?'

'I've told you,' he said, 'because my future depends on it. I owe some men some money.'

'Here, or where you come from?' she asked.

'What's it to you?' He crumbled some plaster between his fingers and mouthed the word 'cunt'.

'It matters to me because you keep threatening me with a gun,' Mumtaz said. 'Before you kill me, I'd like to know why.'

He looked at her, and for a moment she had the feeling that he might just have some understanding about her predicament. But then he said, 'Get battering that wall. We've got all the bits I haven't searched already to do tonight. That is if you're interested in carrying on living.'

'He has to mean the Rogers', don't he?' Vi said to Lee.

A pair of headphones had been purloined for Lee Arnold, 'so

he could also hear what was going on in the Khans' house. He shrugged. 'Who knows?' Then his face suddenly went red. 'He just threatened her. Bastard.' He shook his head. Anger wouldn't do him any good and it certainly wouldn't help Mumtaz. 'Do we have any idea about what he was up to in Bolton?'

The hammering stopped again and they all strained to hear what was being said on the other side of the wall.

A woman's voice that Lee recognised as Mumtaz said, 'What about going to Bangladesh, Mr Khan? Don't you want the police to arrange transport for you?'

There was a pause, and then Abdullah Khan said, 'I'm not going without the diamonds.'

'So you don't want to pay your debt to bad men . . .'

'What I want to do ain't none of your business!' he shouted. This was followed by what could have been the sound of a slap. Lee winced. He half rose to his feet and then sat down again.

'Don't hit her!' another female voice cried. Nasreen Khan.

'Shut up!' Then there was nothing until Abdullah Khan said, 'What would I want to go to Bangladesh for, eh?'

'Well, it's where your family . . .' Mumtaz began.

'Nobody over there wants me!' he said. 'Why would they want me? Eh?'

'Well, I don't know, I . . .'

'Well, shut the fuck up then!'

For a moment they all went silent. It was obvious that Abdullah Khan was becoming more agitated. Night had fallen and he had to be tired, but his thoughts were unclear now too. He'd told the police initially that he wanted transport to Heathrow and a flight to Bangladesh, and he'd implied that if that didn't happen he'd kill his hostages. But suddenly Bangladesh was no longer on the agenda. Suddenly he only seemed to have hatred for the place.

Where did he want to go and what did he really want to do with the mythical diamonds – if he ever found them?

The banging resumed. Lee said to Venus, 'He doesn't know what he wants.'

'I wonder if he ever did,' Venus replied. He looked at his watch. Khan hadn't made contact for nearly two hours.

Vi felt cold. The sound of the hammering bruised her nerves; so did the thought of Mumtaz smashing away at something that made her captor ever more angry every time she failed to reveal what he wanted to see. She thought too of Nasreen Khan, the man's wife. How was she?

The hammering stopped. There was a moment of utter silence and then the most terrifying scream. A woman's scream.

Liquid was suddenly everywhere. Without even looking at Abdullah Khan, Mumtaz ran across the room to Nasreen and took her in her arms. She looked up at what appeared to be the bemused face of her husband and said, 'Her waters have broken, we have to get her out of here.'

'So her . . .'

His phone rang, but he ignored it.

'She's going to go into labour!' Mumtaz shrieked. 'Didn't you ever go to any antenatal classes with her?'

He said nothing, his silence telling her everything that she needed to know.

Shaking now, he said, 'But if I let her go, then I lose one of my bargaining chips.'

'She's not a chip, Mr Khan,' Mumtaz said. 'She's a human being. What do you want to happen here? Do you want her to die on the floor in front of us? Do you want your child to die too?'

He said nothing. His phone stopped ringing and then started up again immediately.

'You'll still have me,' Mumtaz said. 'While you have me you still have one bargaining chip, right?'

He'd walked in on the women, clearly unprepared for Mumtaz's presence or her insistence upon staying with Nasreen. The arrival of the paramedics, who had then called the police, had to have stunned him. But why, if he hadn't known that he was going to be in any danger, had he come into that house with a gun in his jacket? Because he had entered the house with that gun, Mumtaz remembered it distinctly. And then, for no reason she could imagine, he'd fired off a round.

She looked down at Nasreen, whose face became very red and then she screamed again. 'Oh, it *hurts!*'

Mumtaz held her as the second contraction took hold of her and Nasreen's legs flopped open. Khan's phone stopped ringing.

'She'll have this baby whether you want her to or not, Mr Khan,' Mumtaz said. 'Now . . .'

He pointed the gun at her head and then took his phone out of his pocket. Nasreen, wet with amniotic fluid and sweat, looked up at him with terrified eyes. 'What's he doing?' she said. 'Who's he calling?'

Mumtaz continued to hold her. Then she heard Khan say, 'Venus? My wife is going into labour. I need you to come and get her – now.' Then there was a pause and he said, 'No, the other woman stays with me.' He looked across at Mumtaz and added, 'Isn't that right, Mrs Anwar?'

31

Shazia couldn't sleep. Her Amma's Amma had gone to bed hours ago, as had the old man, but she was glued to News 24. DS Bracci had offered them someone called a 'Family Liaison Officer' which Lee had urged them to take, but the old people had insisted they could look after their own. Shazia hadn't wanted some police officer about the place either if she was honest. But now she wasn't so sure.

Breaking news on the TV was that a woman had been taken away from the Strone Road siege house. She was thought to be a young woman who had gone into labour. Mrs Khan, not her Amma. Shazia watched as men with guns escorted two men with a stretcher on wheels up to the house and then waited for the front door to open. Briefly, she thought she saw her Amma's face, but then the camera followed the stretcher as it sped away from the door, towards a waiting ambulance. Its sirens screamed into the night as the police lifted their cordon to let it go through. Then there were just men with guns in the street again and the front of that terrible house, which had returned to stillness once again. The reporter doing the voiceover said that the woman was being taken to hospital. Shazia hoped that she and her baby would be alright. Then she offered up a prayer for them and for her Amma. It had been many years since she'd prayed. The last time had been for her own mother's soul.

'Who are you?' he asked.

Nasreen had gone now and Mumtaz was alone with her captor.

Abdullah Khan's phone rang, but he ignored it.

'My name is Habiba Anwar,' Mumtaz said. 'I told you.'

'What do you do?' Abdullah Khan, his eyes red with sleeplessness, sat on the edge of his bed and levelled the gun at Mumtaz's chest.

'I am a widow,' she said. 'I have a daughter.'

'So you don't work?'

'No.'

He stared into her eyes and Mumtaz returned his gaze without blinking. Abdullah shook his head. 'I don't know why I don't believe you, but I don't,' he said. 'Maybe it's like the Americans say, you should never try to kid a kidder.'

'So, are you a kidder?' she asked.

He looked away.

'Well?'

He looked back at her again. 'Depends,' he said. 'I was kidded, that I do know.'

'How?' He didn't respond and so she repeated, 'How?'

He tipped his head towards the hammer which was now lying on the floor and said, 'Pick it up, we've got a lot more wall to do.'

His phone rang again, and again he ignored it. Then, as soon as it stopped it rang again, and still he ignored it.

Mumtaz sighed, and then she picked the hammer up and said, 'So what do you want me to smash up now?'

Superintendent Venus had tried to call Abdullah Khan three times in the last ten minutes but he hadn't picked up. Now the hammering had started again. He took his headphones off and frowned. 'Doesn't he want to know that his wife has arrived safely at hospital?'

Vi Collins, who had just come off the phone to Greater Manchester Police, said, 'Well, Abdullah Khan's got no record, but he is known to GMP.'

'In what capacity?'

Vi looked down at her notes. 'He liked to leave the nice leafy suburb of Bolton, where he lived, called Ramsbottom, and go and play in the city,' she said.

'Manchester.'

'Ran with a few juvenile gangs in Moss Side. Nothing more'n kids' stuff. Then he went to uni there, where he did a law degree,' Vi said. 'But he didn't go on to practise.'

'So what did he do?'

'First off, he got a job in a pawn shop,' Vi said. 'Then he went to work for a firm of landlords, not unlike Rogers and Ali. He did that for some years.'

'So why did he stop?' Venus asked.

'Because GMP shut down his employers – Macaulay's,' she said. 'Drugs, people trafficking, extortion, you name it. They had a man on the inside, but he only fingered Khan as a debt collector. Nothing criminal. So he wasn't in trouble with the law, but GMP reckon he had some heat from his previous employers.'

'Why?'

'Because he got away scot-free,' Vi said. 'He was the only one who did. GMP reckon he got threats that came from inside Strangeways. Words like 'grass' were bandied about. Also there were rumours that when GMP closed the Manchester firm down, Khan had it away with some of the rent he'd collected for them.'

'So he owes these people.'

'Yes, sir.'

'These diamonds he's looking for . . .'

'Maybe he owes money to more than one set of bad men,' Vi said.

Venus's radio crackled into life and they all heard the voice of SFO Dalton say, 'In position.'

Underneath the bay window in the Khans' bedroom was a windowsill and a set of wooden panels which reached down to the floor. The hammer went through them easily, allowing Mumtaz to pull them away from the brickwork behind. While Khan looked at what had been exposed she sat down on the floor, panting. It was just past midnight and she was exhausted. She wanted to tell him that she needed to rest but she couldn't. How he would react to such a request, she couldn't know, and with every passing moment he was becoming more and more desperate and unstable. She knew that a point would eventually be reached where he would feel he had nothing left to lose.

'Fuck!' He smashed the handle of the gun down on the floor in frustration and Mumtaz winced.

To distract him – and herself to some extent too – she said, 'We must tell the police that we'll need *suhoor*.'

His eyes were hooded. 'How can you think about food?'

'Because we'll both be fasting again when the sun rises. If we don't eat *suhoor* we'll be starving and weak by midday.'

He said nothing.

She changed tack. 'I wonder how Nasreen is – and the baby,' she said. 'He could be born soon. Born in Ramadan. That's wonderful.'

'Is it?'

It was an odd thing to say. 'Of course it is, for a Muslim child.'

'For a Muslim child, yes,' he said.

'Well, your child will be a Muslim, Mr Khan. That's why I said what I did.'

He looked away from the cavities underneath the bay window and sat back against the brickwork. 'But will my child be a Muslim, Mrs Anwar?' he asked.

'Well, of course,' she said. 'I am sure that you and Nasreen will bring him up to be a good Muslim. You both seem to be – observant.'

And then he laughed. 'Oh, I'm observant alright, or I try to be. My wife?' he shrugged. 'A jeans-wearing virgin when I met her. Thought I was in love. 'Thought. Then I thought it through. You don't get to wipe out the past with a pretty face and a bit of a fast at Ramadan, do you.'

'A good Muslim must try to be virtuous at all times,' Mumtaz said. 'But we can only try, we're only human.'

'Yeah, but trying can only go so far, can't it? Can't do anything about contagion in the blood, can it?'

She didn't know what he was talking about and was too tired to even speculate. He slumped lower down the wall. He too was clearly exhausted now. He looked down at the gun in his hand. 'You know we can't sleep, don't you, Mrs Anwar? You know that we have to stay awake.'

'You do.'

He straightened up again. 'I am you and you are me for the

time we're in here, Mrs Anwar. If I don't sleep, you don't. But I'm not a fool, I can see that you need a rest now. Why don't I tell you a bedtime story? It won't put you to sleep. If anything it'll wake you up and haunt you for the rest of your life.'

Venus was still talking to SFO Dalton. Everyone knew that the house was surrounded. Everyone also knew that Khan hadn't spoken to the police since he'd called them to come and get his wife. Now all the hammering had stopped too and Khan and Mumtaz were talking.

Lee Arnold looked at his watch. It was nearly one in the morning. He leaned across and lifted up one of Vi's headphones. 'They'll need to eat before sunrise,' he whispered, reiterating what Mumtaz had said to Abdullah Khan.

'He'll have to ask for it,' Vi whispered back. Then she nodded towards Venus and Dalton. 'Confab.'

'If Khan won't talk . . .'

She shrugged. What Khan had asked for, transport to Heathrow Airport and a flight out of the country, was never going to happen and Khan had to know that. He'd told Mumtaz that he didn't even want to go to Bangladesh. But he still wanted those diamonds. Even if he found them, though, how did he plan to get out of the house and away, with them in his possession?

Venus ended his conversation with Dalton and put his headphones back on again.

And then Lee, Vi, Venus and Tony Bracci all heard Khan's voice say, 'This is the story of my life . . .'

*

'Apart from the fact that I never knew my late mother, I had an ordinary Muslim childhood,' Abdullah Khan said. 'My dad had an electrical shop in a town called Ramsbottom in the back end of Bolton. Nice little place, but as soon as I was a teenager I wanted to go into Manchester where there was some life, you know.'

'I hung out with other lads who liked to take cars and muck about selling bits of weed and doing a bit of robbing. Asian lads they were.'

'What did your father make of that?' Mumtaz asked.

'Me dad never knew,' he said. 'He knew I went into the city from time to time, but . . . Anyway I grew out of all that. I went to uni in Manchester. I spent a lot of money while I was there and so after my degree, I had to get a job to pay off me debts.'

'What had you spent the money on?'

He shrugged. 'Shite. Stuff. I dunno, enjoying meself. I've always needed money, I've only ever been happy when I've been spending. So I had a crap job first off, then I got debt-collecting for these white middle-aged gangsters. I was good at it and they paid me well. But I spent what they gave me just like I'd spent me student loan and so I robbed them to keep me head above water. I couldn't do it for long, they found out. That was when I had to come down here to London to stay with me uncle. When I had to go back to Ramsbottom when me dad was dying early last year, I couldn't go through Manchester just in case anyone who knew me before recognised me.'

'When I saw me dad, I knew he was on morphine, so you have to remember that, just as I do. But he were lucid, or he seemed to be.' He shook his head. 'He had cancer, it were . . . Dad told me things, about himself.'

'What things?'

There was a pause. Then he said, 'He wasn't who I believed he was. He wasn't called Mursel Khan, he hadn't been born a Muslim, he wasn't even Asian.' He shook his head again. 'Then he told me he was skint too. I nearly lost it. I'd banked on money from his shop to pay off me debts. I told him. I said, *What the heck did you spend it all on, you silly old man? And what you doing telling me all this crap about yourself?* And it was then that he told me.' He looked into Mumtaz's eyes. 'About the diamonds.'

'The diamonds you say are here in this house?' she said. 'How did your father know about them?'

Abdullah Khan looked down at the floor. 'Because they'd belonged to his aunt,' he said. 'He wasn't northern either.'

'He was a Londoner?'

'No, he weren't even that.' He said.

Mumtaz didn't know what to say, but in her head connections of an almost unthinkable nature had begun to form.

'You know that when I bought this house there were a small pile of wood that had once been a little building in the back yard. Right at the back, almost against the wall of the cemetery. I knew instantly what it was as soon as I saw it.'

'Did you?' Her voice was tight now but, as he had predicted, she was wide awake.

'It's still there,' he said. 'What's left of it.' He leaned towards her, smiling, his gun aimed at her heart. 'They call them sukkah, the Jews. They're temporary shelters they build to celebrate the festival of Sukkot which commemorates the time they spent wandering in Sinai with Moses. You know the story.'

'Yes.'

'I looked up everything to do with Jews once I'd spoken to me dad. I knew fuck all about them. Do you know why I did that, Mrs Anwar?'

'No.' But she did – or she thought that she might. Mumtaz hardly dared to breathe.

'Because my dad wasn't a Muslim, an Asian or a northerner, or anything else he'd told me about himself over the years. He was a Jew and his name, his real name, was Marek Berkowicz.'

32

Venus used Tony Bracci's headphones while he shared with Lee Arnold, and Vi listened on her own. For the moment, SFO Dalton and his team had fallen silent.

'My dad left London in 1955,' Abdullah Khan said. 'One night, in that December, he told me, he saw something he shouldn't in this house and so he left.'

No noise came from Mumtaz. She, Lee Arnold knew, just like him, was thinking *Did Marek Berkowicz just leave? Is that really possible?*

'His stepfather, a Christian called Reg Smith, was left alone with my dad and my dad's aunt, Sara. His mum and his little brother had gone out. Me dad was supposed to be asleep, but he wasn't. He heard a row between his dad and his aunt. His dad kept on shouting at her to tell him where they were. The diamonds.'

He stopped for a moment.

'Aunt Sara had come to England to give her sister, my grandmother Lily, these diamonds. Their father had been a jeweller, and although Sara had given the Nazis almost everything she had, including her body, to keep herself out of the camps, those four pink diamonds remained. Lily had been in a camp and so when Sara eventually found her over here she gave them to her.

Reg wasn't supposed to know because he was a drinker and violent, but he found out and he shouted at Sara to tell him where they were hid. But she wouldn't and so he strangled her.'

Silence.

'My dad went to help her, but it was too late. He stood in the doorway of the living room and watched Reg Smith choke the life out of Sara, and Reg saw him. Dad said that their eyes met. Reg looked like an animal gone mad, so me dad ran. Out of the house, up the street, eventually on a train to anywhere. He never paid, he had no money. He only got off when he was thrown off, which was in Manchester. At first he lived on the streets, robbing and going down bins. He kept around the old Piccadilly Station because that was all he knew of the city.

He didn't realise for a while that one of the guards was watching him – the man I always thought was my grandfather. He tried to get Dad's name and who he was out of him, but all he'd ever say was that he was a refugee and that all his family had died in the camps. My granddad took him in. He believed him. Later, I believed him. Me dad told me the truth about himself because he was about to die – no one lies when they're just about to die – and because he wanted me to have the diamonds.'

Abdullah paused, and then he said, 'I know you think I'm just a greedy bastard – and I am – I've only myself to blame for the mess my life has become, but I did right by my dad. He lived as the Muslim he became when he went to live with the Khans, but when he died I got a rabbi from Manchester to say Kaddish for him. He wanted that and I got it for him. Know what Kaddish is?' There was silence. 'It's the Jewish prayer for the dead. And I honoured my father by doing that last thing for him. But it means I'm not a real Muslim. My blood's wrong, which is why I'm like this.'

'That's nonsense. And anyway, like what?' they heard Mumtaz say.

'I don't know,' he said. 'I've never managed to find the right words for it, but it makes me unhappy. It means . . . It means . . . I can kill people.'

'What people, Mr Khan, have you . . .'

'I think we should look for those diamonds now,' he said calmly. 'I do the talking, Mrs Anwar, and I do it when *I* like, not when *you* like.'

Lee Arnold tried to speak but found that he had no saliva.

Vi said, 'He is clearly off his rocker. We need to get Mumtaz out of there.'

He took her into a small boxroom behind the bedroom he'd once shared with Nasreen. Its walls were not pockmarked with holes like so many of the other rooms. He told her to make a start by the door and work her way around. She should, he said, tap the walls gently at first to try and locate any cavities.

Mumtaz tapped. Occasionally, she glanced at him, and thought he looked more awake. He had also started to smile. Was he experiencing relief now that he'd got the truth about his father – if it was the truth – off his chest? And what did he mean about killing people? Who had he killed? Perhaps Nasreen had been right, and he had murdered the Afghanistan veteran John Sawyer . . . But why?

Outside in the street, and at the back of the house, there was an unknown number of police officers. Mumtaz wondered whether she knew any of them, and also whether Lee was with them. He'd been a police officer and so he might be. Having found no cavities, Mumtaz hammered. At the very least, Lee had to know what was happening, and she knew that he would have organised care for Shazia. Poor Shazia, she was probably terrified. And her parents! She hadn't thought about them earlier; now she saw their faces in her mind.

Plaster flew up and made her cough as she smashed away at the walls. She looked over at him and heard him say, 'Carry on.' She carried on.

What would he do if he didn't find the diamonds? Why did he think they were in the walls of the house? Reg Smith might have found them, or Lily Smith could have taken them to her grave – or sold them ... But then why was she even thinking about jewels that couldn't possibly exist? And then, being a private investigator and knowing what she did about surveillance, Mumtaz realised that even if the police hadn't been listening in to their conversations earlier on in the day, they had to be by this time.

She stopped hammering.

Abdullah Khan said, 'I've not told you to have a rest.'

She said, 'How do you *know* that these diamonds you're looking for are behind these walls?'

For a moment he said nothing, then he walked over and stood in front of her. Mumtaz felt her heart begin to pick up its beat. 'I don't,' he said. 'But I've had everything else apart in this house. Floorboards, doors, units, the garden – even that old Sukkah at the bottom, the Jew's shack. All I found there was her body.'

'Whose body?'

'Auntie Sara's body. Some old tramp that my wife liked to feed had dug it up.' He jammed the pistol against her forehead. 'I killed him before he got to her diamonds.'

Mumtaz made a conscious effort to breathe as evenly as she could. He really had killed that man, John Sawyer. 'But you don't have any diamonds and so he—'

'I couldn't let him live,' he said. 'I didn't know if the diamonds were on her body or not. Not then.'

'But they wouldn't be, would they? If Reg Smith killed her he would have found them.'

'I had to be sure,' he said. 'I always have to be sure. And that is why my bosses have so much confidence in me.' He pushed the gun into the flesh on her forehead and made her gasp in pain. 'I clear up after myself. I leave no stone unturned.' And then he smiled at her. 'Here and now are no exceptions.'

'Mr Khan,' Mumtaz said, 'why did you come here today with a gun in your hand?'

He said nothing for a long time. Then he said, 'Because I'd been clearing up after myself this morning, then I came home, Mrs Anwar.'

'Killing . . .'

'Why not? I'm a Jew and we all know there's no Paradise for them in the hereafter, don't we?'

'Wendy Dixon has to be a contender.'

'For his victim.'

'For one of them,' Vi said. 'We heard him say he killed John Sawyer. He admitted it. That skeleton we found with him may well have been Khan's aunt.'

'This is an extremely dangerous man who has lost his identity. He's only got one thought in his head, so what he'll do if the diamonds aren't in that house doesn't bear thought.' Superintendent Venus shook his head. 'We have to bring this to a conclusion and get Mrs Hakim out of there without killing Khan – unless we have to. We need to find out whether he just killed for his own purposes or whether his actions were part of his remit from the Rogers brothers.'

Vi's eyes ignited. 'We could bring them down . . .'

'Don't get excited, DI Collins,' Venus said. 'I think the man is more mental health case than gangster.'

Lee Arnold, who had been listening to their conversation, said, 'But where do the diamonds come into the story? Really? Assuming that Marek Berkowicz was in fact Abdullah Khan's father, how could he have known that his aunt's diamonds were somewhere in that house? He left. He never went back. Did he know himself where the diamonds were before his stepfather killed his aunt? There's a bit missing here that . . .' He stopped. SFO Dalton had come into the room and was looking at him and Lee looked back.

'We have to get Mumtaz out of there,' Venus said.

'Yes, sir,' Dalton answered, then said to the Superintendent, 'Khan's got nothing to lose, not even Paradise.'

'I know, and we also have to assume that the diamonds don't exist,' Venus said.

'Because they are unlikely to do so?'

'What do you think, Mr Arnold?'

Lee shook his head. Of course Abdullah Khan had to be delusional, although how he had come upon this particular fantasy, he couldn't imagine.

Venus looked at the SFO. 'Have your men managed to break in the back door?'

'Yes.'

The phone that Venus had dedicated to calls from Abdullah Khan rang.

'Yes?'

Dalton looked at Lee Arnold. 'We need to think about when Khan might be alone,' he said in a low tone. Then he turned to

Vi. 'DI Collins,' he said, 'would a man like Khan risk letting Mrs Hakim visit the bathroom on her own?'

Vi, frowning, looked at Lee. 'I don't think she's been to the toilet, has she?'

He shook his head. 'Don't think so. What if he watches her go? What then?'

'We have to separate them somehow,' Dalton said. He rubbed his face. 'We have ingress at the back of the property now but we can't just go in. He'll shoot her.'

'Then what can we do?' Lee asked.

Venus, off the phone now, said, 'He wants some food.'

He wouldn't think twice about killing her. But only after he'd found the diamonds. There was not, however, much chance of that, Mumtaz thought. If Marek Berkowicz had left that house for the last time the night that Reg Smith had killed Sara Kaminski, then how could he have known where the diamonds were? If the story was true, Sara had died rather than tell Reg their location. Had Marek known, surely he would have told his stepfather where the diamonds were in order to save Sara's life? The diamonds had to be a story, nothing more.

And where, if anywhere, did strange Eric Smith, Marek's younger half brother, fit into the story? People talked about Eric 'guarding' something in that house. But what was it? The diamonds? Sara Kaminski's body? Eric had been out with Lily when Sara was killed so what, if anything, had he known about any of it? And, anyway, wasn't this all just a tale? A good one, which fitted some of the facts admittedly, but no more. Mumtaz smashed another hole in the wall and stood back to let Abdullah Khan look at it. He'd finally asked the police to provide some food for the early morning meal known during Ramadan as *suhoor*. And, although really too anxious to be hungry, Mumtaz knew that she should eat and drink more than she had done for *iftar*.

Khan moved back from the wall and told Mumtaz to carry on destroying the fabric of his house. She was finding it very hard to focus now so, also with half her mind on the police and what she hoped they could hear, she said, 'Wasn't the body of the man in your garden found in the old cemetery?'

'I dragged it over the back wall,' he said. 'Keep working.'

She pounded the wall. 'The police found a skeleton with it.'

'I dumped him, why shouldn't I dump Sara? She had nothing on her,' he said. 'Actually I tried not to just dump them, to be honest. I tried to lay them out decently, but when I got in there the place was full of kids desecrating graves and then some lunatic shouting his head off.'

'But you can't have been seen, or the police would have come for you.'

He laughed. 'Oh, I was seen,' he said. 'Just not by the police.' He looked at what she'd done, put his hand in the hole and said, 'Shit.'

She said, 'What happens to me if you don't find your diamonds?'

He didn't say anything.

'Will you kill me?' she asked. 'Will you tidy me up after yourself?'

Again he didn't say anything, but this time she waited. He looked her straight in the eye and said, 'You and I will leave in that case, and when I've got as far away as I can I'll either let you go or I'll kill you. Same if I do find the diamonds.'

*

Lee Arnold shook. He looked down at the food that was about to be taken into the house next door and realised that he was not only anxious and tired but he was hungry too. In spite of having just heard Abdullah Khan say that he was likely to kill Mumtaz, he was still hungry. He found it odd and disturbing, and he couldn't convince himself that he liked himself for it.

He went and looked out of the back window at the darkened garden of the house next door. If he hadn't known that anyone was in there, he would have thought that it was empty. Vi, just off her mobile, came over to him and put a hand on his shoulder. 'Nasreen Khan's baby boy was stillborn,' she said.

'Oh, fuck.'

'Good news is they think she'll be alright.'

She started to move away, but he stopped her. 'This'll work, right?'

She sighed. 'We either move when the food goes in or . . .' She shrugged. 'The hammering's given the FOs in the garden cover to get the back door open. Khan's concentrating on Mumtaz and his diamonds. If we're lucky, when they go downstairs to get the food, we'll have a chance . . .'

They called up to let him know that the food was ready this time. Abdullah took Mumtaz with him to the window and pressed the gun to the side of her head.

He watched as a figure wearing a helmet and a bulletproof vest put something down in front of the door and then left. Last time an officer had handed the food over to Mumtaz at the door. Why the change? He was suspicious. He called Venus. 'What's going on?' he asked.

'What do you mean, Mursel?'

'Leaving the food on the doorstep. Last time it was handed over.'

'Do you have a problem with it being left? We thought if we left it for you, you'd feel less concerned about what our officer might be doing at your door. It's supposed to be less confrontational. For you.'

Abdullah Khan thought about it. When the *iftar* food had been delivered he had worried about the possibility of the police officer who had delivered it grabbing Mrs Anwar and taking away his bargaining chip. This way, that couldn't happen. But he was still suspicious, even though he said, 'Alright,' to Venus and then ended the call. Unlike last time, this time he was hungry. Maybe it was because the woman had talked about food and woken his stomach up. He looked down at Mumtaz with hatred in his eyes. Who was she, and why had he spent so much time talking to her? He'd spoken to the police hardly at all, why had he spoken to her?

He pulled her away from the window and pushed her onto the landing. 'Go down the stairs in front of me,' he said. 'And don't try to run when you open the door.'

She said nothing as she began descending. Following her, he wondered – and not for the first time – why he'd let that shot off through the bedroom window when he'd first come into the house. Had he still been hyped up after Wendy? Had he been upset after Wendy? Maybe, in a sense. He'd never initially planned to kill her. She'd just been a lot of sexy fun, until he'd realised what she could know, until his vulnerability through her had been revealed when the police raided Sean Rogers's house. Sean didn't know yet, and Abdullah wondered how he'd feel when he did. Wendy had been one of what Sean always called his 'pigs'. Abdullah had liked that about her. Women were mothers or dirty whores, they couldn't be both.

By the time they reached the hall, Abdullah knew about the bedroom window. He'd shot it out because he'd needed to stay in the house to find the diamonds. Sean and Marty were getting impatient for the money they'd lent him. Once the paramedics had seen Nasreen's legs they would have called the police anyway. It was obvious she'd been left like that for days. The shot had bought him time.

'Open the door,' he now ordered Mumtaz.

She unclipped the latch.

'Don't pull it wide open, just . . .' He positioned himself behind the doorway into the living room so that he could see outside the front door without revealing himself. ' . . .open it enough so you can get the tray and then get back in again.'

She opened the door. He pointed the gun at her back and moved it downwards as she bent to retrieve the tray. He heard rather than saw her pick it up. And then suddenly there was a pain in his shoulder.

Mumtaz heard a noise behind her, but she had no idea what it might be. She was straightening up when all the commotion began. First there was shouting, none of which she could decipher, and then a figure appeared from nowhere, ripped the food tray out of her hands, threw it to the ground and picked her up in one smooth movement. The figure was matt black with no face, just a shiny visor. But it told her not to be frightened and she believed it.

Then, from inside the Khans' house she heard a sound that made her blood still in her veins. It was a howl which was furious, wretched and heartbroken all at the same time.

33

'If your father, Marek Berkowicz, left what had been his house, now your house, in Strone Road, East Ham, in 1955, what made him think that his aunt's – Sara Kaminski's – diamonds would still be in the building?' Vi leaned across the table and looked into the blood-stained face of Abdullah Khan. He'd put up quite a fight, even when an SCO19 officer had jammed a gun against the side of his head. 'Eh?'

Superintendent Venus, who was sitting beside her, cleared his throat. He wasn't comfortable around emotion, and that included gloating. And Vi did like a gloat.

'Sean and Marty Rogers, your employers, don't just buy people houses for the hell of it,' Vi continued. 'We could hear every word you said, Mr Khan, and you said that you had to get the diamonds because you owe some men some money. You said your future depended on finding those diamonds. If that isn't, in some way, to pay off Sean and Marty, then I don't know . . .'

'Sean and Marty kindly lent me the money to buy Strone Road, but they never knew why I really wanted that particular place,' Khan said. He looked up. 'They've got nothing to do with any of it.'

'Really.' Vi looked down at her notes. 'But you told Mrs Mumtaz Hakim, and I quote, "I owe some men some money." What men?'

Abdullah Khan looked up at the ceiling. He'd been told who Mumtaz Hakim was and what she did at the beginning of this interview. When Vi had uttered the words 'private detective' he'd laughed. A Muslim woman who did *that*?! But he'd known about her, he'd even had her pointed out to him once, by one of Sean's Asian handymen. He knew he'd known that woman all along.

'What men?' Vi repeated.

He looked away, and Vi looked down at her notes again. Tony Bracci had placed a pile of relevant paperwork beside her own stuff just before the interview had begun. It was six o'clock in the morning and Vi hadn't been to bed, so a lot of the words she was reading were a bit blurry. But she made out the picture of the Strone Road house in the ad that had been placed by the auction house in the *Recorder* the previous November.

'You bought the place, with Sean and Marty's money, just after you got married to your wife, Nasreen.' She paused for a moment and then she said, 'Did you love her, or did you marry her just to give yourself an air of respectability? You do a dirty job, don't you, Abdullah – or is it Paul? – tossing Sean and Marty's tenants out of their homes, parting poor people from their extortionate rent?'

'What I do is quite legal.'

'Oh, so says the lawyer!' she laughed. She checked her notes again. 'You did the same gig for the Macaulay family up in Manchester, didn't you?'

Again he didn't answer.

'My understanding is that Christopher Macaulay, the head of the family, is still in Strangeways and you still owe him money,' Vi said. 'And as I'm sure you as a lawyer know, Mr Khan, criminals in one nick can and do get word out to criminals in other nicks about who they'd like to hurt. Just because Chris Macaulay won't be able to get you hisself, up there in Manchester, don't mean to say that you won't be got. Know what I mean?'

Abdullah Khan was silent.

'By your own admission you killed a man called John Sawyer who, you suspected, may have beaten you to the diamonds,' Superintendent Venus said.

'Yes.'

Vi looked across at her superior. He wanted Khan convicted of the murder, or murders, he had committed and then moved along. Talk about organised crime, in this case in the shape of the Rogers brothers, unsettled him. Talk of that nature always did. Was it really because he didn't possess the stomach for taking on gangs or was there a more sinister reason? Vi had never trusted him, but was she just allowing her prejudices to obscure her vision? Venus was irredeemably middle class, and with a penchant for very young women, but did that necessarily make him corrupt? Would he even have the wit to take bungs from people like Sean and Marty Rogers, even if his latest bit of totty did want a holiday in Barbados . . . ?

Leaning back in her chair now, Vi said, 'I still want to know how you knew about those diamonds being in that house. Until I understand that, I'm either gonna think you're a fantasist or mental. What is it, Abdullah, are you a—'

'My dad came back,' he said.

Vi leaned forwards. 'When?'

'I don't know exactly,' he said. 'But his mum were dead by then. He saw his brother and he told him?'

'About the diamonds?'

'Amongst other things, yeah.'

'But if Eric Smith knew where the diamonds were . . .'

'He didn't.' Abdullah looked up. 'That's what he told my dad.

What was more, he didn't want them. Eric knew his dad had killed his auntie over them. He and his mum knew on the night Reg killed her, they saw her dead when they got in from the cinema. Eric wanted nothing to do with those diamonds.'

'But your dad did?'

'No!' He shook his head which hurt just like his eyes, which had been punched when he'd fought the coppers who arrested him 'No, he wanted nothing to do with them either. He told me about them because he wanted me to have them. I wasn't involved, like, and so if there was something of value there . . .'

'Why didn't he tell you about the diamonds before?'

Abdullah Khan's face changed then and he looked at Vi with contempt. 'Well, why'd you think?' he said.

'I dunno. Why?'

'Because for me to understand, he had to tell me I was a Jew,' he said. 'And he didn't want to do that.'

Mumtaz hadn't been able to see Nasreen. She'd been transferred from Newham General's maternity department over to the burns unit at the London. Her parents, who had been contacted by staff at the General, had gone with her. This had left Mumtaz on her own, to be checked over by doctors at Accident and Emergency while an armed officer waited for her outside her cubicle. Until Abdullah Khan had been properly interviewed there could be a danger from whoever he had been working for or with, although Mumtaz believed that he had operated, at least in the Strone Road house, entirely on his own. When she'd met him he'd been at the height of his obsession with that house, entirely in thrall to a fixation he believed would save him both on a financial and a personal level. He believed that those diamonds were his right.

Compensation, Mumtaz thought, for the loss of identity his father's story had engendered in him.

In reality, Abdullah Khan wasn't Jewish at all. Judaism passed only through the matriarchal line, and it was Abdullah's father who had been Jewish, not his mother. Besides, what difference did it really make? In the brief moment that she'd seen Khan before the police had taken him away, she'd seen a man who had resisted arrest and been beaten. Jew or not, he bled just like anybody else.

She'd had a far more civilised route out of the Strone Road house. Although grabbed roughly by the SCO19 officer who had taken her to the house next door and safety, she had been quickly placed into the care of Lee Arnold. Then, and only then, had she cried.

'If your dad was such a good person, why didn't he tell the police about how his stepfather had killed his aunt?'

Abdullah Khan looked down at the floor. 'Because his brother didn't want him to. He'd spent his life protecting his parents' memories – and his aunt's body.'

'Mr Khan, my predecessors searched that house and garden for your aunt's body back in the 1950s,' Vi said. 'They didn't find it.' And yet, so Abdullah Khan claimed, John Sawyer had found Sara Kaminski's body in his garden.

'Reg Smith buried her in the graveyard at the end of the garden until the heat was off,' Khan said. 'Where'd you think I got the idea from for putting the soldier, and the remains of Sara, in the graveyard?'

'So why'd Reg dig her up again?'

'Apart from the chance that next time there was a funeral at the Plashet Cemetery, some grave digger might find her? My grandmother Lily wanted her close. As soon as I saw that sink outside the back door, I knew she was probably in the garden somewhere. Jews always have running water at the entrances to their cemeteries. That sink were plumbed in for a reason.'

Vi knew that, but she didn't say anything.

'I saw what could have been the remains of a Sukkot sukkah,' he said. 'That's the temporary building Jews make every year to commemorate Sukkot, when Moses was wandering with them in Sinai. But I never thought she might be buried under it. I thought she'd be better hidden than that. Anyway, that tramp lived in it. I was going to wait until he was away from the garden one day and go and have a look to make sure but the bastard beat me to it.'

'So you smashed him over the head, you searched the skeleton for the diamonds and then you decided to do what Reg Smith had done and lob both bodies over—'

'I never lobbed, I—'

'Whatever.' Vi dismissed his words with a wave of her hand.

There was a knock on the door, followed by the arrival of a uniformed officer holding a piece of paper. He gave it to Vi and then left. 'Abdullah, you ever heard the old saying about how anyone who doesn't learn from the mistakes of the past is doomed to repeat them? You walked right into that one, didn't you, son,' she said, reading with a frown on her face and Venus looking over her shoulder. Then she looked up, 'So tell me about Wendy Dixon then,' she said.

'Wendy . . .'

'The woman you shagged up at Sean Roger's gaff,' Vi said. 'The one who liked to call you Paul. The one this ballistics report tells me you killed.'

*

Tony Bracci looked over at Lee Arnold and wondered what was going through his head. The DI, the Super and Tony himself had seen Arnold just about hold back tears when Mumtaz Hakim came out of the Strone Road house alive. Tony knew that they were close, but he hadn't realised until that moment that Lee felt as strongly as he clearly did.

Lee's phone rang. He took his fag out of his mouth and Tony saw him smile. 'Alright,' he heard him say, 'I'm right here. I'm not going anywhere.' Then there was a pause and he said, 'See you soon.'

Tony looked at him and said, 'Was that . . .'

'Mumtaz, yes,' Lee replied. 'She's got a clean bill of health. She's coming back here.'

'Sean tell you to kill her?'

He paused but then he said, 'I killed her.'

'But on Sean's orders . . .'

'No, why . . .'

'Oh, you know why!' Vi said. 'Wendy was one of Sean's pigs who owed him money, who sometimes defied him, and she was looking rough. What was the fucking point, eh?'

'No, no it wasn't . . .' He stopped. He frowned.

'What you thinking, Abdullah?' Vi asked.

Was it just in her head or did Venus suddenly look worried?

She pressed home her advantage. 'We can look after you, you know,' she said. 'Just as the Macaulays can get in jails other than Strangeways, we can put people places where they can't be found provided—'

'I killed Wendy because she was pregnant,' Abdullah said. 'She did it deliberately, to trap me. She loved me.'

'Oh and why was that?' Vi asked.

'Because I was . . . I was nice to her,' he said.

Vi looked down at the table in front of her. 'So you told her you loved her as you stuck your nob up her arse.'

She heard Venus draw in breath. Vi looked up again. Abdullah Khan was not denying anything. Vi shook her head. 'So let me get this straight,' she said. 'You killed John Sawyer because you thought he might have found your diamonds, you—'

'I hit him over the head. I'd taken a kitchen knife to stab him, but he saw me coming and so I punched him, then I smacked him over the head. I thought I'd killed him, he wasn't breathing, and so after I'd looked for the diamonds I pushed him over the wall – with – her.'

'The skeleton of your aunt.'

He looked across at her, and for the first time he seemed to be showing some sort of real emotion. 'But then he started to come round.'

'In the Plashet Cemetery?' Forensics had said that Sawyer had actually died in the cemetery.

'Yeah. And there were other people in there . . .' He looked both surprised and also confused by his own words.

'And so you . . .'

'He started to sit up.' He ran his hands through his hair and shook his head. He looked down at the table again, and panted. 'I heard voices. I punched him in the head to get him down and then I stabbed him in the back.'

'What with?'

'The kitchen knife.' He shook his head again. 'I'd proper lost it by then. I ran. But the voices still kept on coming. I got out of there just before some kids arrived. Like Goths or something they were. I saw them, but they never saw me.'

Vi narrowed her eyes. 'You sure about that are you, Abdullah? I thought the kids were already in there,' she said. Bully Murray had been killed pretty soon after the events that Khan was describing and he did, after all, adhere at least in terms of his ethnicity to the 'other man' that Bully had briefly described to her. In addition to that, Abdullah had told Mumtaz Hakim 'I was seen' when he'd 'confessed' to her back at Strone Road. Bully Murray had almost certainly seen him.

But he looked her straight in the face and he said, 'Yes.'

Vi sighed, but let that go. Bully Murray's murderer had been caught and was now dead himself. What, really, did it matter any more? It mattered because maybe Abdullah had told the Rogers brothers and maybe they had organised Bully's death. Maybe . . .

'So just to get this straight then,' she said, 'you killed Wendy Dixon because she was needy, possibly pregnant and you killed John Sawyer because he appeared to be threatening your fictional diamonds—'

'They're not fictional, they're—'

'Real?' Vi smiled. 'So if they're real, where are they? You knocked seven shades of shit out of your house for months on end, and you didn't find them.'

He didn't say anything.

'No.' She shook her head. 'I don't know what the fuck you thought you were doing, Mr Khan,' she said, 'but prospecting for diamonds in East Ham was not one of your better ideas. Now one more chance, Mr Khan, why did Sean and Marty order the deaths of John Sawyer and Wendy Dixon? She was a pig and so I can kind of understand that, but him? What did the Rogers boys have against a tramp?'

'I told you I was looking for d—'

'Yeah, yeah, the bloody treasure of the Sierra Madre,' she said.

She stood up, looking at Venus as she did so. 'Think we're probably done here for the time being, sir.' Then she looked back at Abdullah. 'Psych evaluation next I think, son.'

Venus, apparently relieved, smiled.

Part Four

34

Lee looked out of the window down onto Green Street. A group of men who normally smoked continuously outside the front of their small restaurant now gathered around an old-fashioned portable TV balanced on a footstool. The Olympics were having a good effect upon Ramadan fasters. It was taking their minds off their bellies. Sadly they also seemed to be having a somewhat adverse effect upon the need for private investigation services. But Lee comforted himself with the notion that once the feel-good effect of the Olympics was over, people would start being suspicious of one another all over again.

On a personal level, he was surprised at how much of the Games he was watching on television. And it wasn't just because Chronus got excited whenever he saw people run. Lee's mother had made him watch the opening ceremony with her, which he had found surprisingly affecting, probably because it was so very 'English' – odd, and rather slanted towards the ordinary person. Thereafter, he'd been suckered at various times into watching cycling, swimming and athletics. The only events he'd switch off immediately were equestrian competitions. What did he, or anyone he knew, know about dressage?

Lee walked through his office to the front door and sat down on the metal staircase outside. Just as he was lighting a fag, he saw Mumtaz coming up the stairs.

'Morning.'

She looked up at him and smiled. 'Morning, Lee.'

'How'd it go?' he asked.

She carried on climbing until her head was level with his. She shrugged. 'I don't know,' she said. 'They liked it, but . . .'

'The boarded-up windows are putting them off.'

'Of course.'

'But you haven't . . .'

'Had any more trouble? No.' She walked past him and went into the office. 'Tea?'

'If you don't mind making,' Lee said. She was still fasting.

'I don't mind making.'

Mumtaz walked into their small office kitchen, switched the kettle on and then put her head in her hands. The latest couple to view her house, that morning, had looked around as if they had bad smells under their noses. Then, on her way from the house to the office, her estate agent had rung to say that the viewers would be interested in the house if she dropped the price by fifty thousand. They, like most of the borough, had read the story about the window-pane shootings in Forest Gate just over three weeks before, but Mumtaz couldn't drop that far. If she did, she would end up truly potless, possibly even still in debt. She listened to the kettle come to the boil, then pulled herself together. Whether the house sold or not, the bills – including Ahmet's debt to the Sheikhs – had to be paid, and so she was obliged to work. She put a teabag into Lee's mug and poured on the boiling water. He'd just given her a pay rise of a hundred pounds a month, bless him. She knew that he couldn't afford it.

'Lee, do you want sugar today?' she called out, as she poured milk into the cup and removed the teabag. Sometimes he wanted sugar and sometimes he didn't.

'Yeah, please.'

Then, as she was spooning two heaped teaspoons into his mug she heard him say something else. 'What?'

Straining her ears, she thought she heard another voice, talking to Lee. She didn't think anything of it until she came out of the kitchen with the tea in her hands. Through the open office door, and Lee's thick cigarette smoke, she saw the thin, pale figure of Nasreen Khan.

There wasn't even a pretence of subterfuge. One of Abduljabbar Mitra's sons came out of what had once been his father's greengrocer shop on Green Street, and handed a pile of bank notes in through the window of a BMW parked outside. Inside the car, Vi easily recognised the bulky figure of Dave Spall, Marty Roger's minder.

Once the cash had been passed, Vi threw her cigarette butt down on the ground, crossed the road and let herself into the BMW beside the man who, on seeing her, stuffed the money hurriedly into his pockets.

'Hello, Dave,' Vi said with a smile. 'How's it going?'

Spall's face whitened. 'Get out,' he said. 'This is a private car, you've no right to get in here.'

She ignored him. 'Better drive on, Dave,' she said. 'You're on double yellows. Don't want to get nicked by a warden, do you?'

'Yeah, but you're . . .'

'Drive on or I'll find a warden,' Vi said.

Dave put the car into Drive and pulled out, heading north towards Forest Gate.

'I don't know about you, but I quite fancy a little trip up to Wanstead Flats,' Vi said. 'Head for Capel Road, just off Woodford Road. Know it?'

Dave made a half grunting, just about affirmative noise.

'Good,' Vi said. Then she sat back in her luxurious leather seat and enjoyed the view. Ramadan or no Ramadan, Green Street was buzzing.

Mumtaz put a mug of tea down in front of Nasreen and then sat. Because she'd lost her baby and been ill afterwards, Nasreen had not been allowed to fast for Ramadan. Getting her strength and her life back were more important to God than her strict adherence to one of the Five Pillars of Islam.

'My legs will be scarred,' she said. 'But that's nothing.'

Mumtaz looked at Lee, who she saw was equally at a loss as to what to say.

'I will be able to have children again.'

'Oh, that's good news,' Mumtaz said.

And then suddenly Nasreen smiled. 'I'd be dead without you, Mumtaz,' she said.

'You would have found a way to get out of there.'

'No.' She looked at Lee. 'She's too modest, Mr Arnold.'

'Oh, tell me about it, love,' Lee said.

She laughed. 'It's so good to see you both,' she said. 'Even though I feel a fool about not believing you about Abdullah.'

'He's your husband, why—'

'He won't be my husband for very much longer,' Nasreen said.

Since she'd arrested Abdullah Khan, all Vi Collins had told Lee and Mumtaz about him, beyond what was in the public domain, was that his psychiatric assessment had been inconclusive. Logically, some of his ideas and beliefs about people around him, his past and his family were quite outlandish. But whether they were actually untrue was very difficult to ascertain. His father, Mursel Khan, hadn't looked at all like either of his parents or the one sister, now deceased, he had been raised with. But on the other hand, Mursel had possessed what was at the time, before the formation of Bangladesh, Indian birth documents. According to these he had been born, under British rule, in Sylhet in 1940. Could such documents have been falsified by the Khans for their stray Jewish boy in what by then must have been 1956?

'You're divorcing him.'

'Eventually,' Nasreen said. 'As you know he's been charged with John Sawyer's murder and the killing of a woman called Wendy Dixon.' She looked down at the floor. 'He was having an affair with her. She was a prostitute.'

That had been another blow to Nasreen's pride, and neither Mumtaz nor Lee considered it politic to tell her what they knew about Wendy.

'That he killed a total innocent like John over a delusion . . .' She shook her head. 'Diamonds!'

Once Khan had been arrested, the police had also looked for the diamonds and found none. In addition, the skeleton thought to be that of Sara Kaminski showed signs of the kind of wear associated with a hard life. On that basis, the notion that she had been the daughter of a rich jeweller who had then comfortably sat out the Second World War seemed unlikely. At some point Sara Kaminski had worked, and worked hard.

'The police have asked for Abdullah's father's body to be exhumed so they can compare his DNA to the skeleton,' Nasreen said. 'It's all so horrible.' Then she looked at Mumtaz. 'Do you think that my husband is mad?'

'I'm not qualified to say.' Abdullah Khan had been in the grip of an obsession that had caused him to kill when Mumtaz had come upon him, but whether that made him insane or not was another matter.

Nasreen drank her tea.

'DNA testing like that'll take time,' Lee said. 'Where old bones are involved, they generally have to look at mitochondrial DNA through the mother's line of inheritance, and that is not done in five minutes.'

'Yes, the police said it would take some time.'

'So what about the house?' Mumtaz asked. 'What's happening about that?'

Nasreen put her cup down. 'Abdullah's employers paid for it and so they own it. I thought that the deeds were in our names but they're actually in the name of Sean Rogers.'

Lee snorted.

'Yes, I know he's a gangster, and his brother too, but I have to say he's been very kind to me,' Nasreen said. 'I mean, when you think about all the damage Abdullah did to the house it has to be worth less now than when it was bought. But Sean Rogers is planning to do it up at his own expense and has already told me that I don't owe him anything.'

Lee and Mumtaz exchanged a look. Given the circumstances, with the police investigation in the affair still on-going, the Rogers boys could do little else.

'So you're back with your parents?'

'Yes,' she smiled. 'It's such a relief after . . .'

She looked for a moment as if she was about to cry, so Mumtaz placed a comforting hand on her arm. Nasreen smiled. 'I'm OK.'

'I know that. You're strong, Nasreen. Look at what you've come through.'

'Yes.' She didn't allude to the loss of her child and neither did Mumtaz, but for a few moments its loss sat in that office and chilled the air around all three of them.

Nasreen lifted her handbag up onto Mumtaz's desk and began to sort through its contents. 'I actually came to give you this,' she said.

A clunk of metal against wood signalled the return of the mezuzah to the Arnold Agency's office. 'The police have taken the photograph they think might be of Sara Kaminski, but they didn't want this as well and neither do I.' She smiled. 'Or, rather, I don't know what to do with it. If you assume that Reginald Smith did kill Sara, and then hid her body with what had to be the collusion of his wife at least, then hiding her photograph behind the mezuzah must have been like keeping her memory alive in just one very small place.' She turned the mezuzah over in her hand for a moment. 'You know, I read that the Jews consider the fixing of a mezuzah to a door as an act of kindness to the world. Maybe hiding Sara's photo behind this mezuzah was an act of kindness to her. Maybe Lily, her sister, did it.' She put the mezuzah back down on the desk again and said, 'Will you keep it for me – and for Sara too?'

Mumtaz's eyes were fixed on the thing. She'd almost forgotten about the mezuzah. 'Of course we will,' she murmured.

Much to Dave Spall's disgust, Vi lit a fag inside Marty's car.

'You can't . . .' he began.

'Oh but I can,' Vi said. She looked out across Wanstead Flats at a happy scene of families, dogs and teenagers playing in the sunshine. Nice weather for the Olympics, which was where most of her colleagues were.

'I got a whisper that the Mitra family on Green Street were in hock to your bosses,' she said.

'A whisper? What . . .'

'Oh, I never reveal my sources, Dave, you know that.' Murderer Noakes had told her that he'd heard through one of his 'Paki' mates that the late Abduljabbar Mitra paid protection to the Rogers. Now, seemingly, so did his heirs. 'Anyway, I saw one of the Mitra kids give you cash with me own eyes. But what the Mitras decide to do is up to them,' she continued. 'I mean, the old man was a murderer . . .'

She looked across at Dave, who just fanned her smoke out of his window with his hand and said nothing.

'Fancy a mild-mannered bloke like Abduljabbar knocking off a racist nut-job like Bully Murray,' Vi said. 'Don't make a lot of sense. Men like Abduljabbar usually avoid trouble, but then he said that Bully goaded him and so . . .' She shrugged. Dave, she noticed, was sweating. 'And so soon too after Bully saw the person who killed that tramp, John Sawyer, in the old Plashet Cemetery. You know, your mate, Abdullah Khan.'

Dave still said nothing.

'Occurs to me,' Vi went on, 'that maybe someone didn't want Khan to get caught. Also occurs to me that maybe Bully Murray tried to make a bit of dosh out of his nugget of knowledge. Know where I'm going with this, Dave?'

He didn't look at her. 'No.'

She leaned in towards him. 'Well, let me spell it out for you, shall I? I think that Sean or Marty or Abdullah Khan, or all three of them, persuaded Abduljabbar Mitra to kill Bully Murray to shut him up. I don't think that any of those three gentlemen wanted Mitra to get caught, but they reckoned without Abduljabbar's moral compass. You do that when you haven't got a moral compass yourself.'

'That's bollocks,' Dave said.

'Is it? Maybe. I mean, I think it's a bit dodgy in light of the fact that Mitra's kids are still paying you money. I'd think that if you topped somebody for someone then all debts would be cancelled. But then that's me and, let's face it, I'm not a psycho, am I.'

Dave went back to saying nothing.

'Of course, because Mitra's dead, I can't prove any of this,' Vi said.

'Then why . . .'

'Just like I'm finding it hard to prove even the existence of a Russian girl called Tatiana . . .' She watched Dave's face carefully. He visibly reddened. Vi smiled. 'Ringing bells?'

'No.'

'No? Well, Wendy Dixon . . .'

'Khan killed her. She was up the duff to him.'

Vi shook her head. 'No, she wasn't actually, Dave,' she said. 'Wendy might have wanted to be pregnant, but she wasn't. I think that Abdullah Khan killed her because it occurred to him that she, if she wanted, could finger him as the shooter that Saturday night up at Sean's place.'

'Khan weren't . . .'

'Oh, but he was there,' Vi said.

'Did he tell you he was?'

'Didn't need to, Dave,' she said. 'The bullet we found at Sean's matched the gun that Khan killed Wendy with. Not rocket science, love. But to get back to my Russian girl, do you know where she went to?'

'I don't know any girl called Tatiana,' he said.

'Strange. She lived in that house you used to go and visit when you was sweet on, what was her name . . .'

He said nothing.

Vi chucked her fag out the window and lit another. 'No, I forget her name too,' she said.

Some kids over on the Flats screeched with delight. Vi looked at them. One little boy was running hard, laughing with the joy of it.

'Think he thinks he's Mo Farah?' Vi asked. Even she had been pulled into the Olympic 'nonsense' as she still liked to call it. She looked over at Dave again. 'Well, anyway,' she said, 'whether Tatiana's back in Moscow or underneath the A13 somewhere, until she turns up, there's nothing I can do about her. I know she existed because, as I don't suppose I have to tell you, Dave, she and I knew one another.'

'So, if you . . . What's the . . .'

'The point is, Dave,' Vi said, leaning in so close to him that her head was actually on his shoulder, 'that I know your bosses aren't little angels, and I know that because of both Abduljabbar Mitra and Tatiana. Hard proof is thin on the ground, but I can't actually make sense of the death or disappearance of either of those people without some involvement from your bosses. Know what I mean?'

Dave sweated and said nothing.

Vi said, 'But anyway, now that's off me chest, you can take me back to the station.'

'What?'

She looked at the stunned expression on his face and smiled. 'Take me back to Forest Gate nick,' she said. 'I've had enough of all this green outdoors stuff. Your problem if Sean and Marty see me in their car. Quite honestly, Dave, you spineless wanker, I couldn't give a fuck.'

35

Because the flat was empty, Sean Rogers looked even bigger than he usually did. Dolly Dixon watched him walk from room to room, apparently making sure that she and her aunt and uncle hadn't nicked anything that belonged to him. Down on the street her Uncle Wazim waited for her in his taxi, ready to transport her and her brothers to a new life, away from the violent ghosts of the past.

Dolly, though only fifteen years old, had asked to go over the flat's inventory with her dead mother's landlord because she'd wanted to make sure, once and for all, that her family's business with the Rogers brothers was well and truly at an end.

Sean looked down his list of fitments and fittings and then he said, 'You know you still owe me, 'cause of your mum, don't you.'

Dolly, shaking, was nevertheless defiant. 'Mum's dead, killed by one of your men. You owe us.'

He looked at her and raised his eyebrows. 'Feisty.'

'You'll never get a penny off of us,' Dolly said.

He walked towards her, watching with pleasure as she backed away from him. 'Sure about that are you, kid?'

'Yeah.'

'Mmm.' He stopped. 'Hate your aunt and uncle to have bother where they live.'

Dolly shouted, 'You leave them alone! You leave all of us alone!'

Sean laughed. 'We'll see,' he said. And then he walked away from her and opened the front door to the flat.

'So is that the inventory done now?' Dolly didn't move.

The gangster turned to face her. 'Yeah, I guess so,' he said.

'So you going now or . . .'

'Yeah.' He moved through the door and began to walk down the stairs. Dolly followed him but then, suddenly, he stopped. Turning, he smiled, which caused Dolly to fight for breath again. Then he said, with a confidence that made her blood freeze, 'One day you'll sell your hole, just like your mother. It's in the blood, Dolly love, trust me on this.'

And then he laughed.

Mumtaz felt her eyes drawn to the mezuzah and so, she noticed, did Lee. But neither of them said anything.

Halfway through the afternoon, Lee went out to an appointment with Brian Green, who was having some sort of issue with an employee. When he returned, however, his eyes went straight back to the mezuzah.

'How did it go with Mr Green?' Mumtaz asked, when she gave him his afternoon tea.

'Brian?' Lee tore his gaze away from the mezuzah and frowned. 'He's got a new gardener he suspects smokes dope. Wants us to confirm or deny. Simple surveillance.' Then he shook his head. 'But I don't know what he's doing.'

'Brian Green?'

'As I left, Marty Rogers arrived. They looked pally, you know?'

'You think . . .'

'Brian might be up to his old tricks? I doubt it,' Lee said.

'Might've been perfectly innocent, Brian's Sean's neighbour, but
. . .' He shook his head. 'Oh don't mind me, I'm starting to see
the hands of Sean and Marty everywhere. Though I agree with Vi
in that I think Abdullah Khan is shielding Sean and Marty.'

'But Khan killed John Sawyer and Wendy Dixon, he admitted
it, and there is forensic proof,' Mumtaz said. 'He's going to prison
whatever he does.'

'Yeah, but when you're inside, organised crime can get you
very easily,' Lee said. 'By not grassing up the Rogers boys, Khan
could just be ensuring his own survival in Stir.'

'But if he won't talk . . .'

'We'll never know,' Lee said. And then he sat down and looked
at the mezuzah.

Mumtaz began, 'Lee, I . . .'

'Yes,' he said, 'I want to open it too.'

They stared into each other's eyes, wondering who would make
the first move and when.

Marty Rogers didn't accept Brian Green's offer of champagne
because he was driving.

'I thought that Dave usually drove for you,' Brian said, as he
settled himself down on his sofa with a vodka and tonic.

'He's out collecting,' Marty said.

'Business good?'

He shrugged. 'Could've done without all the Khan nonsense. I
tell you, that's the last time I employ a Paki. Too fucking unstable.'

Brian laughed. 'You're in business with a Paki, you daft twat!'

'Yunus? What does he do?' He shook his head. 'He puts in a bit
of money and he takes a bit out. Sleeping Pakis I can handle but
full on . . .'

'Yeah, but he done the right thing by you,' Brian said.

'Oh, yeah.' Marty looked out into Brian's neat and finely sculpted garden. He had one very like it himself. For a moment he watched the young man who was Brian's latest gardener pull up weeds from a flower bed.

Following where he was looking, Brian said, 'That's Ricki, he's Brazilian.'

'Oh, right.'

'He's why I had Lee Arnold here.'

'I wondered why you was talking to him. He doing something for you, is he?'

'I found what might have been the end of a joint in the green-house last Friday,' Brian said. 'I've asked Lee to see whether Ricki's got a little habit.'

'Oh.'

Brian downed what remained of his vodka. 'I don't want the law knocking on my door over some South American pooftah, not at my time of life.'

'So why'd you give the job to Arnold?'

Brian Green smiled. 'Well Marty, indirectly, I do owe Lee Arnold.'

'How's that?'

'Well, Amy of course. Come on, mate.'

'Oh, yes.'

'Lee was the perfect witness. The poor PI on watch over some old man's wife sees her and her lover boy get killed by an unknown driver. Meanwhile, said old man sits at home hoping his suspicions about his wife are unfounded.'

Marty shook his head. 'I know she was your missus, Brian, but she weren't half a little slapper.'

'If only she'd kept her knickers on I'd've give her everything she'd ever want. But I couldn't have her fucking chauffeurs and shagging little wide boys,' Brian said. 'Word was getting out.'

'You don't have to explain it to me.'

Brian smiled. 'Your Paki boy done a good job there. I'd think carefully before you say you'd never get another one. Mind you, when he went on to shoot—'

'All the young lads want guns these days,' Marty said. 'You can't get any of them to work for you unless you throw in a clean shooter.'

'Where'd you get 'em?'

Marty smiled. Brian Green was old school, he didn't approve of guns. 'Why'd you want to know, Brian?'

The other man said nothing.

'We got rid of your problem and you paid us well, Brian.'

Brian looked up through bloodshot, yellow-tinged eyes. 'Yeah, you did, you helped me get back my good name,' he said. 'And for that I'm grateful.' Then he stood up. 'But I do want you to go now, Marty, if you don't mind.'

Marty shrugged. 'It was only a courtesy call, Brian.'

'And it's appreciated,' Brian said. 'But Marty, I hope you won't be offended when I say that I do hope that we don't meet again.'

Marty Rogers pushed himself out of Brian Green's overstuffed armchair. Still smiling, he said, 'The days of old lags, truncheons and faithful trophy wives are over, Brian. That's the past.'

'So now it's all guns, Toms taking it up the arse and crack, is it?'

'Yup.' He began to walk towards Brian's hall. 'You wanna try it sometime, Brian. Feel a gun in your hand, come on a tart's face, live the modern dream.'

Brian watched him walk down the hall and then, just before Marty opened the front door to let himself out, he said, 'No, think

I'll pass on that, Marty mate. Might kill some innocent by accident.'

Marty laughed. 'Brian,' he said, 'grow up. There are no innocents any more.'

'I think', Mumtaz said to Lee, 'that *you* should open it.'

'Why?'

They were both leaning on her desk, staring at the mezuzah. Their heads low, they looked as if they were stalking it.

'Because you're an atheist,' she said.

'Meaning what?' Lee asked. 'Why's that significant? And anyway, I'm not so much an atheist as an agnostic. I don't believe in religion but I can't discount some sort of Being who's in charge of the universe. Not even scientists can really disprove that.'

'Yes, but if I open it, as a Muslim . . .'

'What do you think's gonna happen?' Lee said. 'You think smoke's gonna come out followed by outraged Jewish spirits? This isn't *Raiders of the Lost Ark,* this is you and me, Mumtaz, trying to find out what's in there.' He tapped the mezuzah with his finger. 'Just in case it's . . .'

'Don't!' She turned her face away, but then she turned it back again.

Lee flipped the holy lump and saw that the back was secured by tiny screws. They were rusty, and when he put his fingernail into the groove across the top of one of the screws, ginger-coloured dust puffed from it down onto the desk. Lee shook his head. 'Can't use a screwdriver on this, it's too small.'

Mumtaz sat back in her chair. 'Maybe we should just leave it alone.'

'Oh, and never know, yes, that's smart.' Lee shook his head

and then tried to move a screw with the top of a ballpoint pen. 'Shit!'

'It's not going to come, Lee. Maybe we should give it to the local synagogue. I think that might be best.'

He put the mezuzah down. He looked at her. 'What, and never, ever know? You could live with that, could you?' He shook his head. 'Apart from anything else, if this contains what it just might, but probably doesn't contain, we'll have a duty to tell the police. This could change things for Nasreen Khan, this could . . .'

'Who would they belong to though?' Mumtaz asked. 'Really?'

Lee shrugged. 'Dunno.'

She shook her head again. 'I'm just not happy about this. I *am* curious but I feel that it's wrong and I don't know what to—'

'I'll give it one more try,' Lee said. He inserted his thumbnail in the top of the other tiny screw and pushed down hard. 'If this doesn't work this time, I'll stop.'

'OK.'

They both saw the screw begin to give at exactly the same moment. He looked into her eyes and she looked into his, and Lee ventured a smile. 'It's . . .'

'Oh my, it's . . .'

As the small screw came out so its opposite number on the other side of the mezuzah snapped in half. Lee took a deep breath and slid the metal backing plate away.

There was paper. Parchment by the look of it, old and yellowed and folded up into a sort of a lozenge.

'That must have the prayer written on it,' Mumtaz said. 'We shouldn't disturb it, not now that we know.'

Lee sighed. 'We've come this far,' he said. He looked at her. 'While we're here, we might as well see it.'

She shrugged. She wasn't happy about what some Jews would

almost certainly deem desecration, but Lee wouldn't be content until he'd had the mezuzah apart.

He picked the lozenge of paper up between his thumb and his finger and placed it on the desk. Bits of dust accompanied its transit and it was only when this had cleared that Lee and Mumtaz could see what was behind it.

Three large, and one very large, very purple pink diamonds.

Acknowledgements

Grateful thanks go to Melvyn Hartog, Head of Burial at the United Synagogue as well as to Leonard Shear who very kindly showed me around Plashet Jewish Cemetery. Other heroes and heroines who provided help, advice and succour to me on my *Act of Kindness* journey included Vivian Archer and all the staff at the fantastic Newham Bookshop, the staff at the Kalavara Restaurant, Upton Park and everyone at The Boleyn Pub. Other 'persons of interest' include Jim Reeve and Teri Varhol, Steve Grant, Kathy Lowe, Sarah Bancroft and Darragh Carville. Finally I'd also like to thank Jane Wood, Katie Gordon and Lucy Ramsey plus Mark, Dan and Caroline at Quercus. Thank you for continuing to have faith in what I do.